THE BLACK KNIGHT

BOOK TWO OF THE EXCALIBUR KNIGHTS SAGA

LUKE MITCHELL

Cover art & design by Tom Edwards

tomedwardsdesign.com

Thank you for reading.

PROLOGUE - TENTH HELL

It was another arid day on Demeter-12. The kind of day that made it abundantly clear why even hearty Atlantean staples like the much-loved turba root struggled to survive here. Not that Lena was surprised as she stepped out of her climate-sealed quarters into the hot sun, morning-baked clay soil crunching underfoot.

Sometimes, hostile environments were just the cost of keeping their beloved Empire rich in all the rare metals and heavy elements required for places like Olympus and the Triton shipyards to continue functioning.

Lena took a stifling breath through her filters and looked around at the dusty prefab sprawl of her desert home "town." She momentarily allowed herself to indulge, as she did each morning, in the fleeting fantasy of seeing this place after a few decades' worth of work from the terraforming engines. She smiled at the brilliant, dusty horizon, sharing an inside joke with an old friend.

The engines would never come to this place. Demeter-12, otherwise known as Tarkaminen Colony Outpost D-12 to the outside world and as "the tenth hell" to some of their less enthusiastic colonists, was far too arid in both climate and reputation for the Empire to ever bother with a full terraforming effort. Not when there were more temperate choices a few dozen lightyears in any direction.

Demeter-12 had begun as nothing but a rich dig site. It had grown into a convenient staging ground for the burgeoning mining operations taking shape in the expansive and aptly named D-12 asteroid belt. And so it had reached the apex of its cultural development.

Not that Lena had felt any particular qualms about having been promptly assigned here after her vat birth and mandatory socialization period back on New Atlantis. Everyone had to learn their trade somewhere, after all, and the Castors were wise. They'd spliced her in vitro with every genetic advantage she'd need to tolerate the dry, brutal heat and the long shifts at the probe controls.

The Empire was wise. And life wasn't bad.

"Get hopping, dig-whig," called a voice that set her smile to widening. She turned to show that smile to Gurrin Soldiercaste as he passed her by on his morning patrol, like he always did. His handsome face wasn't smiling this morning.

"What's going on?" she asked.

He shook his head, clearly in a hurry. "Dunno. Console jockeys probably just jumping at ghosts again, but uh…" He finally paused, glancing back at her. "Just keep your head down over there in your hole today, yeah?"

He was gone before she could give him so much as a nod. It was only then she noticed the other Soldiercastes marshaling in the barren town square with hurried movements and serious looks. Something was going on. But that *something* was probably little concern of hers, she reminded herself. Especially not when she was already flirting with being late to the pod.

Five minutes later, she was roaring across the open desert in her dune skimmer, relishing the freedom of speeding across a land so thoroughly unpopulated. They couldn't do *this* on the overcrowded city-world of New Atlantis, she told herself, even as the rational side of her brain pointed out that that was a clear exaggeration. But so be it. She drove on, enjoying the ride, already forgetting the odd exchange with Gurrin and beginning to look forward to another day of scouring and cataloging D-12's finely-stocked innards. Enjoying the ride so much, that her brain simply wasn't ready to process what it saw as she roared too fast over the next high dune.

A ship.

A big, looming black ship like nothing she'd ever seen, hanging too low overheard. She gasped, mind reeling. Too late, her eyes fell back to the sands and registered the dark figure kneeling ahead, dead center in her path. Too late, she slammed the brake jets. Time seemed to slow, her senses cutting out completely but for the lasting glimpse of a sinister, jet-black helmet turning her way, capped against the pale desert sky by a streak of blood-red plumage.

Then, impact.

For one furious moment, there was nothing but the jarring crunch ripping through her bones, and the crushing push-and-pull of her restraints fighting to save her life or collapse her chest in, whichever came first. Then time lurched from stand-still to too-fast, thoughts jumbled, ragged breaths too loud in her ringing ears.

She'd hit him at nearly full speed.

She gaped through the spiderweb-cracked windshield, shaken brain taking in the details one at a time, attempting to fit them together. The skimmer's smashed hood and shattered plates. The pattern of crumpled internals, imploded in around the extended dark gauntlet that had somehow just stopped a speeding skimmer. The horrible black mask watching her now through the cracked windshield, watching her with a quiet weight that left her breathless.

The engines were dead, she realized numbly—the skimmer hovering not under its own power, but solely by the dark stranger's hand. Dimly, she registered that his other hand was still resting on the interface display of the data relay node he must've called up from its subterranean housing along the ground lines.

A data scavenger? Here?

The thought was preposterous enough on its own, but it paled laughably next to the sight of the dark titan setting her vehicle calmly down to the sands by the power of his arm, casually as if he'd just caught a small pup from running over the edge.

"You are a prospector."

She gasped at the sound of his voice, some part of her jarred brain having convinced her that this was no mortal man, but rather some dark, voiceless demon of the Synth, conjured straight from the old ghost stories.

That part of her wanted to point out that she was merely a fledgling apprentice. Somehow, the detail felt suddenly paramount. But her mouth wouldn't move. Not until the towering mountain of dark armor and sharp edges stooped down closer, and a soft whimper escaped her lips.

"Do you know what it is you truly seek here, child?"

"R-r-resources," answered a thin, airy voice. Her voice. Her hands shaking on the restraint buckles she couldn't undo, mouth refusing to obey. This was no mere data scavenger. She didn't know *what* he was, only that she'd never been so frightened in her life.

"Resources for the Empire," she finally managed breathlessly, hoping that was enough. Hoping this unflinching dark god wouldn't simply crush her then and there for having struck him.

He didn't even seem to hear her, his menacing black helmet scanning the horizon, settling on the direction of the homestead. Her eyes trailed to the dark fortress of a ship hanging overhead, casting them in shadow.

"There are navigators and historians in the village beyond?"

"The… the Starcastes?" she heard herself asking, not understanding.

That dark helmet bowed once, red plumage sweeping the air like a bloodied scythe blade. "And the Chronocastes, yes. I have need of their archives."

It occurred to her that she shouldn't answer. That to do so may well be betraying her friends back in the homestead. What she needed to do was warn them somehow. Get free. Get out of here. But she couldn't seem to do anything but tremble as he fixed his eyeless gaze back on her and leaned in close. She flinched as he reached out with one jagged-finned gauntlet and tore the warped skimmer door free from its hinges like plucking a flower from the stem. He idly tossed the carbon weave plating across the dune. She sat there uselessly, paralyzed with the fear that he would turn back for her next. Pluck her from the skimmer, aboard that frightening ship, and off to gods only knew where.

"Please," she heard herself whisper, eyes falling shamefully to her lap.

Something heavy settled atop her head. His hand, she realized. The same hand that had just palmed a speeding skimmer to a halt. It was enormous. Big enough to crush her skull like an overripe chelsen berry. She waited, too frightened to look up—hating how frightened she felt. Hating that this could be the end.

She closed her eyes, closing out the world.

"Lady's Blessings be your way, sweet child," said that deep voice. "This will all be over soon."

And then… nothing. Nothing at all.

The world simply went dark, so quick and unexpectedly that she barely had time to wonder if death could really be so painless. Then her eyes cracked open a moment later, head throbbing with the familiar ache of heat exhaustion, skin hot, shallow pulse racing. She felt like she'd been baking in the sun for hours. But she was alive.

And he was gone.

She squinted out at the empty desert stretch. He was gone, and so was the ship.

She raised her arm to check the wrist display of her omni, found her suit's water reserves were all but gone, and that she'd been out for hours. There were missed messages, too, but no active comms. For a long moment, she sat there, head throbbing, thoughts churning like reconstituted gravy. The fear lingered, clutching at her insides like a physical thing even as her business-as-usual brain tried to tell her that there'd been some mistake—that she'd simply imagined the whole affair.

But she *wasn't* imagining the imploded front end of her skimmer. Nor the freakishly unprecedented levels of atmospheric radiation currently ravaging the comm lines, as if the hells themselves had reared up in the wake of that dark titan's arrival. She turned in her crash-tightened restraints, telling herself to be reasonable, scanning the dunes for anything out of the ordinary.

Her breath caught at the dark plume of smoke on the eastern horizon, lingering fear spiking to urgent panic in her chest.

The homestead.

"No," she whispered, her voice a parched rasp. "No."

She clawed at the crash-warped restraints, wild emotion mounting, bursting from her burning lungs in a string of gasping sobs as she fought to escape. Fought until she tumbled out of the skimmer into the hot sand, scraping her palms on the way. There she lay shaking, gasping through her filters, staring helplessly at the rising smoke as her mind screamed on to tell someone. Get help. *Do* something. Too late.

Too late.

"No," she sobbed, again and again, the prayer useless, the realization as tangible as the burning sand beneath her. She pulled herself upright anyway, nose running, checking her omni and trying to gather her wits. Comms still down. Hardline node slagged.

She rose to shaky feet, looking from east to northwest and back again, gauging distances to the pod and the homestead, trying to think of her next steps. A sound split the air, harsh and keening. It was a sound she'd never expected to hear outside of training drills, resonating through her skull with its long call before reeling slowly back down for another crescendo.

The invasion alarm.

She looked up breathlessly, not sure what she was expecting. Pirates. More black ships. An entire fleet of them. What she saw instead was a great dark cloud descending on the arid planet that rarely formed clouds of its own, and never ones so dark.

No cloud at all, then, some clinical part of her brain informed her, as she dialed her omni's limited optics in for a better look at the descending cloud of… not ships. Not like any she'd ever seen.

It was a swarm.

A veritable ocean of what looked for all her uncomprehending shock to be nothing but trillions of rocks and accumulated space dust, descending from the upper atmosphere under some kind of external drive, moving with a singular coordination. Like the D-12 asteroid belt had grown a blackened will of its own and decided to fight back.

She staggered backward as the first brilliant column of emerald destruction lanced out from the homestead's surface-to-air batteries, slagging through countless tons of rock and ore and showering the desert far below in a red-hot rain of superheated metals. The swarm continued on, perfectly unperturbed, filling the hole like so much shifting sand. To the east, she could just make out the tiny blips of ships rising from the homestead. Their colony transports, she realized, with a twinge of disbelief, were evacuating.

This was really happening.

The thought echoed again and again, like a challenge daring her to look away or to prove it all wrong as that impossible swarm shifted and morphed, hurling untold tons of asteroid deluge at the rising ships with a supersonic roar. She watched in horror as the attack brought the entire evacuation down in one fell swoop. Uncomprehending. Numb. The bright desert day pulsing brighter with another blast from the defense batteries, and another. The clatter and distant winks of smaller weapons joining the fray as the swarm descended and punched into the planet's crust like a force of nature, bound for the homestead like a landborne tsunami.

This will all be over soon, that blackened voice echoed in her mind.

Tears streaming down her cheeks. Her body frozen in place.

Too much. It was all too much.

But someone was still alive, said the next brilliant emerald flare.

Her people were still fighting.

So Lena Minercaste set her sights for the impossible wave of destruction sweeping toward her home, and she started running.

～

"Justicar."

On the other side of the galaxy, roughly three light minutes outsystem from the Golnak relay, Malfar allowed himself one centering moment before turning from his main display to face his incessant first officer. He already knew what the perpetually-frowning Atlantean was going to say.

"G-Sec is asking for an update."

G-Sec is asking for an update, SIR, some civilized part of Malfar wanted to correct him. The rest of him, the part that was native-born Troglodan to the core, spotted runt or no, longed to do the more sensible thing and simply squash the good lieutenant's tiny head to a fine meat paste.

"Then update them, Lieutenant Shelton," he said instead, turning back to his displays in a clear invitation for Shelton and the rest of his crew to piss right back off.

Perfect silence reigned as the lieutenant debated whether to press the issue and ask (yet again) what exactly he should tell G-Sec—what it was they were actually *doing* out here at the edge of the Golnak system, other than wasting fuel and manpower.

"Justicar," the Atlantean finally murmured, turning back to his console.

Lieutenant Shelton Soldiercaste knew damn well what they were doing here. They all did. While their presence here *was* admittedly something of an impromptu detour from their expected return to Forge Station, it didn't take an Alliance justicar to deduce that the uncertain glances behind his back had more to do with his hide than with his orders. He could practically smell their growing unease. Ripening suspicions that they'd come all this way for nothing. That *this* was the time he'd finally prove he was naught but a savage brute, unfit for command.

How his native people of Trogarra would've raged to see the way the civilized galaxy balked at being ordered about by a Troglodan. How they would've howled for obedience from these sneering Hobdans and these coldly disapproving Androtta. How they would've bayed for the punishment of this damned Atlantean—this weak, fragile little vat clone—with his constant second-guessing.

And how they would've turned that teeming disgust right back on Malfar the moment any such perceived injustices were rectified. For such was the life of a spotted runt.

It didn't matter that he was one of a very small handful of Troglodans to have ever ascended to the rank of justicar. At the end of it, Malfar's so-called kin cared no more for his accomplishments than his own crew cared for the fact that he'd never once led them astray, or that he held one of the most decorated case records in recent history for any justicar of his career age.

He'd always be a thick-hided brute in the eyes of his crew, just as he'd always be a blighted reject in the eyes of his own people. But it hardly mattered. His so-called kin could kindly see fist to ass. And respectful or not, his crew would do their duty when the time came. Just as he'd do his.

It was to that end, with Lieutenant Shelton obstinately reporting to G-Sec in the background that they were "*still* waiting," that Malfar returned to the preliminary report he'd been scanning from the Tarkaminen sector, where one of the Atlantean mining colonies had gone comms dark a few hours ago, mid-distress-call.

Pirates, his bridge of fools would've guessed, had he put it to them. Partly because they'd just finished putting away a particularly slippery ring of such brigands out in the system's rim. Mostly because they *always* said pirates, no matter what. So much so that he'd stooped to making the use of the phrase *by Blackthorne's tits* punishable by imminent filter scrubbing duty in a feeble attempt to rein in the verbal flatulence. Not that it had made much difference.

Malfar frowned at the Demeter-12 report a few minutes longer, feeling that familiar behind-the-brain tickle of something not quite adding up, then finally flicked the report closed and shut his eyes to think. He had more than enough to worry about without beleaguered Atlantean colonies.

A rumored, full-on illegal incursion on Terra, for instance. Thrice-cursed Excalibur Knights running wild, slagging one another's ships *and* the all-precious mining installation that was home to the one thing keeping the Golnak sector in relay proximity with the rest of Alliance space. And now—

"You lot see this Atlantean colony what went dark out T-Sec way?" muttered one of the Hobs over at weapons, clearly thinking he was being quiet.

"Blackthorne's tits if it isn't pirates muckin' about," muttered his fellow Hobdan turret jockey, like clockwork. Agent Azjgar, if memory served.

Spirit of Justice, he needed to speak with Central about ironing out a more permanent crew. Preferably one less obsessed with pirates.

"It's probably just a solar flare," said the Atlantean female at comms, looking at least marginally worried about her distant kinsmen. "That's all."

"A distress call was logged," pointed out their Androtta voice of reason over in systems, making no attempt to lower his mechanical voice.

"That's what I'm sayin', ain't it?" Azjgar said, more loudly this time, emboldened by the stirring conversation. "What else but pirates, eh? Black-thorne's t—"

"Agent Azjgar," Malfar rumbled, tapping one murderous finger at the universal translator chip by his ear, dimly wishing the thing could somehow just momentarily eradicate his brain's intrinsic ability to understand their low-spoken Common.

The Hobdan looked around like a child who'd just been caught at the sweets. "Yeah, Boss? Sir."

"The waste filters."

"Aw, but Boss, I was just—"

"Go."

Agent Azjgar went with all the brimming moodiness of a petulant broodling. The rest of the crew, with a few level-headed exceptions, looked no less surly about the exchange.

Children.

He was surrounded by impulsive children, more enamored with departmental politics and galactic hijinks than they were with the sober, disciplined pursuit of True Justice. But that was no surprise. Such was the way of the Alliance—more and more, it seemed, with each passing year. They might as well have emblazoned such words across the recruitment banners.

Malfar turned back to his displays, dismissing the disgruntled looks and focusing his thoughts back on their outsystem progress, and on the matter at hand.

They would come. He had no doubt of it. No more than he doubted his already short leash would be promptly yanked tighter by C-Sec, or perhaps removed completely, if he was wrong. But he was not afraid. They *would* come, these so-called Knights, fresh from whatever worldly catastrophes they'd wrought amid their power-drunk squabbles.

The only question was when they would arrive, and what they'd have to say for themselves when they did.

Which one would be first, he wondered: the Gorgon or the Troglodan? The legendary Huntress of Kalyria, or the one they called Dread Knight— the simultaneous pride and shame of the Troglodan people, depending on whom one asked.

That hardly mattered either.

By their precious Lady's Light, they would come.

And by all of the True Justice in the galaxy, Malfar would be waiting.

CHAPTER 1

FOREPLAY

"**C**ome on, kid," came the voice of Nate's new full-time tormentor through the swirl of pain and disjointed thoughts. "Whole world's watching."

"We're... in space," Nate grunted back, head still spinning from impact with the cell wall, too thoroughly pinned by his two attackers to even collapse.

By way of reply, Lt Col John Jaeger freed one hand from the near-dislocation act on Nate's shoulder and tapped pointedly on the clear cell pane beside Nate's face. Nate didn't need to look to know most of the *Camelot's* new crew were still standing there, gathered in the cargo bay to bear witness to the end of the carnage that was Nate's "daily training."

Nothing like getting your ass kicked for a live studio audience.

Then again, most of them had already had their turns. In twos and threes. *After* they'd made sure he was pre-exhausted with a world-class weight lifting session—and thrown him into the e-dim dampening cell where he'd be unable to call on his handy Excalibur toys for aid. Frankly, the entire situation was starting to seem a little unfair. But that was kind of the point.

Four days and counting of this bullshit.

Perhaps it wouldn't be so bad if you stopped losing, came the gruff voice that lived in his head these days, whether he liked it or not. The voice of the Eighth Excalibur, long may the synthient superweapon live... and suck it.

I heard that. Words hurt, you know.

Nate was about to point out that pummeled cheeks and ribs and dislocated shoulders all hurt a hell of a lot more when Jaeger hauled back and smacked his head into the cell wall, and things went a little fuzzy.

"—think he's gonna fight back, or what?" Jaeger was saying as things sharpened back into focus.

A noncommittal grunt was all the reply he got from the burly airman helping to pin Nate to the wall back there—the enormous, perpetually scowling monster the team all called "Elmo" for reasons unknown and surely ironic.

"You gonna fight back, kid, or what?" Jaeger spoked directly to Nate this time, flicking his cheek like an honest-to-Christ schoolyard bully. Which was probably exactly what the deranged bastard had been. It wasn't hard to imagine an eight-year-old Jaeger spending recess plucking the wings off of flies and gut-punching anyone who thought to tell him otherwise.

Stop sniveling and kick his rectum, Nathaniel!

It didn't sound like the worst plan, aside from his shoulder's screaming insistence that it would be leaving its socket if he so much as twitched. Then Jaeger rewarded his silence with an encore head slam, and the lizard brain took over. He bucked against their combined grip. Felt his humerus threaten to tear free. The pain only made him angrier. He planted his feet on the wall and kicked off as best he could, determined to break free, no matter what.

His shoulder gave way with a sickening pop, a fiery knife of pain plunging in. He cried out, dimly noting a few of their spectators clamping hands to mouths in *oh shit* shock. Then strong hands slammed him back into the wall, head first. He blinked, pretty sure his eyes were still open but strangely incapable of making sense of much beyond the floor-tilting churn and the prickly darkness clouding over everything.

Funny to think that Jaeger and Elmo might've been the only things holding him up at that point. Funny to think he was powerless to stop them when, outside of that e-dim dampening cell, with Ex's power at his call, he could've easily taken ten Jaegers, and at least a few Elmos.

But inside that cell, barring what enhancements Ex had already made to his baseline physiology, he was still only human. A far hungrier, faster healing, more muscular human than he'd been a few short weeks ago. But human nonetheless. And dead exhausted at that.

"You done?" Jaeger asked, so close he felt the man's breath on his cheek. It smelled like goddamn spearmint.

Nate wanted to tell him to shove it. Wanted to fire off some perfectly witty quip, then dig deep and come out swinging with the inner badass warrior that every movie he'd ever geeked out to had told him should be there, lying dormant in even the meekest Chosen One, buried beneath the self-doubt, waiting for precisely such a moment to rear its dramatic head. But he *wasn't* a Chosen One. Not really.

Not this again.

The random-ass human who'd happened to be strolling by when a drunk wizard had stumbled into town with an extra Excalibur in tow. That's what he was. The chump who'd been naive enough to yank the surly sword from the metaphysical stone, mistaking the simple capacity to do so for the true test.

Earth had been the true test. The Beacon. The Troglodan invasion. Bonding with Ex. All of it.

Now this part was the test too. And a man like Jaeger wasn't simply going to be beaten by a guy like him on the grounds of supreme will and divine intervention alone.

So instead of fighting like a gritty action hero, Nate heel-kicked Jaeger's shin, ripped his good hand free, and thrust it forward, willing the cell wall to part for him. The ship—*his* ship—responded to his will almost as smoothly as his own limbs might've… had he been severely under the influence. But it was enough.

"Hey!" Jaeger growled, shifting his grip to yank them back from the wall.

But Nate was already calling his armor from e-dim, watching with grim satisfaction as the first repulsor gauntlet unfolded from thin air to encase the hand and forearm right up to the edge of the cell's higher-dimensional interference. Whether it would've kept coming from there, he didn't know. Jaeger ripped them away from the ill-formed opening before they found out. Or started too, at least, before Nate's hand caught on something that snagged them both to a halt.

His sword, he realized in a flash, caught in the small opening by the pommel and elaborate crossguard like a dog trying to run a stick through a doorway. Except Nate's stick was broken—the once sweeping blade neatly truncated right where the Black Knight had all too recently hewn it clean in two.

He traded a surprised look with Jaeger, part of him wanting to clarify that no, he *hadn't* intended to shiv the good Lt Col just to prove a point. Jaeger punched him in the mouth before he could open it. Nate ducked his head against a second strike, releasing the sword and letting rip with the repulsor gauntlet. A round of indignant shouts sounded from the crew outside the cell. Nate was too busy rocketing into his startled opponents on the inside with a string of bodily thumps. He took the rest of the cell at a wild spin, losing track of up, down, and pretty much everything else until something—deck or wall, he could hardly tell—broke his flight, hard.

"Son of a..." Jaeger growled somewhere nearby.

Cheater, added the Excalibur.

Nate didn't care. He was done losing. Done with all of it. So done that he almost wasn't surprised when he sat up to find Jaeger lunging toward him with a knife.

More by lucky reflex than anything else, he caught the blade with his armored hand. Good sense took over, and he squeezed down, crushing the blade like a pneumatic press and ripping the weapon from Jaeger's hand. Unperturbed, Jaeger went for the forehead sucker punch.

This time, Nate *was* surprised to see his hand shooting up, deflecting the punch, and snaking right into a solid grip on the back of Jaeger's head, almost like he knew what he was doing. Then a dark boot swept in from the side and kicked the better part of consciousness clear from his head.

Elmo's boot, Nate dimly processed, as Jaeger slipped free, and the huge outline of his scowling SAS crony appeared beside him, cocking his huge boot to kick again.

Nate thrust his repulsor gauntlet up at that dark scowl, knowing even as he did that he couldn't possibly attempt a non-lethal blast. At least it bought him a moment of hesitation from the huge man. He used it to aim a ground kick at Jaeger's chest, but the Lt Col deftly caught his leg and pinned it beneath one armpit, stepping down on the other leg to hold him still for Elmo.

Desperate to escape the impending stomp, Nate threw his repulsor hand overhead, parallel to the deck, and let loose with another hard thrust. His arm nearly buckled under the force, but he held on. He plowed into Jaeger's legs. Maybe Elmo's too. It was hard to sort out through all the jostling thuds. There were curses and a few hard skips across the deck. He tried to roll to his feet and crashed straight into the far wall instead. He scrambled up, heart racing, rounding on his opponents with repulsor raised, fully expecting to find them both charging back in.

Across the cell, Jaeger calmly finished picking himself up off the deck and turned to offer a disgruntled-looking Elmo a hand up before turning his frown back to Nate's gauntlet.

"What?" Nate asked, glancing down at the readied repulsor and back up again. "You gonna tell me I broke the rules of engagement or something? Like this was supposed to be a fair fight?"

Jaeger held him on the end of his stare for several tense seconds. "Actually, I was just thinkin' you'd better learn to open that shit up *without* fifteen minutes of foreplay next time. But if you wanna get all bitchy with the people flying across the galaxy to protect your ass, well then…" He shrugged, his frown giving way to a weapons-grade smirk. "I guess that's your prerogative, Mr. Excalibur Knight."

Nate stared, some part of him categorically counting how many parts of that statement were just plain unfair, the rest fixated on a single souring thought.

He'd won.

He'd *won* dammit—finally beat Jaeger and Elmo, just like they'd been daring him to do, day in and day out. He'd cleared the final boss level, and they *still* didn't give a shit. Still weren't going to give him a break, even for a second. He could see it in their eyes.

He glanced out to the rest of the watching crew and saw much the same. Snuffy, at least, looked a touch empathetic, and Tessa shot him a lazy wink that might've been sarcastic or congratulatory. The rest just looked supremely underwhelmed and moderately hostile.

The 501st Space Aggressor Squadron, Ladies and Gentlemen. The people who'd flown across the galaxy to protect his ass.

You consider their sacrifices inferior to yours?

Coming from Ex, the statement was an unexpected slap to the giblets. Nate looked back to Jaeger and Elmo, cheeks heating. He hadn't asked these people to join the mission. Still wasn't sure he wanted them here at all (not that anyone had bothered asking once Iveera had given the White House the green light). But here they were, saddled up right beside him at a moment's notice to chase an unfathomably powerful Black Knight into the unknown reaches of Alliance space… and maybe beyond.

None of them truly understood what they were flying into. Most of them were still busy trying to wrap their heads around the fact that they weren't even the first humans to make the trip. Not since the so-called Atlanteans had set sail from good old terra firma over four-thousand years earlier, coaxed out by the Merlin to establish their own empire among the stars.

He was hardly the only one who'd gotten more than he bargained for here. He had to remember that. So, with a force of will on both fronts, he willed the cell walls to dissipate around them and turned back to his two opponents, trying to look amicable. "Are you guys okay?"

Elmo's only answer was his unwavering scowl. Jaeger just gave him one of those short *kid, I've killed better men than you with my pinky* laughs.

"Great," Nate muttered, turning to go, feeling all the more irritated as he caught sight of the sad excuse for his Excalibur sword lying there on the deck and felt his cheeks burn hotter. "So glad I asked."

He stooped down to snatch up the broken sword, willing it to return to e-dim along with his repulsor gauntlet, and started across the bay, feeling more battered and alone than he had since they'd left Earth.

"Carter," Jaeger called before he'd made it more than a few steps. "Pop the kid's shoulder back in."

Nate faltered. Ex must've been masking the pain. Or maybe he'd just been too flustered by everything else to notice. It hardly mattered. All he knew was that it rankled the shit out of him, the way Jaeger didn't even bother to *pretend* as if Nate had any say in the matter. Rankled him almost as much as the look in the steely medic's eyes as she stepped forward to bar his path—the same look they all had.

"I've got it," he growled, storming past Emily Carter's allegedly healing hands and putting his back to those persistent stares. The stares that silently asked who the hell he thought he was, taking up a vast alien power in Earth's name when every soldier aboard this ship so clearly outclassed him.

As if he'd stepped into this mess on purpose. As if the Lady had spelled it all out for him before he'd plucked that sword from the stone and invited Ex in. As if he wouldn't have given just about anything to be safely back at Penn State right then, obliviously playing Battle Royale with his roommates, or exploring where things might've gone with Gwen after he'd finally found the stones to tell her how he felt.

The thought of her smiling face agitated the familiar hole in his chest, the bitter duology of longing for everything he'd left behind even as some part of him admitted that he never would have stolen that kiss, never would have cared about all of it so dearly, had events not unfolded exactly as they had.

Somehow, the thought didn't quite make up for the fact that he'd swapped his best friends and the girl he loved for a crew of abrasive airmen. A crew that respected him about as much as they might respect your average millennial legacy billionaire. A crew that clearly wasn't going to accept him just for winning a few fights.

But a crew nonetheless, some part of him pointed out, as he reached the wide threshold where the cargo bay opened to the lower of the two main corridors that ran the length of the *Camelot*.

He slowed, feeling their eyes on his back, knowing he should probably turn around, apologize, and accept Carter's help with his shoulder. No one said a word. Nothing but their silent judgment on his back. His feet made the decision for him.

∼

WELL DONE, Nathaniel, Ex said as Nate rounded into the corridor, setting off at a brusque march for he didn't know where. *Not only did you manage to—*

I don't wanna hear it, Ex. Not now.

To his mild surprise, Ex didn't press the matter. He supposed his companion could already see how frustrated he was. It wasn't like he didn't understand how this childish defiance would only further incinerate what precious little goodwill the 501st held for him, or how he was being irrational, wishing for his old life back. He certainly wasn't under any delusion that life on Earth had simply gone back to normal the moment they'd blasted off.

Lazy Penn State weekends. Classes. People's jobs. Hell, maybe even war, for all he knew. However things shook out in the wake of the Troglodan invasion, the only certainty in all of it was that Earth would never be the same again. He knew that. Knew it perfectly well. But no amount of cold, hard logic would ever drown out that wistful voice of what-ifs in his heart.

The interesting thing was that Ex almost seemed to be coming to accept that. It was like they were reaching some kind of middle ground, with Ex growing marginally more tolerant of Nate's profoundly human emotional chicanery even as the simple presence of the synthient super-intelligence living in his head made Nate ever more cognizant of his every illogical tic.

Almost like they were becoming bona fide partners.

Lady spare me your squishy sentiment.

Nate caught himself before he could make the mistake of shrugging and instead leaned gingerly against the corridor wall, weighing the options of going to Iveera for help or just hiding in his quarters, where no one would hear him scream.

You DID fight well, for what that's worth, Ex added, as if the soft-and-cuddly side of his algorithms had just alerted him that Nate most likely required some form of compliment. *For you, at least.*

Nate gave a bitter huff at the backhanded compli-sult, thinking idly of his broken sword but not wanting to talk about it. *I thought you said I was a cheater.*

The two are not mutually exclusive.

Nate arched an eyebrow at nowhere in particular, waiting.

... Even if the one DOES make you somewhat of an embarrassment to the title of Excalibur Knight.

There it was.

Good thing I already had that part going for me anyway, huh?

That's the spirit, Nathaniel. Ex hesitated. *As for the sword, you should know it's—*

All in my head? Nate interjected, pretty sure he already knew the answer.

All in OUR head, if that sounds better. But yes.

Nate sighed and pushed himself off of the bulkhead, not wanting to think about the sword or the terror that still clung to his insides every time he thought of the Black Knight closing in on him, raining down thunderous blows—raining down an entire damned city on his head. He glanced toward Iveera's quarters. Toward his own. Back again. His heart was beating too fast. *We still have a few hours before Golnak, right?*

Perhaps you should ask your ship.

Nate frowned at no one in particular, knowing Ex was right. He closed his eyes, fingers drifting to his temple like Professor X in a half-cocked attempt to help him focus and clarify his shoddy bond with the *Camelot*, forming the question and—

HOURS. The ship's mechanical yet oddly frenetic voice sounded off like a klaxon in his head, eliciting an involuntary jerk. *FOUR HOURS POINT THREE-THREE-TWO-FIVE—*

Nate yanked back from the roaring stream of mechanical ship-speak, wondering (not for the first time) if something hadn't gone a little *off* with the ship in the thousand-odd years it had been floating around, waiting for a new Knight.

No more than something went 'off' with that hamburger you call a brain on the day you were born. You are simply not listening properly.

Pretty sure I heard that one just fine. It said four hours.

Congratulations, Nathaniel, you have decoded the most superficial of the roughly eight-thousand data points contained in that message.

Nate frowned. *Eight-thousand? You're making that up.*

We will arrive at the Golnak outskirts in 4 hours, 19 minutes, and 57 seconds, bearing roughly 8.7588, 41.9928, and 237.0192 degrees at approximately 7,495 kilometers per second, Golnak system relative. Crusher drives currently operating at approximately 35,652-fold efficiency, yielding a current subjective of roughly 891—

"Okay, okay!" Nate said, throwing his hands up at the empty corridor. *Well, why didn't the ship just say that, then?*

DID.

This time, Nate at least managed to stifle his jerk of surprise. He stayed poised there, waiting. For what, exactly, he couldn't say, but waiting. *How many data points were there in that one?*

One, came Ex's flat reply. *Obviously. Pay attention, Nathaniel.*

Nate sighed.

"Talking to our girl?"

He stiffened, whirling to face the speaker just as Ex gave an amused, *By the way, there's someone behind you.*

"You suck," Nate hissed under his breath as he caught sight of Tessa Kalders posted up against the corridor wall, arms crossed and mischievous grin in place, like she'd been enjoying the show.

"Can I help you?" he asked.

She didn't answer right away. Just watched him like some kind of jungle cat, sharp hazel eyes scanning his face, studying the underworkings. He hadn't really told anyone about the full extent of his bond with Ex and the *Camelot*—a gut decision that neither Iveera nor Ex had seen fit to challenge —but nor had they missed out on the fact that he seemed to do a lot of talking to himself.

Tessa, who'd already begun forming some affinity for the *Camelot's* erratic on-board intelligence, seemed to be the most curious about it all. That, or she just enjoyed trying to make him squirm under her scrutiny. He wasn't sure. He drew up to his full, unsquirming height just to be safe.

She seemed to get a little kick out of that too.

"I'm all good, Mr. Knight," she said finally, uncrossing her arms and approaching with confident steps, stopping just a hair too close. "Just wanted to—" She frowned, looking up at him. "Are you getting taller?"

"I… don't know," he said, starting to shrug, pausing at the pain. Had he *not* been imagining it? "Who can tell anymore?"

Her, apparently.

It was Nate's turn to frown as Tessa shrugged off his non-answer. *What? What do you—*

The gentle touch of Tessa's hand on his triceps drew him back to the moment.

"—ust wanted to let you know," she was saying, leaning closer still. Close enough that parts of him started doing funny things. "There's nothing wrong with fifteen minutes of foreplay," she whispered softly.

"Huh?!" he sputtered.

Then her hands tightened on his arm and wrist. A sharp tug and a flash of panic, then a soft, wet pop, and relief. Sweet, painless relief from the shoulder that'd been biting at the edge of his consciousness more angrily than he'd even realized until that moment.

"Fuck," he whispered.

A satisfied smirk pulled at her lips. "It was good for you too, then?"

Before he could so much as close his gaping mouth, she gave him a grinning pat on the cheek, and turned to strut off toward the bridge like that was simply that.

"Wait," he said, more out of reflex than anything.

She paused and glanced back, waiting. "He didn't send me," she finally said. "If that's what you're wondering."

It wasn't, really, but it was still good to know this wasn't Jaeger's doing. For a second, she looked like she wanted to say more. Nate wanted to say more too. A *thank you*, for starters. All he mustered, though, was grateful nod. She considered him a moment longer, her demeanor shifting back to that of the assessing jungle cat, then she returned his nod and continued on her way.

He watched her go, not really sure what to make of the entire interaction, oddly grateful for the distraction anyway. For a moment, he almost felt… normal.

Then he remembered that he needed to go talk to their Gorgon passenger before they reached the Golnak system and the so-called Beacon relay that was supposed to cannonball them across the galaxy in pursuit of the renegade Black Knight, and that equilibrium safely vanished.

There was too much he didn't know about what came next. Too much Iveera hadn't yet told him. Too much she'd avoided during her stiff lectures on Knightly duties and Alliance politics. Like what the hell they were going to do about the mysterious and possibly sinister "corruption" that may or may not still be lurking within their Excaliburs from the Battle of Atlantis.

But they had a few hours before Golnak. Time enough, he decided, for a short stint of the mildly magical rejuvenation Ex had taken to calling "super sleep" as they'd bounced from one ass-kicking to another these past days. Maybe he could even sneak in a quick q-node call to his friends.

An hour's rest. No more. Then he'd have that word with Iveera. Maybe even two if she'd spare them.

~

"You want me to have a look at that, sir?"

Doing his best to mask the wince, Jaeger turned his frown away from the cargo bay exit Kalders had just marched through and back to an obstinately hovering Emily Carter. He pulled his shirt back down over the mottled bruising on his ribs, shaking his head. "Nothing's broken."

He was pretty sure. Not broken enough to fuss over, at least.

It wasn't so much that he loathed bringing attention to the fact that he was flesh and blood like the rest of them, or that he'd just had his ass half-kicked by a kid who barely knew how to make a proper fist. Admittedly, those parts did irritate the shit out of him, but that wasn't the crux of the matter.

"Kid's pretty damn strong, huh?" Carter asked, missing nothing.

He frowned harder at the medic. "Kinda hard to say, seeing as we've got no goddamn clue what one of us could do with that Excalibur shit riding shotgun."

Carter just gave him that steely-eyed *momma knows best* look of hers—the one that always hit him with a confusing jolt of emasculation and arousal—and knelt down to peel his shirt up and have that look of hers, protests be damned.

Definitely more on the *arousal* side today, he decided, as she leaned closer, running her dark fingers across his ribs. He stowed that thought, and let the pain of a particularly firm prod pull him back down to that damned crux. The team beat him there, with Snuffy unsurprisingly taking lead in the complaints department.

"How much longer are we gonna keep, you know..." The unlucky mechanic waved his hands, searching for the words.

"Gang-banging the kid?" Ramirez offered.

Snuffy turned palms up in a shrug, accepting the verbiage.

"Like he can't fucking take it," Pierce said, looking more than a little disgusted that they'd even think of sympathizing at this point.

"Seriously?" Snuffy asked, with an unusually confrontational cross of the arms.

"I dunno," Ramirez said, his half-thoughtful, half-jovial tone somehow dispelling some of the tension before he even spoke his mind. "He *did* look kinda..." He waved a hand, searching for the words. "Well, the sword thing, you know?" he said, jabbing one finger up as if to skewer his point right there. "I mean, what's that about? Kid can conjure fresh armor in the blink of an eye? But the man's sword…" In lieu of words, he merely curled his rigid finger through a passable impression of a man's droopy detumescence.

Snuffy gave a begrudging huff of amusement. Elmo came dangerously close to smiling. Jaeger shot a sideways glance at Carter, curious whether she'd roll her eyes at having to listen to yet another complex problem boiled down to the metaphor level of *man's genitalia*, but she just shot him an *oh, please* scowl and returned her eyes to his bruised ribs.

"I still say we're taking it too easy on him," Pierce said.

"Yeah, well tell that to my internal bleeding," Snuffy shot back. "Never mind the moral quandaries of gang-banging a civie for a second. What about us? We're not freaking spec ops in here."

That drew eyes to Jaeger and Carter, who'd both done stints here and there, though maybe not quite enough to merit the predictable glances that always followed any mention of the special forces.

"Okay, *most* of us aren't freaking spec ops in here," Snuffy amended. "I mean, I'm supposed to be a goddamn mechanic, not a bruiser."

That, at least, broke some of the tension in the room as everyone had a good chuckle at the timeless joke of Snuffy the Mechanic—no doubt the most butter-fingered, hapless, downright unlucky one the Air Force had ever seen.

"I'm just saying," Snuffy muttered, frowning down at his boots as the amusement spread. "A guy's only got so many kidneys."

Jaeger wasn't entirely sure whether Snuffy was referring to Arturi or himself. Either way, he was painfully aware of the point. Lieutenant Tessa Kalders clearly was, too. She'd left without a word. Not even a single zippy comment. Which, for her, was kind of like forgetting to breathe.

He had a feeling she'd gone to comfort Arturi. Maybe even help him with that shoulder. He couldn't quite decide if he hoped she succeeded or not. Either way, she seemed to have a soft spot for the kid, and that was a potential problem waiting to happen.

He made a mental note to have a private word with her later. He didn't blame her, exactly. He might've even liked Arturi himself if the kid wasn't such a full-time pain in his ass. But they needed to be unified with the goal here.

"You sure he can take much more of this, sir?" Carter asked, pulling his shirt back down, inspection complete.

Jaeger didn't know how to answer the question. Luckily, she'd had the courtesy to speak quietly enough so as not to be heard by the rest of the team, who'd happily shifted their collective attention to their favorite pastime of dicking around with Snuffy.

The only thing he was really sure of was that it was a damned good thing the diplomats back on good ol' terra firma hadn't had time to cram an international grab-bag of specialists and black site operators onto this ship like the UN had proposed in their emergency meeting. Political equilibrium, they'd called it. Or world peace, or some such bullshit. As if they weren't already sitting on enough of a powder keg here. Black Knights and wizards and end-of-the-world hoodoo, and one greenhorn American supersoldier caught in the middle of it all, in desperate need of record-time training.

Arturi had some spunk, that was for sure. More than Jaeger had given him credit for upon their first meeting. With time, it was even possible the kid might be shaped into something approaching *useful* in shit storms like the one they'd just weathered back on Earth. But time seemed to be the one thing they couldn't count on.

Do whatever you must, the Gorgon Knight, Ser Katanaga, had told him in private at the outset of their voyage four days earlier. *He will survive it. He must.*

That could've been that, as far as Jaeger was concerned. He didn't like it, but he was at least a moderately competent soldier, and he knew enough to recognize that he had no earthly idea what the hell they were truly dealing with here. It was what the Gorgon *hadn't* said that troubled him, the unspoken alternative he could've sworn she was thinking when she'd said it. *He will survive it. Or he won't.*

He still wasn't sure what to make of that.

"Colonel?"

He came back to the cargo deck, where Carter was watching him with serious eyes. Across the bay, he glimpsed Kalders stalking past the wide doorway, headed from wherever she'd been back up to the bridge and to her new obsession of learning the ship, in and out. *Befriending* it, she kept insisting. He shook his head, thinking about how far they were from home, and how far they'd already deviated from best-practice guidelines of physical and psychological stresses with Nate Arturi.

Could the kid take much more of this?

"I don't know, Carter. I don't. But I have a feeling we're gonna find out."

CHAPTER 2
AWOL

They faced off in the low, windswept ruins of some ancient village under a broodingly stormy sky, two veritable gods of the Light Side and the Dark. Both titans in their own right. Both with swords drawn.

On the left was a tall, devastatingly fearsome Excalibur Knight whose golden armor shone like a brilliant sun, casting pure defiance at the darkening maelstrom above. On the right, the unnatural gloom of the Black Knight's armor devoured that golden light whole, annihilating it, his jagged armor and hellish blade an antithesis to the Knightly splendor of his opponent. A dark bundle lay on the ashy ground before them.

When they crossed swords, the entire world shook and—

SHIP. WAITING SHIP. HEADING SHIFT.

The words rang from the howling wind itself, frenetic and mechanical.

Ahead, the two Knights turned like they'd heard. Turned straight toward him.

"Nathaniel," whispered the wind.

WARNING: INTERCEP—

~

NATE SNAPPED awake to a sinus-searing hit of adrenaline and a confusing jumble of dream fragments and sound.

"What the shit?" he hissed, lurching upward before he'd even finished processing where he was.

Ah, there you are, Ex said as Nate's feet touched down on the hard deck, and his bearings began flooding back in. *You were having quite the dream.*

He scanned his bland *Camelot* quarters with sleep-stained eyes, mind feebly attempting to hold on to the fading images of the two Knights facing off in that stormy hellscape. At least until he noticed the softly pulsing amber light directing his attention toward the door.

Ah, yes. You'd better make your way to the bridge. We'll be arriving at the Golnak system momentarily.

"You…" Nate blinked at the familiar *oh-shit-I-forgot-the-homework* feeling settling in the pit of his stomach. "You let me sleep for four hours?!"

I am not your mother, Nathaniel. Besides, you looked very tired.

I told you to wake me!

An attempt was made.

You knew I wanted to—

What, Ex cut him off, *snivel? Pace? Pointlessly harry Ser Iveera with your insatiable worries rather than recuperate for what comes next?*

Nate scowled at the wall, trying to gather his thoughts. He'd *wanted* to talk to his friends. And it wasn't as if the rest of his *insatiable* worries were baseless.

Hmm, Ex said, considering Nate's thoughts like a choosy art critic. *Or perhaps you merely wanted the time to go canoodling with Lieutenant Kalders in the middle of the corridor again.*

What are you trying to—Canoodling? Seriously? There was no… canoodling. Jesus. He rotated his arm and hand, noting the relative lack of roaring pain from his re-located shoulder. No worse than every other square inch of his battered body, at least. *And since when do you…*

He paused, blinking down at his hand––his *armored* hand.

He was fully suited for battle.

Ex, did you happen to—

Before he could finish the thought, the entire room crooned with the descending hum of massive machinery powering down. The soft tug of deceleration greeted Nate's stomach past the inertial dampeners, deck shuddering underfoot. They were coming out of the jump, he realized, back to real space, or whatever one called the opposite of the spatial collapse chain reactions generated by their so-called crusher drives.

Ex gave a weary sigh, probably at his sadly inferior understanding of their flight mechanics, but Nate only half-heard, caught up as he was in the sudden, uneasy memory of that dream, and the voice he'd heard on those howling winds. Mechanical. Urgent. The *Camelot's* voice.

SHIP, the *Camelot* cried—not a dream. *WAITING SHIP. HEADING SHIFT. WARNING: INTERCEPT COURSE.*

"Shit!" he cried, lurching for the door on a fresh surge of adrenaline.

The door sprang open by some extension of his will, clearing the way for him to barrel into the corridor. Straight into Iveera, he registered, as something caught his charging mass effortlessly on the end of one long, deceptively slender arm.

"We've got trouble," he croaked, looking up at the seven foot Gorgon and dimly noting by the presence of her copper armor that she was probably already aware of the fact. He turned for the bridge, expecting her to fall in with him. She caught his arm before he could take a step, and spun him back around like a slack-jawed rag doll.

"They are not enemies, Nathaniel," she said, perfectly calm by all alien appearances. Her hairlike jin paused around her head mid-swirl, as if considering her own words. "They have not come to slag holes in your ship, at least."

It was only then that he noticed the holo projection of the unfamiliar ship hovering over her palm. "How do you know?" he croaked. Christ, his throat was dry.

"Because that is a justicar ship," she said, releasing his arm and gesturing to the holo. "Alliance law enforcers. And it's still twenty minutes out at current velocities."

Nate studied her face—not so radically different than a human's barring the green skin and phosphorescent blue eyes—and wished yet again that he knew how to read those non-expressions of hers. He noted the subdued writhing of her jin instead and was opening his mouth to ask why she didn't seem too happy about the fact when the plunking thud of running boot steps cut him short.

There was a low hum from the gravitonic lift a little ways down the corridor, the Snuffy burst out of the lift well, red-faced and scurrying fast enough that he nearly wiped out when he saw them and tried to stop. "Guys!" he cried, catching himself on the wall. "We've got incoming."

"Yes," Iveera said, in a tone that might've been intended to soothe. "Thank you, Airman Killian."

With that, she stalked off down the corridor, leaving Nate to shoot a clueless shrug at a wide-eyed Snuffy before turning to hurry after her.

"So why do you look like you'd rather it was a Troglodan raiding party out there?" he asked quietly when he'd caught up.

"Because crushing a Troglodan raiding party would be infinitely less bothersome than diplomatically excusing ourselves from a justicar," Iveera said, not slowing. "Especially a Troglodan one, considering."

It's right here in the ship log, Ex said, before Nate could even ask. *Current commanding officer of Alliance Justicar Vessel D679: Malfar, Clanless One. Troglodan. Alliance Justicar, Third-Class.*

Nate was about to point out that he couldn't *see* this magical ship log when it occurred to him that that was probably exactly the kind of thing he could've summoned up via holo display. He jerked in surprise as Ex did him one better and somehow projected the data right across his visual feed in neat orange letters.

Iveera was still moving.

"Does that mean, uh…" He started, hurrying after her. "Wait, why is the law waiting for us?"

"Likely because we are the first arrivals in the wake of brewing rumors of conflict on Terra." A flutter ran through her jin. "And because I did not leave this system on amicable terms."

"Amicable terms?" Nate echoed. What did that even—

"Hey," he said, surprising himself by reaching out and grabbing Iveera's shoulder. She paused so abruptly that he nearly ran into her. "What the hell's going on here? I thought we were the good guys."

She pointedly shrugged his hand off before answering. "We are the sometimes revered, often mistrusted agents of the Lady, currently riding the blade's edge between a political firestorm and the only three entities with which the galaxy should truly be concerned at present. If you were expecting a trillion hearts and minds to simply fall in line with the righteous importance of our mission, you've come to the wrong Alliance."

With that, she turned back for the bridge.

"But then—"

"Uh, Nate?" came a new voice, seemingly straight from his own brainstem. Tessa, he registered, coming to him via ever-freaky Ex radio right at the center of his noggin. "We seem to have an angry alien ship hailing us now that we're all done… breaking physics or whatever. Looks like a—"

"Justicar Vessel D679?" Nate asked, drawing Iveera's attention back from the bridge.

"That's the one," Tessa said. "I think they're asking for the Excalibur Knight, but these interfaces are… well, you know."

"We'll be there in a sec," Nate said, following Iveera up the ramp toward the bridge. "Just, uh, standby, I guess."

"Roger that, Mr. Knight," Tessa chimed, somehow managing to sound chipper about it. More chipper than he could imagine his good pal Lt Col Jaeger was feeling at that moment. He killed the comms with a thought, focusing back on Iveera, wanting answers.

"Best we attempt diplomacy first," she said, before he could even compose a question. "We cannot spare the time to submit to a full inquiry, but justicars and fleet admirals are not fond of being brushed aside. Hiding behind the protection of the Round Table Accords will only complicate matters." She looked pointedly down at his torso. "As will that armor."

"What?"

"You should hide your armor," she said, calling up her holo interface.

"But why?"

She made no sign she'd heard him, fidgeting with her holo until she gave up and turned to him with an unmistakable frown. "Your ship is under the impression that I require your permission to accept incoming communications."

"Well," he said slowly, confused and mildly irritated, "maybe you should tell me what's going on if you wanna play with my toys."

It felt like a stretch pretending like he was the one in control here, or that the *Camelot* even truly belonged to him just because the Lady had allowed it for the time being. But at least he managed to not flinch as the Gorgon stared him down.

"In addition to ascertaining why I slagged Ser Groshna's ship and fled the system three weeks past," she said, electric blue stare hardening, "the justicar will no doubt wish to know what has transpired on Earth. It is possible the galaxy is still largely ignorant of the invasion, depending on how much of my limited report the Council has elected to distribute. Regardless, the one thing of which I am certain is that we must not broadcast the facts that the Merlin is missing and that he has furnished a defenseless boy with an Excalibur, ripe for the reaping."

Quickly as he bristled at her words, her jin fanned out like a stop sign, calling for peace.

"I am only trying to protect you in the wizard's stead, Nathaniel. Allow me to send this ambitious justicar on his way. If all goes well, he will stand down and pass along his recommendation for the relay fleet to grant us safe passage without additional questioning, given the urgency of our mission."

I believe she speaks wisdom, little hobbit.

"Fine." Nate shrugged, not liking it but also not really sure what else he'd been expecting from an entire galaxy's worth of cooperating governments and militaries. "We'll take the call on the bridge. I'll keep my mouth shut."

He started to move, but she was still waiting for something.

"Your armor," she said.

He hesitated.

"Until you are prepared for the considerably dangerous attention that comes with the mantle of Excalibur Knight, it is best that no one outside this ship knows who you are, or indeed that you even exist."

He had a number of questions to that—not the least of which being just how dangerous *considerably dangerous* was, why she felt they couldn't even trust the Alliance Space Police, and how Ex felt about hiding their existence —but before he could ask anything, Jaeger came marching off of the bridge, clearly looking for them.

"Lt Col Jaeger," Iveera said, sounding every bit as if she'd been expecting him. "If you wish to protect your asset, you will pretend to be the captain of this vessel until this situation is resolved. No one is to make mention of a new Knight. You have your translator?"

It was only at that last bit that Nate registered she'd switched from her Gorgon tongue to English. Ex's on-the-fly translations were good enough that it was easy to mistake them for the real thing. The small translator disc that Jaeger slipped from his pocket, on the other hand—while plenty sleek and apparently fairly ubiquitous throughout Alliance space—was definitely a step down from Excalibur tech where smoothness of delivery was concerned.

"Understood," Jaeger said, not complaining about his intergalactic Rosetta stone one bit as he slid the small disc in place behind his ear, where no one would notice it unless they were right beside him. "I'll *pretend.*"

The word practically had air quotes hanging from it, a not-so-soft reminder that no one aboard this ship really counted Nate as anything other than the snot-nosed owner of the *Camelot*, and certainly not its captain. It irked the crap out of him, but not as much as Jaeger's expression as he took up position beside Iveera, both of them staring Nate down like they were expecting something.

The armor.

Goddammit.

What was the point of even *being* an Excalibur Knight, if he was just going to be shoved into the corner at the first sign of danger?

To fight for duty and justice? To protect all life in the galaxy from deconstruction at the hands of the Synth? I'm just spit-balling here.

Nate clenched his jaw, wanting to argue with all of them, feeling all the more childish for it.

Our time will come, Nathaniel.

Stifling a sigh, he willed his armor to recede and watched the pristine plates peel from his body, folding safely back into e-dim with a soft whir. When it was done, he stood on the deck, just another harmless Earthling.

"Hey, you did fix that shoulder," Jaeger noticed out loud. "Nice going, kid."

Nate half-expected the smug bastard to pat him one square on said shoulder, just for maximum machismo in-your-face-ness. He fondly imagined paying the Lt Col right back with a knee to the groin, then muttered a neutral thanks and stepped past Jaeger and Iveera for the bridge instead.

"Not to interrupt, guys," Tessa was calling as he entered the bridge, her head half-turned toward them, eyes still riveted to the consoles like she couldn't look away, "but can anyone tell me why we just got hit with about thirty more pings on the comms?"

The rest of the SAS team looked equally curious. Which was to say most of them were glancing around from their crash couches and consoles like they half-expected to find the *Camelot* had already been boarded.

"It's the relay patrol fleet," Iveera said, stepping past Nate and up to Tessa's station on the raised command deck, her jin flicking toward the front of the bridge and somehow calling up a small ocean of bright blue dots across the viewport, each coupled with a few strings of text and small but detailed holos of the warships themselves. "They're several light minutes in-system. They would've hailed the moment they saw us."

"And how the hell'd this one know to be waiting for us out here?" Jaeger asked, nodding to the holo display over Tessa's consoles that showed an intercept countdown ticking at around twelve minutes.

"Perhaps he is merely proficient at his craft," Iveera said, her holo coming back to rest on their impending justicar neighbor, one long jin poised over the Gorgon symbol that, with a little focus, shifted before Nate's eyes into an *answer* icon he could understand. "Let us find out."

She paused, looking back first to Jaeger, then to Nate.

"Do not speak unless you must."

Jaeger gave a grim chuckle. "My first wife's standing order."

Nate just held her gaze in stubborn silence until, apparently satisfied, she turned back to her holo and accepted the hail.

~

"Knight ship *Camelot*," boomed an unmistakably Troglodan voice before the huge command deck hologram even finished resolving, "this is Justicar D679 of the Galactic Alliance. You have entered a controlled access system harboring a fugitive of the Alliance and are hereby ordered to power down your drives and prepare to be boarded."

Nate glanced at Iveera, wondering just how understated her not-so-amicable escape had been. When he looked back to the hologram, it had clarified into a dark gray Troglodan. He was on the smaller end of the trog size chart if the holo was to scale, and outfitted in well-worn but neatly maintained armor of royal blue and gray, with several muted decals and emblems etched across the chest and shoulder plates. Nate recognized the blazing star and overlapping crescents of the Alliance emblem front and center, but it was the several large splotches of discoloration on the trog's wide face that his eyes drifted to—a raw, agitated pink that leapt out from his gray hide.

Blight spots, Ex explained.

"There are no fugitives aboard this ship, justicar," Iveera replied in her perfect calm. "I have committed no acts in excess of my order's mandates, and as for the former point, you will find this ship is permanently cleared for unrestricted access to any and all Beacon ports, Golnak included."

The justicar looked none too impressed. "Then you deny that you destroyed Golnak mining installation C-73? And that you were thereby directly responsible for—"

"The altercation was unlawfully instigated by the former Excalibur Knight, Ser Groshna," Iveera said, "as evidenced by the records transmitted to Elder Teedath on Kalyria shortly after the incident."

"Then you do not deny that it was indeed your order which was responsible for—"

"The *former* Excalibur Knight, Ser Groshna, was acting outside of our mission mandate, and against the will of the Merlin. In the name of the Lady, this injustice has since been rectified."

The justicar paused at that. "Please explain, Ser Katanaga."

Iveera's jin flattened in what might've been remorse or caution. "You have no doubt already heard the rumors."

"I do not make a habit of trusting all that I hear on the nets."

There was a subtle shift in Iveera's face as she studied the Troglodan, like she'd just confirmed something important. "In the order of my duties, I was forced to slay Ser Groshna on Terra. It is in the order of those same duties that I must now request you stand down and allow us to continue in pursuit of our quarry."

Across from them, the justicar had gone so still that Nate wondered if the holo hadn't frozen. "I see," he finally said, touching absentmindedly at one of his angry pink splotches. "I see." He gestured dazedly to someone outside of the holo, then focused back on Iveera. "And what quarry am I to take it you pursue?"

"The one who used Ser Groshna as a puppet in the theft of the Terran Beacon. Beyond that, out of no personal disrespect for you, justicar, I am disinclined to speculate on the identity of the thief at this time. I only request that you stand down and forward your clearance to the relay fleet ahead."

The justicar was a stone wall as he chewed over Iveera's words. "Very well," he finally said, and for a second, Nate thought that would be that. Then the pockmarked Troglodan turned to someone outside of the holo. "Prepare to board, at speed."

"Hey," Jaeger said, taking a step forward.

Iveera silenced him with a raised hand, not looking away from the holo, where the justicar's own crew seemed to be equally surpised and confused.

"You would not let the Terran speak in the matter?" the justicar asked, ignoring his people. "I find that curious, Ser Knight. Nearly as curious as—"

"Justicar," Iveera said, "you are wasting my time and yours. I will invoke the mission-critical compliance clauses of the Accords if I must, but if you merely consult with Elder Teedath of Kalyria, you will no doubt—"

"Elder Teedath is dead."

The look on Iveera's face was one Nate had never seen before. Open surprise, and anger, and… horror? He couldn't tell. Her emotions were too muted to begin with. But he was pretty sure of one thing: whoever Elder Teedath was, this wasn't supposed to have happened.

"Elder Teedath is dead," the justicar repeated, "your story cannot be corroborated, and you are aboard a Knight ship that is not your own, admitting to having slain another member of your order in pursuit of an unconfirmed Beacon which was allegedly thieved by an unidentified individual. Tell me, Ser Knight, how would you proceed, were you in my position?"

Nate watched, waiting for Iveera to invoke that mission-critical authority—to remind this lone stubborn justicar that she was an *Excalibur Knight*, dammit. A legendary hero fighting for the fate of the very galaxy.

But Iveera's silence only loomed, amplifying the tension until Nate was positive it would explode into violence. Above Tessa's consoles, the intercept display had skipped under the five-minute mark.

Should he do something?

"Elder Teedath," Iveera finally said, her voice quiet. "How did she die? When?"

Hammer of Justice or not, the trog sobered a little at that. "I know only that her death was reported across the nets in the days following your incident here with Ser Groshna." He hesitated. "My condolences if this news carries personal weight, but now it is I who must insist that you submit to…"

It was only as the justicar trailed off that Nate noticed Iveera's fingers and jin flitting across the holo controls, and the faint tickle the gravitonic dampeners couldn't quite hide from his stomach. The *Camelot* was accelerating and changing course. He felt it in his mind and stomach just as surely as he saw it in Tessa's raised brow, looking from him to Iveera to Jaeger for some kind of instruction as the intercept timer ticked up, up, up beside her.

"Kill your engines immediately, Ser Knight," the justicar growled in the holo. "Do not make me open fire."

"You know as well as I that your efforts would be wasted, justicar," Iveera replied, not looking up from her controls.

"Ser Katanaga," Jaeger said, his tone as inexplicably flat as his expression. "A word?"

She ignored him too.

"Iveera," Nate heard himself say, hand half-raised to nothing in particular. "Just…"

Just what?

He didn't know. Didn't have a damn clue what was at stake here—what this could mean for them, for Earth. All he knew was that Iveera was supposed to have had this shit under control, and now they were cutting and running from Alliance law enforcement, and *under control* was the last thing this felt like.

They were still accelerating. The justicar was ordering a targeting lock. Jaeger was giving him a funny look. To do something? To step back and shut up? It was only then that he remembered he was supposed to be an anonymous fly on the wall here.

But screw that.

Iveera was preparing to q-jump them right to that tiny speck of the Beacon relay he saw on the viewport, dead center of the fleet. He felt it somewhere deep in his gut as he extended his thoughts to the *Camelot*, preparing to act.

Are you certain of this? Ex asked.

Not even close. But this was going too nuclear, too fast.

Mute the justicar and tell him to hold fire, he thought to Ex and the ship. *Blank our video feed for a minute and kill the engines.*

A minute to talk. That was all they needed.

The reaction was instantaneous. The ship slowed, and the justicar's voice cut out mid-sentence, the SAS crew looking to Iveera in confusion even as she rounded on Nate with a soft hiss and an electric blue stare, jin gone rigid. For a second, he thought she was going to strike. Then her jin sank, flattening against her head, shoulder slumping.

"Dammit," she practically whispered.

Then a sleek golden ship warped into existence dead ahead, so close it eclipsed the entire viewport, and a voice like gilded steel rang through the bridge without so much as an incoming transmission request.

"So, the *Camelot* truly has returned. Delightful."

Nate was reaching for the *Camelot*, still trying to process who, what, how, and why when the shimmering hologram appeared at the edge of the command deck, tall and proud and far more coherent than the pale justicar beside it. Nearly lifelike. So lifelike that Nate could only gape.

It was the golden Knight from his dream.

"Now," he said, lazily scanning the bridge as if he were actually there and could see each and every one of them, "what is this I hear about my Knights causing a disturbance?"

CHAPTER 3

FIRST KNIGHT

Everyone on the bridge swiveled to Iveera in unison. Everyone but Nate, who'd skipped the question of *who* this newcomer was in favor of the much more unsettling one of how in the hell he could've somehow *seen* him before actually *seeing* him.

Perhaps your dreaming mind merely accessed some snippet of my data banks. Ex sounded less than certain.

Did it?

A moment's hesitation. Ahead, the golden Knight's eyes finished scanning the crew with all the care of a bored window shopper, then focused back on Iveera.

No, Ex admitted. *Not that I can tell. But this is—*

"Ser Kelkarin," Iveera said, surprising Nate by dropping to one armored knee and bowing her head mechanically.

Ser Zedavian of the Eldari House Kelkarin, Ex amended. *First Knight and de facto leader of our order in the Merlin's absence.*

The golden Knight certainly looked the part as he stared down at Iveera, high cheekbones, slender golden face, and long, immaculately braided hair all giving him the look of some regal high elf, albeit nine feet tall and substantially more intimidating than Nate had ever imagined any yellow-eyed elf could be.

So *this* was an Eldari. One of the oldest and most powerful species in the Alliance, according to Lesson Time with Ex and Iveera.

"Where is the Beacon?" Ser Zedavian Kelkarin finally asked, all earlier traces of smug playfulness gone from his tone.

"Taken," Iveera said, rising smoothly to her feet like she'd been waiting for the chance. "Which is why I implore you to—"

"Taken by whom?"

Iveera couldn't have straightened any further, but she sure seemed to as her jin gave a sharp flick. "That is what I am trying to tell you. The incursion on Terra was orchestrated by a foe the likes of which I have never seen. A Black Knight whose—"

"Show me."

Nate watched right alongside Jaeger and the others, almost too riveted to even remember what was at stake here. It was bizarre, seeing Iveera spoken to like this. The unstoppable Knight who'd stared down an entire Troglodan army and sent them running. The one who'd clearly had no qualms blasting off from their waiting justicar. And Nate had stopped her. Why?

"Ser Kelkarin," she said, almost softly, "I believe—"

"I do not require your personal conjecture, Seven. You will transmit all records of the Golnak incident and your time on Terra directly to me, and then you will bring the *Camelot* to the Forge, where—"

"I must—"

"You will bring the *Camelot* to the Forge," the First Knight said, his golden hologram striding closer until he towered head and shoulders over Iveera. "You will report to the Council and dance without complaint until such a time as they are satisfied. Do you understand, Ser Knight?"

The tension was so palpable, Nate forgot it was a hologram standing before them. Iveera stood perfectly still, caught in some internal battle. Nate waited for her to spit it out—to tell this so-called First Knight that some evil bastard was running around out there with the Merlin and a stolen Beacon, and that nothing else mattered.

They were all on the same side here, weren't they? If they could just make him understand what was happening…

"Yes, First Knight," Iveera finally said, head bowed as she drew up her holo controls.

What are you doing? Nate thought, which—as Ex quickly pointed out— was probably a little chicken shit, seeing as he couldn't seem to find the stones to speak his own mind. Or breathe. Whether or not she actually heard his paltry attempt at Ex-powered silent radio speak, her eyes flicked his way as her slender fingers paused over the holos.

"The Merlin…" she started, then paused at the sudden suspicion in the First Knight's eyes.

"The Merlin was there, Zedavian," she finished. "On Terra. He was captured by the same Black Knight who absconded with the Beacon. With respect, the Council's squabbles will be of no concern if we do not catch them before—"

"Before what?" A hint of amusement was creeping back into the First Knight's tone. "Tell me, Seven, what is it you think this fabled Black Knight could do with a Beacon?"

"He used it to jump clear of the Sol system."

Ser Kelkarin studied her evenly, betraying nothing.

"He possessed other unprecedented abilities," Iveera pressed on.

"The power to imprison a wizard, no doubt."

I do not think he believes her, Ex said.

Nate didn't argue. The First Knight's comment was flat. Disbelieving. Like what he'd just suggested was clearly impossible. For a second, Nate thought Iveera would go a step further just to prove she wasn't screwing around—confess that they'd been touched by the synthient corruption that had infected Groshna's Excalibur and turned him puppet to the Black Knight. That they still weren't sure it was gone.

"The Merlin feared this Knight to be an ancient member of our own order," she finally said, "turned to darkness by the hand of the Synth."

"The Synth," Zedavian echoed quietly, seemingly lost in thought. "What do you know of the Synth?" He stirred and held up a hand to stop her before she could mistake the question as an invitation to speak. "We are finished here. Submit your records and report to the Council, Ser Katanaga. That is an order. I will dowse the relays and assemble my own wild speculations, and you will stay put on the Forge until I say otherwise. Understood?"

Iveera stood silent, jin flexed rigid against her head.

The First Knight leaned closer, reaching down to clasp her ivy green chin between golden thumb and forefinger. "Do not make me hunt the mighty Huntress," he said, in a soft tone that suggested he would've enjoyed nothing more.

Nate wasn't sure she actually felt the contact—still wasn't even sure how the First Knight had arrived out of thin air on top of them and back-doored his way in with this hyper-realistic holo connection—but if the curling of Iveera's lip and the faint crimson glow seeping from her jin were any indication, she was hardly flattered by the touch.

Zedavian looked rather pleased about it all.

"Now, slave your controls and let us be on our way," he said, straightening and turning as if to exit through the invisible holo door he'd first appeared from. He paused midway, bright yellow eyes scanning the crew once more, then settling straight on Nate. "This one?"

Nate stood frozen beneath his gaze, some tiny part of him wanting to step forward with a haughty *that's right, Elrond,* and explain to the First Knight how he was making a huge mistake and how he needed to listen to them, dammit. The rest of him was stuck under the weight of that all-seeing stare, and the fact that he didn't actually have any idea what he was talking about here. And hadn't Iveera told him to hide his identity anyway?

Did it even matter? Maybe this First Knight knew something they didn't. And that dream…

Blackened hands, will you do something?

But Zedavian was already moving on with one of the most disinterested sounds Nate had ever heard. "The controls, Terran," he added, not looking back.

I believe he is asking you to surrender the Camel—

I know what he's asking, Nate shot back, looking to Iveera for some kind of guidance. She might as well have been catatonic. Fuming internally, maybe. Or engaged in some furious discourse with her Excalibur. Either way…

"Do it," she said softly, not breaking from her vacant stare.

Zedavian turned like he had choice thoughts about his subordinates deigning to advise one another on whether or not to follow *his* orders. Like maybe he should remind them who was First Knight here.

Follow his ship, Nate found himself thinking toward the *Camelot* more by flinching reflex than anything else. *Do what he says.*

AFFIRMATIVE.

Nate felt his shoulders slump and waited for Ex to step in with a cheeky remark on the merits of cowardice, but there was nothing. Ser Zedavian Kelkarin didn't give so much as a confirmatory nod. He just stared at Iveera for a long moment, then vanished.

"Well, that was fun," Tessa muttered into the stark silence.

"Just a lovely goddamn barbecue," Jaeger agreed, turning his frown to Nate and Iveera. "Now, does someone wanna tell us what the hell's going on?"

Nate followed Jaeger's deepening frown to the viewport, which was busily zooming itself in on that tiny, distant ring labeled *Golnak Beacon Relay.* The optics zoomed across what the zipping display numbers declared to be millions of kilometers, past ships that pinged with titles like *ASF Gilderoy* (Reconnaissance-Class Corvette, Triton Shipyards) and *ASF Rahgamesh* (Nova-Class Battlecruiser, Seventh Star Industries) and estimated crew counts from the tens up to the tens of thousands. In and in, until…

"Huh," Tessa said, as they all gaped at the viewport.

It felt about as adequate a thing to say as anything else as they all seemed to realize in unison just how completely out of their depths they were here.

To say the Beacon relay was a sight to behold felt a bit like saying it was *kind of* nice, finally sharing a kiss with the girl you'd secretly been in love with for three years. Understated, at best. But neither the thought of Gwen nor the business with Ser Zedavian Kelkarin were enough to pull Nate's attention away from the miracle of a sci-fi geek's wet dream floating in the viewport.

At its essence, it was a ring––an unfathomably titanic ring that had been visible to the naked eye at over thirty million kilometers, granted. One that dwarfed even the orbiting thirty-thousand-crew dreadnought several hundred, maybe several *thousand*, times over. But a ring, nonetheless, formed of dark matte panels whose size Nate could only wonder at, and positively teeming with a network of metal arms and girders that spanned several hundred kilometers inward from the outer superstructure, giving the entire thing the vague look of some kind of steampunk dreamcatcher, pulsing here and there with crackling arcs of azure light.

"We're flying *through that*?" someone asked.

"Shut it, Snuffy!" someone else replied.

"Let's batten down the slack jaws and buckle up people," Tessa called over her shoulder, before turning to Nate and Jaeger and adding in a hurried whisper, "But seriously, we're flying through that? Now?"

"Assuming we make it past those," Jaeger said quietly, almost absent-mindedly, his eyes glued to the tactical layout of the potentially not-so-friendly Alliance forces arrayed before them. He turned to Nate, remembering himself, and Nate didn't need to ask what it was.

Their scheduled check-in call with Earth.

They'd explicitly told their people—told the freaking president of the United States, not to mention Nate's friends—that they'd report back before flying off into this big mysterious relay. And now…

"Q-drives initiating," declared bold cyan text across the viewport display. "Prepare to jump."

Now it was happening.

Nate looked to Iveera, desperate to snap her out of her funk, to do *something*, for god's sake. She was already watching him, eyes wider than he'd ever seen, glowing red jin pressed flat to her head, like she'd just had a troubling realization of her own.

"Give me comms to that justicar," she practically hissed. "Now."

～

HALF A MILLION KILOMETERS AWAY, Malfar stood at the helm of his ship, watching his main display as the two cursed Knight ships, *Camelot* and *Eldest Stone*, held their privileged secret council. What in nine hells the First Knight was doing out here, away from his posh throne of power on Forge Station, Malfar didn't know. But he had a sinking feeling this entire mess was about to be re-branded with a big fat *out of your jurisdiction*.

Destroyer take the entire damn Order Excalibur. Pompous bastards. Over-inflated relics of a forgotten (and almost certainly embellished) Great War. And as for the Dread Knight Groshna—the allegedly *deceased* Dread Knight Groshna…

"Justicar?" came the voice of Lieutenant Shelton Ordercaste, who'd been uncharacteristically silent ever since the *Camelot* had punched out of crusher space and put all of his earlier complaints to shame. "Word from Vice Admiral Var'lain. We're to stand down and allow the Knightships *Camelot* and *Eldest Stone* safe passage to the relay."

Malfar let out a sigh, clenching and unclenching his powerful fists. "Send our acknowledgment to the vice admiral," he told the Atlantean, eyes never leaving the two Knightships on the tactical display. "And remain ready for anything, lieutenant," he added, suppressing the urge to order his excitable Hobdans to maintain weapons locks as the two Knightships spun in unison, orienting in-system, toward the relay.

"Sir," his first officer acknowledged, wielding the elusive word of respect both as if it were foreign to his tongue but also as if he almost meant it.

Nothing like a shared disdain for Council-legislated law-breakers to bring them all together. Not that a single frustrating brush with the red tape was going to magically disperse his fine crew's resentment for good. No. The First Knight would abscond with his little Gorgon terrorist until such time as the Council could declare Katanaga's chaos on Terra and at the Golnak mining station to have been "within the lawful realms of Knightly peacekeeping duties." And just like that, the fine crew of *Alliance Justicar Vessel D679* would once again find itself sitting through another long, fruitless burn in Golnak space, wondering what in nine hells their big dumb Troglodan commander had thought he was playing at—trying to apprehend a Knight.

No one took down a Knight. Not like that.

For a bitter moment, he wondered why C-Sec had even bothered giving him permission to come out here as a tertiary investigator in the alleged incidents. *To fail*, was the most tempting answer. To let him prove himself right out of a job that the galaxy would've rather seen filled by a more civilized pair of boots. But that was only his overdeveloped sense of persecution talking.

In truth, no one had stopped him coming out here because no one knew what was actually happening on Terra, and because he'd left his assignment request sufficiently vague. C-Sec didn't tend to question their justicars all that much, even the Troglodan ones, and his unique interest in the case was hardly something that would be readily flagged by anyone who wasn't intimately familiar with the Trogarran capital brood lots, circa 5,022, GTE reckoning.

Regardless…

In the distance, he watched the Knightships light the darkness with twin flares of acceleration burn, itching for one fleeting moment to throw it all to hell and give the futile order to open fire. Just to remind the bastards that no one was above Justice, even if they *were* above the law.

A crackle of noise drew his good senses back to the muted holo connection he'd nearly forgotten. The bridge view of the *Camelot* sputtered back to life on a crew that looked rather unanimously shaken. It was an easy expression to recognize in Atlantean faces—or Terran ones, rather—once one learned to look for it.

There'd been some kind of disagreement. The dark-eyed youngling looked especially disgruntled about it. Far more so than his older, hard-faced superior. And as for Ser Katanaga…

"No time," the Gorgon cut him off before he could even open his mouth, barely bothering to look up from her holo controls.

He felt his lip curling itself into a snarl, felt the red-rimmed Troglodan rage flaring bright.

"If you are truly the servant of justice I believe you to be," Ser Iveera Katanaga pressed on, "you will turn your attention to the data I am transmitting and—"

"I am not your servant, Knight," he growled before his higher brain could even process what she was saying.

"The timing of Elder Teedath's death," she continued like she hadn't heard him, almost as if she were speaking to herself. "The arrival of Groshna's personal fleet on Terra a mere three weeks later." Her electric blue eyes flitted elsewhere, then back. "The First Knight's intervention. Something is amiss."

He faltered, failing to mask his hesitation. It had been hard to miss, the rather troubling timing of the rumored invasion—timing that suggested it had all been long months in the planning, far longer than the Terran Beacon had even been awakened, as far as he understood it. But that was all it had been. All it *was*. Rumors and hearsay. Rumors from the one who now claimed to have slain the Dread Knight Groshna. And until the Alliance Justice saw fit to dispatch orders otherwise—

His omni buzzed against his wrist, his display pinging the summary notification of what looked to have been a rather vast multi-format data transfer. It didn't make any sense. None of this did.

"The data is in your hands, justicar," the Gorgon said. "It should be enough to begin your investig—"

"I AM NOT YOUR SERVANT, KNIGHT!"

The ringing in his head, coupled with the ensemble of shocked expressions from his crew, told him that the roar had been every bit as ferocious as he feared.

Dammit.

He forced out a breath, demanding control of himself. He could practically hear the thoughts bouncing around the bridge. *There* was his true beastly nature, rearing its head. *There* was the spotted savage, proving he wasn't fit for the station of justicar. The thought made him want to smash his console to a sputtering heap and bite one of their damned heads off. In the pulsing red flash of his mind's eye, he *did* do those things. Back in the perfect quiet of the bridge, though, under the tense watchfulness of his crew, Malfar set his gargantuan shoulders and focused back on Ser Groshna's killer with a deadly calm. "By all the gods in the universe, Ser Knight, I will see you delivered to the hands of—"

But the holo winked out of existence before he could finish, the *Camelot* and *Eldest Stone* both dropping off of the displays, perhaps lost to one of the Knight ships' mythical q-drive jumps, or perhaps merely shrouded by cloaking technology beyond the rest of the galaxy's wherewithal to penetrate. It mattered not, Malfar decided, staring through the dark void on his main display, and the softly pulsing notification of Ser Katanaga's waiting data bundle.

He turned to the forward bridge display, only distantly aware of his tensed crew awaiting his orders, and watched as the two Knight ships blipped back into existence at the massive Golnak relay minutes later. Probably, the jump had only been mere subjective seconds for the Knights with their godly q-drives. Half a day's sub-light burn in the blink of an eye, and here sat Malfar and his pitiful crew, unable to so much as visually confirm the fact until the photons arrived at the ship's optics from the relay at the boring old speed of light, a ghostly afterimage of those fleeing titans, who were as unbounded by Alliance law as they were by the laws of mortal physics.

His fist clenched as the twin blips reached a small sub-port of the relay ring and vanished again on a faster-than-light trail of crackling azure energy, bound for the Forge.

More minutes stretched, broken only by the soft hum of shipboard electronics and the periodic glances of his crew, not-so-subtly wondering what in nine hells had just happened, and what they were going to do about it. Then the message came, the emphatic ping at the first officer's station entirely too energetic for the order it no doubt carried. Malfar wasn't sure how he'd known it was coming at all, much less so quickly. Subconscious intuition, he supposed—incomplete details churning in the back of his head, infinite possibilities and branching pathways, somehow all converging to a single overwhelming likelihood.

"It's Central," Shelton said, confirming Malfar's sinking suspicion even as the Atlantean frowned at the display, re-reading the message like he was sure he must've gotten it wrong the first time. "They want you to report in person." He glanced up from the display, and Malfar's whirring background brain was mildly surprised to note the Atlantean actually appeared a tad concerned for his blight-spotted brute of a commanding officer. "They want you there immediately, sir."

Malfar let the words hang undisturbed, not really needing to wonder what they meant. Something had clearly gone wrong. Was actively going wrong still. Something big. Maybe something small, too. And he'd just stepped straight into the steaming pile of it all.

He scowled down at the slowly winking alert on his personal display, aware of the grim, battle room silence of his waiting crew, knowing he should immediately flag the Gorgon's files to Central's active investigations database, yet hesitating all the same. *Something is amiss*, she'd said, right before beaming over the mysterious data packet. It felt like an understatement, staring at the winking packet that suddenly seemed far more likely to hold the final seal on his personal and professional doom than any substantial answers.

"Set course for the relay, then," he heard himself say, dropping his hand from the untouched display, "and prepare for max burn."

Flag the files, his lawful mind insisted as the crew snapped to make good on his orders. *Do it now, and what will come will come.* Because that was the job. Because there was truth to be found and Justice to be served. For Ser Groshna's killers. For the unlawful aggressors of Terra. For all of them. Justice was due. It didn't matter whose hand served it. And if Malfar went down in the process... well, he'd hardly be the first.

That was the job.

And yet his fingers lingered over that data packet, held in place first by the tightening crash couch restraints as the ship began its burn, then by something else entirely. Something even the whirring processor of his subconscious couldn't resolve as the minutes ticked slowly by, one after the other, until the burn began to taper off, rousing his attention.

It had been three hours.

Spirit of Justice, what was he even thinking?

He flicked the holo controls to life, determined to flag the files to C-Sec and be done with it before that pesky tickle at the back of his mind could distract him again.

In his defense, it didn't.

That honor went to the choir of proximity alarms that cried out across the bridge as an entire Troglodan war party dropped out of crusher space, barely two light-seconds ahead of them.

An explosion of surprised curses chased the chirping alerts across the bridge. Malfar was too stunned to think twice about the lack of decorum. In-system, the relay patrol fleet was scrambling all over again to respond to this new development, the slow trickle of relay-bound traffic rapidly decelerating as the space before the superstructure came alive with maneuvering battle cruisers and preliminary scout wings of Alliance fighters.

The bridge was a lightning storm of chatter.

"—ere'd they even—"

"—shit's going on with—"

"—not even any—"

"Control yourselves," Malfar boomed, loud enough to bring the bridge to a full stop.

"Clearances say they're headed out T-Sec-way," someone finally said.

"What kind of clearances *are* those?" someone else asked.

"Those right there're *don't fuck with us 'less you're looking to start a gods-damned civil war* clearances, ain't they?" said a Hobdan voice.

Malfar barely registered any of it, distracted as he was by the way that subconscious tickle of intuition was catching to a full-on blazing inferno as he processed the information populating across his displays.

"Those are the emperor's credentials, aren't they?" asked the Atlantean at comms, openly frowning at the Troglodan fleet on her readouts. "Isn't that the war paint of—"

"Clan Groshna," Malfar confirmed, his gaze still glued to the blood-red insignia painted across the most fearsome of the three Nova-class dragonhead capital ships. Custom jobs, straight from the Trogarran shipyards. Which might've explained how he knew that ship, even before he spotted the words *Blood Moon* laid across his display in tiny letters.

"That's—"

"The personal flagship of Ser Groshna's next-of-brood sire," Malfar finished, insides curling with dark disgust at the memory of the last time he'd beheld his divine majesty, Varga, Clansire Groshna. "Yes."

"The Dread Knight's heir?" asked Lieutenant Shelton.

Destroyer take his hateful hide, Malfar thought.

"Blackthorne's tits," Agent Ajzgar muttered, before remembering himself and shooting a guilty glance at his commanding officer.

Malfar just stared on, head spinning with hows, whys, and perfectly suspect timing as his kinsmen's three enormous warships and their dozen-plus not-so-small support craft boldly accelerated toward the Golnak relay superstructure, the Alliance patrol fleet, holding, holding, then slowly beginning to peel apart, clearing the way as if urgent word had just come down the chain of command.

What in nine hells was going on here?

Something amiss, Iveera Katanaga's cursed voice rang in his head.

Something galactically fucking amiss.

CHAPTER 4
CHITTER CHATTER

In the musky depths of the dungeon, ensconced in the unrelenting stench of mildew and excrement and the maddening trickle of a leak that had never once ceased to pitter *nor* patter, it might've been easy for one to forget that one was in fact aboard a one-of-a-kind starship, hurtling through the cosmos. Even easier still to lose one's mind completely.

Which, reflected the filthy old man as he flexed fruitlessly against his oppressive armada of chains and shackles, was precisely the point.

Anyone who'd lived a few thousand years could attest that it was all but inevitable: the slow creep of madness. Even with an entire galaxy of novelties at one's fingertips, the best of sentient minds would go at least a touch eccentric with age. Hells, even a synthient mind would. He'd seen it. You might as well simply call it "growing up."

But put a man (or a synthient) in a place where he/she/it is left with nothing—*nothing*—but the endless dark, and the biting pain of claustrophobically tight bindings, and that Lady-damned undying pitter-patter of dripping water—dripping, dripping, like the filling pool of his own madness... and that was where one began to fear the line between a *touch* of eccentricity and a writhing nightmare of full-blown insanity. The kind of place where one might find himself longing for the decadent novelty of simply being allowed to piss himself, just for a change of pace.

The Merlin had been here before.

Or, maybe not *here* before. But… close enough. Close enough to know that such a defiance would've been nothing but an atrocious waste of his dwindling resources. Not that that especially mattered either. When his blackened captor had plundered his e-dim larders, so to speak, he'd left the Merlin only enough to sustain his body for nine days. Perhaps ten, but nine was the intended number, he had no doubt. Nine hells. Nine days. Just long enough to get to wherever they were going, he imagined. Or so the bastard wanted him to think.

Knowing this particular brutally cunning creature as he did, though, the Merlin had no doubt that if he'd been given sustenance for nine days, he could damn well count on the journey lasting for at least eighteen, and quite possibly longer than that. They both knew he wouldn't actually *die*, after all. Just like they both knew he would've perished long, long before now, had it been so easy as that. And so it was to be the madness of *hope* instead, right up until that hope finally dried out and blew away, and it was nothing left but plain old madness, simple and sweet, and drenched in unfathomable agony.

The thought made him want to go on and piss himself right then and there, just to prove he could. It would be absolutely luxurious—an act of defiance for the ages. But also pointless and illogical. No reason to expedite the onset of the agony of starving to death—or to deathlessness, rather.

The Black Knight truly was an immortally devious old bastard, the Merlin decided.

But perhaps it took one to know one.

"Mordred," the Merlin called—or croaked, at least—through the papery tissues that had once (so long ago, it seemed) been his throat. "Mooordred, is that youuu?" Voice like a dry-rotted balloon hemorrhaging stale air. "You won't fiiind it…"

He continued on like that for what could've conceivably been days or hours, rattling his chains, croaking his taunts and that cursed name over and over. Possibly, it was eons. Over and over. He felt like he'd been here before. Over and over. Maybe he'd always been here. Over and over.

Until something pierced through his half-starved daze and yanked him to a full halt.

A sound.

A sound?

Illusions, whispered a voice in his head. *Trickery*.

Plain old hallucinations, he thought back. No reason to complicate matters.

Click-clack, went the darkness. Click-clack.

"Are we there yet?" he asked softly, and nearly let loose a delirious giggle.

Nothing. Nothing. Silence. The Merlin stared into the nearly complete darkness, sinking into it, mirroring it. Not moving. Not breathing. Not afraid. Only waiting. Waiting.

The faintest chitter.

Click-clack. Click-clack.

Devious bastard.

Click-clack. Click-clack.

Something rustled against his chains.

Hope—cursed, stupid, pathetic *hope*—sprang like a leaky fountain in the Merlin's chest, and he peered closer, reaching for his inhibited power, coaxing his sight to expand just a touch further into the spectra. Just another touch, and…

A jabra rat?

He blinked at the bony little bundle of fur that was perched on its haunches by his feet, snout raised to the air, whiskers curiously whisking.

Can it really be? asked a voice in his mind.

Why not? asked another. It was a jabra rat, after all, not a ham sandwich. The dungeon was probably crawling with them. Or so he reasoned, right up until he remembered that he was actually aboard the *Avalon Eternal*, most likely cruising through crusher space, and that the dungeon wasn't even *real*, as such. Nothing more than an elaborate reconfiguration of one of the ship's decks, a hateful throwback façade to the dank torture dungeons of his people's olden days.

His people?

Their people. His people. Whose people?

He was losing himself in here. And for all his mighty, paranoid logic, there stood the jabra rat, watching him go, sniffing at the filthy air, every bit as convincing as the real thing.

"He's looking for something," he croaked, insisting at first that it was only himself he was talking to. But his gaze remained locked to the rat, that pitiful spark of hope stoking the words in his throat. "Did… Did he send you to find it?"

He watched with a critical eye as the furry critter pawed its way closer. He would've seen it if this was some hyper-realistic hologram illusion. He was sure of it. Even if it was something more sinister—remote neural stim, or mind-altering drugs. If anyone in the galaxy would've seen through such shrouds, it was him.

Right?

It is as you say, my love.

An involuntary sigh of relief escaped his lungs at the sound of that voice. That voice like the sweetest sip of cool mountain water. That voice like the sour bite of harker acid.

He covered up his sound of quickly-curdling relief with a dry snort, loathe to give his ethereal companion the satisfaction. She said nothing. She rarely did these days. Sometimes they went years without speaking. Especially during his centuries-long stints of naive abandon. As if he could ever escape. As if either of them could.

Two peas in a fate-bound pod, they were.

Quite out of the blue, the Merlin thought of Nathaniel Arturi—the most peculiar ripple of all in this latest changing of tides. Not a stray thought either, he realized. There was something there. A faint raised note amongst the endless ocean of the Light, gone before he could properly tune in. Blackened hands, but his senses were growing rusty. *Everything* was growing rusty. He needed to look no further than his current predicament to remember that.

He'd waited too long to rejuvenate.

And now he was at the mercy of this blackened specter, with his only real hope resting on his loyal Knights, chasing after him into darkness. That must've been what he'd just felt, he realized. Nate's first proper journey into the Light. That faint whisper of fear and overwhelm and sheer, jubilant power. And something else with it. Iveera, he supposed. But also something… discordant.

He thought of the oily corruption that'd been in possession of Groshna's Excalibur, Samael, when he'd met them at Golnak and wondered with a sinking feeling whether there was any chance his clever Huntress had escaped the clash of Atlantis untainted.

Probably not. Doubly unlikely for Nathaniel.

How could they have defended themselves? They had no idea what they were up against. The Merlin didn't even fully understand himself yet what manner of creature had crawled back from the depths wearing the black armor of his long-dead protégé. The way the Black Knight had clearly harnessed the Light to create a prison capable of holding the Merlin. The way he'd tapped the power of the Beacon back on Earth—directly, effortlessly. And the empty void the Merlin felt whenever he tried to focus his senses on the thing beneath that black helm…

Click-clack. Chitter. Click-clack.

There was the jabra rat staring up at him, waiting for something.

"He won't find it," he croaked, more to himself than to his furry visitor. "He'll never find it."

But he wasn't so certain. If the corruption *had* spread... If his loyal Knights fell prey to this Black Knight's will...

The jabra chittered again and moved closer still, so curiously interested.

"What's that? You'd like to know *why?*"

Chitter-chitter. The jabra rat went up on its haunches, listening attentively. The Merlin stared down at the rodent, shaking his head, thinking of all the many ways a foe of Mordred's skill—if that was indeed what he was up against—might use such bait to extract what he was looking for. The shaking slowed, though, as the first workings of a counter-plan began to alight at the edge of his mind.

Maybe. If he was careful.

Maybe. If he worked backward from what little bits Mordred had already revealed of his hand, and if his trusty Knights truly were on their trail...

Maybe the Lady really *did* work in mysterious ways, the Merlin decided, leaning through his two centimeters of shackled freedom to smile his most kindly, positively deranged smile down at his attentive visitor.

"Perhaps we can help one another, my furry little friend."

CHAPTER 5

ONE SMALL STEP

I t started like an accidental trip down the stairs—and ended with a plunge straight into the cheery infernos of hell.

One second, Nate was watching Justicar D679 pledge to hunt them to the far reaches of the universe. The next, the justicar was gone, and the *Camelot* was obediently q-jumping across the Golnak system on the *Eldest Stone*'s leash, the bridge half a shade shy of losing its shit as they blinked back to normal space speeding straight for one of the many thousand spindly-armed gateways that networked out from the superstructure's external ring.

Nate was distantly aware of Jaeger shouting at him to buckle up, even more distantly aware of Iveera standing there without restraints, clearly unafraid, her attention fixed to a holo pane on the starboard wall, where a distant passing structure that looked to be half-asteroid was labeled *Golnak Mining Installation C-73.*

Then something snagged him tight. The *Camelot*, he realized, cradling him into a kind of half-standing crash cocoon, apparently spurred on by whatever string of breathless *holy shits* was roaring through his mind. On the viewport, the *Beacon Relay* countdown ticked under ten seconds.

"Shit's about to get weird!" Tessa announced, hands clamped in a white-knuckle grip to her useless control consoles.

"Keep it tight, people," Jaeger called in a tone that might've been admonishing if he hadn't been so busy gaping out the viewport himself.

Nate looked to the SAS crew and saw nothing but clenched jaws and pale faces. *Tight* was one word for it. The tension on the bridge was one-hundred-fold what it'd been when they'd first engaged the crusher drives two weeks ago.

That had been terrifying. But this was a jump across the freaking galaxy.

So help me, Nathaniel, if you pass out...

The counter ticked to four seconds.

Ahead, the reaching arms of the gateway were crackling with an unnatural blue energy, the open aperture shimmering like an oil-slicked film set across a background that was unmistakably disjointed from the rest of the star-strewn darkness behind it.

Gwen's face flashed through his mind, followed by Marty, Kyle, and Copernicus.

You just need to—

ENJOY THE LIGHT, NATHANIEL, came the *Camelot's* exuberant cry.

Right, Ex added. *Which is to say—*

Then the Camelot punched headfirst through that shimmering gateway film, and Nate's entire body screamed.

HE'D CAUGHT FIRE. Or taken a ship-sized bolt of that crackling blue energy straight to the everywhere. For one terrible instant, all he knew was that every cell of his body had been spontaneously electrified with a brilliant, blinding, all-encompassing *blue*—too pervasive to even be called light. Or pain. For that instant, he wasn't even sure he existed anymore.

Then the flood of bottomless, infinite azure evaporated in an instant, and the fire morphed in his body—not fire at all, he realized, as the sensation receded at the sharp edges and calmed to a kind of luxurious, effervescent full-body tingle. Not pain. Just pure, unadulterated *power*, blazing through his every cubic centimeter.

He moved to stand, caught up in the building rush of it, and something gave way with a string of wrenching snaps. His crash cocoon restraints, he realized, just before he caught sight of Iveera beside him and forgot everything else.

She was glowing. Literally. Back arched. Fingers fully extended. Jin swirling in languid contentedness. She basked in the glow of whatever had just touched them, azure energy radiating from the lines of her copper armor, and even from the surface of her green skin. She turned to look at him then, and there was something in her eyes he'd never seen before—a kind of warmth and reverent wonder. And it wasn't just her eyes. Her entire body was electrified in his mind. Practically singing to him.

The faintest smile touched her lips, and then that soft glow began to recede, and her stern composure crept back in. Nate took a shaky breath and realized both that he'd inadvertently summoned his own softly glowing armor from e-dim… and that, for reasons he couldn't even begin to shake a stick at, he'd grown fully aroused beneath.

It's a perfectly natural reaction, Nathaniel, Ex said as Nate shifted, trying not to blush.

I—That's not… He glanced around at the rest of the crew, thanking all the gods in existence that he *had* accidentally called his armor. *What is this, sex ed?*

No glowing crew members, as he'd half-expected. No noticeable erections, either. Just a few wide-eyed *what-the-hell-was-that* looks traded around the bridge, and several expressions of slack-jawed awe fixed dead ahead.

Ex was pulsing with something like laughter. *Amusing as your infantile defensiveness is, I am merely pointing out that the Lady's Light is quite stimulating.*

Lady's Light. That's what that had been. Sure. That actually kind of made sense. Not even Ex and Iveera seemed to understand all that much about how the Beacons worked, or where they'd come from, but if they were connected to the Lady's power—her Light—much as the Excaliburs themselves were, then maybe hopping through the relays was akin to toggling from *battery power* to *plugged in.* Or whatever.

It all kind of felt woefully unimportant, as he followed the crew's stares out the viewport.

If calling the Golnak Relay a sight to behold was an understatement, applying the phrase to Forge Station was an outright joke. At first glance, Nate could barely even process what he was seeing. Then the enormous mass began to resolve into its constituent shapes and pieces, and he beheld a city the likes of which he'd never imagined.

Even calling it a city felt like a joke. Forge Station was a small world in its own right—an expansive network of enormous floating islands, all drifting together on some celestial tide. It didn't really click in Nate's head how they were even suspended until he remembered that they were in space and that those "islands" might not be floating so much as in orbit together, probably held tight by gravitonics or some scaffolding he couldn't yet see. As to what they were orbiting…

It was the center of the goddamn galaxy.

Not that Nate would've recognized that fact if Ex hadn't already told him where Forge Station was located. All he saw behind the gargantuan mass of the station was an even more incalculably expansive sprawl of stars and light and nebulous space dust that shone with more colors than he'd known existed. Against that backdrop, even Forge Station looked rather small and unimpressive.

Taken all together, it was absolutely breathtaking. More vast and vivid than words alone ever could've captured, though the first person to speak on the bridge made a valiant effort.

"Oh my god," Snuffy said quietly.

"That's..." Tessa started to say.

Then Ser Zedavian Kelkarin's mellifluous voice cut through their moment of awe, bringing the bridge right back to the reality where they'd been ordered to stand down and involuntarily detoured from a trail that had already gone too cold.

"I trust I needn't hold your hand to the docks," the First Knight said, not bothering to appear via holo. "Your appointment with Elder Representative Kaiyosh has already been arranged, Ser Katanaga. Report to the Council assembly." There was a moment's pause. "And do not say anything of this Black Knight. Not until I've returned."

Nate looked to Iveera, expecting to see some iota of his own surprise reflected in her expression, but she only watched impassively as the *Eldest Stone* pitched around and began accelerating back toward the gateway that had ejected them from a relay ring superstructure that was, if anything, even larger than the Golnak ring had been.

"Right," Jaeger said, peeling off his compression restraints and rising to his feet as Zedavian's *Eldest Stone* hit the gateway and fired off across the galaxy on a wispy trail of blue. Behind them, Carter was on her feet too, checking on the crew and helping them out of their restraints. Jaeger shot a curious frown at the crash restraints Nate had accidentally torn free from, then turned to Tessa. "Status?"

"Fully torqued, sir," Tessa replied absently, staring out the viewport in wonder for another moment before remembering herself. "That is, uh, ship looks good too, sir." She pursed her lips, looking back at her displays. "I think. You all good, Cammy?"

Cammy?

Nate didn't need to check Tessa's displays to feel that the *Camelot* was humming happily along, jubilant from its dip into the Light, but he was still surprised when the ship saw fit to reply with a neat list of pertinent updates on Tessa's main display, capped with a final, "GOOD, TESSA. THANK YOU."

That was new.

So far, the *Camelot*, much like Ex, had seemed to abide to the hard and fast rule that it would only speak directly to its own Excalibur Knight. That hadn't stopped it from working with Iveera through the holos, or from indirectly communicating with the others via a helpful guiding light here, or spawning an impromptu couch crash out of the deck there. There'd already been more than a few amusing stories of the ship scaring the crap out of the crew with its skittish helpfulness. But until now, communication had been extremely limited.

It seemed Tessa's quest to befriend the *Camelot*—and to *nickname* it, apparently—wasn't going half-bad, and Tessa seemed to know it.

"Can we get a course overlay to that station, Cammy?" she asked, running her hands affectionately over the consoles.

The *Camelot* responded with gusto, throwing a bright blue trajectory and a ton of other information up on the viewport like an energetic pup who'd just been waiting for the chance to show off its new trick.

There was no maybe about it. The ship definitely liked Tessa. Which was fair enough, Nate decided, as the magnetic pilot looked over and shot him a wink that made him avert his gaze.

Perhaps she would like you too if you paid her any attention.

Nate was already firing back with an indignant *I have a girlfriend, remember?* before it hit him that Ex had been talking about the *Camelot*, which now that he thought about it, he'd really never thought of as anything but an *it*, or just *the ship*.

And yet you think of me *as a* he. *Curious. You should know, Nathaniel, that misogyny is considered to be an indicator of extreme societal immaturity amongst the dioecious species of the civilized galaxy.*"

I'm not a... Wait, what? Die-yeesh... Huh? You're technically both sexless synthients, aren't you?

Not as sexless as our hapless Knight, it seems.

Nate gaped, too blindsided to produce a comeback, eyes darting back to Tessa of their own accord.

I believe they call that a burn, Nathaniel.

Now the voice in his head was going to start knocking on his lack of a sex life?

Buuurn.

He sighed, focusing back on what came next for their derailed mission, and nearly jumped out of his armor when he realized Iveera had appeared at his side, silent and mirthful as a ghost.

"What did you think you were doing?" she asked quietly, her tone not aggressive so much as suggesting she was genuinely uncertain whether he understood where he was and what he was doing.

Which, given that he didn't understand what she was even asking, was kind of hard to prove at the moment.

"You wrested control of the Camelot from my hands at a critical moment," she added, sensing his confusion. "You may well have compromised our mission."

Nate swallowed, insides tensing for fight or flight—he didn't know which. In all the excitement, he'd nearly forgotten that Zedavian had only caught them with their pants down once Nate had done the yanking and stopped the *Camelot* mid-flee. Jaeger was watching them now. Suddenly, the whole bridge was watching.

"I... I just thought I was giving us a second to talk things out before we ditched that justicar and ended up on the galaxy's most-wanted list." He looked to Jaeger for some kind of support. "Right?"

"This is not a democracy, Nathaniel," Iveera said. "You are my charge, and if you will not allow me to protect you and your crew as I see fit aboard your ship, I will pull the *Kalnythian Wilds* from e-dim storage and take you aboard my own. By force, if I must."

"Setting aside my obvious qualms with you threatening to kidnap our asset," Jaeger said, "I think we're past all that now." He turned to Nate. "Lesson learned, right?"

Nate only stared back, not really sure what lesson he was supposed to have learned here. He'd only been trying to help, to keep the situation from going to full-on dumpster fire status.

"Lesson learned," Jaeger decreed. "Rule number one on foreign soil, kid. Much as I appreciate the team spirit, when shit starts going sideways, you don't ignore the guy who speaks the language. Or the Gorgon lady, as it were." He looked at Iveera. "Though I'd sure as shit appreciate an explanation and some fair warning next time. Now..." He looked around the bridge like that was that, and it was time to take stock of their next steps.

But Nate wasn't done.

"And what about you?" he asked Iveera. "I'm not the one who just bent the knee and gave up when that Zedavian guy showed up."

"He is our First Knight, Nathaniel. The highest voice of authority in our order, so long as the Merlin is missing."

As I said, Ex pointed out.

"So the Alliance Space Police can shove it, but you won't bend the rules with that golden…" Nate hooked a thumb toward the relay gateway the *Eldest Stone* had disappeared through, lost for a proper insult. "I mean, we know the Black Knight's out there, right? We *know* we have to stop him. What does it matter whether this First Knight believes us or not? Aren't you—"

"It is our duty, Nathaniel. Our duty to the Lady, and to all life in the galaxy. Without order, without duty"—her jin sliced the air decisively—"we are naught but agents of chaos. Black Knights in the making."

Which might've sounded reasonable, except they were talking about saving the Merlin here, weren't they? Not invading Earth and heisting a Beacon. Nate looked to Jaeger for some backup, but of course, the Lt Col agreed with her. Duty and honor. Good, obedient soldiering and all that.

Was that all the Excalibur Knights were at the end of the day? Just more soldiers, marching to the beat of yet another drum?

Iveera was watching him. They all were.

This wasn't helping, was it?

Do you trust Ser Katanaga's judgment beyond your own in this realm?

Nate let out a heavy breath, wilting under the weight of the bridge's collective stares. Of course, he trusted her judgment over his own. How could he not? He didn't *have* any judgment out here. None based on experience, at least.

"Okay," he said, nodding, forcing himself to meet her eyes and not stare at the deck like a scolded child. "Lesson learned. I messed up. I'm sorry." He looked around at the crew. "That goes for everyone. I know this hasn't been… easy."

"Hey, we get to see all this," Snuffy pointed out, nodding toward the miraculous viewport cosmos.

"Boldly go where no man's gone before," Ramirez added, like he was listing perks.

"Aside from fucking Poseidon and his posse," muttered the one they called Pierce, bringing the room back down to a resting unease.

"Food's not bad," Elmo finally grunted.

That seemed to decide it. The SAS crew broke into grins, content for the moment that they'd survived their first brush with this vast new galaxy.

Carter remained somewhat stoic. Pierce was the only one who looked actively irritated.

Jaeger gave Nate a somber nod, and for a second, Nate felt a flicker of something very much like that elusive team spirit welling up. He looked to Iveera and saw—if not approval—at least a lack of disappointment in her muted expression. Briefly, he wondered if he shouldn't mention his Zedavian dream to her just to make sure it wasn't somehow important, but now didn't really feel like the time. Given that Ex didn't argue with that assessment, he settled instead for looking out the viewport and caught another hit of the cosmic *dust-in-the-wind* effect.

Who could really care about petty rights and wrongs with all of *that* floating before their eyes? Undeniable proof of just how goddamn small and insignificant they truly were.

"About an hour, at present speed," Tessa was saying as he brought his attention back to the bridge. "Not sure with all that traffic up there, though." She glanced over at another display. "Looks like they're already hailing us."

"Allow me to handle the communications," Iveera said, calling up her holos with a meaningful look toward Nate.

Whatever she wants, he thought toward the ship. *Let her at it.*

AFFIRMATIVE.

Ahead, Iveera's jin gave a satisfied flick.

Thanks. Cammy.

WELCOME, NATHANIEL, came the perfectly pleasant reply as Iveera began rattling off a formal-sounding request to dock at Forge Station. He noticed her gaze lingering on his torso as she ended the transmission.

"Stow the armor?" he guessed out loud.

Iveera's jin sliced the air in a negative. "We will obscure it beneath a disguise, but do not for one second think of removing that armor while we are anywhere in this system."

Somehow, that answer didn't make him feel any better. Nor did the wary look in Jaeger's eyes as he turned from them to scan the crew with a deepening frown.

"Look sharp, people," he said. "We represent the entirety of Earth in T-minus sixty."

CHAPTER 6

WARM RECEPTION

I f the arrival of representatives from a new planet was cause for excitement on Forge Station, the voices of Station Control certainly didn't let on to the fact as they approached the docks. As far as Nate could tell, *dock control worker* might well have been the galactic equivalent of *Jersey toll booth operator* where jovial service was concerned. Of course, there might've also been a few things lost in translation, seeing as he couldn't even tell what *species* he was listening to as Ex worked his translation magic.

That was a Svendarian, Ex provided. *Fairly logical creatures, except where their blind sense of unerring honor is concerned.*

So great traffic controllers, then?

Just as one might expect from a septapod.

Nate's brain faltered over the word, then caught up with a mental image of a seven-legged insect scuttling around behind the Forge control consoles, mandibles clicking all the while.

Svendarians are in fact the species upon which your mythological centaurs were based.

The image in Nate's head shifted to one of a galloping horse-man with seven legs. He shook his head, trying to focus back on the mission but mostly just staring at the thickening clouds of space traffic instead, wondering at how infinitesimally small his known world had been—and still *was*—compared to everything that was out here in the galaxy. Around the bridge, the rest of the crew looked equally flummoxed.

Excited or not, the Svendarian on the other end eventually accepted Iveera's lengthy list of credentials and cleared their final approach to the central docks of the Capital with a berthing assignment somewhere in the diplomat wing. Whatever that all meant. Nate was still preoccupied with studying the swarm of station traffic pouring in and out of the station vicinity. Ships of all shapes and sizes, many bound to or from the system's two massive Beacon relay superstructures or to the shipyards and other satellite stations scattered throughout the system, others only moving from one island to another within the main continent of the Forge.

Nate tried to parse out some of their functions as he watched them pass —a cargo ship here, a private yacht there. A few island-sized warships were hovering off in the distance, keeping watch over it all. Ex dutifully stepped in to let him know where he was right or wrong, flashing schematics and ship tags to the holo above Nate's palm.

It was only at Iveera's stern look that he killed the holo and pulled his not-quite-US issue tactical gloves back on, completing the full body disguise Ex had rigged from e-dim, marking him down to surprising detail as just another one of Iveera's SAS escorts along with Jaeger, Ramirez, Elmo, and Snuffy.

He looked around the bridge, wishing he'd had a proper chance to talk to his friends before they landed. In all the rush to suit up and get their stories straight, they'd barely even had time for the lightning-round check-in they'd managed with Earth, which had basically consisted of a terse *be careful, try not to speak for Earth, and for the love of god, don't piss anyone off.*

They'd done a bang-up job of that last one so far. But there was nothing for it. They'd check back in once they were safely situated on Forge Station. Maybe even once they'd docked if there was time. For the moment, though, it was all any of them could do to stare as they closed in on one of the many shimmering blue-green atmosphere seals dotted across the bulky exostructure of the central docks.

With the sheer volume of traffic teeming in and out of the docks, it seemed a minor miracle there weren't a few hundred collisions every second. Then again, he'd once had the same thought about the superhighways of Atlanta, Georgia, so maybe he was easily impressed. Either way, even Tessa, who'd been chomping at the bit the entire voyage to take the controls properly, looked perfectly happy at the moment to be letting Cammy do the flying, no questions asked.

No one breathed as they soared through the shimmering atmos containment seal, into the first cavernous but densely packed hangar. Aside from one prolonged, "Uhhh…" from Snuffy, no one spoke as Cammy whisked them on, across the hangar, through multiple corridors and conduits Nate was sure were too tight for the ship.

By the time they finally arrived at their allotted berth, and to the unsettlingly firm *thunk* of magnetic docking arms clamping onto the *Camelot*'s hull, it felt like a safe bet that Iveera was the only one on the bridge who could've honestly checked the "unclenched" box on her personal rectal status. Assuming that was even anatomically possible.

Gorgons DO have—

That-that's okay, Ex, Nate thought, trying to look innocent as he met Iveera's questioning gaze. *One mystery at a time, please.*

He sobered as he realized she was double-checking to see if he was ready to step out onto the station, where battle armor was apparently a prudent precaution. He glanced down at the dark battle suit veneer he and Ex had conjured over his armor. Not at all SAS standard fare, he'd gathered, watching Jaeger and the others suit up. Apparently Washington had airlifted the good stuff over—space worthy and everything—in the few hours they'd had to prep their brave pioneers for Earth's first interstellar military operation.

"Come," Iveera said, stepping past them for the bridge entryway. "The sooner we make our report and have done with it, the sooner we might be on our way."

"All right," Jaeger said, pulling on his helmet. "You heard the lady. On me, Alpha Team."

With a careful thought, Nate conjured his own helmet to match and fell in with Jaeger, just another one of the SAS gang.

THEY GATHERED by the port airlock on the main deck, half the crew preparing to take their one small step while the other half remained behind to keep the ship safe and ready. No one griped about their assignments, though Nate also hadn't missed it when the good Lt Col had quietly asked Iveera why they shouldn't just leave Nate on the ship too if she was so concerned about his safety out there.

"Nathaniel does not leave my side," she'd said just as quietly, simple as that.

Nate wasn't really sure what to think about the exchange, other than that his hearing was apparently sharpening right along with the rest of his abilities, and that they were probably just being overly paranoid anyway. Ex certainly seemed to think so, muttering on about frightened rabbits and such.

Luckily, the final round of checks was lightning quick, mostly because there really wasn't much to check. Weapons were technically forbidden on the station, save for those individuals with the proper clearance—Alliance peacekeepers and military personnel, mostly. Excalibur Knights too, if for no other reason than that it was quite hard to deprive a Knight of their weapons. That didn't stop Iveera from conjuring a rather drab woven cloak to conceal her armor from plain sight. Clearly, she was content to keep a low profile.

Jaeger, on the other hand, didn't look too thrilled to be walking into the unknown with nothing but his fists and his winning personality.

"How many people actually abide by this no weapons bullshit?" he asked, arms crossed over his sparse gear vest, scowling through his lightly-tinted helmet visor.

"All law-abiding citizens," Iveera said.

"And how many non-abiding citizens might there be, crawling around this station's seedy underbelly?"

Iveera's jin swirled thoughtfully. "Do not worry, Lt Col Jaeger," she said, moving to the hatch controls. If Nate hadn't known better, he might've thought there was a twitch of a smile on her lips. "I will protect you."

Jaeger's scowl tracked from the back of the Gorgon's head straight to Nate, silently ordering him to shut his trap about it. Nate raised his hands in surrender, and the scowl swiveled on to the rest of Alpha Team, then to the gear locker where their weapons and spare oxygen masks were tucked away.

Iveera had already assured them that the air on Forge Station was compatible with Terran needs, and Tessa had confirmed as much from the *Camelot's* readings. Nearly every species on the station breathed oxygen at one concentration or another, and while a few of the lower islands would apparently be less than ideal for human physiology, it sounded like the atmosphere on the Capital was more liable to get them high than hypoxic. Add to that that the team's suits were all equipped with sophisticated oxygen filters and modest personal reserves baked into the armor layers, and that still left them all looking about as comfortable as cats in deep water.

Nate was surprised to find he felt more calm than his comrades looked as Iveera paused to look back at them, long fingers poised over the door controls. "Remain calm, and follow my lead."

"You heard the lady," Jaeger said, what little apprehension Nate read on his face bleeding away as the Lt Col stepped front and center to the door. "Keep it tight, hooah?"

He got a tense round of answering *hooahs* from Snuffy, Elmo, and Ramirez, Iveera keyed the *Camelot*'s hatch controls, and that was that. The hatch hissed open, the low roar of dockside activity pouring into the ship, and…

Nothing happened. Nothing at all.

Which was to say, business on the dock carried right on without so much as a lull or a curiously cocked cranial appendage. Nate wasn't sure what else he'd been expecting. A roaring welcome parade, perhaps, complete with fountains of champagne and a banner that read, "Welcome, Earthlings," with the word "Terrans" comically crossed out right before that. Maybe just a solitary Alliance recruiter, waiting to take Earth's signatory pledge of allegiance down on the dotted line.

Instead, they got the ordered chaos of the apathetic docks and the palpable wave of relief at not being met by an immediate explosion, or cut down in a hail of blaster bolts.

Those came the moment after.

Iveera was only two steps down the boarding ramp when the fiery red bolt came sizzling through the air, straight for Jaeger's head. Iveera caught the bolt on her raised palm as casually as if someone had lofted her the car keys, then swatted down the next two bolts—bound for Nate and Snuffy— and threw herself across the dock before Nate could manage so much as an, "Oh shit."

She cleared two berthed ships in the blink of an eye, sailing straight for the scaffolding where his sputtering brain informed him the shots must've come from. He spotted the spindly, masked shooter the moment before Iveera crashed into the creature and drove him into the scaffolding nearly hard enough to bring the entire thing down.

It had barely been a full second since the first shot.

"What the piss?" someone finally managed to hiss from the corridor behind. Ahead, the general sentiment seemed to be echoed in the several alien cries spreading through the steady roar of the docks.

Nate was already stepping forward, thinking about flight thrusters and blaster wrists, when Jaeger barred his way with a rough forearm.

"Eyes peeled below, Ramirez!" he snapped. "Pierce, Carter, weapons!"

They snapped to action, Ramirez taking covered lookout at the open hatchway while the others hurried to the weapons locker. Across the dock, Iveera had their would-be assailant by the throat, dangling him over the scaffold edge with one hand while she held his long rifle safely in the other. She seemed to be saying something to him.

"She's got him, kid," Jaeger said quietly at Nate's ear. Almost gently. "Take a breath, maintain your cover. Eyes peeled for the next one, hooah?"

Nate had started shoving Jaeger's arm away before he could even think, not sure why he was suddenly so angry—only that he could barely see straight for the thundering of his heart, and that he'd be damned if he was going to let Jaeger treat him like another *hoo-ahing* airman to command when that shooter had come here to...

To what?

To kill an Excalibur Knight? To kill *him*? The gunner had fired three bolts. He saw it clearly in his memory even as Ex pointed it out. Three bolts. Jaeger first. He'd been gunning for every human he could, ignoring Iveera. Why?

"Sorry," Nate mumbled, releasing Jaeger's arm. "I..."

"Eyes peeled," Jaeger repeated, clapping him on the shoulder and turning to receive a rifle from Carter. Outside, the shouts of panic were leveling back to a steady roar of activity as some attempted to flee and many more gathered around, pointing up to the sight of Iveera and the shooter. Nate took a breath, reaching to open communications with her.

"Sir?" Ramirez called from the open hatchway. "We've got incoming on our platform. Looks like station security, maybe." He glanced back to face them, expression tight behind his faceplate. "And I don't think they're coming to tickle our Elmo, sir."

CHAPTER 7

MELTING POT

Nate shifted uneasily at the hatchway, wondering if he should keep his head down or if the station would respond more favorably to an Excalibur Knight.

They appear quite edgy with one Knight already, Ex pointed out. He wasn't wrong. Outside, the entire docking bay had ground to a halt.

"Great," Jaeger muttered, looking out the hatchway first toward their incoming company, then toward the growing crowd of spectators pointing up at Iveera from the next several platforms over. "Just great."

The Lt Col leaned back in from the hatchway, glancing to where Pierce and Carter were whipping out more rifles like he wasn't sure whether to belay the *to arms* order, or tell them to double time it. Iveera thunked down at the base of the boarding ramp before he had to decide, assassin and rifle both still in tow.

"Peace," she called—toward the *Camelot* or their incoming company, Nate wasn't sure. Her voice was loud enough that everyone in the surrounding area probably heard it, despite the fact that she somehow managed to sound as if she'd barely raised her voice at all.

The docking bay fell silent.

"Shit," Jaeger muttered, glancing out and back, and finally giving a *what the hell* shrug. "Standby, people. Keep those weapons on board."

And with that, he turned and strode down the ramp to join Iveera before Nate or anyone else could argue. Without prompting, the *Camelot* called up a holo beside the open hatchway to let everyone inside have a better view of the docks and the approaching... he didn't know what.

Those are Androtta, Ex said. The closest thing to robotic life the Alliance has trusted since the Synth Wars. The pair behind them are Hobdans. The Troglodan, I trust, you recognize. And those last two, if you hadn't guessed, are Atlanteans.

Nate followed along, taking in the vaguely crystalline faces of the Androtta—seemingly lifeless but for the orange-violet sparks in their eye sockets—and the orangish skin and knobby features of the Hobdans. The hulking gray form of the Troglodan was indeed recognizable enough, and more than a little strange to see here among so-called civilized company after what had happened on Earth. As for the Atlanteans that followed in the Troglodan's wake...

"What the actual fuck?" someone murmured. Pierce, Nate thought. And for once, he was actually on the same page with the moody airman.

A bay full of alien life before them, and Nate was positive the entirety of the *Camelot* was suddenly riveted to those two Atlanteans. Because as unbelievable as it'd been hearing that the long-lost descendants of Earth had spent the past few millennia building their own empire among the Alliance stars, actually *seeing* them here amid the booming chaos of alien civilization...

It was impossible.

They just looked so *human*. Flawlessly human, in fact. Walking gods of men if ever Nate had seen them. They didn't even look particularly small or puny walking behind a Troglodan.

"Goddamn," came an appreciative mutter from right beside him. Tessa, he realized. He hadn't even noticed her there. She tore her wide eyes away from the holo like she'd just remembered this wasn't a runway show. "Should we be ready for blastoff in here?"

"No," Nate said quietly, turning his gaze back to the holo. He meant to say more—that Iveera would take care of this mishap, or hell, that *he* would if he had to. That they needed to make their peace with this Council so they could get back on track. But the words faltered as he spotted more Atlanteans peppered here and there among the crowds, his brain picking them out now like shiny objects. "I don't... No. We've got this."

"Okay, then," Tessa said.

Outside, their welcoming party was drawing closer in their matching armor—blue and gray, the cuts and pieces differing to accommodate morphologies, but the color tones all perfectly consistent across the eight bodies. Definitely station security, Nate decided, even as Ex confirmed as much.

"Hark!" called a high voice as the security force drew to wary attention, Androtta, Hobdans, Troglodan, and Atlanteans all parting to form a column on either side of Iveera and Jaeger, permitting the speaker clear passage. The speaker glided forward, a tall, golden being that moved with other-worldly grace and poise, slender hands clasped elegantly at the hemmed sleeves of his royal blue robe. Another Eldari, like Zedavian.

Except *not* like Zedavian, Nate decided, as the speaker drew closer. Tall and graceful as this one was with his sharp cheeks and pointed ears, his thin frame and dignified airs were nothing compared to the First Knight's devastating presence.

"Fellow beings of the Alliance," the Eldari called, projecting his steady voice to all of the docking bay, "we do apologize for the disturbance and ask that you return to your duties with good assurances that the danger has passed."

As he spoke, one of the Androtta leaned in and tossed a pair of matte gray discs at Iveera's weakly struggling prisoner. Iveera pushed the shooter forward as the discs came to life, casting out wriggling gray tendrils to ensnare his wrists and ankles, then engaging gravitonics to lift him until he was suspended half a meter above the platform, drifting by his humming restraints.

The Troglodan who'd been stepping forward like he intended simply to toss the lanky assassin over his burly shoulder instead gave a bored grunt and dragged the hovering captive aside to clear the way for the Eldari speaker, who spread his delicate hands wide and showed Iveera something resembling a smile.

The entire exchange had all the cheerful tone of a frozen lake cracking underfoot. Which was why Nate was only half-shocked when Iveera responded by cocking back and tossing the assassin's rifle to the Eldari envoy hard enough to crack his gleaming white teeth. Only it never struck. The Eldari plucked the speeding rifle from the air and twirled it around for inspection as casually as if he were stifling a yawn. "Something to tell me, then, old friend?" he asked, peering back up at Iveera.

"With all due respect, herald," Iveera said, with a meaningful look at the watching crowds and a tone that said anything but *old friend*, "it is a matter to be discussed in private." She looked at the floating assassin and back to the Eldari. "I trust you know what to do with that one. Now, if you'll excuse me, I must report to Elder Representative Kaiyosh."

The Eldari didn't move to clear the path. Nor did any of the blue-and-gray security squad.

"Your special friend will be coming with you?" the Eldari asked, studying Jaeger curiously. To Jaeger's credit, he didn't bat an eye under the intent scrutiny. None of them, Iveera included, seemed overly perturbed by the fact that someone had just attempted triple murder.

"All of my special friends are dead, Herald," Iveera replied, as the Eldari's inquisitive gaze drifted to the *Camelot*. "Now, I must go speak with the Elder," she added, a hint of command slipping into her tone. "My allies will accompany me."

"Including Nathaniel Arturi?"

Nate froze mid-turn to Alpha Team, locking surprised stares with Carter of all people, his mind scrabbling for some explanation.

The First Knight, Ex said. *Iveera's records. He must have passed your identity on before he departed.*

Which made sense logistically, Nate supposed. It just didn't answer the gaping question of *why* Ser Zedavian Kelkarin would've gone out of his way to out him to an apparently hostile station, unless…

"—still aboard the *Camelot*, yes?" the Eldari herald was saying out on the platform. "Or did you expect no one would recognize one Terran from another?"

"Guess that's our cue," Nate said, looking from Carter to Elmo and Ramirez. The so-called Alpha Team shot him a round of *we don't take orders from you* looks, but no one tried to stop him as he turned and started down the ramp. He might've even felt a hint of satisfaction as they fell in behind him, if not for the sharp eyes of the Eldari, tracking him down the ramp. Whatever was at play here, the jig was clearly up.

"We are finished here," Iveera said, beckoning for Nate and the others to join them so they might be on their way.

The herald roused from his hawk-like study of Nate, turning smoothly back to Iveera with a shallow bow. "Very well, Ser Knight. May our paths cross again soon."

For a second, Nate thought that was that. Then the herald straightened and gestured to his posse, who started cautiously forward as he spoke. "In the meantime, these peacekeepers shall escort the new initiate to—"

"That won't be necessary," Iveera said, taking a decisive step between the parties as Nate and the others scooted up to join Jaeger. The herald's peacekeepers faltered, turning wary looks from Iveera to the Eldari and back again. One of the Hobdans shot a nervous glance back to the head of the platform, where several more uniformed guards were waiting.

"To the contrary," the Eldari said, handing the assassin's rifle off to one of the Atlanteans, and folding his hands delicately at his front once more, "the Council was quite emphatic that it was. Seeing that they are well within their amended treaty rights to assess any and all new initiates to the Order Excalibur, well..." He spread his hands palms up as he trailed off, as if to demonstrate how out of his control the matter truly was. "They wish to hear your report within the hour. Chancellor Adamus, meanwhile, awaits his appointment with the Terran. The Atlanteans will begin the assessment, as is their right."

"I was not made aware of any such appointment," Iveera said, her face a sea of tranquility that Nate was pretty sure was boiling beneath the surface.

"No?" the Eldari asked, in a tone that made it perfectly clear he wasn't surprised. "Hmm. Well, perhaps you might make use of the time to take a brief preliminary congress with Elder Representative Kaiyosh. I imagine the two of you could use a chance to straighten your respective stories."

He said it with a kind of surgical politeness that would've made even the finest of Earth's politicians blush. Nate looked at Iveera, feeling ten steps behind and wondering what the hell kind of assessment they were even talking about here.

Blasphemy is what they're talking about, Ex growled. *Bureaucrats and gamesters, prying their slimy fingers into the Lady's business. They have grown too bold in this false peace.*

"I do not have time to play these games, Herald," Iveera said.

"Nor time, it seems, to inform the Council of a newly awakened Knight," the Eldari replied. "Nor to report of other interesting... developments, shall we say, amongst your sacred order. Developments, some may argue, that leave the authority of your individual agency somewhat in question."

Iveera was silent long enough that Nate half-thought she might just say to hell with it and give their entire welcoming party a good taste of that *individual agency* right then and there. He was pretty sure it'd take a lot more than a few handfuls of Forge security cops to stop her. The shamelessly gaping spectators on the surrounding platforms seemed eager to find out.

"Sounds like maybe we should report to the Council, then," Jaeger said, probably speaking more to dispel the building tension than anything else. It caught the herald's interest.

"Ah, the modern tongue of Terra," the Eldari said, glancing briefly back to his Atlantean guards, who were both wrinkling their perfect noses at

Jaeger. "We have not heard your speech in person for some time. If it should please you, perhaps we might borrow source samples from your collections while you are here, that we might more effectively update our records and facilitate any future communications between Earth and our fair Alliance."

"Sure," Jaeger said, slowly, like he was trying to make sure he actually understood the request and its implications. "Yeah, I'm sure we can find some good—"

"Excellent," the Eldari interjected, focusing his attention back on Iveera. "Shall we proceed to the Hall of Reason as your ally suggests then, Ser Knight?"

Nate glanced sideways at Iveera and saw with some relief that she was relenting, jin resuming their gentle swirl as if all was well, or at least would be. "Lead the way, Herald," she said, beckoning to Nate and the others to follow.

"Splendid," the Eldari purred, gesturing to his peacekeepers.

Nate was stepping forward to fall in line with their awkward little welcome parade when Iveera spared him the first brief look since he'd stepped off of the ship.

Be ready, that look said.

Ready for *what*, Nate didn't know. But somehow, as they started off down the platform surrounded by blue and gray uniforms, he suddenly had the feeling that an assassin's blaster bolts had only been the beginning of the dangers they might face that day.

ON THE FEW occasions Nate had found time between lessons and "sparring" match beatdowns to envision what their eventual arrival to the heart of the Alliance might actually look like, he'd never quite pictured things like this. Marching along in his dark faux cover armor, squished between a towering Troglodan and a sneering Hobdan, both bearing Forge Station Security insignias. No gleaming Excalibur armor on proud display. No wondrous stares at the coming of a new Knight and his Earthly brethren.

Which wasn't to say there were no stares at all. They just weren't all that wondrous.

Apparently, there'd been plans to save time and face by heading straight to the maglev tubes that served as primary transit around Forge Station, just as apparently there'd been some kind of major malfunction with the Capital island's control systems earlier that day. Whether or not that malfunction had anything to do with the general fog of chaos and discontent that pervaded over the docking bay, Nate didn't know. All he knew was that there were plenty of stares to go around.

Eloquently inquisitive stares from the diplomats they passed in the docking bay, bustling about with airs of importance and flowing robes that brimmed with vibrant colors and shimmering inlays. Distrustful stares—and a few downright angry ones—from the station dock hands who stomped about in gray-and-blue jumpsuits, ferrying luggage and goods on gravitonic sleds and working ship maintenance with tools that looked as alien as the beings using them. Plenty more stares that Nate couldn't even begin to decipher because they were just too alien. And all that by the time they reached the edge of the chaotic docking bay, the crowd parting before them all the way, all the better to keep staring.

"You would be wise to relieve us of your hounds," Nate could just make out Iveera saying to the Eldari herald ahead, her electric eyes sweeping briefly back to their armed escorts. "If we must walk, we needn't paint the mark so brightly for curious eyes."

"Come now," the Eldari said, gesturing to the parting crowd as if to ask whether she truly believed anyone on this station would *dare* raise a finger against his golden glory.

Bureaucrats, Ex grumbled.

Nate, suspecting the crowd's respectful distance had a lot more to do with their caravan's snarling Troglodan and considerable artillery than with the Eldari's magnificence, didn't disagree with the sentiment. Iveera said nothing. Just continued on, indifferent to the sneers from their Hobdan and Atlantean escorts.

Why is it starting to feel like we don't exactly have many friends out here? Nate thought toward the back of Iveera's head as they marched toward the high archway on the bay wall and the explosion of noise and intriguing smells pouring out from the next wing of the station.

True friends of our order are few and far between. You would do well to remember that.

Nate blinked at the resonant lilt of Iveera's voice in his head. He hadn't really been expecting an answer. Hadn't even been sure she'd actually heard the first few *who-what-whys* he'd tried beaming her way. At least he was getting slightly better at the Excalibur stuff.

And this assessment? he wondered toward her. *What does this Chancellor Adamus want from me?*

You would do well to keep that *question front of mind any time you find your-self dealing with a politician.*

Hear, hear, Ex agreed.

Nate was about to point out that that wasn't really an answer when they passed beneath the archway and the cresting roar of voices buffeted all other thoughts from his mind.

The space that stretched out before them was huge and absolutely frantic, like some kind of intragalactic bazaar straight out of the movies. Thousands upon thousands of beings, more species than Nate could count, all swarming to and fro beneath the astoundingly high vault of the ceiling, haggling at stands and storefronts for food, clothes, parts, and a thousand other things Nate couldn't begin to recognize.

It was too much to process. Complete visual overload, and it extended up through multiple floors of vendors. Some were built into the walls above, while others floated alongside the networks of intersecting pathways that went up, and up, and... Jesus, the *smell* too. It was as inescapable as it was erratic. A pocket of eye-watering spices here. A divine splash of florals tinged with a strange musk there. All of it infused with a subtle dry chemical smell that told of overworked air filters, churning on in futility in the face of this galactic melting pot.

Nate didn't realize he'd stopped walking until his Troglodan escort poked him. Jaeger and the rest of Alpha Team had faltered too, all staring, ignorant of the knowing smirks the Atlanteans were shooting them.

"Come," the Eldari herald said, beckoning them on with a knowing smile, like elvish Willy Wonka. *Come, children. The Great Chocolate River awaits.*

Nate fell back in step with the others, too mesmerized to hardly even remember where they were headed. He spied children of three or four different species running through the crowd, encased in pale blue holo armor and crying out in delight as they blasted each other with toy laser guns that sent ripples of red cascading across their target's armor. He saw what must've been a Svendarian plodding by on four legs while it used the remaining three to tear at a charred hunk of god knew what kind of meat.

There were Atlanteans among the throng, too. Every one of them as aesthetically flawless as their two peacekeeper escorts——an entire race of photoshopped supermodels walking around in dull rough-spun garments. Some paused to glance at Nate and his SAS companions, first with double-takes and slight frowns, then with growing expressions of surprise and maybe even disgust as they got a better look at their long-lost Earthling brethren behind the faceplates.

Maybe they'd never seen such ugly faces in their lives. Nate didn't know. But they were hardly the only ones who gawked. A small cloud of stasis seemed to follow them through the bazaar, all manner of creatures pausing to murmur and point like *who are these stupid bastards and what did they get themselves into?* Others gaped at Iveera and the Eldari herald like they knew exactly who they were looking at, and were properly astounded to be doing so.

The rest of the bazaar kept churning right on like an unstoppable wheel of capitalism and raucous sound. One short brown creature that looked vaguely like a big, mustachioed ant actually worked up the bravery—or the indomitable spirit of salesmanship, at least—to press up to their security wall, chittering benevolently and offering a pot of some steaming stew as the Hobdans shooed it away.

Nate saw all of this and more. So much novel *otherness* packaged up in such strangely familiar tones that, for several minutes, he nearly forgot to be afraid for himself and the crew. Especially when he finally peeled his eyes away from the crowd long enough to look up to the ceiling—which, while impressive enough in its own right, with its high, vaulted architecture, was nothing compared to the sight its broad panes opened up to.

Stars.

A breathtaking canvas of light, dancing in full spectra across the nebulous space dust above.

"Holy shit…" Ramirez muttered beside him, apparently having followed his gaze upward.

That pretty much summed it up.

If you are going to be this awestruck every time you happen across a simple, flea-ridden marketplace, this is going to be a very long and annoying voyage.

Nate huffed a shallow laugh. *Well, excuse me for being a sad little human.*

I do, Nathaniel. Every single day of your unfortunate affliction.

Nate just shook his head, surprised to find a smile pulling at his lips as he continued to explore the wonderfully exotic bazaar with his eyes—and, whether he liked it or not, with his nose too.

They might not have come here by circumstances of their choosing, and there were clearly dangers on the station—both physical and political, it seemed. Nate had no doubt he was woefully unprepared for all of it. But as he watched the vivacious ocean of alien life from the center of their safe little guard bubble, he actually found himself starting to relax a little.

Because it was also pretty damn amazing to be here.

He turned his smile to Ramirez, realizing as he did that he actually felt lucky, despite everything. Lucky to be here. Lucky to have Jaeger and the SAS crew with him, busting his balls and watching his back. And Iveera too, he decided, watching the graceful Gorgon striding along beside the Eldari herald ahead. He couldn't really imagine a version of himself that would ever reach the point of not batting an eye when someone tried to kill him and his friends, but as long as she was around…

He looked around at the infectious energy of the bazaar. Maybe everything was actually going to be okay. Maybe this detour was nothing but a minor speed bump. Hell, maybe Zedavian would come back from his little private investigation with all apologies and call in the cavalry to saddle up with them for the hunt. Nate wouldn't hold his breath on the last bit, but it didn't matter. One way or another, they would get through this bureaucratic shuffle and find the Black Knight. They'd take back what he'd stolen. Everything was going to be oka—

Something slammed into his chest, driving him clean from his feet before he could so much as blink. He slammed down to the deck on his back, his assailant thudding down on top of him—*Iveera* thudding down on top of him—just as a string of sharp hissing coughs cracked through the air all around them. Screams followed. Shouts and frenzied activity. Nate tried to sit up, mind whirling, struggling against Iveera's weight, trying for words, time slowing, sound receding to a dull blur as he took in the bodies. Blurring motion. A furious roar and Iveera on top of him, clutching her chest right at the spot where her armor had somehow ripped open, soaking her hands in dark blood.

"What—" Nate gasped.

Then the air rippled beside them, and something thrust a wicked-looking gun straight in his face.

CHAPTER 8

WRAITHS

"Ex!" Nate cried, praying for shields to bolster his helmet even as it hit him that this thing had just blasted through *Iveera's* defenses. He felt the whine building through the half-transparent weapon as some invisible hand shoved it straight to his helmet.

Then Iveera's weight lurched on top of him. There was a flash of light, a sizzling hiss, and a sharp screech, and a pale hand appeared from thin air and thunked to the deck beside Nate's head, still clutching the now fully revealed pistol.

Nate had all of a second to gape before another ripple touched the air right behind Iveera, a second apparition coming for her turned back. He raised his hand, summoning his wrist blaster and firing in the same frantic motion, almost before Ex finished tuning the spectra on his HUD enough to show him what he was even aiming for.

He had a faint glimpse of long, spindly limbs and a twisted posture, all ghostly blue even to his enhanced helmet vision. Then the bolt took the thing in the shoulder, and it staggered back with a hideous screech, ducking into the crowd.

Iveera was already rolling to her feet, her bloodied armor morphing on the fly, mending its damage, thickening in areas, and coming alive with shimmering layers of energy shields all at once.

Half of their security detail was already dead. Two more peacekeepers fell before Nate could even pull himself up from the deck, their attackers flitting in like a deadly wind that left behind nothing but sliced throats and a blinding panic in Nate's chest.

"Back to back!" someone shouted right beside him. Jaeger, he registered, right as the Lt Col grabbed him by the arm and yanked him into a huddle with Elmo. "Carter, check Ramirez!"

Nate's gaze tracked dumbly from the blasters the two must've grabbed from the fallen guards over to the limp form Carter was dropping next to—— Ramirez. Alien cries of panic and terror spilling through the bazaar. Nate swept the stampeding crowd, insides pure ice, looking frantically for whatever was attacking them.

They're using spectral shrouds, Ex said. *Good ones.*

Nate only half-registered the words, gaping down at one dead-eyed Hobdan peacekeeper while Jaeger barked something about keeping his head down, and the Troglodan rushed past them with a low bellow, chasing something into the crowd. Nate turned, looking for Iveera, only dimly aware of the pressure of Elmo's grip on the back of his neck, trying to wrangle him closer.

He caught a glimpse of Iveera standing over a dead *something*, double-sided gaija spear in hand, the air crackling around her with multi-hued energy barriers. The Eldari herald lay dead on the deck nearby. Elmo tugged harder, and Nate whirled on his ally just in time to see the big man yank his hand free like he'd been burned.

There! Ex called, just before Nate caught the faint HUD-blued specter detaching from the frenzied crowd to dash straight toward them.

Nate raised his wrist blaster and fired off two bolts without thinking. One of them hit, staggering the creature's rapid approach and setting its spectral shroud flickering, revealing a sputtering glimpse of bony limbs, sickly pale flesh, and a nightmare face partially obscured by dark goggles. Jaeger put two more sizzling blue blaster bolts into the thing's chest before it could so much as cry out in pain.

The pale nightmare thing hit the deck, and no one spoke, blasters still raised, all of them trying to look every direction at once for any more ghostly apparitions charging from the crowd. There was too much commotion. Too many moving bodies still packed in around them, even as desperately as the stampede was struggling to evacuate the area.

A flicker here. A false start there. Nothing. Nothing but chaos, slowly waning as the crowd thinned.

Then Ex called another warning just as something small and dark landed at Nate's feet with a heavy *thunk*, and a tiny red flashing light. Nate had a split second to appreciate the icy certainty that the object was going to detonate before Iveera came flying across the deck and plopped heavily on top of the thing.

For one terrifying moment, Nate was sure she intended to sacrificially absorb the blast with her own wounded body. But then there was a faint whine of power, and Iveera pushed herself up from the deck, looking warily around at their thinning surroundings.

The bomb was gone, just gone. Nate didn't have the bandwidth to worry about where. He checked around to confirm there weren't any more HUD specters actively charging in, and then he reached to help Iveera up.

She didn't need his help. She rose to her feet like a Gorgon possessed, steadily as if she'd suffered no more than a few good punches, and certainly not whatever it was that had left a gaping bloody hole in her torso moments earlier. But something *had*. He could still see the blood plastered around the freshly mended section of her copper armor as she whirled to go find the ones responsible.

I wouldn't—Ex started, but Nate was already reaching. He caught her arm before he could think better of it, and was rewarded with an arm-numbing shock from her shields.

"You're hurt," he said, shaking his numb hand loose and taking an involuntary step back at the cold fury radiating off of her. It oozed from her darkened faceplate and tight shoulders, her jin glowing faint crimson through whatever armor membrane coated them. It was frightening enough that it came as a relief when she turned to scan the thinning crowd for their attackers.

I believe they've retreated for now, Ex said, but he didn't argue as Nate continued looking around for himself. He didn't see anything other than frightened aliens running for their lives, some of them beginning to glance back now that the abrupt storm of violence seemed to have abated. Ex seemed to be right about the things retreating. For a second, Iveera looked like she might take off after them. She looked back to Nate, around at the pile of their dead, and seemed to come to some realization.

"Dammit," she said softly.

Nate stowed the reflexive urge to apologize, unsure what it was he'd even be apologizing for. He was still too busy trying to process what the hell had just happened, gaping at the dead security force all around them, and the dead Eldari herald, and the pale, lifeless nightmare *thing* laid out at Jaeger's feet.

It's an Ooperian, Ex said. *One of the primary inspirations for Earth's vampire legends.*

Of course it was, Nate thought, idly aware that he should pass the information along to the others—that he should do *something*, at least—but stuck instead simply staring at the elongated corpse. The goddamn *alien vampire* corpse, with its creepy dark goggles and razor-sharp claws and fangs. Elmo was watching it too, blaster still trained on the thing like he half-expected it might rise from the dead any moment. Which, all things considered, who the hell knew?

A wet, awfully *human* sputtering sound drew Nate's attention over to where Carter was on her knees, bent down over…

Ramirez.

Shit, how had he forgotten?

"Easy, Vic," Carter was saying, rummaging in her pack with a stark intensity she somehow managed to keep out of her voice. "Eeeasy breaths."

The look she shot Jaeger over the man's bloody chest made it plain enough that it didn't matter one damn bit what kind of breaths he took. Ramirez was dying. That didn't stop her from making some adjustments to his suit's breathing apparatus and starting in on the bloody mess of his chest with some kind of foam spray. Nate gaped as that foam expanded like bloodied shaving cream, wanting to help, wanting with sickening desperation to undo it all.

Jaeger was on the comms, saying something to their crew back on the *Camelot*, giving a terse order to Elmo. Heavy approaching thuds drew Nate's shell-shocked attention over to where the Troglodan peacekeeper was jogging back toward them from the crowd.

"Lost mine," the Trog grunted as he reached them, addressing the words to Iveera.

"And your squadmate?" Iveera asked.

Nate looked around, uncertain which of the peacekeepers had even survived, wanting to point out that Ramirez was dying, damn it.

"Pursuing his," the Trog said. "Reinforcements inbound. Ordered me to regroup with survivors. Protect as needed."

"Lovely fucking job of that so far," Carter growled, her eyes and hands not wavering from her work on Ramirez, who was looking too gray and vacant beneath his faceplate.

If the Troglodan took issue with Carter's attitude, he didn't bother saying so. If anything, the big brute looked bored now that the action had passed. Jaeger, on the other hand, looked more deadly serious than Nate had ever seen him as he squared off with Iveera and the Troglodan.

"We need medical responders and escort back to our ship. Now."

"Orders to take you to Hall of Reason once safe," the Troglodan said, watching the crowd like this was just another day at the office.

"All due respect," Jaeger said, "but you can take your orders and go shove 'em up whoever's ass is in charge of this shit show. We're not going anywhere but our ship until—"

"Peace, Colonel," Iveera said, earning herself a level glare.

Beside her, the Troglodan was frowning idly down at the dead Eldari herald as if he couldn't quite remember whose ass *was* next in line.

"That's two shots on my people in ten minutes," Jaeger was growling at Iveera. "We're getting the piss out of here until—"

"Colonel," Iveera cut in, with enough of an edge to give even an inflamed Jaeger pause. Or maybe it was just what Jaeger saw when he followed Iveera's pointed gaze that made him hold his tongue.

Reinforcements were coming. And they didn't look happy.

"Status?" asked the Androtta that arrived at the head of the incoming security wave. Its voice was mechanically flat, the orange-violet sparks of its eyes trained on the presiding Troglodan peacekeeper. Displeased? Robotic? It was hard to tell.

"What in nine hells happened here?" added one of the arriving Atlanteans, looking around at the carnage with subdued shock and none of the sneering smugness that had radiated from the others.

Dozens of blue-and-gray uniforms were converging on the scene now, some combing through the crowds for trouble, others hurrying their way with packs of supplies and what looked like gravitonic stretchers.

"Orders to take them to Hall of Reason," the Troglodan guard replied. "Ambushed along the way."

"Ambushed?" The Atlantean traded a look with his crystalline-faced partner, looking surprised enough for the both of them. "Ambushed by— Why wasn't…?" He shook himself clear of some momentary jam and turned to the squad at their backs. "Call for more backup and tell Central we're gonna need more med pods out here. Do it!"

As the guards snapped to comply with his orders, two of the medics— one Atlantean and one a long-faced, multi-tentacled creature apparently called a Kelgen—approached Carter and Ramirez, carting along what looked a little bit like a transparent glass tanning bed or a hyperbaric chamber built onto a grav sled. One of those med pods, Nate prayed.

"You may return to the ship if you wish," Iveera said quietly, taking Jaeger discreetly aside and gesturing for Nate to follow as the Troglodan began to give a more detailed report to the relief squad, "but if you want Airman Ramirez to live, I recommend you allow the medics to transport him to their facilities. Nathaniel and I will continue to the Hall of Reason."

"You gotta be kidding me," Jaeger said, glancing from Iveera to Nate as if expecting him to step in and remind the Gorgon that he was barely more than a helpless college kid. Which, admittedly, wasn't far from what Nate was thinking at that moment.

Several trained soldiers had just died. Ramirez looked about two shades away from joining them. Elmo, Nate realized only then, was bleeding freely from a nasty forearm wound, his face blanching whiter by the second. Nate was almost certainly lucky to be alive, as were Carter and Jaeger. And yet...

"She's right," Nate was surprised to hear himself say.

"What?"

Nate looked from Jaeger's rare expression of surprise to Iveera's calm eyes. She'd cleared her armor of the blood, but it struck him that her insides must still be at least partially ground meat right now, no matter how much her Excalibur would eventually repair.

She has doubtlessly known worse pain in her life, Ex pointed out, as if he could see the decision forming in Nate's head almost before Nate saw it himself. And there it was:

They couldn't just turn tail and hunker down on the *Camelot.* And even if they *could* outrun this, it'd only land Lady knew how many more cross-hairs on their heads.

They had to find out what was happening here—who was trying to stop them, who was trying to *kill* them, and why. And until they knew more, the safest place his crew could be was away from him.

It was an arrogant thought. One he could hardly believe belonged to him —to Nate freakin' IT Guy Arturi. But there it was, and whether he imagined it or not, he got the impression Iveera was thinking the same thing.

"Someone gave them disrupter rounds," she said quietly. Gravely.

Bleeding edge tech, Ex replied to Nate's silent query after a slightly longer than usual pause. *Highly secretive. I had to scour the Net to find even a few fringe references just now. Highly encrypted. Initial findings suggest munitions designed to circumvent a broad range of energy-based defenses, including several extradimensional modalities.*

Designed to shred Excalibur armor, in other words?

So it seems. Certainly effective for penetrating a wide range of our available barriers.

So they could add *invisible vampire assassins toting bonafide Knight-killer rounds* to the list, then.

"Should we tell the peacekeepers?" he asked Iveera, keeping his voice low.

Jaeger was watching them like he couldn't quite believe what he was seeing. He was hardly the only one, either. The bazaar was slowly beginning to creep back to life around them—alien heads peeking out from shops and stands and whatever other cover they'd found in the fray, craning necks and various cranial appendages from safer distances above and below, assessing whether the madness had indeed ended. A few particularly ambitious shopkeepers were even opening back up for business.

Too many eyes, though, were trained on Nate and Iveera. Less-than-surreptitious stares from security and civilians alike. It was only then that Nate realized his disguise wasn't doing much good with the shimmering radiance of his overt kinetic barriers still raised. For a second, he thought to hide the telltale sign and resume his cover. Then he thought of cloaked Ooperians lurking in the wings, watching, waiting for their chance to strike again.

If it really was him and Iveera they were after, at least he could make sure they didn't get their Terrans confused. With a thought and a nervous ripple in his gut, Nate released the disguise completely, revealing his true Excalibur armor in plain sight and drawing a new wave of attention and murmurs from the crowd. If Iveera took qualm with the move, she didn't say anything.

"Take Carter and Elmo and make sure Ramirez is safe," Nate said to Jaeger. "We can regroup when we have some answers. Figure out what to do next."

He was half-tempted to add a sardonic *hooah?* when he realized how much it sounded like he'd just given the good Lt Col an order, but Jaeger already looked sour enough. He tore his frown away from Nate, to where the medics and Carter were sealing Ramirez—helmet now off—into the transparent med pod, which was coming alive with all manner of holo vitals, most of them orange and red.

"Piss on that," he finally said, beckoning Carter over before glancing at Nate. "I'm coming with you."

He turned his back before Nate could even think to argue and launched into a fast and furious series of murmurs with Carter, who looked progressively less and less thrilled by the second, gesturing first to Ramirez, then to Nate with a darkening scowl. Finally, she nodded and went to say something to Elmo, who looked up from the bandage the Atlantean medic was dressing his arm with long enough to favor them with his own wary frown.

"Let's go," Jaeger said, turning away from his people to focus back on Nate and Iveera.

Nate looked to Iveera, not really sure whether to argue or be relived.

"Very well," she said, slowly rousing from her thoughts like she'd nearly forgotten they were there—and wasn't really all that happy to remember. She spared an empty look at the lifeless face of the fallen Eldari herald. "Let us be on our way. Some of the chancellors will still be waiting for us."

"Some of them?" Nate asked, as she started to turn.

"Yes," she said, barely bothering to pause or look back. "The ones who didn't just try to have us murdered."

CHAPTER 9

PECKING ORDER

By the time Malfar arrived at Central, the only thing that had become clearer with any certainty was that whatever self-important drama was unfolding among the Excalibur Knights wasn't over. There'd been some kind of attack over in the Capital marketplace. Multiple Forge peacekeepers dead. More wounded, along with several non-combatants. Two shiny Knights allegedly at the center of it all, allegedly unharmed. As for the rest of the details trickling in…

Ooperians.

Malfar huffed a tired breath, stepped into the never-ending bustle of Central's main bullpen, and set his sights for the lift wells on the far wall, inviting the room's dull roar to wash away his troubled thoughts. It wasn't that he didn't believe the legendary killers had struck here on the Forge. He'd always known they were out there, even if he'd personally never seen one. They'd left too many bodies across the galaxy to be pure myth.

It was more a question of whether this latest madness was any professional concern of his, or if he had bigger concerns entirely. It wasn't so easy to tell, what with wild Troglodan war parties and cryptic Gorgon data packets appearing without warning.

A paranoid sort might've jumped to conclusions by the looks he drew from some of his so-called comrades as he crossed the hectic ocean of personal holo displays, stale desk-side snacks, and tired-looking peacekeepers. But then again, those looks had never *not* been there. Especially not since Central's favorite spotted runt of a peacekeeper had gone and joined the scant list of those audacious souls who were both Troglodans *and* justicars.

Paranoia, he'd soon learned, quickly became untenably exhausting when the entire galaxy had long ago decided you weren't to be trusted, no matter what badge you wore.

He reached the lift wells and keyed his way up to the admin level most colloquially known by various translations as "the ass grinder." There really weren't all that many reasons an officer ever got called to report in person, after all, justicar or otherwise.

No matter. He'd done nothing wrong, broken no regulations or mandates. Or almost none, he amended, remembering what was riding in his gear pouch. But that was barely even a bent technicality. He pushed it aside as he reached his destination among the sparse, repetitive hallways and paused at the door, listening—more an ingrained investigator's reflex than anything. One never knew what manner of secrets they might pick up if they merely listened before knocking. But this was the chief justice's office. It was soundproofed and secured, the outside monitored from within, which was why Malfar wasn't all that surprised when the door hissed open to permit him entry.

What did surprise him was the sight of Ser Zedavian Kelkarin's holo projection standing beside the Eldari chief justice, staring at the open door like he too had been awaiting Justicar D679's report. Malfar stared right back, too stunned to do anything else.

"Leave us," the First Knight said.

Had he not been so off-balance by the entire thing, Malfar might have been miffed at being dismissed so summarily—shooed off before he'd even stepped inside. He was doubly resentful at the way his mindless feet shuffled an obedient half-step back at the order. Then his brain caught up, and he realized that the chief was shooting his Eldari kinsmen an irritated frown and stepping out from behind his pristine workstation. The chief justice strode to the door, straight for Malfar, pushing past him with a warning glare, and suddenly the door was closed, and Malfar was standing alone in the chief justice's office with the First Knight's holo.

"I know she sent you records of what transpired on Terra," that holo said, before Malfar could manage so much as a dumb blink. "I'm sure she told you a few things as well. Troubling things, perhaps."

Something had changed.

With an effort, Malfar closed his stupid mouth and looked around the well-appointed office, allowing his brain a second to sputter back online and recalibrate. Gorgon Knight allegedly kills Troglodan Knight, only to be plucked from the hands of Alliance law by Eldari Knight and delivered into failed Ooperian ambush, at which point Eldari Knight comes sniffing after Gorgon Knight's data packet because… Why?

Why had the First Knight separated from his charge in the first place? Where had he gone? What had he seen? And why bother with Malfar now? He was a lowly third-class justicar. His detaining Katanaga had been a long shot in the first place. No way he was a threat to Zedavian Kelkarin unless…

Something had changed.

"It's not my job to speculate, Ser Knight," Malfar forced himself to say, trying to sound like a good peon. He *was* a good peon, dammit. That's what had gotten him here. And yet something *had* changed. "The records were relayed to the proper channels," he pressed on. "Anything beyond that is above my station."

He didn't meet the First Knight's eyes as the Eldari studied him. He just stared straight ahead like a good peon, mind whirling like a one-Trog rattler barreling down the side of the Death's Head peaks back home.

"Hmm," Kelkarin finally said. "A judicious Troglodan. What a rarity."

Malfar ignored the bait, eyes forward. What in nine hells was going on here? What could possibly be so important that—

The holo was there before he knew it, across the room and in his face in less than the blink of an eye. Malfar staggered back, his entire torso tingling with the proximity of the apparition. Tingling like—

"You will forget whatever she told you," Kelkarin said. "You were never there. Do you understand me?"

Malfar could only gape, as certain that he'd just felt the buzzing power of this holo apparition as he was that such a thing was completely impossible. Theatrics and trickery. Some sophisticated remote device here in the chief's office. It had to be.

"The records were relayed to the proper channels," Malfar repeated, his voice admirably calm, not at all like he felt, as he pointed out the obvious wrinkle in Kelkarin's plan of denial.

"It's already been handled," the First Knight said, supremely unconcerned. "You will be too if you fail to heed this conversation." The holo went into a jittering standby like Kelkarin had frozen it to mask his activity on the other side. "I am arriving at the Capitol now, justicar," said the motionless apparition. "Do not concern yourself anymore with these affairs. Do not give me a reason to track you down in person."

And with that, Ser Zedavian Kelkarin was gone.

Malfar was still staring at the empty space he'd just vacated when the door hissed open behind him, and the chief justice jerked a hand from the hallway in what couldn't have been a clearer sign for, *get the hell out of my office, you damn dirty runt.*

Malfar was too rattled and off-balance to question the sentiment. He turned and left, eyes to the deck, before he could incur the threats of any more monumental authorities.

"If I ever have cause to see your hide up here again…" the chief started as he passed, his voice too low and angry to manage more words at first. Malfar hardly begrudged him that much. He imagined he'd be pissed too, had he climbed all the way to the office of Chief Justice of Forge Station only to be dismissed from said office on the casual whim of a thrice-cursed Excalibur Knight.

Not that he and the chief were about to hold hands and bond over the injustice. He wasn't even sure why he turned back to face the chief, other than some dutiful sense that he should allow his commanding officer to finish the threat, should he so choose. But the chief didn't look threatening anymore. Just dead tired.

"I checked your assignment request."

The words were oddly speculative and light-handed, given the circumstances.

"What were you looking for out there?" he finally asked, when Malfar made no reply.

"Justice, sir."

The words left his mouth without his really thinking about it—far from the complete truth, admittedly, but not at all a lie, either. The Eldari considered him for one contemplative moment before his Chief Justice face slipped back on, and he nodded to himself like he'd just confirmed something.

"Right, then. You're suspended until you hear otherwise. Effective immediately." The chief cut him off with a hard look before he could manage so much as a *but sir.* "Just be grateful it's paid. It's more than you deserve, digging around in Knight business. What did you expect would happen?"

Malfar didn't know what to say. Couldn't do anything but gape dumbly as the Eldari's expectant look faded, replaced with building frustration and disgust.

"Just turn over your cases and get out of my station."

"Sir," Malfar distantly heard himself say, back in the real world where this was really happening.

Suspended.

Something had changed.

Him, a justicar, suspended.

"Malfar."

The voice brought him back to the corridor, where the chief was still watching him from the office doorway, clearly thinking twice about whatever he was about to say.

"I'm telling you right now because I know how your kind are: don't go fucking with this one. Drop it now, or say goodbye to the badge." He thought about it for a moment, then shrugged. "I really don't give a shit."

The door hissed shut once more, and Malfar was alone, deck swaying beneath him, insides cold with something he scarcely recognized. Something like fear. The fear of having awoken in a crowded room only to find that he was suddenly drowning and that no one else could be bothered to notice or care.

Something had changed.

Justicars didn't *get* suspended. Not over anything less substantial than a capital offense. And they sure as hell didn't drop cases. Not true justicars. Not ever. That was the entire point of the office. And now… Now, he carefully lowered the curled fists that had been preparing to dent the wall plating on the rising tide of brutish rage that was his only real birthright— his one true companion in life.

He needed someone to talk to, now more than ever.

There was no one.

The halls of Central passed him by in a detached blur on the way out, full of noise, devoid of meaning. Even his churning thoughts couldn't seem to scrounge up a lick of that. Thinking without thinking. A dull roar of nothingness, with the sneering face of Admiral Varga and his Clan Groshna war party floating by in the background. No coincidence. No…

It was only when he found himself sinking onto a familiar stool at the closest thing he had to a favorite cantina that he even really processed what he was doing. He needed to hand over his case files before anyone made a fuss. Release his vessel's command credentials back to Central, too, assuming they hadn't already been changed remotely. His crew would be gods-damned thrilled.

Instead of opening his omni to get things started, though, he found himself sliding the tiny data key from his belt pouch. Suddenly, he didn't care if he was alone, if anyone was watching. He set the infernal little chip on the table in front of him. It felt unconscionably bold, like going all-in at a life-or-death-stakes game of garrick. Doubly so as he beckoned for the Svendarian behind the sparsely populated bar to bring him a drink right there at the scene of the crime.

But he didn't care in that moment. He just stared at that damned data key, waiting, silently cursing himself for having made the clone at all, and then again for not having looked at it sooner, back in Golnak, when the damned Gorgon's mystery message had still been his rightful jurisdiction.

When he hadn't been gods-damned suspended.

The thought rocked him, rippling through his troubled mind, lapping messily up against swirling snippets of rogue Knights, unlawful incursions, Ooperian assassins, and now shadowy Troglodan fleets, and Varga, and the sins of the thrice-damned father.

Quite out of nowhere, the thought of that Atlantean mining colony flitted to the surface.

Where had Kelkarin disappeared to after yanking Katanaga free from the law only to deliver her to waiting assassins? Where, for that matter, had Varga's fleet been headed? It wasn't hard to guess what that deranged warmonger was after, but...

Drop it now, the chief's voice rang in his head. *Or say goodbye to the badge.*

He scowled down at the drinkless table, knowing that he was well beyond grasping at straws anyway, and that he'd soon be barred (if he wasn't already) from Central's database besides, and left with nothing but hearsay and grog to fuel his half-spun hypotheses.

No official resources.

No jurisdiction.

But he *did* have at least two contacts on active duty out there with the T-Sec relay fleet, didn't he? Contacts with working eyes, and perhaps even working tongues. And there was that damned data key, too, sitting right there through all of it, teasing him with the Gorgon's infernal mysteries. Something amiss. Sins of the father. A mighty empire, no doubt inflamed at the news of their fallen hero. And yet, how had they known? How had Varga's fleet arrived so quickly? Unless...

"I am not your servant, Knight," he muttered at the chip, feeling petulant and more than a little frustrated.

"Bad day?" asked a deep, knowing voice from entirely too close. Malfar forced himself to unclench as the Svendarian barkeep slid a tall mug of dark grog in front of him. Then he grabbed the mug and took a pull of the thick liquid with an intensity that surprised him. He relished the glugging swell of bitter fire. The barkeep, not exactly an acquaintance but at least familiar with his patron's vocation, eyed Malfar's self-made chugging contest, then the data key, then Malfar again, caught between curiosity and professional discretion.

"Big case?" he finally asked.

Malfar pulled the mug from his lips, dimly surprised to note it was already half empty. He looked at the Svendarian, searching for a sufficiently dismissive answer, then back down to that infernal data key, and the simple but infinitely damning forking paths it represented. One way the path of a career shit-stain riding the waves of office politics and the other that of a true justicar, a servant of Justice. One way kowtowing to Zedavian Kelkarin and his obedient chief justice, and the other…

He scowled into his mug, thinking of Katanaga and her band of pet Terrans. The Svendarian, finally yielding to that professional discretion of his, was turning to leave his patron in peace when Malfar looked up at him again.

"Big case," he agreed, plucking the data key carefully from the table and brandishing his half-empty mug. "I think I'm going to need another."

CHAPTER 10

RESPECT, AND ELDERS

"The chancellor is nearly ready."

Nate straightened from his post in the corner of the waiting room, stiff to the gills after nearly three hours of standing there, and glanced up at the disembodied speaker voice. In the adjacent corner, Jaeger did the same. They traded an uncertain look.

"Still beats the DMV, right?" Nate asked.

Jaeger gave a half-hearted huff.

They'd barely spoken since Iveera had reluctantly departed to go meet her Elder Representative Kaiyosh in one of the nearby offices. Mostly, they'd just stood there, both on guard, both sure that this preposterous wait couldn't go much longer. An hour ago, Jaeger had finally gone out to check with the eerily gorgeous receptionists, who were oh-so-sorry about the wait, and profusely insistent that they'd be seen at any moment.

Any other day, Nate might not have minded taking a load off here in the lavish offices of Chancellor Adamus Statecaste, where the thick carpets and rich dark woods were quite well matched with the pillared splendor and decadent atriums they'd witnessed on their way in through the Hall of Reason. The waiting room was perfectly cozy, and with the exception of the wait, the service had been accommodating to a level that might've made Nate blush had either of them actually taken advantage of it. But with Ramirez off in some alien medical facility and Lady knew how many Ooperian assassins still on the loose out there, they hadn't really felt like now was the time to try a cup of the local joe. Especially not since Jaeger had been stripped of his commandeered weapons at the door, and Nate had had a chance to tell him exactly what those pale-skinned *things* had actually been.

So they'd waited, keeping the full room in view, backs firmly planted to the walls. Nate still wasn't entirely convinced those creatures wouldn't simply come phasing through anyway, with a ghostly sigh and a *poof* of reapparition.

For the last time, Nathaniel: Ooperians are not ethereal. You're being such a human about this.

You know that's not—

"The chancellor will see you now," chimed that perfectly pleasant speaker voice.

Nate looked uncertainly at the door and finished his thought. *You know 'human' isn't a curse word, right?*

That depends entirely upon which lexicon one consults. In my summary acclimation to modern Alliance affairs, I've already encountered several instances of Atlanteans using the word as a derogatory slight against their Terran ancestors in the interest of distancing the Atlantean people from their, ah... humble beginnings.

Nate drew up to the Chancellor's door beside Jaeger. *Seriously?*

Seriously, dude, Ex shot back in the tone he always used when Nate asked a particularly daft question.

"Well, that doesn't really bode well, does it?" Nate muttered.

Not when they were fixing to go have a chat with the closest thing to the King of the Atlanteans.

"Maybe dial it down on the talking to yourself, kid?" Jaeger said. "It's not getting any less weird. Just in case you were wondering."

Nate shot him a sarcastic salute and turned his frown to the door's access panel, wondering what came next, whether the King of the Atlanteans would apologize for having kept them waiting for three damned hours, or if it had been a deliberate power play. The door slid open as Jaeger reached for the panel, revealing a sleek but sparse office space that wasn't nearly as kingly as Nate had been expecting. *Space station chic,* Zach would've called it. Elegant in its simplicity.

The thought of his dead friend hit as unexpectedly as it had every other time, leaving him standing at a loss before the man he'd come to see—the man who apparently had the right to challenge his selection as Excalibur Knight.

"Chancellor Statecaste," Nate said, setting Zach's image carefully aside and trying to compose himself.

Chancellor Adamus, Ex corrected. *First names for Atlanteans, not caste titles, remember?*

"Chancellor Adamus," Nate added quickly, as if he could cover the slip-up that had already sent their host's sculpted lips curling into a faint smirk at the head of the long table.

If the office was elegant in its simplicity, then Chancellor Adamus was built to match. Physically, he was as flawless as the rest of the Atlanteans in the room, albeit visibly older with his salt-and-pepper hair and the slight wrinkling around his eyes. But he also seemed to have taken care to keep his adornments as simple as possible—a well-fitted charcoal tunic, trousers to match, and a single golden pin on his chest, featuring an Atlantean trident laid across a barebones version of the blazing star and overlapping crescents of the Alliance emblem. When he brandished a hand toward Nate in invitation, he didn't stand from the table like the others did.

"Come. Join us, Terran. Let us be brief."

Brief?

Nate scanned the rest of the waiting faces—senators, aides, and advisors from a host of Atlantean worlds, according to Ex's on-the-fly database queries. Most of them dressed with far more color and ornamental flare than the chancellor. He stepped into the room beside Jaeger, eyeing the humming blue holo window that stretched across the back wall, looking out over an enormous amphitheater Ex identified as the Council assembly chamber. It was stacked tall with ascending stadium rings of offices, much like this one, most blurred from view with opaque barriers, others revealing mixed cadres of alien ambassadors mingling over drinks and data streams and vigorously waving appendages.

"Chancellor Adamus," Nate repeated, forcing his attention back to the room. Even with all the alien novelty outside, it was still strange being stared at by so many uncannily beautiful humans. Like he'd accidentally stumbled onto the set of *America's Next Top Model: Space Politico Edition* in his Saturday morning sweats. He glanced at Jaeger, who faintly nodded for him to proceed.

"People of the Atlantean Empire," he continued, turning back to the room. "My name is Nathaniel Arturi. This is Lt Col John Jaeger of the Terran Air Force. We're pleased to make your acquaintance."

The words felt overly formal on Nate's tongue, but this seemed like an overly formal kind of setting. He watched their faces for any cue or reaction, but no one spoke.

"We were told you wish to assess the candidacy of the Terran Knight," Jaeger added when the silence continued to stretch. "We would also like to extend the respectful greetings of the combined governments of our homeworld."

Some of the Chancellor's entourage might've smirked a bit harder at that, but it was kind of hard to tell, what with all the preexisting condescension cluttering the air.

Adamus gestured for his people to sit with all the dead calm of a school teacher preparing to correct an obvious error while the rest of the class giggled behind their notebooks. "The Galactic Alliance recognizes no such Knight at this time, Lt Col John Jaeger." His gaze flicked to Nate. "Only a confused initiate. But thank you for your greetings."

That definitely drew a round of knowing smirks from the table. Only one man—dark-haired and dressed as simply as Adamus himself—looked uncertain about the comment.

So it's to be a verbal contest of perceived phallic magnitude, then, Ex grumbled. *Splendid. Blackened bureaucrats.*

"Now," Adamus continued, "I do believe we've had our mandated look. If there's nothing else"—he gestured to doors that led to the reception area—"I'm sure the Council will be in contact soon."

The dismissal was so abrupt and unexpected that it took Nate a moment to realize what was happening. Brief in-freaking-deed. Jaeger was watching him with a look of brimming *if you don't, I will.*

"Chancellor Adamus," Nate started, grasping and failing to find any of the numerous lines he'd rehearsed during their long wait. "I do admit to being somewhat unclear on the details of this assessment process…"

Other than that it all looked a lot like *bullshit*—a few vague lines in their precious Round Table Accords that had apparently only ever been employed once, in the supreme Alliance oversight that had led to the Knighting of Ser Groshna, who'd gone on to commit such noble deeds as flying off the rails, defecting to the Black Knight's banner, and leading the invasion of Earth. He almost wished Iveera hadn't told him those bits on the way over.

"… But I *have* mastered my Excalibur," he continued, trying to sound confident.

Mastered, Ex chuckled. *That's a good one, Nathaniel.*

"I am bound to him, just as he's bound to me," Nate pushed on. "And you should know that our time here comes at the expense of delaying a mission of dire importance."

Christ, he sounded like he'd walked straight out of a fantasy RPG.

I think it's cute.

"So, I'd appreciate it if you could tell me what it is you'd like to see from me before you'll feel comfortable recommending the Council approve the Lady's edict to appoint me as a Knight."

A few of the Atlanteans traded unreadable glances across the long table. Jaeger gave him a slight *that'll do* tilt of the head. The chancellor just stared. And stared.

"No," he finally said. And just like that, he turned his attention pointedly back to the surface of their meeting table, where green and aquamarine streams of data were scrolling across the dark surface. "Now, Senator Zodaya. You were saying, pertaining to these T-Sec abnormalities..."

The one who must've been Zodaya shot an uncertain glance Nate's way, then turned and started rattling off a breakdown of how an unprecedented solar event could have theoretically led to the failure of multiple *something-or-anothers* in Demeter's orbit, disrupting operations, but how none of that accounted for this reading, and that report, and this...

It appears they've recently had a mining colony go dark, Ex said, right around the time Nate was deciding it was all too fast to follow. Meanwhile, Adamus was holding up a hand to pause Senator Zodaya, glancing at Nate and Jaeger like they were interrupting. Which—Nate realized as more stares turned their way—they totally freaking were. Because Adamus had clearly called them in mid-conversation. And as potentially not good as a dark colony sounded, Nate couldn't help but focus more on the bit where it sure felt like the King of the Atlanteans had just let them sit around for three hours so he could invite them to politely go fuck themselves.

Jaeger seemed to have arrived at a similar conclusion, his expression caught somewhere between the persona of Earth's first diplomat and that of the guy who was sorely tempted to see how many Atlantean asses he could kick before security got in here.

"We have private business of some urgency to attend," Chancellor Adamus said, eyeing them both like he couldn't quite grasp why they were still standing there intruding on their lovely little tea party.

The room was silent, the first signs of discomfort creeping onto a few of the Atlantean's perfect faces.

"Well, forgive our intrusion," Jaeger said, with a hint of the drawl that crept into his tone when he was being especially sarcastic. "We must be a tad turned around, what with the attempted assassination and having been invited into the room and all. Just for the record, is it customary here to keep your guests couped up for three hours just to tell them to piss off?"

"What I think Lt Col Jaeger is trying to say…" Nate started, not really sure where he was going with it.

Adamus cut him off anyway with crisp words and mounting irritation. "I was ordered to meet with you and to provide my honest opinion to the Council. I've done the former. I'll gladly do the latter. That concludes our business here, Terran."

Nate felt his knuckles cracking, the urge to raise his armored fists and smash their nifty little data table to a heap nearly overwhelming his better senses. They hadn't fought through invasions, justicars, and assassins—hadn't lost friends and watched Ramirez rushed off to medical, half-dead—just to walk away now, smiling politely in the face of this bureaucratic bullshit. They needed to get the hell off of this station. Back to the *Camelot*. Back after the Merlin.

But Iveera had made it maddeningly clear that submitting to Zedavian's and the Council's little games and assuaging their doubts was the fastest way to do that.

Thrice-blackened politicians, Ex grumbled.

"What's the shakedown here, Chancellor?" Jaeger asked, calm and controlled. "You have the leverage. We're obviously strangers to your customs. What do you want from us?"

Adamus studied them both. "You've already caused several deaths on this station," he finally said, as if it were really all there was to say.

"That's hardly fair, Chancellor," said one of the Atlanteans, drawing a round of surprised looks from the table. It was the same dark-haired man who'd looked put-off by Adamus' earlier comments. He was conservatively dressed. More slenderly built than most of the other men, his features more refined.

Calum Statecaste, Ex provided, *junior senator of Triton.*

"They were attacked in public without cause or warning," the outspoken senator added when the stares remained. "Last I checked, self-defense is no crime."

Nate felt a begrudging stir of gratitude for the senator's defiance, but Chancellor Adamus only shook his head softly, like he'd barely heard. "The Atlantean Empire is not interested in witnessing the honor and respect we've built through millennia of service and toil upended by the ancestors of those who'd have brained us with sticks and stones for heresy had our own ancestors lacked the courage to take to the stars."

"Yes, Chancellor," the senator agreed, "but if we could only—"

"That's enough, Calum," Chancellor Adamus said, with a pointed look at the dissident senator. He turned back to Nate. "I have fulfilled the mandate of my current orders, Terran. If you have a problem, you will need to take it up with Supreme Chancellor Priatus. Otherwise, I must ask you to"—his eyes flicked to Jaeger with the faintest hint of glib amusement—"kindly piss off, I think the phrase was. Our people require our full attention at the moment."

Behind them, the main doors hissed open in time with Adamus' pointed gesture, inviting them to leave the Atlanteans be. Nate traded a look with Jaeger and saw his own growing defeat mirrored in the Lt Col's eyes. They started to turn by some unspoken agreement, maybe to go regroup, maybe to go fleeing to Iveera's skirts. He didn't know. He just blurted the words before he could think better of it.

"I didn't ask for this."

Jaeger shot him a look of soft warning. Nate turned anyway and found Calum and Adamus both studying him, the rest of the assembled Atlanteans trading their own looks around the table—so perfectly human in their reactions, no matter what they said.

"I didn't ask for the honor of bearing this Excalibur," he pressed on, finding his voice. "How could I? I didn't even know the damn thing existed before the Merlin found me. But it's mine now."

The words sent a soft ripple through the room. Maybe because he'd mentioned the Merlin. Maybe because he'd just raised more questions than he should've. He didn't really care at the moment.

"The duty is mine now, and you need to know I'm gonna do my job no matter how many old laws and ancient grudges you throw my way."

He let that statement hang a moment, mildly surprised himself to hear the words coming out of his mouth with such gravity, already thinking he should probably follow up with something more amicable before he left. An assurance that he didn't want to fight, maybe. That he'd rather move forward as allies rather than adversaries.

"I hope your colony is okay," was all he could think to say when the moment came. "We'd be happy to lend whatever aid we can."

To his surprise, Adamus gave him a slight nod just before he turned to leave with what dignity he had left.

"Maybe you're not so hopeless after all, kid," Jaeger murmured quietly as they marched out the room.

Nate was biting back a half-giddy retort and trying to simply focus on making that dignified exit when Ex bubbled up to the surface with a big, fat, *Ahhh...*

He frowned. *Ah?*

Yes, ah. Ah as in, ah, I just finished scanning all available data pertaining to this Demeter-12 colony, and I think it might behoove us to have a closer—

"Terran," called a voice behind them.

They turned to find the one called Calum walking quickly after them across the lobby.

"Nathaniel," the senator amended as he drew up to them, seeming to decide his first word had been too unfamiliar. He extended a hand. "Senator Calum Statecaste, of Triton. It's a pleasure to finally meet you."

The senator made it sound like Nate hadn't been Knighted—or *initiated* —mere weeks ago. Like he'd in fact been following Nate's career for years with great interest.

"Uh, thanks," Nate said, taking the offered hand. "Likewise."

His grip was strong, but then again, Nate doubted that was uncommon for these god-people. He glanced uncertainly past Calum as Adamus' office doors slid closed once more. "Aren't you missing your meeting?"

"Oh, we'll be at it for hours in there," Calum said, waving Nate's concern away and turning to take Jaeger's hand next. "I hope neither of you will think too harshly of us for this less than fortunate reception. As you seem to have intuited, one of our smaller mining colonies recently came under attack."

"Attack?" Nate asked.

"That sort of thing common out here?" Jaeger added.

Calum's brow furrowed like he'd only just realized what he'd said. "I spoke carelessly. We're not certain it was an attack at all. I only worry."

This data IS highly erratic, Ex said, as if the senator might be right to worry.

"At any rate," Calum was saying, "I merely wished to extend my welcome, and to let you know that my door is always open to you, should you need anything."

"That's awfully kind of you," Nate said. It might've come out a little more suspiciously than he'd intended, after what they'd just been through with Adamus.

"Not to sound unappreciative, Calum," Jaeger said, apparently having similar thoughts, "but does your boss in there approve of you befriending a pair of troublesome Terrans?"

Calum glanced around to make sure they were out of earshot of the receptionists, then showed them a knowing smile. "Probably not," he said, a little more quietly. "But then, there's a good deal on which I don't see eye-to-eye with the chancellor. He speaks of maintaining the empire's reputation as if what peace and prosperity we've brought to the Alliance hasn't already already been marred by such embarrassments as our birthing of the Asgardians. If I'm to be honest, I sometimes fear my people will one day pass into history, remembered more for pirate cults and vat birth reproduction rates than for any good and noble cause."

Nate and Jaeger were still sharing a look as if to say *did he just say Asgardians?* when Calum stirred from his own thoughts and pushed on.

"All of that to say, there are those among us who do rejoice at the coming of a human Knight, Atlantean or not."

"Thank you," Nate said, meaning it this time, and actually starting to feel a little better about their chances here.

Calum nodded, looking pleased. "I should get back to it, but I'll reach out soon. Rest assured, I'll do what I can to bend the chancellor's ear your favor. And in the meantime, if there *is* anything I can do to ease your transition here, please…"

The Atlantean trailed off, looking slightly confused, then flat out surprised, at whatever he'd just seen over Nate's shoulder. Nate was already whirling, Jaeger going tense beside him, when the voice cut in from behind them, elegant and unmistakable.

"So sorry to interrupt the pleasantries."

For a moment, Nate could only stare in awe at the sheer deadly presence of the golden titan standing in entryway. Then his brain caught up and he took in Iveera floating there, dejected, stripped of her armor, and confined to a transparent e-dim dampening cell. He tensed, thinking to help her, then froze as Ser Zedavian Kelkarin aimed one ominously glowing palm at his chest. An empty cell unfolded from thin air in front of him, and the Eldari tilted his golden head at it, a casual, almost bored smile stretching his lips.

"I'm going to need you to surrender your armaments and come with me, Initiate."

CHAPTER II

EMPATHY

"This is jatara shit," Iveera growled at Zedavian's back as they floated into yet another large, swanky room on his flanks, and the door hissed shut behind them.

It was the first thing Nate had heard her say since he'd been taken. The first thing Zedavian had allowed her to say, he was pretty sure. As if the First Knight had finally pressed the *unmute* button on her cell now that they were alone in this… whatever it was. A dungeon fit for kings, Nate decided, staring dumbly around the richly furnished room that felt to be at the bottom of the world. Or the bottom of Zedavian Kelkarin's preposterous estate, at least. But at least Iveera finally sounded angry with her precious First Knight.

It might've been a comforting thought if they hadn't both just been kidnapped.

"I know about your Excaliburs," was all Zedavian said.

Nate froze, waiting for more.

They were the first words Zedavian had spoken since Adamus' offices, excluding the brief orders he'd given the peacekeepers outside to see that Jaeger and the rest of his Terran brethren in medical were all safely moved back to the *Camelot* to await further processing under a generous guard detail.

Nate had spent the cell ride through the Hall of Reason hoping they'd be okay. There hadn't been much else to do, aside from trying to catch Iveera's eye for some confirmation that this was all just a colossal misunderstanding. Now, though, those five little words struck like the first nail in the coffin, and he couldn't help but wonder if he shouldn't have at least tried to put up a fight.

You did the right thing, Ex assured him. *Now stop sniveling about it and find out what he wants.*

"Did you honestly believe I wouldn't notice this festering *corruption* of yours?" Zedavian asked, turning to Iveera.

That settled it, then. Nails Two through Fifty, firmly sunk.

A tired, humorless smile stretched Zedavian's lips as he studied Iveera. "No. Of course not. You didn't even attempt to hide it, did you?"

"There is nothing to hide, my First Knight," she said, tall and proud in her cage. "There has been no evidence the corruption permeated either of our defenses."

"No?" He leaned closer until their faces were separated only by the transparent cell wall and scant inches of air. "I can smell it in your blood, Seven. You are tainted. Tainted with *him.* Both of you are." He leaned back from the cell, appraising her from head to toe, making some remark about what a pity it all was as the space behind him came alive with the unfolding walls of a larger e-dim prison.

Nate was too busy trying to process what he'd just said.

Tainted with *him.* Like Zedavian had already known. Like he was in fact so intimately familiar with this mysterious Black Knight that he could recognize the bastard's scent from across the galaxy. Which meant...

"Can you prove what you say?" Iveera asked, calm as ever despite the nice little prison unfolding around the two red-cushioned benches at the center of the room, promising a long stay. "Can you prove that we are truly afflicted?"

"I don't have to," Zedavian said, not glib or haughty. Just very matter of fact. Behind him, the e-dim prison finished its self-construction. "We shall have our proof soon enough."

Nate's hovering cell started forward as Zedavian spoke. Iveera's too. Both of them gliding over to the larger prison. The cell walls merged where they met, opening like a pair of atmos seals to dump them into their new home. Nate spun to face the freshly-sealed wall, stomach tight, panic surging at the thought of being imprisoned in this asshole's basement while the Black Knight did gods knew what with the Merlin, and Zedavian...

Zedavian was already halfway to the door.

"Hey!" Nate slammed a fist to the transparent wall, mind racing with a disjointed whirl of assassination attempts, betrayal, and ominously prophetic dreams. He felt Ex at the edges, silently bidding he calm himself even as he opened his mouth to shout it out anyway.

Was it you? Did you try to have us killed?

"Will you not help us?" Iveera called before he could form the words. She was still calm. Too calm. Like she was asking for nothing more than an extra hand with the groceries.

Zedavian slowed and turned. He studied them intently, maybe even remorsefully. "I cannot."

"Then let us go after the Merlin," Nate blurted. They both looked at him. "If you can't help us…" He glanced uncertainly between the two senior Knights. "Couldn't the Merlin? Can't you let us try, at least? What's there to lose?"

Aside from two Excaliburs and two Knight ships, that was. And all of it compounded by a whole burning boatload of unknowns.

Zedavian gave another one of those tired smiles, clearly seeing that and more. "I would say you have much to learn, Terran, were it not already so doubtful you possess the remaining time to learn it. Be at peace," he said, gesturing to the room's splendorous artwork and decorations with an all-encompassing wave as he began to back away. "We'll have our answers soon enough."

"Wait!" Nate cried, pounding the wall again.

But the door was already hissing shut behind the First Knight, leaving them together alone, side by side with the most profound silence Nate had ever known.

"WHAT DID HE MEAN, we'll have our proof?" Nate asked sometime later, frowning down at the untouched pitcher of water a soft-spoken Gorgon—one of Zedavian's servants, it seemed—had brought them earlier. His throat was dry, his voice hoarse. He looked over at Iveera. "What's gonna happen to us?"

She remained silent, staring through the wall and into nothingness, as she had been for too long now. It might've been an hour or two. Maybe more.

Not quite two, Ex said.

Not quite two, then. And she'd barely said a word, aside from a few pacifying *I don't know*s early on, and one slightly less tranquil *quiet your tongue and give me a moment to think.*

It had been one long-ass moment since then.

"Iveera?"

Peace, Nathaniel, Ex said. *You know what he meant.*

Nate sighed and rolled back into a laying position on the modestly-padded bench, idly wondering if maybe something—or several somethings—hadn't been lost amid all the seamless translations that allowed him to speak with Iveera, Zedavian, and every other non-Terran on the Forge. Magical as it all seemed, he couldn't help but wonder how many intricate little details fell to the wayside every time one of them opened their mouths. It might explain at least part of why no one on this station seemed to be making one damn lick of sense right now.

Sure, blame the translators for your shoddy interpersonal skills. No small wonder you ended up here.

Nate huffed at nothing in particular, knowing that neither of them were being truly serious. The thought was merely a momentary distraction from the more pressing questions of who had tried to kill them, and why, and whether or not Zedavian was right, and they were actually corrupted and... what? Bound to go full Groshna? Or to drop dead within the week if they failed to bend the knee and pledge themselves to the Black Knight as the Troglodan had done?

Ex had been unusually reticent to speculate. Nate could tell it bothered his companion—the inability to resolutely confirm or deny the presence of any such corruption within his subsystems. The thought that he, a being of supreme inorganic logic and reason, might not be as in control of his faculties as he so vehemently believed.

Maybe it really was best for everyone, them being locked up here in e-dim prison with no choices left to them. Zedavian was clearly confident enough that they weren't to be trusted, and from what he'd seen, Nate doubted the rest of the station would feel much differently. Chancellor Adamus certainly hadn't been too stoked at the thought of a Terran Knight running around. The Troglodans were almost certainly yearning to turn both of them to jelly after the disgrace they'd suffered back on Earth. And then there were the Ooperians, and whoever the hell had sent them—assuming it hadn't been any of the above parties, which was admittedly pretty damn far from a sure thing at this point.

"We should have just run when we had the chance," he murmured, mostly to himself. But it was that, of all things, that finally got Iveera's attention.

"I tried," she said, jin absentmindedly swaying his way like they secretly longed to grab hold of his throat. "You interfered."

"I said I was sorry for that," Nate pointed out, wishing it didn't sound so useless. "But I wasn't the one who insisted we obey his Golden Imminence and come here after the fact."

The words just sort of slipped out, a hot poker of accusation thrust forward by his own guilt at having failed to let her flee that justicar and jump them clear when they'd still had a shot at avoiding all of this bullshit. He probably would've apologized for them if he'd had the chance. Probably immediately. But Iveera was faster. Faster than he could even comprehend.

Next thing he knew, he was gasping for air, body ringing with the violent impact of the cell wall she'd just slammed him into.

"No," she hissed, jin ensnaring his head and neck, immobilizing him. "You are the one who lives only because I have kept you alive more times than bear counting, you ungrateful hatchling."

For a second, Nate could only gape, twice frozen by the ferocious strength in her arm and the sudden bite in her voice. Then his hands caught up and began clawing for precious air, vision already darkening, soft voices whispering to him from the other side of consciousness. He felt oddly calm about it all.

Listen carefully, Nathaniel, Ex said, his tone admonishing.

Nate blinked, hands pausing at their ineffectual attempt to free himself from her crushing death grip, feeling calmer still. Disturbingly calm.

They watch, whispered Iveera. *They listen.*

He blinked again, every bit as sure he'd heard her words as he was that her lips hadn't moved, which didn't make sense—not with all of his Excalibur goodies locked up in e-dim. But there was no denying the voice in his head.

Feel my presence, Nathaniel. You do not need your suit. You require nothing more than your mind for this bond.

She speaks the truth, Ex said.

Nate stared, feeling half-drunk with the unerring calm that filled him. Radiating, he could almost swear, straight from where Iveera's hands clutched his throat. He opened his mouth to say something. He didn't know what.

She threw him across the room like a Ken doll before he decided. He landed heavily, something shattering under his weight, momentum carrying him on for another whirling revolution before he crashed into the opposite wall of their cell.

"What the fuck?!" he growled, as he scrambled upright, disoriented eyes finding their shaky focus back on the Gorgon. His bench lay shattered on the tiled floor between them. Iveera stepped over the splintered ruins and stood over him.

"Consider it payback for the wounds I sustained coming to your aid."

He paused. Somehow, it hadn't even occurred to him she might be angry about taking a few disruptor rounds to the guts to knock him out of the line of fire. But something about the way her jin rippled when she said it, almost like a flinch, turned his thoughts back to Earth—to Groshna on the bridge of the *Kalnythian Wilds*, to Iveera bound and trapped, her crew dead all around her.

Say something aloud, came her voice in his head. There was something there in her electric blue eyes, something he'd never seen before. *They're listening.*

"I… Fine," he forced himself to say, rubbing gingerly at his half-crushed throat as he tried to make sense of any of it. "I'll be more careful next time."

"If there is a next time," she said aloud, turning to stride back to her corner. "I would prefer we arrive there without any more of your incessant speaking."

Something is wrong here, she added in his head, staring out at one of Zedavian's odd displays—a slowly undulating tentacular blob of a sculpture. *I fear our position here is even more compromised than I'd realized.*

Nate watched her turned back, uncertain what to say or how to say it, and more than a little off-balanced by her split personality act.

I believe she was merely employing a convenient charade to jump-start nonverbal communications using her natural empathic abilities.

Convenient? That was one way of putting it.

Still doesn't mean she had to beat me up, does it?

Ex huffed. *Perhaps she wished to demonstrate a lack of emotional sympathy for whoever might be watching. Not that I'm in any way implying she didn't also thoroughly enjoy calling you a hatchling and smacking you around like a… what was it, a Ken doll? What is a… Oh. Oh, yes. I do see the resemblance now. Particularly in the scrotal region. Fascinating.*

Nate scowled at Iveera's back, wondering where to start.

I'm not certain what the First Knight is after, she continued in his head, as if she'd been speaking all along. *Whoever hired those Ooperians was unusually meticulous in covering their tracks. I shudder to imagine what the Black Knight is doing with the Merlin out there. And the Council...*

Ahead, her jin worked the air in an agitated wringing motion, but she didn't turn. If he hadn't known any better, he might've thought she sounded overwhelmed herself.

What became of your meeting with Chancellor Adamus? she asked. *Speak as if I were your Excalibur*, she added, when he was silent too long. *And if you are begrudging my display just now, you should know that I required the physical touch in order to establish an empathic connection with your untrained mind. It was nothing personal.*

Told you so, Ex said.

Yeah, he thought back at both of them, not particularly caring whether either or both heard. *Because a hug was obviously out of the question, right?*

He felt a flicker of amusement from Ex.

It is to our advantage to allow them to believe we are less than fond of one another, was all Iveera said.

What a tough act that would be.

He thought of the out-of-context calmness he'd felt cascading from her hands, not so unlike the soothing act Ex had once pulled on him when he'd been unduly freaked at their first meeting. Was that what Ex meant by empathic abilities?

Clearly, I wasn't referring to her warm and cuddly side.

Well, mark that one down on the list of things to be wary of, then. He focused back on Iveera, who was still watching the sculpture, awaiting his response.

Adamus basically said the Atlanteans will never support a Terran for Knight, he thought, focusing the words her way. *He seems to think we're all Stone Age savages.*

So I suspected.

Well, that might've been useful to know walking in. There was one senator who seemed sympathetic toward our cause, but Ser Golden Halo showed up before we had much chance to talk. Is there any reason you and I couldn't have gone over all this two hours ago, by the way?

Her jin made a kind of shallow genuflection, then continued their thoughtful swirling. *I was thinking.*

And now? He crossed his legs and leaned back against the cell wall, frowning at a piece of perspective-shifting holo art outside. *What's our next step here?*

I do not know.

He suppressed a bitter laugh, maintaining the silent charade. Nothing to see here. Just a bored Terran staring at the wall. *I don't suppose you're ready to bust us out of here yet?* He tried not to furrow his brow, considering the raw strength in her arm against that of the unforgiving cell wall. *I mean, could you bust us out of here?*

Iveera was silent for a stretch, maybe considering.

There are reasons—strong reasons—that I will not defy the First Knight's orders without absolutely damning evidence. An odd ripple passed through her jin. She looked uncertain. Almost like she was trying to convince herself. *You will come to understand one day, should we—*

What, should we survive that long? he suggested. *Should the corruption not consume our souls first?*

Her flattening jin were hardly a comforting reply.

What's really going on here? he asked. *Why are they treating us like we're the enemy? And how come Ser Golden Halo gets to strut around like Emperor of the Galaxy?*

Well, he is Eldari, for starters, Ex said.

Because he is Eldari, Iveera echoed, almost at the same time. *And because he has been saving worlds and currying favors for nearly as long as the Galactic Alliance has existed. Over three thousand years, according to most records.*

Nate blinked, trying to process. *He's that old?*

One of only two living Knights to have fought in the Great War, Iveera said.

Nate looked down at the floor, trying to process a being who could've been polishing off a centuries-long intergalactic war and celebrating his first millennium of life around the same time baby Christ had been popping onto the scene. It was too much to wrap his head around. He glanced back up at Iveera, suddenly wondering how old she was. Fifty? Five-hundred? Two-thousand?

Alliance records indicate Iveera Katanaga was Knighted roughly 637 years ago.

He swallowed, feeling dizzy. Ex had mentioned more than once that Knighthood drastically extended one's "natural" lifespan, but he clearly hadn't grasped the enormity of that statement. He looked around the room at the illustrious art collection, wondering how many thousands of years of alien culture it represented. *You think he would've picked up a touch of humility along the way.*

Hard to come by when you are one of the most powerful beings in the known galaxy, Iveera replied.

Other than who? The Merlin?

She didn't answer.

What the hell happened between him and the Alliance, by the way? Why do they act like the station's gonna catch fire if someone says his name?

They fear him because they do not understand him. Because no one does. The Merlin is the oldest mystery in the galaxy, save for the Lady herself. The oldest sentient one, at least, and he has been gone too long. Most of the beings on this station have never seen him. Many question whether he exists at all. Multiple generations of chancellors have passed through entire careers in his absence. To them, the Merlin has become little more than a dark cloud ever hanging over their heads, and in the dusty interstices between ancient bylaws—an unceasing reminder, however distant, that their authority, their power, was built by one unlike them. One who could return at any moment to collect his dues. Needless to say, they do not appreciate such notions.

A small flutter passed through her jin as she said the last bit, some unspoken thought making itself known.

What is it?

My meeting with Elder Representative Kaiyosh... did not bear encouraging fruit.

He waited for her to expand on the statement. It took a while.

There was a time, she finally said. *A time when the Council wouldn't have dared question the Lady's will in the choosing of a new Knight. A time when the power of assessment was merely a formality—a cautionary provision in response to damages wrought by a few of our less compassionate predecessors at the end of a long and bloody war. That power was never meant to be wielded.*

Nate studied her, waiting for more, but she was a wall of distant eyes and lightly swirling jin. *So what happened?*

The Synth were defeated. Polite society was allowed to rear its head once more. Over the centuries, we Knights became little more than lingering oddities in the eyes of the Council—powerful weapons which might serve the interests of the Alliance, or at least those of deep pockets and clever tongues, if only we could be more reliably controlled. If only the Merlin would step aside and allow civilization to progress out from the shadow of the Synth. For a thousand years, the Alliance has been seeking any excuse to solidify their power over the Knights. And no small wonder. Silas and Dalnak destroyed an entire moon in a petty squabble. Imagine what damage the Knights could do were the Merlin to lose control—or, worse, to turn on his Alliance. Then came Groshna. A Troglodan brute if ever there was one, selected to wield such vast power. The seeds of doubt truly sprouted. The first assessment was called. With a good deal of extortion and bribery on the part of the Troglodan empire, the assessment was passed, and so began the eight-hundred year descent to the state of affairs today. No one thought twice when I ascended to Knight two centuries later. No one cared anymore, save for whether or not they could buy my loyalty. Civilization carried on. The Merlin grew disinterested with anything that couldn't be found at the bottom of his cup. Eventually, he disappeared completely. Centuries passed. The Synth faded in memory—nothing more than a phantom excuse paid lip service by generations of ships and weapons engineers attempting to emulate Excalibur tech in the pursuit of the ultimate destructive power. We have become a farce of an Alliance.

It was only when she stopped speaking that Nate realized he was leaning forward, staring at her, waiting for more. It was already more than he'd ever heard her speak before, and it made his head spin, how much he had to learn, how much history and intergalactic baggage he was stepping straight into.

Kind of gave him an inkling as to why the Merlin drank so damn much.

Do you really think the Synth are coming back? he wondered, thinking of that terrible swarm he'd witnessed during his brief mental trip across the universe with the Lady, prior to taking up his Excalibur.

Iveera's jin were switching back and forth, sampling the air. *I think they never truly left. I think it is a matter of no small wonder how readily our so-called civilization has set aside the memory of what awaits us in the darkness, just beyond the firelight.* Her jin sliced the air. *And I fear this is only the beginning. Rogue Knights and unlawful incursions. Whispers of outer colonies going dark without warning. Something is coming.*

For the first time since their little "mock" scuffle, she turned and looked at him, electric blue eyes piercing, intent.

The Council is going to abolish the Merlin's authority.

"What?" Nate whispered before he could stop himself.

Insolent curs! Ex cried. *Thrice-blackened bureaucrats and pig-swindling cowards, the lot of them!*

Elder Kaiyosh told you this? Nate attempted to ask Iveera over Ex's continued string of insults.

The notion has been many years in the making. It was hardly a secret that it might well happen someday. But the vote is coming. Change is in the air. The fools all feel it, even if they cannot say why.

We must do something, Nathaniel, Ex said. *We must show these impudent cretins where they can shove these petty votes of theirs. Vote the Merlin down from power? Ha! They might as well...*

What about Zedavian? Nate asked Iveera over the ruckus of Ex's ongoing rant. *If he has so much clout here, why doesn't he step in and stop this vote?*

Why indeed? Ex said, pausing from his rant to agree.

Come to think of it, Nate pressed on, *why do I get the impression he doesn't even give a shit that the Merlin's been captured?*

Hear, hear! Ex cried. *Something is afoul here. I said it all along.*

They watched Iveera together, waiting for some answer—some rational explanation as to why their First Knight might be compelled to play it cool while their entire order caught fire, and why Iveera remained loyal despite the fact. But she only turned back to her quiet study of the undulating sculpture.

Iveera, Nate prodded.

I do not have the answers you seek, Nathaniel. We have come to a treacherous place. The terrain is shifting quickly underfoot. If they knew the Merlin was in enemy hands—that he'd been defeated by a mortal opponent, no less, and possibly an ex-Knight at that... Her jin sliced the air as if to kill the thought. *Well, perhaps it is no longer any concern of ours. If the First Knight is correct about our condition...*

Nate frowned at the trailing thought, waiting for her to finish. In his limited experience, Iveera Katanaga was about as far removed from self-doubt as a person could be without venturing into full-blown ego-mania. If she truly was questioning herself based on Zedavian's word...

He wasn't sure what to think of that. Ex didn't seem to know either. The more he tried to bring himself to ask her, the more a quiet fear grew within, snaring him in place until he gave up and rested his head back against the wall, attempting to process in silence, and getting nowhere fast. Nowhere, that was, aside from the growing certainty that, whatever he'd been expecting from this voyage, he'd been expecting wrong.

Approaching the Golnak system, his biggest fear had been that they'd actually find the Black Knight waiting for them there—that they'd have to cross blades with the dark titan again before they were ready. He'd been terrified. He still was. Except now, the thought of a straight-forward fight was actually starting to sound appealing by comparison, even if it was with the Synth's own black-armored demon. Because as it was, they were in a freaking pickle-and-a-half.

The *Camelot* was grounded—the Black Knight making his hassle-free escape to Lady only knew where. Even before the churning mess of scornful politicians and unhelpful First Knights, their best plan had basically been to fly out like a pair of Excalibur-powered dowsing rods, sniffing out the stolen Beacon until they got close enough to pull Iveera's (hopefully repaired) ship out of e-dim and start triangulating. The plan had always been a crapshoot at best. But now...

Now, some part of him almost hoped Zedavian would "accidentally" leave the door open for those Ooperian assassins, wherever they might be lurking tonight—or whatever you called the dark-and-spooky hours of a giant space station's diurnal period. At least things would be quicker that way. Because even if the freaking space vampires didn't get him—even if Ser Golden Halo was wrong about the corruption sneaking through their veins—he'd still be at the mercy of the Council's obviously rigged assessment, Judge Adamus the human-hating human presiding. He'd still be facing the handy little bylaw Ex had plucked from their beloved Accords— the one declaring that, in the event of an initiate's failure to pass a Council-mandated assessment, should the Merlin not be present to offer any defense or counterargument, it fell to the First Knight to assemble his Excalibur Knights and gather a vote.

Retrain the initiate, or reclaim his Excalibur?

Nate had little doubt which way that decision would go if it came to it. No more than he doubted what it would cost to separate an Excalibur from its bearer.

Maybe the Ooperians wouldn't be so bad after all.

And here we had been making so much progress on the sniveling, Ex practically sighed. *Keep it up, and I'm going to start broadcasting a "come kill me" sign on all frequencies.*

Yeah, Nate thought back, smiling a little in spite of himself, *but aren't we insulated in here?*

One may always try.

Nate sank more heavily into the wall, not bothering to argue that the great philosopher Yoda might take qualm with that one. He touched at his aching throat, staring idly at the shattered wooden bench—or the synthetic hydrocarbon one, or whatever the hell the thing was made of. The silence was a physical weight, only compounded by Iveera's detached presence, but he felt oddly calm despite the fact. Not content, exactly, but… calm. Accepting, even. More relaxed and accepting than he could recall having ever felt, even sitting home at Penn State, in the safety of his room.

The thought cast ripples across his calm, marring the smooth surface with pangs of longing and thoughts of what he wouldn't have given to be there now—Christ, to be there with Gwen. With Marty, and Kyle, and Copernicus.

He closed his eyes, picturing the worn beige hallways of the State College house and thinking of the q-node Ex had begrudgingly agreed to leave behind—the one point of quantum contact on Earth, disguised from all eyes so that they could safely maintain communications. There were only two connections as far as anyone needed to know: one with the White House, and one with the UN. But it was the third connection Nate thought of now. The one that only three people on Earth knew about.

He pictured the node. Pictured where it would be, down to every last detail, until he could see it there in the dark space behind his eyelids. Until he could practically feel it. Somewhere on the periphery of his mind, he felt Ex stirring with curiosity, and maybe something else. Something like... pride?

The mental image was on the verge of waning to Nate's curiosity when he heard it: the achingly familiar *click-clack-click-clack-click* of tiny nails trotting across the faux hardwood floor. His vision was moving now of its own accord, a first-person camera feed rushing down the hallway to the faint sounds of panting.

He let out a shaky breath, too surprised and delighted to worry about how this was possible. He was too focused on that blessed old hallway, which had frozen in place at the sound of his exhalation, pitching clockwise a few degrees, supremely curious.

Hi, boy, Nate thought, carefully willing the words into existence. *How's it going back home?*

The reaction was immediate. The "camera" jumped two feet in the air and landed with a wild spin, sounding off with a rapid-fire string of ecstatic barks.

Easy, boy, easy!

But the video feed was spinning tight circles now, *clickity-clacking* Nate straight toward a bout of motion sickness, barking like a fiend all the way.

The most sophisticated piece of communications technology on Earth—the single link to the planet's first native representatives to the Galactic Alliance in over a thousand years. They would've had a collective heart attack if they'd realized where he'd intended to leave it. But damn if Copernicus wasn't excited to hear his voice.

Nate shook with silent laughter imagining the scene on the other end, then felt a pang of guilt as the corgi continued spinning, clearly still looking for the mysterious speaker. With another deliberate thought, Nate willed the one-of-a-kind "tag" riding along on Copernicus' collar to produce a small holographic projection of his likeness.

"Copernicus?" came a voice from nearby—a voice that instantly deepened the longing ache at Nate's core. "Copernicus, what the—What?! Guys! Hey... Hey, guys!"

The video feed ceased it's whirling, and then there was Marty, gaping straight at the camera, still restraining an overly excited Copernicus, judging by the shaking perspective. "Nate?" he gasped. "Guys—Guys, it's Nate!"

Copernicus whined, wriggling harder for freedom. In the background, there was the sound of heavy footsteps fast approaching, then Kyle bowled into view and slammed into the wall on one raised hand, apparently having tripped in his hurry. Gwen appeared behind him a moment later, wide-eyed and flushed, and breathtakingly beautiful as ever.

Gods, was she a sight for sore eyes.

They all were.

It felt like years since he'd seen there faces. Long enough that, between the stress of his ship-board training and all the chaos on Forge Station, he'd forgotten what day it was back there. Forgot right up till the moment his dad stepped unexpectedly into the frame, and Nate registered what they were all wearing. Black suits for Marty, Kyle, and Dad. A modest black dress for Gwen.

His heart fell, the moment of joy evaporating like a volatile gas. Distantly, he felt his leaden body slacking back against the cell wall.

Today had been the day. And he'd forgotten.

"Nate…" Gwen whispered.

For a long few moments, no one else seemed capable of finding words. Why Nate chose to look to his dad for answers, he couldn't have said. The poor man just stared at Nate's holo apparition with a slack jaw and dead-ened eyes, like he couldn't even bring himself to fully register what he was seeing, for fear that it might actually be true. It might've hurt to see his dad look at him like that if he hadn't already been too busy drowning in guilt.

Zack's funeral.

One of his three best friends in the world.

And he'd forgotten.

"I'll get Mrs. Arturi," Marty said, starting to stand.

CHAPTER 12

FAMILIAR FACES

Marty hadn't made it more than two steps to fetch Nate's mom before Nate's dad caught him by the shoulder, stopping him. "She's... She needs time. After..." He shook his head, lost for words. Just lost. "And after everything today, too. She just..." He focused back on Nate, like he'd only just remembered his son was there. "They're... They're treating you well?"

Nate actually jerked a little, he was so taken aback by the question. Treating him well? Where the hell did he think his son was right now, freaking daycare? Prison? The sixth-grade field trip?

I'm an Excalibur Knight, Dad, he wanted to say, *not a prisoner of war.*

Except he wasn't quite so sure about either of those statements right at the moment. But he *had* helped save the planet from the Troglodan invasion, for the love of god. He knew that much. *Just ask the President of the United States, Dad,* he wanted to say. Blindsided as he was, though, his dumb head just defaulted to a dumb nod. It seemed to be all his dad was looking for, anyway.

"Good," he said, numbly bobbing his head as well. "That's good." He looked older than Nate remembered. "We're... We're worried about you. Just, umm... Just be safe and come home, will you? For your mother?"

Another dumb nod. Brain powered down, on standby.

Come home. For your mother.

Sure thing, Dad.

"Good," his father said. "Good."

He backed out of the hallway, past the gaming shrine and out of sight, nodding to himself all the way. In the hallway, Marty, Gwen, and Kyle all stared at each other, trying to parse what had just happened, but no one spoke until they'd been granted permission by the sound of the front door opening and closing.

"Well," Gwen said quietly, "that was…"

"Weird," Kyle provided.

"He's just…" Marty started, before remembering himself and turning back to address Nate directly. "Your parents are just shell-shocked man. By all of this. I should've—Your mom does wanna see you, Nate. I'm just gonna…" He started to turn as if to run outside and try again.

"It's okay," Nate said quickly, trying to convince himself he meant it. "It —It doesn't matter right now. Just tell me about…"

"The funeral?" Kyle asked.

Nate swallowed and forced himself to nod. Marty came and crouched back down in front of Copernicus, moving carefully, like he might accidentally break something. "It was…"

"A funeral," Kyle finished.

"It was… good," Gwen said, frowning at her own words almost before they'd left her lips. "Healthy, I mean. Half the world still seems to be trying to pretend the Troglodans never happened at all. It was good to face it today."

"Time to wake up and do something about it," Marty agreed, his expression grim.

"We just wish you could've been here with us," Gwen added, with a sad smile.

Nate took a breath, thinking to say that he wished the same, and to ask how they were all holding up, and how Zack's parents were doing, and a thousand other things. The questions all hung in his chest, too constricted to find their way out. He let out a long sigh, deciding they were all futile in the moment anyway.

"Can I see Copernicus too?"

A minute later, his friends had liberated Copernicus from his Excalibur-powered collar, set the thing on the coffee table, and gathered up on the couch so that Nate could see them all.

"So you're out of crusher space?" asked Marty, who'd been soaking up every update and bit of lingo Nate had given them. "Does that mean you're about to make the relay jump?"

Kyle shot him a look like, *You're really gonna ask the dude about space right now?*

Marty shot him a look right back that said, *You'd rather us fixate on our dead best friend?*

"Yeah, about that," Nate said, mostly just to break the staring contest. It was only when they all focused back on him that he realized he didn't know what to tell them. "We, uh… Well, there were a few complications."

Marty nodded like he'd been expecting as much. "I thought you guys were running behind with this call. What happened? Everything all right out there?"

"Yeah, we were just uh…"

Just intercepted and led across the galaxy to be attacked, judged, attacked again, judged again, and finally thrown in goddamn Excalibur prison for make-believe maladies and unfathomable political agendas.

"… It's nothing major," he heard his lips saying, well before he gave them the order. "Just shaking the dust off the *Camelot*. She was kinda rusting it out on the moon for centuries before this."

"Yeah, no biggie," Kyle agreed, shaking his head. "Just sitting on the dark side of the—Dude!" He sat up straighter. "Pink Floyd knew all along!"

"Indubitably," Gwen said. She and Marty both looked a bit skeptical about Nate's story.

Can you show them the relay? he thought privately to Ex, figuring a picture —or a small holo, as it were—was probably worth more than a thousand of his tongue-tied words right then. Ex must've complied, because a moment later, the skeptical looks averted to follow the source of Kyle's impressed, "Holy shit! That's the thing?"

Thank you, Nate thought to Ex. *For the diversion* and *for opening this link. I didn't know we could do this in an e-dim cell. Or without our gear.*

Quantum entanglement communications are not so easily shielded against, Ex said. *It is one of the largest draws of the technology, second of course to the unparalleled speed over vast distances. But I didn't initiate this link, Nathaniel. You did.*

If his friends had been watching his holo, they probably would've wondered at the look of surprise that crossed his face. Fortunately, they were all still leaning in to study the Beacon relay he was apparently going to pretend he *hadn't* already jumped through several hours ago.

"That's right, boy," Kyle was murmuring to a softly whining Copernicus, absentmindedly stroking the corgi's head as they both continued to study the relay. "One small step for doggo…"

Copernicus barked in agreement, and despite everything, Nate almost smiled. Then his attention settled back on their funeral attire, and the rest of reality came settling back in.

"I should've come with you," Marty blurted, bringing it home, decidedly not smiling. His tone took Nate by surprise. They weren't the whimsical words of his nerdy best friend naively lamenting a lost chance to see something that sounded cool on paper. It sounded more like the disillusioned declaration of someone who'd woken up to a world he was no longer happy with. Someone who was ready to do something about it. It was unsettling.

"Maybe next time, buddy," Nate said, not really sure he meant it—or that there'd even *be* a next time—and thanking all the celestial beings above and below that he hadn't dragged his friends into this shitstorm with him. "For now, just…"

"Stay in school?" Kyle asked.

They all shared a terse laugh. All but Marty.

"Anyway," Nate said, grasping for more, wanting to tell them the truth if for no other reason than to actually feel like he had his friends there—and maybe even to bask in some goddamn sympathy for a moment. But what would it accomplish? "I guess I just wanted to see you guys. Just in case. I'm…" His throat constricted. "I'm sorry I wasn't there today."

It was impressive how unified their response was—shaking heads and critical looks. Bit lips and a clear air of *don't you dare beat yourself up about this*. But still, no one found the words to fill the big, fat silence spanning the twenty-some-thousand light-years between them. Kyle gave up and dropped his gaze to the Copernicus. Marty stared off through the wall, lost in some dark thought. Not sure what else to say, Nate focused on Gwen, numbly documenting the exact shades of her blond hair and sky blue eyes. The soft curves of her cheeks. The way he knew they'd dimple when she smiled. Burning it all into his brain. Just in case. She held his gaze right back, possibly having similar thoughts, neither one of them willing to break the silence.

"I always thought having a superhero best friend would be cooler," Kyle said, staring at the floor now. He roused and focused back on Nate. "Not, uh —Not to bash, man. You're a rock star. And that Iveera chick, I mean, hot damn. It's just, uh…" He looked to the others for help.

"Sitting on the bench blows goats," Marty provided, not breaking from his thousand-yard stare.

"ALL of the goats," Kyle agreed. "I'm up to my neck in…" He frowned at whatever was about to leave his mouth. "You know what, never mind. Point is, we miss you, buddy. And, uh… Well, I'm not sure exactly how one says,

'Be careful hunting down the Dark Lord Sauron Clone who dropped a whole Atlantis on your head,' but, uh… yeah."

"I'll be sure to wear my helmet," was all Nate could think to say. If he ever escaped e-dim prison, that was. He opened his mouth to add something about them keeping his seat warm until he got back, then decided it probably wouldn't make them feel much better, what with all the talk of riding the bench.

Gwen looked between Kyle and Marty, her hand drifting toward the collar on the coffee table. "You guys mind if we have a word?"

Kyle tilted his head in a *be my guest* kind of way.

Marty was still zoned out until Gwen reached a little further.

"Nate," he said, snapping out of his ruminations to catch her arm. He was silent for a stretch, clearly trying to settle on the right words. "You can do this," he finally said.

The words settled in Nate's chest with an odd tumult of emotions. For a second, Marty looked like he might say more, but then he conceded the floor with a tilt of his head and sat back, releasing Gwen's arm. Nate held his friend's gaze as Gwen scooped up the collar from the coffee table, unsure what to say, hoping that Marty could see that he'd heard him and that it meant something.

"I'll talk to you guys soon," he said. It felt woefully inadequate, all things considered, but they didn't seem to mind. Marty gave him a solemn wave as Gwen started off down the hall.

"Hey, you'd better bring me back a Holy Grail if you find one out there!" Kyle called after her.

Nate smiled, then sobered as he watched Gwen silently carrying the camera down the hallway and into his abandoned bedroom. Even halfway across the galaxy, the sight of her in that room made his heart beat a little faster.

"Just the two of us, then," he said, mostly because he didn't know what else to do. "Fancy that."

She studied him, concern etched across her brow. "Are you okay, Nate?"

He opened his mouth to say he was fine, then caught the reflexive answer and did her the justice of at least thinking about it first. "I'm surviving," he finally said. It felt honest enough.

She nodded, and the care in her eyes threatened to crumble him from inside out. He dropped her gaze to keep his heart from giving out and looked around his not-so-old room for anything to latch onto. His gaze settled on the bed. "Guess it kinda figures," he muttered, before his brain could veto the action.

Her eyes tracked to the bed and back to him, the beginnings of a knowing grin pulling at her lips. "What's that?"

"Nothing," he said quickly. "Just, you know." Christ, he hoped the q-node holo didn't portray burning cheeks faithfully. "You spend all these years wishing you could get someone alone in your room, and you kinda figure it's a given you'd actually *be* there. Like, physically."

She arched an eyebrow, that grin threatening to spill over. "Years, huh?"

Nate huffed out a nervous laugh, rubbing the back of his neck. "Did I say years? I meant, uh… you know. The other thing."

"Oh, yes," she said, nodding in emphatic mock-agreement. "The other thing. Totally." The wry smile returned to her lips. "Well, I guess I'll just have to wait for you right here, then."

In the not-so-distant past life, those words would've left him in a bubbling puddle on the floor. Now, though, they only brought reality crashing down that much harder.

"It, uh… It might be a while, Gwen. Months, maybe."

Or maybe the rest of his life, however long or short that might turn out to be.

She shrugged the comment off with a kind of forced casualness. "I'm not in any rush over here. I just…" She teetered on her next words, then let out a soft huff, shaking her head.

"What is it?"

"Nothing. It's just—I want us to be able to help you, to really *be there* for you, you know? But I just… have this feeling we're never going to be able to really understand what you're going through, out there. I mean, *really* understand it. You tell us you're about to hop halfway across the galaxy, and…" She bit her lip, trying to regain control, tears welling in her reddening eyes. "I just miss you, Nate. I just… miss you. I'm sorry."

Nate swallowed against the sudden ache in his throat, wanting to tell her that he was the last person she ever had to apologize to for anything. That this, right here, was more help than words could explain. That he *loved* her, dammit, and that he was going to get out of this mess, finish the job, and get back to her, no matter what. But the words all stuck in his throat, clinging there with every shallow breath.

"Gwen, I—"

A discordant roar tore through his head like a sounding alarm, sending the room spinning, vision blurring.

"Shit!" he gasped, eyes snapping open reflexively, dumping his brain back into their illustriously-decorated-art-gallery of a prison cell even as his mind clung to the image of Gwen in his room, head throbbing with an instant migraine for the split effort.

"Shit?" asked the ethereal Ghost of Gwen from beside the shattered bench, looking worried as she dabbed quickly at her eyes with a loose black dress sleeve.

Well, that was new, Ex said, as if he were observing a moderately interesting bit of weather. Nate was too busy trying to bring Gwen back into focus, trying to get back to that room.

"Nate?" Her voice was distant and jumbled now, like she was calling down a long, echoing hallway. "Nate, what's—"

Another wave of sensation smacked his brain, an all-consuming blare riding in on a wave of pure blue and burning turkey breast. He was having a goddamn stroke. Gwen was barely a wisp on the air now, hovering in front of him. Fading.

"No," he whispered. "Gwen, I—"

A brain-numbing roar. His mother's face and a roaring jungle waterfall, swirling into… nothing. He was back in the cell, sinuses itching with the smell of sulfur, and Gwen was gone. Just gone.

I… might not do that, Ex said, just as Nate was preparing to close his eyes and search for the q-node connection more carefully, *unless you'd like to be disrupted again.*

Nate looked suspiciously around the cell as if he might spot a rogue Stroke Fairy hiding in the corner with a poised shock collar remote. *I thought you said quantum communications couldn't be blocked.*

I said they are not so easily shielded against, which is true.

Well then, what the hell was that?

Extremely precise electromagnetic pulses, as far as I could tell, remotely employed to induce neuronal flux as a crude means of disrupting your so-called 'transmitter,' if you will. Transcranial magnetic stimulation, in other words, he added a few seconds later, when Nate was still frowning into space.

Oh, blackened hands! Someone just used magnets to give your brain a hiccup. Is that better?

Yeah, I get it! Nate snapped. He frowned. *Kind of. I'm just… trying to process.*

Iveera was watching him with a sideways stare, like he'd gone and done something *especially* bothersome or stupid this time.

Perhaps she is merely displeased that you just chose to end our collective q-

comm privileges on a call to your friends rather than with the only reliable allies we have on this station.

Nate stared past Iveera, registering and processing the words on sinking tiers of shameful realization. The *Camelot*. It was bound to Ex just like the q-nodes were. And Nate might've just blown their chance to take advantage of the fact.

Hey, Ex? he thought, numbly raising his hands in a show of surrender to Iveera and to whoever else might be watching.

Yes, Nathaniel?

Maybe next time we're trapped in a cage with a line to the outside world, you remind me about it BEFORE we spend three hours stewing in e-dim prison and ruining everything.

Certainly. I'll add that to the Growing List of Things That Are Most Assuredly Not My Job. Item number 7,473.

Fucking splendid, Nate fired back. *And you know what? I have another one for you, while we're at it.*

Oh, pray tell, Ex said, dripping mock enthusiasm.

Nate ignored the attitude, too busy thinking about home, and the fact that he'd just missed his best friend's funeral. And not just missed, either, but *forgotten*. Completely. He was drifting out here. Drifting frighteningly fast in a world that wasn't his own. A world packed with more landmines and political traps than he could even begin to shake a stick at. And if he didn't find the Merlin and end this damned thing, once and for all...

It didn't matter, he decided, because that was exactly what he was going to do. No matter what. He met Iveera's phosphorescent eyes, willing her to see that, then turned back inward, to his waiting companion.

I need you to help me figure out how the hell we're gonna get out of here.

CHAPTER 13

LULLABY

On the dark streets of the District slums, Malfar strode silently through the living dregs of the so-called polite society above, trying to pay them no mind. It was a futile effort. There was simply no shutting out the decades of duty-honed instincts and pattern recognition, no masking the drunken HUD overlay of his inner justicar voice pointing out that *that* beggar was truly desolate while *that* one was swindling. That those four Hobdans at the streetside hovel of a bar had worked a hard day's shift scrubbing filters, and that the curly-horned Satyrian currently loitering beside their table was an unknown to them, almost certainly fishing to hook them on whatever diluted drug he was currently peddling. That hypnotic spice from Nidavellir that'd been making the rounds lately, Malfar's unwavering inner voice decided, even as his conscious mind pointed out that he had no way of knowing any of this, and his eyes involuntarily scanned the two Troglodans posted at the far side of the bar—both with untouched drinks and poorly-concealed weapons, both watching without watching. It made his hide itch.

He faltered without meaning to, the third voice—that of Justice— decreeing that *here* was a problem with a clear solution. A just solution. Never mind the immediate problems of jurisdiction and protocol. Here was—

Something crashed into his flank, small and apparently angry, judging by the string of muttered curses. Another Hobdan, he saw. Two, actually. A mismatched pair. Another station worker fresh off of his shift, and a suggestively-dressed companion who was likely only beginning hers.

"Watch it, asshole," grunted the station worker. He took in Malfar's blight spots, beginning to sneer with another brimming insult, but his date clutched at his arm, murmuring something in his ear, her alarmed eyes never leaving Malfar.

Whether Malfar actually heard her whisper the word "justicar," or whether that was merely his wary imagination at work, he wasn't positive. Whatever she said, the drunk station worker turned and shuffled off with his companion—his *prostitute*—faster than he'd come, leaving Malfar standing in a deepening pit of his own pathetic self-doubt.

This was despicable. A justicar didn't belong here. *He* didn't belong here. He belonged on his ship, or in the boot-box squeeze of his central-alloted station quarters, processing case files. Not here. And certainly not poring over the illegal data that cursed Gorgon Knight had handed as part of the full Career Suicide Self-Starter Kit.

But pore he had, and now he couldn't unsee what he'd found. The facts had not helped. The grog hadn't either. After everything he'd seen that day —after the whispered rumors he'd heard of the testimony the First Knight had allegedly delivered in a closed-Council session shortly after his remote "debriefing" with Malfar...

Malfar gathered his wits and prepared to move on. What he needed now was clarity. Peace of mind, if only for a moment. He was turning to continue on his way when the Satyrian's hired Troglodan muscle at the bar finally abandoned their *watching without watching* act to fix him with the preemptive nonverbal equivalent of a *do we have a problem here, tough guy?*

He held one of the young bulls' stares, feeling nothing, save for the soft hope that maybe one of them would be foolish enough to press the matter and come harass him. A small opening—that was all he needed to *make* this his jurisdiction, to step into a perfectly legal, mostly-by-the-books opportunity to channel the cleansing spirit of Justice through his ready fists.

The more level-headed side of him pointed out that he hardly needed to bend the rules, here. He could pass it on to station security right now. Except he knew as well as these thugs did that the peacekeepers wouldn't be in any rush to come catch a petty spice pusher in the District slums. No more than a busy broodmother would've been to correct the crying of the last calf in her brood. It was merely the way of things—business as usual.

More of the bar's patrons were turning to look now, tension and curiosity spreading across the small space like an airborne contagion. He turned and left, feeling all the heavier for his brief brush with the indomitable shadow of injustice that always had and always would hold this station in its treacherous palm, right along with the rest of civilization.

There was no escaping it, no defeating it. There was only resisting. Only the daily struggle to hear the unadulterated voice of Justice over the din. But even that much felt nearly unobtainable as he stomped down the grimy pedestrian ways that were becoming too familiar to his feet. Too shameful. Down to the sub-levels where even the thugs rarely had cause to go. Down to the familiar old corner of nowhere, where a neon blue holo sign declared, through the hazy red darkness, "Arden's."

There'd been no reason to add any subtext to the declaration, though if there had been, it likely would've read something along the lines of "Arden's One-Stop Menagerie for the Broken and the Outcast." Those who required Arden's services tended to find them on their own, and usually at the end of a long and arduous road of shame and self-destruction. They didn't need their subtext advertised to the outside world.

Inside, no one made eye contact. No one save for the Atlantean attendant at the front, who acknowledged him with a polite smile and a straight-to-business, "I'll inform her she has a visitor."

Malfar dipped his head in acknowledgment and went to add his brooding silence to the waiting area—the one place in the galaxy his inner voice ever seemed reticent to undress the conditions and moral failings of those around him, perhaps out of pure sympathy. It wasn't long before the attendant caught his eye and waved him on toward the back rooms.

His heart lurched as he stood to march down the dim red hallway. Lurched as it always did, just as he'd always imagined a criminal's might, right before a job. There was nothing intrinsically *wrong* about what he came here to do, he told himself, just as he always did. But that thought was of no true comfort. *If* the indomitable shadow of injustice truly had any potential rivals amongst the ocean of civilization, he decided, surely those rivals were the spirits of tradition and social stigma, for there was no escaping *them*, either.

Luckily, he didn't have to pause at the door, warring with internal resistance. She always left it open—knowing, perhaps, that a closed door might well be enough to turn a paying customer away.

"Come, my sweet sapling," came the soft voice from inside.

It was cozily dim inside, but not so dim that he couldn't see how frail

Heilga looked as she extended a hand in invitation. She'd lost weight since the last time. *Withered* was the word.

"Well, if you won't," she added, huffing a little too heavily as she rose to slide over to the bed, "then I'm going to get comfortable all the same. I am tired, my son."

He didn't mean to bristle at the word—didn't even realize he had until she paused, raising her hands in apology. "Some of the others prefer it, you know."

"I am not like the others."

"No," she said, settling onto the bed with a sigh before weighing him more carefully with her eyes. "No, you're not. Now, will you please come inside?"

He glanced back down the hallway, accidentally making eye contact with the hunch-backed Atlantean—a rare vat clone defect—shuffling into the room a few doors down. Shame pulsed between them like a wave of igniting gas. The Atlantean dropped his gaze and hurried into his own room, head hung low. Malfar felt a rare twinge of regret.

"We are all loved here, child," Heilga said softly, beckoning for him to enter the room. "You know that."

He stepped into the room, closing the door behind him. "I do not come here for love, crone."

She didn't rise to match his moodiness. Only beckoned again, bidding he join her on the bed. With an irritated grunt, he began working his way out of his tunic. Once he was free, with the tunic neatly folded across the back of the chair in the corner, he went to Heilga's bed, approaching cautiously. He laid beside her, reluctantly allowing her to guide his head to her lap.

Then she began to sing, and for a while, nothing else mattered.

A shudder passed through him, as it always did. She smiled, as she always did. He didn't have to look, could hear it in her voice as she sang on, crooning a wordless melody as she began to stroke his blighted hide.

It was indescribable.

Sometimes, at times like these, some quiet corner of Malfar's mind even toyed with the wild notion that, in a way, he was lucky to have been born a spotted runt. For who else could truly appreciate a broodmother's song and touch so much as one who'd spent a lifetime deprived of both, watching his people cringe from his blight?

It didn't matter that the blight had been rendered genetically incommunicable centuries before his birth. The stigma remained. But Heilga didn't care about that. Didn't care that any respectable Troglodan would spit on her name for daring to bless a spotted runt with broodsong and loving touch. It was degrading—an unholy impropriety. Back on Trogarra, the All-Clan of the Destroyer might have even had her on heresy charges for the act.

It only made her touch all the more intimate, her song all the sweeter, in these rare moments of weakness that found him here at Arden's.

He closed his eyes, sinking into the scent and sound of her, into the humming melody that rang through his every cell, resonating back through his lineage. For thousands of years, every capable young calfling had heard these songs, or ones very like them, encouraging them to grow strong. To not be afraid. To become the warriors who would one day make their ancestors proud.

And then there were the Clanless Ones.

After he'd been ousted to the mines for his affliction, once he'd grown old enough to actually begin earning wages for his backbreaking work there, Malfar had spent his first pay on an illegal recording of some random broodmother's song. The seller—no doubt a swindler, in hindsight—had offered him a custom capture job for a small additional fee. Genuine brood-song, straight from the mouth of the birth mother who would've sung it to him herself, had he not been born with his unfortunate affliction. Malfar had declined.

He couldn't have said why at the time. All he knew was that his sire and birth mother had left him at those mines on purpose. In the name of tradition. For the fear of stigma. On purpose, they'd left him to the mercy of a cold world, without so much as a *sink or swim as you may, my bright little bastard*. Left him in spite of the clear duty they'd owed to the life they'd wrought upon the world—the same duty which any biological progenitors ostensibly bore for their progeny in a just universe. Left him merely because their polite society had told them to.

It'd been the first stroke of injustice that'd sparked his journey as an investigator, tracking down those dear birth parents. It'd been the surprise and perverse awe at what he'd found that'd lit the fire in his soul and seen him off-planet to bigger things and nobler callings here at Forge Station. Against all odds, he'd escaped.

And now the chief justice was casting him aside just as his bastard sire and matron had once done. Just as the First Knight seemed intent to do with the hard truth of what had happened on Terra—to the Beacon, to the Merlin, and to Ser Groshna, Clan Groshna, Destroyer take his twisted soul.

Then there was Varga, that bloody tyrant. And as for Justice... Sweet Justice...

Do not concern yourself anymore with these affairs, rang Zedavian Kelkarin's voice in his head. *Do not give me reason to track you down in person.*

But he'd seen. Couldn't unsee.

Drop this case, added the chief, *or say goodbye to the badge. I really don't give a shit.*

He'd seen. And yet... He could still leave it behind. Wait out his suspension. He could still have the rest of his life as a justicar. Was it truly his place —truly an act of moral integrity—to assume that the duty he felt at the core of his being was somehow superior to that he owed the Central Justice? Was it not instead an act of ego, to operate as if his Inner Justice was one and the same as the True Justice of the Universe?

Of course it was.

And he could still leave it behind.

The thought sent another lurch through his heart.

He could still leave it behind.

All he had to do was leave his own Inner Justice behind with it, alone to roam the mines of its own cold, uncaring world. And once he'd done that...

Heilga's melody waned momentarily, her soft groan of discomfort the first indicator that his fists had gone too tight where they clutched at her, holding on for a balance that wouldn't come. His stomach was still turning from the grog, and he was more than a little surprised to find that he was weeping. He hadn't noticed the sensation. Barely even recognized it, long as it had been. But there were the quiet tears of moisture trailing down, absorbing right back into his dry, blighted hide, unbeknown to anyone in the galaxy but him, and possibly Heilga.

"Forgive me," he whispered into the lap of Heilga's rumpled robe.

She laid her hand on his head, still singing.

The next words hissed out before he could stop them.

"Forgive me, Father."

They tasted of bitter ash on his tongue. Incomprehensible. A part of him wished he could take them back. The rest focused on Heilga, who didn't ask questions or pass judgment, just stroked his drying cheeks, her broodsong morphing, taking on a lilting, mournful quality. He closed his eyes and laid there, trying not to think on any of it, knowing deep down that the decision was somehow already made—had *been* made even before he'd thought to come here in his desperation.

When he stood at the end of Heilga's song, wobbling on the unmetabolized remnants of the grog and the soft swells of the deep, existential rage that'd been his only true birthright, he knew what had to be done.

"I am proud of you," Heilga said.

He looked down at the withered broodmother, wondering not for the first time at the pseudo-mystical connection of the broodsong. He'd told himself all his life it was nothing but psychological—the simple boon of a mother's love, enjoyed by those privileged enough to be born normal. And yet he'd never walked out of this room *without* the feeling that Heilga had somehow glimpsed a piece of his soul.

And now she looked so frail.

He adjusted the payment slider on his omni holo up to triple their standard rate and sent the credits her way with a flick of his finger. "You won't be seeing me," he said, when she saw the sum and started to argue. It came out sounding more fatalistic than he'd intended. "Not for some time."

He resisted the urge to say more.

Leaving Arden's, his mind was already whirling with priorities, precautions, and half-formed plans. Knowing what had to be done was only half the battle. The *how* was another question entirely.

His feet carried him on, mind turning, senses faded to the background. So far that he wasn't sure at first why his feet chose to pause before he'd made it back up to the main level. Not until his speeding brain slowed down enough to register the Troglodan he found himself staring at. The same Troglodan from the bar.

His partner and their Satyrian boss man were speaking in hushed tones around the corner, discussing payment, maybe, or—

"What the fuck are you looking at, runt?" asked the bull on lookout.

Behind, his friend twisted around to see what the fuss was and scowled when he saw Malfar. "Get fisted, blight stain."

The Satyrian didn't bother with words, just made an impatient shooing motion, as if he were granting Malfar permission to move on unmolested (this time).

Not his problem, he reminded himself. Not his jurisdiction. Not even pressing, when weighed against the rest of his current problems.

He found himself raising his omni holo anyway, making a point to keep it plainly visible as his justicar badge ID flashed alongside the waiting comm channel. Maybe because it wasn't up to him to decide. Maybe because he simply wanted to see the looks on their faces. And see it, he did.

One moment of pure, priceless shock, rippling across all three of his unexpecting perps like a perfect wave. Then the tension broke, and everyone exploded into motion.

Malfar's stunner was out and coughing a high-voltage electrobolt into the Satyrian's fleeing back before his amateur bodyguards managed to free their poorly-concealed weapons. The first bull went down with a bolt to the chest, overcoat still snagged shut. The second bull was midway through drawing his ancient slugthrower when Malfar lunged forward and smashed the stunner into his face. He kept driving from there, slamming the bull into the wall and following up with a hard knee to the ribs before reaching for a restraint cuff.

Once the bull was secured, he bent over his groggy friend and sealed his wrist to the wall as well, tossing both of their weapons out of reach. The smaller Satyrian was still twitching, mouth sputtering incoherent consonants as Malfar hauled him over and cuffed him to the wall right beside his hired muscle.

That done, he considered his omni, hesitant to call the arrest in through official channels. He looked down at the three criminals, searching as he often did in these moments for some measure of wisdom, some critical understanding that might allow him to fix the problem rather than merely delay the inevitable until these three found their way back to the streets.

"You do your people no honor," was all he could think to say, looking from one Troglodan to the other, knowing full well that the words were woefully inadequate.

"Fuck you, runt," growled the first bull. "You and your traitor sire. Destroyer take him and your whore of a..."

Malfar waited a full breath, letting the tension flow from his fist as the bull went on, spitting the same insults he'd heard all his life. He didn't have to give in. Didn't have to let the rage control him. For a moment, he took heart in that knowledge.

Then he cocked back and punched the bastard silent, just because he wanted to.

Groggy curses followed him down the way as he marched to the nearest public node and keyed in a request for emergency response under the most apt of the available category tags: "Altercation In Progress."

He left them there, knowing damn well he probably hadn't made one lick of difference in the grand scheme—that one didn't simply *punch* the crime out of a criminal. That the problem was one of systemic desperation and immoral opportunity, and that new pushers would be on the same streets within hours, taking advantage of the opening he'd just created.

And Justice?

In that moment, he honestly wasn't sure where Justice landed on the matter. All he knew was that he needed to find Iveera Katanaga. He was going to have to move fast, adapt on the fly. And Justice, if it truly wished to see its will done through the limited means of this particular loyal vessel… Justice was just going to have to adapt with him.

CHAPTER 14
IDLE HANDS

Aboard the *Camelot,* the air was about as warm and relaxed as your average pre-battle flight deck, tinged with baseline adrenaline and apprehensive fidgeting, all set to the arrhythmic tapping of Snuffy's restless leg-bouncing.

Not that Jaeger had really expected otherwise. None of them were going to be sleeping easy aboard the *Camelot* tonight.

"Anyone else feel like we're officially in over our heads right now?" Snuffy finally asked, pausing from his leg bouncing long enough to glance around the crew quarters where they'd assembled.

"Shut up, Snuffy," came Carter's quietly detached response, her brow furrowed in concentration as she peeled back Elmo's bandage just enough to check the big man's arm, which had stubbornly refused to stop bleeding after whatever those Ooperian bastards had grazed him with. "And stop fidgeting over there."

"But also yes," Kalders chimed, drawing Carter's darker-than-usual scowl over to the couch where the young pilot lay staring up at the ceiling, boots propped up on the opposite arm, crossed at the heels and lightly tapping at the air.

Even she was getting antsy. Not a good sign.

Jaeger closed his eyes, searching for grounded thoughts that wouldn't come, quietly hoping his people might somehow rib each other out of this collective funk, but hardly counting on it. It was a tall order, after everything they'd been through. Even taller now that he'd finished explaining how their prized asset had been kidnapped by the so-called First Knight and how they were more or less on house arrest themselves moving forward. Forward to *where*, god only knew, but for now…

He gathered himself and opened his eyes, coming back to the moment—to the sight of a comatose Ramirez resting in his borrowed medpod beside the bunks, and a brooding Pierce watching him from a few bunks down, hard jaw set in an *I-told-you-so* scowl.

"So, what do we do?" Snuffy asked, finally voicing the question they'd all been silently chewing on for well over an hour now. "Are we…" He looked around the cabin, weighing their expressions. "Are we gonna get Nate out of there, or what?"

On the couch, Kalders' boots froze mid air-tap, their owner suddenly attentive. Carter and Elmo traded a look.

"We'd have to get ourselves out of *here* first, genius," Pierce said from his brooding corner. "Did you miss the guard detail out there?"

"Oh, no," Snuffy said, shaking his head in perfect earnestness. "I was kinda just assuming we might decide to go ahead and grow a pair, seeing as we're not actually a boatful of frightened, untrained space daisies, is all."

Despite everything, Jaeger had to fight back a grin at that. Even Carter smiled a little. Much as they all delighted in using Snuffy as Team Punching Bag on a daily basis, it only made it all the better on those rare occasions the unlucky mechanic decided to bite back.

Pierce hardly looked amused with this particular Snuffy Bomb—looked mildly murderous, in fact, as he scowled and laid back on his bunk, dismissing them all from his existence—but Jaeger didn't mind that bit so much, either. The ex-flyboy's tangible mood had been chafing at his patience all evening.

"Seriously, Colonel," Snuffy said, growing abashed once more. "It doesn't feel right. None of this does. I mean, right?" he added, looking around at the others for input.

Elmo conceded the point with a slight tilt of the head. Judging from the still tension of Kalders' boots, she felt similarly but didn't want to say anything. Carter just considered Snuffy, then turned to Jaeger with one of those Mama Bear looks that never failed to make him feel a little funny on the insides—some strange and paradoxical combination of loyally supported, fairly questioned, and mildly aroused.

"Your concerns are duly noted, Snuffy," he finally said, frowning over at Pierce's protruding feet for a thoughtful moment before turning back to the rest of the crew. "And I hear you. But for now, we sit tight. We gather what intel we can and assess the situation before we go putting our foot in it any worse than we already have. Kalders."

"Sir?" asked the couch.

"I need you on the bridge talking to Cammy, keeping an eye on whatever station news she can scrounge up for us."

A hoisting hand appeared on the back of the couch, followed a moment later by Kalders' dirty blonde updo and a skeptical look that silently asked if he *hadn't* been paying attention when she told him she'd already left instructions for the ship's intelligence to contact her with any important developments. He gave her an equally potent, *just do it* stare.

"Sir, yes sir," she said, rolling to her feet and setting off for the door with only a minimal amount of huff. Good girl.

Jaeger had never been one for flexing rank and busting chops without rhyme or reason. Especially not when things were already plenty tense on their own. But if they didn't tighten this ship up, remind themselves who they were, things were only going to start slipping downhill from here. What they needed right now was a bit of order. Something to focus on. A mission—even if it wasn't *the* mission.

Which almost made it seem something of a blessed curse when an urgent chirp-whistle of alarm sounded from the cabin wall, demanding their collective attention. Kalders hadn't even made it out of the room yet. They all turned as a holo pane blinked into existence on the wall, sporting an image of—

"Fuck," Jaeger muttered before he could stop himself.

In his defense, though, the gold-armored Eldari dominating the camera feed had brought them nothing but trouble with his every step. In fact, Ser Zedavian Kelkarin was entirely the reason they were in this mess to begin with. And judging by the busy hubbub evident in the holo's background, the bastard was now standing right outside their ship.

"The fuck's he want?" Pierce muttered from his bunk.

It was a fair question. Maybe even a good one, albeit in need of a touch more healthy respect for the situation. Jaeger glanced from the display to the doorway where Kalders had paused, weighing his options, less than comforted by the way Elmo and Pierce were already fingering their rifles.

"Jets down, people," he said, in his best casual commander's voice. "Let's see what he wants. Cammy, can you patch me through out there? Audio only?"

"AFFIRMATIVE, LT COL JOHN JAEGER," read the bright green text that scrawled across the display. "PATCHING AUDIO IN 3… 2… 1…"

The hectic sounds of the docking bay filled the room in impressive surround sound, nearly convincing Jaeger's brain for a second that he was actually out there. What was more disconcerting, though, was the way Kelkarin's gaze drifted calmly dead center of the holo display, like he'd not only sensed the connection but could also see them perfectly well through the freaking walls, video feed or no.

It was just his imagination, Jaeger told himself. Then the First Knight spoke.

"Greetings once more, Lt Col Jaeger."

Jaeger stifled a dry swallow, doing his best to ignore the creepy-crawlies worming their way under his skin. "Can we help you, Ser Knight? Something tells me this isn't a social visit."

Ser Kelkarin tilted his head in a rather human way. "On the contrary, I have indeed come to make a personal request. May I come aboard?"

"A personal request," Jaeger echoed, not trusting a thing about this situation, and even less certain what the First Knight could possibly want from them.

"Nothing more," Kelkarin confirmed. "Though I am additionally willing to discuss your kinsman's current standing, if you so wish." He showed them an unexpectedly charming smile. "I see no reason we cannot interact with civility here, regardless of the internal affairs of my Order."

Jaeger watched that smile, thinking how it kind of reminded him of a Ted Bundy documentary he'd watched a while back. Charm, charm, and charm—with just a tiny, tiny flicker of something totally fucked deep down in those golden-yellow eyes.

"Give us a moment, please," he said, gesturing at the holo on the cabin wall in the hopes that Cammy would understand. The bay sounds cut off, and a green "MUTED," appeared across the display.

"I don't like it," Pierce said.

"I mean, none of us *likes* it," Snuffy said, before remembering himself and glancing around at his neighbors. "Right?"

Carter didn't dignify that with a response. Elmo just scowled down at his rifle as if categorically blaming the weapon for the clear lack of options it currently offered them against a Knight.

"'Bout as trusty as single-ply," Kalders agreed. "But at least we might get some of that juicy intel you were wanting."

Carter glanced from Kalders to Jaeger. "Keeping in mind, as we consider opening the hatch, that there might also be invisible space vampires waiting somewhere out there."

"And that he might've sent them, for all we know," Kalders added, hooking a thumb at Kelkarin on the holo.

"Whose side are you even on here?" Pierce asked from his corner.

Kalders shrugged. "I wasn't the only one who noticed the sketchy timing between our departing from Ser Midas out there and arriving straight to Assassination Station, was I?"

"You weren't," Jaeger said. "But, keeping in mind that Iveera also apparently tore the Trog Knight's ship in half a couple of weeks ago, I'm guessing we don't really have a choice here anyway."

"Fucking great," Pierce muttered.

"Man," Snuffy said, shaking his head. "Guess it's really two in one hand, three in the other, huh?"

Confused looks turned his way.

"It's six one way, half-dozen the other," Kalders said.

"What is?"

"The… the saying, Snuffy. It's 'six one way, half-dozen the other.' Which also doesn't even make sense here, for the record."

Snuffy furrowed his brow, clearly skeptical. "Those are both the same number, Tess. Why would… Oooh." A look of raw comprehension dawned across his face. "Oh, I'll be damned."

Tessa shrugged. "Two in one hand, you know?"

"Yeah," Snuffy mumbled, then frowned like something had just occurred to him. "But wait, how many birds are in the bush, then?"

Jaeger cleared his throat.

"Right"—Snuffy bowed his head, clasping his hands behind his back like a scolded school kid—"not the issue here. Sorry, sir."

"Jesus," Pierce muttered, shaking his head like he genuinely believed his own moody bullshit to be above the juvenile display. The rest of them just turned their attention back to the actual issue.

On the holo pane, Kelkarin stood at perfect ease, not quite looking at the holo anymore. Not quite looking at *anything*, as far as Jaeger could tell. The First Knight just stood there, looking as if he'd be content to wait for ten seconds or ten centuries if need be, and no hard feelings either way.

Somehow, the patience was even creepier than the smile.

Jaeger looked at his people and met Carter's gaze. He felt the silent understanding pass between them, then out of his lungs on a heavy sigh. She'd know what to do if anything happened. He stood from his perfectly comfy chair, wondering exactly when it was that he'd started feeling so goddamn old. "Hold the hatch until I get there, Cammy."

Kalders scooted aside to let him pass with nothing but a questioning look.

"Wait!" Snuffy called after him. "What do you want us to do?"

"Stay here," Jaeger called over his shoulder. "Listen to Carter." He paused long enough to look back at his team through the doorway. "And for the love of Christ, don't speak unless you have to."

MUCH AS THE analogy irritated the shit out of Jaeger, it was hard not to entertain the thought of the words, *golden god*, when facing off with Zedavian Kelkarin in person. It wasn't *just* that the Eldari was taller than most Trogs, or built with the kind of elven grace and unspeakable confidence that left little doubt in Jaeger's mind he could've torn the entire hangar bay —hell, maybe the entire station—to shreds without breaking a sweat. It was something more than that. Some ineffable depth to his yellow-gold eyes that made Jaeger feel utterly bare, like the scary bastard could see straight into his soul, and beyond.

Jaeger forced himself to step aside and politely wave Kelkarin into the ship anyway. No reason not to, he supposed. It wasn't as if he could've stopped the big scary bastard if he'd wanted to.

Kelkarin strode aboard without a word, his movements eerily silent. So silent that, for a moment, Jaeger felt a sudden and bizarre urge to reach out and touch the Knight, just to be sure he was even there at all. Instead, he stood there like a good little sane boy, waiting in silence himself until the hatch door had sealed behind them, snuffing out the never-ending background chatter of the hangar bay.

Silence hung. Jaeger resisted the urge to fill it, forcing himself to hold the Eldari's gaze.

"I have come to request your music," Kelkarin finally said.

Even Jaeger's hard-earned poker face couldn't keep up with that one.

"Music?" he asked, feeling his eyebrows attempt a handshake.

"Music," Kelkarin confirmed, looking casually around the entryway. "Visual artwork would also be most welcome, whatever paintings or cinemographs you might have aboard, but music... Music is preferred. Whatever styles or methods your people have produced in recent centuries. The more, the better."

Music, Jaeger just managed to refrain from droning out loud again. Ted Bundy the godly Knight Overlord had come all this way, graced them with his divine golden presence, just to ask for some freaking tunes?

Beep, beep, beep, went Jaeger's personal bullshit detector, if for no other reason than that he was sure someone of Kelkarin's apparent political station could've easily sent an underling—or just messaged the *Camelot* directly—with such a request. There had to be some reason the First Knight was here in person.

"And this is…?"

"A personal request," Kelkarin confirmed, reading Jaeger's concern like an open book. "Nothing more. No intricate politics at play."

Jaeger consciously refrained from tensing as the Eldari reached out to offer him a small data disc as it appeared from thin air between his golden fingers.

"I have merely become something of a collector over the years, you see," Kelkarin explained, his expression reassuring. Almost too human. "Your contribution would be much appreciated. And well-rewarded, of course."

Jaeger looked at the data disc, not taking it, not sure what to think about any of this. Maybe the guy was serious. But either way… "Don't suppose I could posit a trade here, then, if our contribution would be as appreciated as you say?"

Kelkarin studied him with those soul-piercing eyes, plainly unsurprised by his less-than-tactful segue. A thought seemed to occur to him. "Am I correct in assuming your young Knight friend failed to inform you of his unfortunate condition?"

He surely *was* correct—every bit as surely as he already knew as much and was clearly fishing for a bite. Jaeger decided to deflect the deflection instead. "I thought my young *Knight* friend was only an Initiate, officially."

Out came that smile, a few degrees more predatory this time. "Oh, but you are a clever one, aren't you, Colonel? A pity the Eighth Excalibur didn't end up in your hands."

Jaeger met that creepy smile, trying not to squirm. "Oh, I don't know. I think the kid might surprise you if you give him a chance."

The First Knight let out an amused huff. "Surprise me? Hmm." He flicked the data disc at Jaeger without warning, flicked it like a bullet. Jaeger caught it by reflex, jerking back a half-step, and Kelkarin's knowing smile only grew. "What a treat that would be."

Jaeger frowned down at the disc, knowing damn well that he'd just lost whatever dick measuring contest they'd had going on. Not that it mattered.

"My aid Sashia will come to collect the disc when you send word," Kelkarin said, turning for the hatch controls. "And since you posit a trade, in addition to the exorbitant amount of credits I will gladly offer, I will also allow you a brief visit with your bright young Initiate once our transaction is complete."

"Thought we weren't supposed to leave the ship," Jaeger pointed out, tilting his head toward the security detail at the end of the platform as the hatch hissed open.

The First Knight paused at the top of the boarding ramp. "Your caution is wise, Colonel, but these agents are here for your own protection. I assure you, I am not the one you need fear here on… what was it?" He smiled that predatory smile. "Assassination Station?"

Jaeger felt his face draining of blood despite his best efforts. Had they not been muted in there? Jesus, had Kelkarin *heard* them talking from outside the ship?

"What witty tongues your people keep," Kelkarin said, turning to depart with a casual wave. "The *Camelot* will know how to send a message my way," he called over his shoulder. "I wouldn't recommend you try to leave otherwise."

Jaeger watched the First Knight stride down the platform like he'd gotten exactly what he'd wanted, wondering…

"No problem," he muttered under his breath, quiet as quiet. "Something tells me we wouldn't get very far anyway."

He watched with an uneasy feeling as the First Knight glanced back from twenty meters away, not breaking stride, and favored him with a smile that said he'd heard the words perfectly well over the din of the bay's night-time crowd. *Very good, Colonel*, that smile seemed to say. *Now you're learning.*

It was sometime in the "early morning" hours of the Capital's light/dark cycle when Cammy quietly pinged for Jaeger's attention on the console ahead. He looked up from the music files on his old phone and the handy data disc interface Cammy had cooked up, blinking through his sleepless headache. Over in her reclined pilot's chair, Kalders shifted in her sleep, muttering something about Snuffy. The rest of the crew were asleep back in their quarters, last he'd checked.

"Whadya got, Cammy?" he quietly asked the console, feeling strange as usual about talking to the erratic ship, and more than a little apprehensive about what might've prompted the alert. His stomach only sank when the ship responded by pulling up a small holo above his workstation.

For a tired moment, Jaeger was sure it would populate to show him the First Knight standing there, come to abandon whatever cutesy game he'd been playing, and to let the other foot fall in earnest. What he saw instead though, when the image sprang to life, was a splotchy-skinned Troglodan. The *same* splotchy Troglodan who'd been waiting for them back in the Golnak system, he registered after a second. The justicar. He was almost sure of it.

"The hell?" he whispered, sitting up straighter in his chair, glancing around the dim bridge as if he might discover some reasonable explanation hiding in the shadows. This night was just getting better and better.

The Troglodan looked… well, Jaeger wasn't really sure what he looked like, given how little he knew about Trogs, but the words *rough* and *shit* still sprang to mind. The furtive glances the Trog kept shooting down the docking platform only added to the sense that something was wrong. The guy—or bull, or whatever—wasn't even wearing his justicar uniform. Whether or not that meant he was off duty or simply in street-clothes-detective mode, Jaeger had no idea.

He scooped up his rifle and stood, looking unhelpfully around the bridge once more, thinking. Probably no reason to wake the crew, now that they'd actually gotten to sleep. But no reason to be stupid, either.

"Come on," he said quietly, shaking Kalders awake by the shoulder.

She blinked blearily a few times, squinted from his face to the gun in his hands, then went from zero to wide-eyed in a split second.

"Oh god, it's just like Alien!" she hissed.

"What?" Jaeger started to ask. But she was already springing out of her pilot's rig. She snatched her rifle from beside the consoles and whirled.

"So help me, if I have to Sigourney Weaver my way out of this bitch, I'll…" She trailed off, looking from the bridge down to her gun, then over to Jaeger like she'd only just realized where she was. "Space vampires?" she asked, as if questioning whether she'd been dreaming that bit or not.

"Just an unexpected justicar at our door," he said, hooking a thumb toward the main hatch. "C'mon, Sigourney."

"Like that's an insult," she muttered behind his back, falling in. "What's the justicar want?"

"Thought we might ask him that."

He chose to politely ignore what snippets he caught of the following stream of mutters—something about mood pills and waking a girl up in the middle of the night. By the time they made it to the main hatch, it looked like their Troglodan justicar was a few mood pills deep himself.

"What seems to be the problem, officer?" Jaeger asked through Cammy's offered holo comm channel, too tired and irritable to particularly care that *justicar* was probably the more proper title. The Troglodan hardly seemed concerned with the minutia anyway.

"We must speak," the creature rumbled in a quick, low voice, tilting his thick shoulders to glance back toward the base of the docking platform yet again. "Better for us both if we do it in private."

Jaeger traded a glance with Kalders. Somehow, he'd had a feeling the trog would say something like that. "If it's all the same to you, I think I've had enough private chats today. Not to mention attempts on my life. How about you tell me through the armored door instead?"

"I need to speak with your Knights, Captain."

"Well, they're not..." he started, right before it occurred to him in a flash.

The data dump Iveera had sent the justicar just before the First Knight had whisked them away from Golnak. Had the trog found something? Realized they weren't the bad guys here? Maybe. But then again, maybe it was more that he *had* found something—and was now looking to come silence the pesky Terran crew before they could rat out what his kin had truly done to Earth.

"... not taking visits right this moment," Jaeger finished, trying to sound casual. "And I'm not actually a captain. So, unless you'd like to leave a message..."

"I am well aware they are not aboard, Cap—whoever you are," the justicar growled, glancing back down the docking platform before letting out a deep breath and stepping closer to the ship. Conspiratorially close. "I need to speak with your Knights," the trog repeated with slow deliberation, as if spelling it out. "And I believe we must help one another if either of us ever intends to do so again."

CHAPTER 15
WILES

They faced off outside the low, windswept ruins of some ancient village, Zedavian Kelkarin and the Black Knight. Swords drawn. The sky brooding and wild above, flashing with… not lighting but something else. Searing streaks of green and blue lancing through the haze. Blinding flashes of orange and white flooding the heavens.

A battle, high above.

The entire world shook, yanking Nate's attention back to where the two Knights had crossed blades. The air hummed around them, howling winds all but screaming with the twin powers of the flaring golden sun and the all-consuming black hole before him, like some twisted yin and yang preparing to tear the planet asunder in their quest for equilibrium.

Only the blows didn't come.

As one, the two titans turned, armored heads swiveling like mirror opposites to look first at Nate, then to the dark bundle which lay on the ashy ground before them. It was only then that Nate realized the bundle was moving—that it was in fact a struggling man in a tattered robe, his face hidden by a tangled mess of filthy gray hair.

It was the Merlin.

Nate tried to move, tried to stand from the dirt where he'd fallen to his knees. His body barely listened. Ahead, the Merlin was saying something to the Knights, something that was impossible to make out over the howling winds. A look passed between the two titans, unreadable behind their gold and black helms.

"Nathaniel," whispered a familiar voice in the wind—or the wind itself, it seemed, as Nate jerked around looking for the absent speaker. The Merlin was looking straight at him when he turned back, watching him with an expression Nate couldn't even begin to fathom.

He had to get up. Had to do something.

The deep boom of the Black Knight's voice drew the Merlin's attention back to the scene ahead. Nate still couldn't make out any words, but something was happening, the wind redoubling its buffeting fury, the air between the Knights beginning to crackle and glow with an eerie blue energy.

"—*will* open it, wizard,"

A wicked black thorn erupted from the ground between them, thickening from the razor-sharp point as it rose up from the crust like some long-buried obsidian shrine. The Merlin said something inaudible. There were other voices too, now. Distant voices, whispering.

"OPEN IT!" roared the Black Knight, shaking the sky with the ferocity of his bellow as he thrust his hand out toward the Merlin. The wizard sprang into the air, weightless as a feather on the Black Knight's gravitonics, and went speeding toward the dark titan. Straight for the thorn.

Nate reached dumbly, helpless to do anything but watch in slow-motion terror.

He knew he didn't actually hear the impact. That would've been impossible over the howling wind. But he might as well have heard it, for the unmistakable wet-thunk jerk the Merlin gave as the thorn impaled him. Nate could only watch, mouth frozen in a silent scream, as the wizard's body settled like a fresh-dead slab dropped unceremoniously on the meat hooks.

A weight materialized in his tired hand, heavier than it should've been. His sword, he realized.

"The choice is yours," the air itself breathed in his ears. Ahead, the Black Knight turned back to his and Zedavian's crackling portal. The First Knight was on his knees now, sword still raised to the Black Knight's, head bowed as if in reverent worship.

Nate gasped a pained breath in, looking for direction, looking for Iveera. It was only then he noticed the broken copper figure collapsed in the ashes nearby.

Nathaniel.

He reached for her just as the air smacked him with a deafening roar of power, casting her copper armor brilliant azure, casting over *everything* until the entire world bleached from view, and—

~

NATHANIEL!

Nate snapped to, in a room that was only vaguely familiar. *A museum,* his rattled brain offered, right before he took in the shattered bench and the transparent cell walls all around them and remembered properly. They were still in Zedavian's palace. His most recent exhibits, in fact. He blinked around the room, unsure how long he'd been out, whether it was even "day" or "night."

Someone approaches, Iveera's resonant voice broke in.

Two someones, Ex added. *An Atlantean female, accompanied by that Gorgon servant. And it is hour 37 of our imprisonment, for the record, approaching the second dark period since our ceremonious arrival.*

I was dreaming, Nate thought blearily in their general direction.

So I noticed, Ex said. *Now, if you'd like to focus on the matter at hand...*

But I saw the Merlin, he thought, focusing the thought at Iveera this time, *and the Black Knight. And it wasn't... It wasn't just a dream. It was more like...* He furrowed his brow, head pounding with a deep ache as he tried to draw the chaotic details back into focus. *Zedavian was there, too. He...*

Nate teetered on the words, face scrunching as he examined the solidifying image of Zedavian kneeling before the Black Knight, sword held high. Had he truly seen what he thought he'd seen? Iveera was watching him across the cell, having broken her ignoring act for the first time to scrutinize him with those bright eyes, jin swirling with a slow, uneasy air.

Later, she finally sent.

He had a moment of indignant impatience, and one more to realize just how damned hungry and thirsty he was. Then the hiss of the opening door tore his mind back to that matter at hand.

"Later," Nate whispered under his breath, supremely uncomforted by the thought. He pulled himself to his feet, ineffectually attempting to wipe the sleep from his eyes and gather his wits for whatever fresh hell came next. What came striding through the door, though, was about the furthest thing from hell he could've imagined.

It wasn't *just* that she was preternaturally gorgeous—though she undeniably was. It was more the uncanny sensation that he'd suddenly found himself looking at Gwen Pearson's Atlantean vat clone.

At the very least, she could've been Gwen's long-lost supermodel sister. Or the Mother of Dragons, maybe, considering how regal she looked with her crisp white full-shouldered tunic and her elaborate platinum blonde braids. Her arms were bare, her chest overlaid with an elegant weave of blossoming silver threads. Nate watched her approach in a surreal funk, distantly wondering if he was still dreaming, or if maybe someone were using those handy magnetic pulses to plant this image in his head. In his mind, he pictured himself lying on the floor, foaming at the mouth, enthralled in some dissociative delusion.

Gwen's pseudo-doppelgänger just kept striding toward the cell, confident and poised, eyes fixed on him all the way, paying no mind whatsoever to Iveera, or to Zedavian's Gorgon servant, who stood in the open doorway behind her, surveying them all with an uncertain air.

"Hello, Nathaniel," the stranger said, crossing the last few feet right up to him and laying her open palm to the clear cell wall, as if in lieu of a handshake. Her smile was warm and entirely too perfect. "My name is Amelia Sundercaste. I'm here to begin your assessment."

"I'm…" Nate heard himself mumble, looking from her hand to her too-familiar face. "… Sorry, wh-who?"

A string of orange bullet-point text appeared beside her face, Ex helpfully detailing the abbreviated professional history of one Amelia Sundercaste. The letters jiggled emphatically, demanding to be read, but Nate was too flustered to take in much more than the words *psychosocial*, *Terran*, and *special consultant*.

Had they purposely sent this woman to rattle him? To get inside his head? How would they've even known?

His visitor looked slightly bemused by his molasses-brained reaction.

Did *she* not know, then?

"My name is Amelia Sundercaste," she repeated. "I'm… to be your primary assessor in the Council's ratification process."

"… For your claim to Knighthood in the Order Excalibur," she added when he failed to make any response.

Ex's information overlay, jiggling like a freaking sea of jumping beans now, finally went up in a tiny poof of ash, carried away on Ex's exasperated sigh.

For Lady's Light, will you stop staring like a mindless buffoon?

To his surprise, the voice was Iveera's, not Ex's.

"R-Right," Nate finally managed. "Yeah."

Amelia gave a tentative nod, looking like she wasn't positive he was actually following. "I'm told I may also be in line to become something of a personal liaison between you and the Council if our relationship should prove agreeable. Provided your Knighthood is actually ratified, of course, in light of current circumstances."

That finally snapped him out of it. Because this was most certainly not a friendly face, no matter how much it might look like the one he knew and loved. This was a stranger, an agent whom someone—probably Adamus—had hand-picked, he wasn't sure how or why, to come and dismantle his claim to the Excalibur from the inside out.

He needed to get it together.

"Right," he said, steadier this time. "So, where do we begin then, Amelia?"

He watched her closely, telling himself that this was almost certainly a serpent he was speaking to, not an ally. But she didn't look like a serpent as she stared back with a curious, cautiously friendly smile. She looked genuine. Too genuine.

"Honestly? I'd be lying if I said there was a correct answer there, Nate. Do you mind if I call you Nate, by the way? I'm told it's your preferred moniker."

Told by whom? he couldn't help but wonder. He just shrugged.

"Okay," she said, nodding like they were making progress. "Well, Nate, normally, I prefer to begin new counseling relationships with a preliminary coupling to get better acquainted, but given our current constraints..." She trailed off like the rest went without saying, which only deepened his curiosity.

"Coupling?"

She gave him an odd smile. "Pardon me. Sexual intercourse."

Nate's lungs did the bone-dry equivalent of a spit-take. "And that's... standard practice?"

For a moment, she actually looked taken aback by the question. "There are few substitutes for so quickly accessing the more... elusive aspects of an individual's inner truth. Provided one knows how to read the thrust of things if you will."

Atlanteans DO love their coupling, Ex offered.

Seems like one of those things you might've thought to mention before, Nate shot back, his throat caught on a dry swallow.

Amelia was watching him, missing nothing. "How does that make you feel, Nate?"

"Umm..."

Your cultures harbor radically different views on reproduction, came Iveera's voice. *A Sundercaste would know that. She is merely attempting to disrupt your balance.*

"... I guess I was expecting more gladiator fight pits out of this assessment thing, is all," he finished.

"You have much to learn of the Atlantean people, then."

"Yeah, I'm starting to get that."

What is this, he added silently to Iveera, glancing around the room purely for a momentary escape from Amelia's scrutiny, *some kind of psych eval?*

This, Iveera replied, *is a thinly-veiled ploy to subvert your defenses and establish an agreeable agent close to you—*

His eyes flicked back to Amelia, tracing her down and up before he could stop the little retinal rebels. Agreeable. That was one way of putting it.

—in the unlikely even that Chancellor Adamus fails to see you slated for reclamation by the end of this assessment, Iveera finished, rather pointedly.

Provided he wasn't promptly put to death, he translated, as Amelia continued to stare him down like she was perfectly happy to wait for him to squirm.

Real freaking agreeable.

"You're trying to make me uncomfortable."

"*Are* you uncomfortable, Nate?"

"Is this all part of your test?"

She watched him with those attentive eyes. "Nothing that transpires between us is exempt from my assessment. Does that answer suffice?"

He held her gaze until he had to look away again. It probably didn't earn him any Knightly Bonus Points. "Fine," he said, begrudgingly putting on his most cooperative face. "So how's this assessment work, then? Do you have a specific set of questions? He who'd cross the Bridge of Death must answer me these questions three, ere the other side he see? That sort of thing?"

She didn't look even a shade amused by that. Which probably made sense, seeing as she'd almost certainly never heard of *Monty Python and the Holy Grail.*

"You don't trust me," she said.

"Should I?"

She studied him, idly tracing her fingers along the transparent cell wall as she allowed the silence to permeate the uncrossable space between them.

"You miss your friends," she finally said, speaking softly. "I can't imagine how overwhelming this all must be for you."

His breath stuck unexpectedly, an unruly harem of emotions threatening sudden and violent revolt from deep within his chest. It was the most human thing anyone had said to him since they'd left Earth. Which, he told himself, almost certainly meant it was also a trap—a calculated sucker punch, inviting him to expose his soft underbelly and all the un-Knightly inadequacies therein. But none of that made him any more sure about how to respond, or what any of this had to do with his candidacy as a Knight when they had a dark-armored psychopath running around out there with a Beacon and a captive Merlin.

"Look," he started, trying to keep his voice calm, "how do we get this thing moving? Was that supposed to be a question?"

"Merely an observation," she said, searching his face, "though I do find it interesting that you've asked three separate times now when and where we should begin. Do you feel that we haven't?"

His mouth worked silently, brain shooting down the first few knee-jerk responses that tried to escape.

"Let me ask you this, then," she continued. "Where would *you* begin, if you were meant to establish whether a twenty-three-year-old Terran with unknown ties and moral proclivities is indeed fit to wield a power that could quite literally grow to world-shattering proportions in the centuries to come?"

Nate glanced helplessly at Iveera, feeling the weight of another big fat *I don't know* resting in his chest. He'd never thought of it that way.

"I understand your frustration, Nate," Amelia said. "It certainly doesn't help that this assessment comes with little precedent, save for Ser Groshna's several centuries ago."

"Which obviously turned out so well," Nate muttered, feeling childishly flippant even before he'd finished saying it.

"Groshna, Clan Groshna was clinically stable at the time of his Knighting," she said calmly. "For a Troglodan, at least. I've read the reports. It's the thinking of most experts that the problem in fact lies with the prolonged lifespan of the average Exalibur Knight, and the novel challenges that lifespan poses to modeling long-term psychological development. The data on the subject is, as you can imagine, rather limited. Which makes my job rather difficult."

Nate searched her face, surprised to find himself almost wanting to believe her. She didn't *sound* like some puppet who'd been sent along to blindly check a few boxes and tell the Council whatever they wanted to hear. But that was probably exactly what she wanted him to think.

"Almost sounds like someone was just looking for an excuse to keep us busy here then, doesn't it?" he asked.

To his surprise, she didn't argue.

"Perhaps you're right. It's no secret that some in the Alliance would rather your entire order simply be retired for good. The Synth have been gone for two-thousand years, after all, with neither sight nor sound, and no reason beyond legend and religious hearsay to believe they'll ever return. It's not such a stretch to understand how one might arrive at the impression that the Excalibur Knights are little more than—"

"Artifacts?" Nate said quietly.

Amelia nodded. "Albeit extremely dangerous ones, and highly valued, of course, by those hands which long to see their will securely enforced throughout the Alliance."

"Hands like the Council's."

Her gaze flitted to Iveera, back to him, then down to the floor almost… guiltily? "More hands than you might imagine."

Bureaucrats, Ex muttered like a soft curse.

Nate just watched Amelia, parsing her reaction with an uneasy feeling. "Who voted for this assessment?"

"Over eighty percent of the Alliance Council," she said quickly, automatically. "But I believe Chancellor Adamus was the one to bring the motion to the floor if that's what you're asking, seconded by Chancellor Targa of the Greater Troglodan Empire."

Nate processed that, not overly surprised by any piece of it. It all kind of just seemed to figure, at this point. "And Adamus sent you? You work for him?"

"I am a public servant of the Atlantean Empire," she said, drawing a shade more upright, almost defensively, "reporting to the Alliance Council for this assignment."

He watched her, kind of wanting to apologize for any perceived slight, but also curious at her reaction. After a few seconds, she continued on.

"Chancellor Adamus did not select me for this appointment, to answer your question. In fact, I suppose there's no reason I shouldn't tell you that you're not completely without friends, here. It was Senator Calum Statecaste who nominated me for this position."

Nate failed to hide his surprise but at least managed to clamp down on the immediate, *why-didn't-you-say-so-please-god-get-us-outta-here* that tried to slip out of his mouth. If she hadn't led with the fact of her affiliation with the friendly senator from Triton, there was probably a reason. Maybe Calum had made this arrangement quietly, hoping to avoid any accusations of favoritism. Or maybe Amelia was just testing Nate's reaction now, all part of the assessment.

"His argument was well-played," she continued. "A Sundercaste was the only reasonable choice to assess a Terran. We specialize in the study and analysis of your people, you see, both ancient and modern," she added, at his uncomprehending look. "It's a small caste, but also one of vital importance in ensuring the Atlantean people remain…"

"Chaste of our dumb Earth monkey ways?" Nate suggested.

"I'll have you know that I have great respect for our Terran heritage," she said, her brow frowning even as her quirked lips attempted to hide an amused smile, "brutish as it's been at times in the past. Regardless, you should likely be thanking Calum. It was bold of a junior senator to speak up to the Council assembly as he did today, and if he hadn't, your assessment most likely would've consisted of little but neural scanners and inflexible judgments."

"You're… friends with the senator, then?" Nate asked.

"We have a healthy working relationship," she said, seeming to sense that he was testing the waters in some way.

"Well, please pass along my thanks to the good senator, then," he said, leaving it for now.

"Perhaps you might pass them along yourself. Senator Calum has expressed his desire to meet you on more hospitable terms once your… confinement is past. I believe he intended to visit you today, in fact, before your current circumstances came to light."

"They let *you* in here," he pointed out. "Why not him?"

"I have Council-mandated jurisdiction to assess you. The senator does not."

"Right."

She gave him a probing look, as if expecting something more. "I don't suppose you'd be willing to explain why it is the two of you *are* being held here?"

"You don't know?" he asked before he could stop himself.

She just gave him a wry *why do you think I'm asking* look. Whether it was simple surprise at her not knowing or just the fact that that look reminded him too much of Gwen, the answer was already halfway to his lips before his brain caught up and reminded him that maybe there was good reason

Zedavian would've kept the details of their imprisonment private and that, friendly veneer or no, she was ostensibly still assessing every word out of his mouth. Maybe even deliberately testing how easily she might coax valuable Order secrets out of him.

He glanced at Iveera and found her electric blue eyes watching him in a way that made him think Amelia wasn't the only one testing his mental aptitude.

"I think that's kind of an internal affair, actually," he said, turning back to Amelia.

"So said the First Knight." She studied him for a few seconds longer, then nodded to herself, seemingly satisfied. "Very well. I think this has been a good start."

He tensed, caught off guard, not ready for her to wander off to her own assumptions. He needed to convince her. Needed to—

"We'll continue tomorrow," she said, reading his expression. "For now, I imagine you must be tired after all the recent excitement, and I need time to compile my findings."

"Findings?"

She just gave him a lovely, perfectly noncommittal smile. "Get some rest, Nate."

"But—Hey!" he cried, as she turned to leave. "How long is this gonna take?"

She slowed marginally, head tilting like she might turn, but it was only when Iveera spoke her name that she froze—almost *flinched*—to a halt, shoulders tightening like she'd nearly forgotten the Gorgon was there. With a clear effort of will, she straightened her shoulders and partially turning to face Iveera, seeming to consciously remind herself that she was ostensibly the one in control here.

"Yes, Ser Knight?"

"What news from yesterday's assembly?" Iveera asked. "What report from the First Knight regarding the events of the Terran incursion?"

Amelia hesitated. "I'm not sure it's my place to say, Ser Knight. The conditions of your confinement were rather unclear. I do not wish to undermine the—"

"What news?" Iveera repeated, in a voice like an executioner's ax waiting to fall. Whether Iveera was actually physically capable of busting through the cell wall and shaking the answers free, Nate was far from certain, but that tone certainly made it sound like a promise.

Amelia turned fully back to face them, critical eyes shifting from Iveera to Nate, and back again, weighing whatever she saw there, genuinely uncertain. "You would truly pretend ignorance in what has happened, then?"

"That depends entirely on what you believe has happened," Iveera said, her jin strained and half-flattened like she already suspected she knew.

"The…" Amelia swallowed, glancing toward the door as if to double-check they were alone. She steeled herself as she turned back to them. "The Merlin."

"What about the Merlin?" Nate asked, with his own sinking feeling.

Amelia hesitated, clearly torn. Finally, though, she decided the risk was worth the reward. "A missing Beacon? A maddened Knight?" She looked between them, testing their reactions against whatever she was about to say. Finally, she splayed her hands as if offering the only plausible explanation.

"The Merlin has betrayed us, has he not?"

CHAPTER 16
CINDER AND ASH

Starvation.

Blinking at the darkness with unseeing eyes, the Merlin considered the word that was slowly bleaching the rest of existence from his mind. It was a fiery rift opening at the very center of him, inch by terrible inch. Ever more gaping. Ever more empty. His mind's eye swimming with feverish phantasms of chasm walls parting wider, wider, spilling forth a river of agony with no end in sight, and with no beginning either, save for the hatred which stemmed from Mordred's blackened soul.

For that was the one thing he was now certain about in all of this. He had no idea how many days he'd been here. He hadn't eaten or drank so much as a pittering-pattering drop. He knew that much. He wasn't sure he'd even slept by any proper meaning of the word, though there had been brief glimpses—troubling glimpses—of Nathaniel Arturi, and crossed swords, and a hellish, crumbling landscape he recognized all too well. Fever dreams, he told himself. Twisted artifacts from his efforts with his furry little friend. Only he wasn't sure anymore that the jabra rat had been real either. The memories were growing too hazy. But he *had* spotted the mountainous jet black figure watching him from the darkness more than once. That much, he was sure of. He'd seen the dark titan pacing about. Recognized his stride. Was pretty sure the Black Knight had even spoken to him once or twice, though it was growing increasingly hard to recall. Still, the fact remained.

This *thing* was indeed Mordred le Faye. Or at least the vengeful spirit of the boy. Man. Thing.

As for where that landed the Merlin...

He let out a rattling wheeze of a breath and tried for a moment to focus only on rolling over to give his aching sores a rest. The simple act proved beyond his means, despite the fact that he was no longer chained in place. Mordred, being quite the virtuoso of sadistic torture, had restored him some small degree of freedom right around the same time his e-dim stores had hit rock bottom, slipping him gently into the exquisitely unpleasant realm of starvation. Where before he'd had only scant centimeters of shackled wiggle room, now he was free to roll about the filthy floor like a spit-bound hog in the dark. Provided he could only find the energy to do so.

There was none to be found, of course. None but the faintest trickle of the Lady's Light, almost entirely muted in this clever prison of Mordred's, but still apparently sufficient to hold his empty body together at the seams. The Merlin wouldn't die of this starvation. Couldn't. Not while *She* was bound to him, and he to Her. And that was the point, entirely. The only reason he was here. The only reason for any of it.

"Are you prepared to end it?"

The voice came from the pitch darkness, hard and heavy as leaden steel, and so abrupt as to coax a surprised twitch from deep in the Merlin's core. It didn't make it to the surface. His body was too broken, his mind too frayed from this latest dip into madness. A thousand lifetimes ago, that voice might've frightened him as he lay there, chained, helpless, and bitterly undying. But now, all the Merlin could think about was when in nine hells the blackened bastard had managed to slip into the room. How long had he *been* there this time, watching, waiting, playing out Lady only knew what visionary manners of un-death to next wreak upon his captive wizard?

Had he ever even left?

It hardly mattered. All that mattered in the universe right then was that Mordred wouldn't find what he was looking for. Not as long as the Merlin refused to let him. And if the blackened bastard truly thought the Merlin's will would be broken by something so simple as a few days' torture at the hands of starvation...

It was an insult. Plain and simple. But then again, Mordred never *had* thought very highly of him, back in the day. Not after Avalon. Nor had he ever tried particularly hard to hide it. At least he'd been an honest savage. Which only made his next words all the more disconcerting.

"Another outpost fell today, wizard. The 12th Demeter colony. Gone.

Assimilated." That towering silhouette surfaced like an inky smudge on the darkness and knelt down beside the Merlin, the eyes of his fearsome helmet glowing like twin embers, waiting for him to confess his sins. "How much longer will you stand stubbornly by? How many thousands more must die when you have but to tell me the location?"

There were many things the Merlin might have told him. That they both knew damn well who was to blame for this latest atrocity. That it was simply too steep a price, risking the multiple *trillions* of lives this galaxy was home to just to save a few thousand. That, even if the Merlin had *wanted* to give up and turn coat on the entire galaxy, asking someone in his current state to form words was an optimistic proposition at best. Most of all, though, the Merlin wanted to tell the blackened bastard that he was hardly the first fool to have come seeking the Grail, so to speak, that he wouldn't be the last, and that at this point, the Merlin would've gladly suffered a thousand lifetimes of this agony for no more reason than to spite him.

A hard impact to the gut robbed him of what little air he had before he could try to say any of it.

He went tumbling across the dank dungeon, chains jingling in happy harmony to the ragged gasps each impact drove from his papery lungs, the pain oddly disembodied, like his nerves were simply too tired to be troubled. He'd barely come to a halt when the darkness lurched downward, strong hands hefting him effortlessly from the deck.

"Why do you do nothing?" Mordred's voice was perfectly calm, completely at odds with the violence of his crushing grip. "Why does she not make you?" Trembling rage building in those hands. "Why do you even *exist*?"

Ugly gasps of laughter seized at the Merlin's lungs, deathly dark amusement wracking him, setting his body to swing in the Black Knight's unbreakable grip.

"Told you..." he rasped, "y'were dealing with... forces... couldn't..." He took a few labored breaths, reminding himself who he was. What he was. Not some mortal prisoner in peril. He was the Merlin, dammit. "No shame in it, lad," he whispered. "You're in over your head. Always were. You have no idea what you're—"

The darkness lurched again—*sideways*, he had the fleeting impression, right before the wall broke his flight with thought-shattering force. Bones broke. Most of them, by the feel of it. The pain, late to arrive before, was suddenly all-consuming and laced with a familiar prickly, sickly itch— abused bones already beginning to knit themselves back together, some part of him knew, weaving pure strands of Lady's Light into a fragile lattice of soft tissues and hard minerals, ready for the breaking all over again.

In time, when the inferno of his blazing nerves dimmed, he'd notice that the bottomless hunger had in fact worsened, the chasm at his center having widened all the more, exacting the perceived balance of his debt to the natural order of things. For the moment, though, the pain of bones broken and un-breaking was all the Merlin knew. Pain and the sight of those twin embers watching him in the darkness. And beneath those eyes…

The Merlin strained to focus on the dim, lumpy mass dangling from the Black Knight's fingers. Dangling by the *tail*, he realized.

A dead jabra rat.

His dead jabra rat.

"How low you've fallen, wizard," the Black Knight said, "to speak of shame when you, the mighty Merlin, have trusted your hopes on a blackened rat. Did you honestly think I wouldn't notice your cheap trick?" When the Merlin didn't answer, he flicked the dead rat casually aside, shaking his head. "You needn't say a word. I already know where to go. I will find her, wizard. And you will watch your precious kingdom burned to cinder and ash. I swear it on my life, I will find her."

If the coppery taste and the tearing pain were any indications, the Merlin might've smiled a bloody smile at that. Judging by the blunt shock that ripped through him the next moment, the Black Knight repaid the affectation with another kick. The Merlin let the sensation take him, basking in the kaleidoscoping pain and darkness, trying not to shake with the manic amusement coursing through him, trying to maintain the charade just a little longer. It was nearly too much.

Mordred was chasing a dead end.

The blackened bastard still had no idea what he was dealing with—no clue what he was even looking for. Avalon. The Merlin shook with more silent laughter. To think his old protégé would be so easily deceived, even after the bastard had spent a full century on Kalyria making a butchered attempt to learn the art of the Gorgon empaths…

Hells, to think he'd just used naught but a jabra rat to convince the terrible Black Knight to go chasing after a largely worthless hunk of drifting rock when in truth he already had almost everything he needed to find what he was looking for—already had a Beacon, and an Excalibur, and the one wizard who could tap them both for this particular feat. All he needed was one or two more Excalibur wielders to help him stabilize the entire process, and… the Merlin sobered, thinking how easily the Black Knight might've ended things back on Terra, had he only known the full truth. Then another thought struck him, and he lay perfectly still.

The corruption.

He still didn't understand it in full. Still didn't know from where it had spawned. But all of a sudden, he couldn't help but see the overwhelming likelihood of what the Black Knight intended to use it for.

Had that blackened bastard been playing him the entire time?

He lay there for a long time, replaying the conversation over and over in the darkness, wondering if it was true what Mordred had said about the Demeter colony. Wondering at the infinitesimally subtle vibrations he'd felt through the impenetrable dungeon walls, and at the equally subtle glint he'd fancied he'd caught of Nate and Iveera chasing after him, and the faint note of wrongness he'd sniffed on their wake. For all he knew, their Excaliburs could be coursing with corruption by now.

But Iveera was strong, he told himself, thinking of the fierce loyalty, level-headed calm, and devastating power that had quickly made her his running favorite ever since their Lady had picked the Gorgon six-hundred odd years ago. She would find his trail. She would bring the boy. Smithy's blackened hands, she would bring the entire damned Alliance Space Force if she had to—though whether in support or pursuit would probably depend on how well she danced her political gymnastics against Kelkarin and the Council.

He felt his lips pulling painfully tight, felt the warmth of dehydrated, sludgy blood blossoming across his lips once more. *Deranged*, most would've called that smile, had they been there to see it. Desperate.

But Iveera was strong. They would come.

I will find her, wizard, Mordred's words echoed in his head. *I will find her.*

Find her, would he? His Lady? *His* Lady.

No. They would come. They had to come.

That deranged smile stretched—stretched until it was unmistakable from a feral snarl. Had anyone been present to hear it, they wouldn't have recognized his voice from the tortured creaking of a weather-worn shack on a howling windy night. But he knew what words he croaked out, and that was all that mattered.

"Not… before… they find you first."

IN THE QUIET depths of the *Avalon Eternal*, in the dim room that had once been a medical bay and had long since ceased to serve any function at all, the Black Knight withdrew his hand from the Merlin's fitful brow, took one measured step backward, then wavered and slumped against the bulkhead. Ahead, against every biological law of the universe, the Merlin shifted and groaned in his so-called sleep.

Even in this state, drugged well beyond mortal limits and buried under multiple levels of technological *and* arcane immersion methodologies, the miserable old bastard was still stronger than almost anything the Black Knight had ever encountered. One of the strongest beings in the galaxy, to be sure. But not the strongest.

Gathering himself, he slipped clear of the multiple containment fields of the Merlin's cell and reached for the Beacon, allowing its strength to flow into him. The artifact responded without complaint, flooding him with life and energy enough to set the room aglow with a thrumming azure.

He had everything he needed.

Or *would*, just as soon as he caught himself another Knight.

The thought very nearly stirred something like excitement as he finished replenishing himself on the Beacon's bottomless reservoir and turned for the door. Quite to his surprise, he found himself pausing at the threshold, turning back to the frail sedated wizard and considering all that he'd just learned. Multiple fabrications deep, and the old bastard was still weaving lies. Even now, his wizened brow twisted and furrowed, like for all the stars in the sky, the wizard was trying to think himself awake past it all.

For the scantest fraction of a second, the Black Knight almost felt something like pity.

Then he bolstered himself and stalked from the room, setting course for a universe where he'd never again have to look upon the miserable fool who'd just failed to stop the Synth for the last time.

CHAPTER 17

AWESTRUCK

Amelia Sundercaste stepped off her third magtube shuttle in the past ten minutes, marveling at the fact that Ser Zedavian Kelkarin had somehow managed to situate his extensive quarters in a place that was so close to the Hall of Reason by raw distance and yet so inconvenient to reach. She doubted it was an accident, especially considering the local lore of the golden figure that could sometimes be glimpsed gliding by through the cold blackness of space just outside the Hall of Reason.

Twenty minutes by foot and magtube.

Twenty *seconds* by personal gravitonics and sufficient Forge airlock access.

No, she decided, turning down the pedestrian path toward the Hall of Reason. Zedavian Kelkarin's inaccessibility was no accident. But it was hardly worth complaining over, given the magnitude of the opportunity she suddenly found herself attending.

An Excalibur Knight.

An honest to reason, Terran Excalibur Knight—or Knight Initiate, at least. And he was all hers, for the moment being. It was hard to wrap her head around.

She smiled in the faintly dimming, sleep-filtered light of the station's descending diurnal dark hours, thinking of all the wild and magnificent adventures and opportunities that might well follow, if only this assessment went well. If only.

Her smile faded, thinking of the First Knight's news at the assembly, and of the way both Nate and Ser Katanaga had reacted when she'd made the questionable decision to fill them in.

The Merlin, a traitor?

At least they'd looked genuinely surprised.

Amelia still wasn't sure what to think about any of it. She felt rather disconnected from the allegation itself. It had been nearly four entire Atlantean generations since the Merlin had even purportedly been sighted in Alliance space proper. There *was* the slightly concerning testimony of one Vice Admiral Var'lain, who claimed an individual utilizing the Merlin's ancient verification codes had met with Ser Groshna at the Golnak Beacon facility just weeks before the terran incursion. But for the legendary wizard to come to light now as some villainous mastermind…

The First Knight might as well have told them the bogeyman had come to play. It meant little to anyone on a personal level. And yet the Council was in no less of an uproar, clamoring for emergency votes to eradicate the Merlin's executive authority immediately. Some were even saying it was time to disband the Order Excalibur completely. Then again, there was never a time when someone *wasn't* saying such things.

Whatever was happening out there—whatever betrayal, or moral failing, or genuine wizardly evil might've underlain the events on Terra—she only hoped that Nate wasn't caught up in the middle of it. That he was merely an innocent bystander, roped—much like her—into a sudden, unexpected, and monumental duty to which he might still do proud service, provided the right care and guiding hands.

Her reasons were almost certainly self-serving, of course. Imagining otherwise would be naive at best. Nate was *her* sudden and unexpected ticket to entire new tiers of prosperity and professional achievement, after all. But even as brief as their time together had been thus far, there was also some part of her that simply hoped he was clean because she liked him.

Maybe she just had a soft spot for Terrans. Most Sundercastes did. But there was something especially quaint and actually rather cute about her new charge. The way he deferred and deflected, utterly devoid of arrogance even with the awesome power of an Excalibur at his fingertips. The way he went red as a turba root at the simple mention of a perfectly casual coupling, like a hungry diner bashfully eyeing the communal helpings at mealtime, fearing that there wouldn't be enough to go around if he partook, or that he'd be judged poorly for his appetite.

Nate Arturi was no servant of evil. Of that much, her instincts were nearly certain. His Gorgon companion, on the other hand… Amelia had no idea what to make of her. Gorgons weren't easy reads to begin with, and Katanaga was ancient by any reasonable standards. It wasn't hard to see why the Council feared the Knights. But Nate…

Nate was good. She was almost certain. He just had much to learn.

Perhaps, if all went well, she'd have the chance to teach him what little she could. Show him what the Atlantean Empire had to offer, and what the entire galaxy would be expecting of him. Show him what to do with that appetite of his, at the very least.

For now, though, she needed to keep her lens objective. Set aside these personal biases and stick to observable facts. Compile her findings from the day and report to Calum, as promised. The only small caveat to the kingly gift of his nomination—the Triton senator wished to be kept abreast of her assessment prior to any public reports.

It might've come across as a questionable request had she not already known Calum as well as she did. Just like a skeptical observer might've cried foul on the grounds of nepotism, had they been privy to her routine personal visits to the good senator's bedchamber. The fact remained that a psychosocially trained Sundercaste was the only proper choice for this appointment. Few other Atlanteans would be equipped to speak to Nate as anything other than the superstitious Terran ape they believed him to be. She was just grateful Calum thought her worthy of the task.

She knew he wouldn't have picked her otherwise, no matter what inner doubt or outside eyes might whisper. Calum Statecaste was not a man who accepted anything less than the perfect candidate for a job. She could read as much in the precision with which he implemented his eccentric coupling practices, and in the way he'd reacted to her willingness to not only be a part of them but to push and explore their boundaries together.

Sometimes, the pain had been excessive. More often than not, though, she was delighted to find it heightened the pleasure beyond anything she'd experienced in the past with even the most skilled partners, adding a flavor of frantic thrill that was often as sensuously delicious as it was terrifying—sensation beyond anything she'd ever imagined. There was a passion at the center of that man. A passion that burned brighter at the height of their throes than anything she'd ever witnessed. A passion no casual observer would've ever dared guess could lie at the center of one so disciplined and charmingly self-controlled. Sometimes, it almost frightened her.

Adept as she was at reading such things, she'd never quite been able to put her finger on the exact shape and direction of that passion. Calum burned to better the Atlantean Empire, certainly, and to protect their people's stake in an increasingly tumultuous Alliance. Sometimes, at the height of their private explorations, it almost felt as if he burned for her, and nothing else.

It was that thought that drew her up short and bade her glance down at her omni bracelet, wondering if Calum were available. Her cheeks actually heated a few degrees as she found her feet shuffling her off the beaten path and into the darkness of an ancillary privacy nook of their own accord, her fingers dancing the familiar path on the omni controls.

Was she truly growing that attached?

She shook the thought off, chiding herself, reaching for the call icon. Stimulus and response. That's all it was. All it ever was. Nothing to blush about. Not unless she'd somehow caught an inkling of Nate Arturi's regrettable shame—which she absolutely hadn't. She'd give Calum the preliminaries. See what he made of the timid Terran for whom he'd quite publicly stuck out his neck. She could compile her findings properly once they'd had a chance to clear their heads together.

She paused at the self-image on the waiting holo, brushing a single errant hair from her forehead before reaching for the call icon. Her body jerked with a reflexive startle before her brain could even finish registering the cause.

Movement just ahead. A shadow among shadows in her periphery, yanking her eyes up from the holo. Up to the tall figure that suddenly stood before her in the intimate space of the privacy nook, appeared from thin air, gangly and misshapen even beneath its long black coat.

A thick fog settled through her brain, clouding the spiking terror.

Listen, child.

The whisper sighed through her on an icy wind, straight into her mind. The thing's lips hadn't even *moved*, some part of her murky brain pointed out. And there was something else that seemed to fit that theory, buried deep down in her internal storage. Something about the thing's build, and the dark goggles it wore, pulled up over its pale, elongated forehead.

Something brushed her cheek, cold and fleshy.

"Sh-sh-shhh," breathed the icy wind, this time in her ear.

An Ooperian, her brain registered through the fog. This was one of the Ooperians, and its goggles were up. That wasn't right, for some reason. She couldn't remember why. Could only stare in wonder at those nebulous amber eyes, floating before her like softly glowing gateways to an all-expansive universe. Infinity in those swirling depths, melting the icy touch on her cheek into something warm and wonderful.

She melted with it, sinking into strong, slender arms, head lolling lackadaisically in her sudden and utterly supreme relaxation. Tender hands cradled her all the way, pale, spindly fingers cupping her face. And those mesmerizing eyes, floating over it all, whispering her senses into oblivion.

She wanted to scream.

Wanted to melt into that luxurious touch forever.

Listen, and obey.

"Yes," her lips whispered.

BACK IN THE master chambers of his quarters, Zedavian Kelkarin stirred and opened his eyes, taking his first conscious breath in over an hour. It smelled gray and ponderously empty. Tasteless. Benign.

He was tired of this charade. Tired of these petty games. So damned tired.

It had to end.

"Come to us, my love," moaned a thick voice from the next room over. He turned to look, not immediately recalling of whom this evening's entertainment consisted.

Saffarin and Ilxa, it seemed. Two of his favorites. He studied Saffarin's immaculate physique. Watched disinterestedly as the Asgardian paused from reaching out to him, face contorting in an involuntary groan as Ilxa's generous hands teased him more vigorously, her sultry grin fixed on Zedavian, and nothing else.

"Join us," she said, an air of would-be command in her tone.

Empty. So ponderously empty.

"No." They all paused at the tone in his voice. *He* paused at the tone in his voice, and took another breath. That was gray, too, tinged with an edge of Kalyrian florals.

"Refreshment then, my Lord?" came Sashia's soothing voice from the doorway. The Gorgon glided into the room with her lithe dancer's grace a moment later, bearing a full tray of once-exotic cuisines. Zedavian let his gray breath out on something too flat and sedated to be called a sigh. How he'd ever thought such a delectable flower of a creature could somehow fulfill his curiosity for the Gorgon Knight... Clearly, it had been a fool's errand from the start.

Sweet as they'd all been, neither Sashia nor her predecessors could ever hope to rival the raw, righteous tenacity of Iveera Katanaga, or the barely-contained loathing he'd seen in her brilliant blue eyes ever since she'd spurned his drunken advances some three-hundred years ago. And without that...

"You must eat, my Lord," Sashia crooned, tipping her tray to one hand as she approached so that she could reach for his cheek with the other, no doubt intending to soothe, or perhaps to pleasure. She was quite a talented empath. Sensual, willing, and entirely too young to even begin to grasp why her pathokinesis, endlessly blissful as it was, could often fail to stir even a flutter of emotion in his ancient bones.

He caught her hand just short of his flesh with a light gravitonic thought—vague ideations of stronger, crushing thoughts dancing in the depths of his mind beside harsh words and even harsher demands. Pointless. All of it pointless. He stood, releasing his gentle gravitonic grip and offering her a soft, mechanical smile. "Not now, my sweet pet. There is something I must do."

CHAPTER 18
EAGLE'S NEST

"The Golden Eagle has left the nest," crackled a tense voice in Jaeger's earpiece. "Repeat, the Golden Eagle has left the—"

"I read you, Snuffy," Jaeger whispered. "Jesus." He scanned the crowded-but-not-quite-packed plaza from their inconspicuous post among the courtyard foliage, lightly shaking his head until he spotted their Golden Eagle. Ser Zedavian Kelkarin was hard to miss, even in a crowd.

"All right, I see him. Now quit your—"

A firm prod on his shoulder yanked his attention over to the Troglodan sitting beside him in the small alcove. Jaeger spread his hands in what he hoped was a universal sign for *what the fuck, pal?* Malfar just tapped his giant sausage finger pointedly to one lumpy ear hole, then sliced his hand through the air in what felt like a clear *quiet down, idiot.* Which was rich and all, considering that that was more or less what he'd been about to tell Snuffy.

Jaeger turned his scowl from the Troglodan to the First Knight's retreating form, at least a good hundred meters away, wondering how anyone—even a fancy-pants Knight—could possibly isolate a single quiet whisper at this distance past the sounds of the crowd. Even after Kelkarin's little trick outside the *Camelot,* Jaeger was skeptical, but when it came down to it, he knew jack shit about what these Knights were truly capable of. So he closed his mouth and settled in to wait, idly hoping that his people weren't standing out like sore thumbs in their hastily procured Atlantean garments.

That they probably wouldn't have even made it past the *Camelot*'s guard detail without Malfar-the-stiff-assed-justicar there swinging the rank hammer seemed to warrant that Jaeger lend some credence to the Troglodan's judgment. But then again, he still wasn't even close to certain they could trust the justicar. For all he knew, they were walking into some elaborate sting operation. But he didn't see what other choice they had.

Assuming, of course, that Malfar hadn't *also* been lying about all the crazy shit he'd pieced together from Iveera's records and station gossip.

"We've lost sight of the Golden Eagle," Snuffy's voice crackled, annunciating each word with ear-punching intensity, "but the Doctor is in. Repeat, we've lost sight of..."

Jaeger closed his eyes and pinched his nose, resisting the urge to snap, internally promising to never again let Snuffy handle call signs. Most of all, he hoped that Carter was equal to the task of keeping inconspicuous while looking out for the return of an Eldari who may or may not be capable of hearing a whisper across a crowded public space.

What the hell had he been thinking, agreeing to move forward with this?

When he opened his eyes, Malfar was watching him with the closest thing to a judgmental Troglodan frown he'd ever seen.

"You are a strange people."

"Yeah?" Jaeger took one more careful look across the plaza and stood. "Well, at least we don't run around bullying less advanced civilizations."

"Yet," the Troglodan countered, rising to stand head and shoulders over him.

Jaeger scowled up at the big brute, fishing in his borrowed Atlantean pocket for their golden ticket. He knew damn well what Earth's best and brightest engineers were already up to with the data and the wrecked Troglodan vessels Iveera had left behind for them, just like he knew damn well what kinds of high-ranking megalomaniacs might one day take the reins on the fruits of their labor. But none of that even came close to making anything about the incursion of Earth forgivable.

He found what he was looking for and keyed his mic, still holding Malfar's stare. "Move in, Bravo. We'll see you inside."

"Commencing Operation Eagle's Nest," Snuffy confirmed. "Watch your tail feathers, team."

Jaeger wasn't really sure whether *smug grins* were part of the Troglodan repertoire, but it sure as shit felt like Malfar was shooting him one as the

Troglodan slipped a compact, loosely pistol-shaped weapon free from concealment, checked it, and slid it back home.

"We must move, Mother Hen."

Jaeger sighed and slipped Zedavian's handy little data disc out of his pocket.

"Sure," he muttered, as the Troglodan keyed his omni and winked out of sight under one of the *Camelot*-grade optical shrouds Kalders had somehow managed to coax Cammy to fabricate. "Let's go find out if this bullshit actually works."

CHAPTER 19

SPOON

At the heart of Zedavian Kelkarin's fortress, trapped inside their palatial little prison square, Nate was beginning to think that maybe the mule had been unfairly judged all these years, right along with the goat and the ox.

Stubborn as a *Gorgon*, the saying should've gone.

How can you still be denying this? Nate thought to Iveera. *Your sacred chain of command is broken. That golden bastard's already shipped us down-river, right along with the Merlin. You heard Amelia.*

I did, Iveera thought back, facing him from her sitting position in the opposite corner, no longer bothering to maintain the ignoring act. *I am also well acquainted with the value of idle words and wild hearsay. And that is to say nothing of the tactics a competent, driven psychoanalyst could well employ in the interest of observing what manner of reactions might boil out of her volatile test subject.*

Now who's being paranoid? Nate thought, but he couldn't help dropping her gaze to scowl at the floor. Because he honestly didn't know. No matter how many times he played the conversation back in his head, the only conclusion he arrived at was that, despite being pretty damn sure she'd gotten exactly what she wanted from the exchange, he still had no idea whose side Amelia Sundercast was actually on.

But Amelia's news was only half of the picture.

I'm telling you, Iveera, these dreams are freaky-real.

Perhaps you should tell them to Amelia Sundercaste. I'm sure she'd find your conjecture quite riveting.

On the surface, she looked as disinterested as she sounded. But there was something else there. Something about the slight tick that flickered through her jin at his words, mid-swirl. His dream wasn't insubstantial to her. Not completely, at least.

Prescient visions are not wholly unprecedented among the Knights, Ex said. *Perhaps she is merely concerned that you are in fact correct. You organics DO have quite the penchant for denial.*

Really? Nate asked his companion, sitting up a little straighter.

Of course. Take, for instance, your radical refusal to accept the reality of our cohabitation back in State College. Or, more recently, your stubborn refusal to admit your attraction to—

I meant the vision thing, Ex, Nate snapped, pumping his hands out in exasperation and drawing a disapproving jin-shake from Iveera. *Obviously.*

Ah. Well, in that case, yes. There are records of confirmed clairvoyant episodes among the Order. Quite rare, but not unheard of.

And how do you tell? How would I know this is... that, and not just some weird dream?

Well...

What? Nate felt Iveera watching him from her corner just a little too intently, like she was trying to see inside his head.

You aren't going to like it, Ex said.

Nate gave an amused huff. *Well, that'll be a first. What is it?*

Well, there IS one certain way to separate prescient visions from convincing dreams. And one way only.

And that is? Nate asked, pretty sure he saw where this was going.

Prescient visions, by definition, will inevitably come to pass.

Nate sighed and rocked his head back against the cell wall. *So I'll know it was a proper vision after it actually freaking happens? Real helpful.*

I'm glad you think so. Personally, I couldn't make heads or tails of what was happening in there.

Sarcasm, Ex. That was sarcasm. And what about, like, cause and effect? I do something because I thought I saw it, and thus random dream becomes prescient vision?

Hmm, yes, Ex said, sounding thoughtful. *Well, if you're going to miss the point, I suppose you might as well do it completely.*

Any chance you could just tell me this magical point?

Ah. The thing is...

My puny human brain isn't capable of comprehending it?

I figured that went without saying, Ex replied with a hint of amusement, *but if I had to put it to one hopelessly inadequate word, I would say I believe it boils down to a matter of faith.*

That *was* a rather inadequate word.

Forgive me. It is merely more convenient than saying 'your individual reading of the subconscious-weighted probability distribution amassed across your pathetically limited perspective of this fleeting frame of the infinitely branching realities within Light-space-time,' Nathaniel.

That's... fair enough, Nate admitted, preemptively throwing in the towel on even trying to unpack what the hell that meant. *But what about your reading, then? If it's a question of faith, I mean... Aren't you one with the Light too? You saw my dream. Was it real?*

I am powered by the Light, Nathaniel. You are... He deliberated. *Privy to it, perhaps. There is no clear word, but I assure you, it is not the same between organic life and inorganic synthience.*

Nate sat by, waiting for him to answer the real question.

I can parrot back every detail of what you saw, Ex finally said, *but I cannot tell you what your dream means, Nathaniel. No one can. Distinguishing between prescience and mere manifest trepidation is—*

A matter of faith, Nate supplied, feeling strangely disembodied.

Just so.

Nate looked to Iveera, found her still watching him, practically dissecting him with those phosphorescent eyes. Not knowing what else to do—and figuring there was little reason to keep any of it to himself—he reached out and began to tell her about the dream, starting from the beginning this time, and including every fine detail he'd left out in his first mad rush at trying to explain himself.

We have to do something, he declared, when he'd finished, and she was still watching him, jin swirling, expression unchanged. *I'm going to do something.*

She only crossed her arms, silently inviting him to have at it with his big talk and show her what he was going to do about any of it.

I left Earth to help you save him, Iveera.

You left Earth because you had no choice.

But I did choose, didn't I? I could've tried to run. Maybe I would've surprised us both and actually slipped your grip. But I got on the Camelot, and I left my world behind without your ass-kicking. I got on that ship to come find the Merlin and set things straight, and after what I just saw... He shook his head, at a loss. *He needs us, Iveera. I don't understand what's happening out there, but I'm sure about that much. Now more than ever. I'm seeing this through.*

He considered her flat expression, weighing his next words.

Plus, your ship is still in Cammy's cargo, so unless you want me jetting off with that, you know...

Something in her demeanor shifted in a way that left Nate holding his breath.

You attempt to threaten me?

For a second, the words made him want to flinch. But then her demeanor subtly shifted again, the idle eddies of her jin rocking with a trickle of what might've been amusement.

To his surprise, he felt a small grin pulling at his lips. *More of a friendly logistics reminder, really.* He sobered a little, the moment passing all too quickly. *I know you didn't exactly sign up for this either. And I know... I know you're only stuck with us because you lost your people.*

He watched her jin swirl on, felt the tension building more in the air between them than in her perfectly disciplined posture. It was the first time he'd mentioned her dead crew outright since she'd nearly drowned him in the Atlantic Ocean over her losses. Losses she'd suffered while cleaning up his mess and fighting for his planet.

Duty is duty, Nathaniel, she finally said. *A true Knight does not pick and choose in which circumstances they wish to uphold it.*

He bowed his head, eyeing the polished tiles. *I think that's what I'm trying to say. For better or worse, we're in this together now, and I think... Whatever Zedavian's playing at, I think...*

You think that you are special.

What? No, I—

You think that after three thousand years of his loyal service, the Lady has chosen you, a fresh-faced Terran with naught but a few weeks' experience to illuminate the corrupt failings of our First Knight?

Nate stared at her, unsure how to respond, unsure where this was suddenly coming from.

It hasn't even entered your mind yet, has it? That the First Knight is correct about us.

It hadn't entered his mind. Because the bastard *wasn't* correct, dammit. They'd checked, time and time again. Done the scans, ad nauseam. And yet...

And yet, Iveera said, like she could see his exact thoughts unfolding, *how does one ever truly trust the results of a measurement when the measuring tool itself is suspect?*

For a long moment, Nate sat there wanting to argue that that logic proved nothing. All he could do was stare dumbly, feeling… he didn't know what. Sick, for starters. Hopeless. Betrayed.

Betrayed by himself or by her, he couldn't really say. Both, he supposed. Betrayed by his own wavering sense of confidence. Because he'd *known*—still *did* know—that he'd meant what he'd said, just a minute earlier. Didn't he? Where was the faith he'd been so certain he felt only a moment ago? Displaced to the murky edges of his mind like so much formless vapor, hovering right beside Ex, who watched uncertainly, saying nothing, not refuting Iveera's words.

We are touched by corruption, she said. *I feel it festering within my Excalibur as certainly as I begin to smell it in yours. I was a fool . And as for these allegations, and this vision of yours…*

Nate was still waiting for her to finish the thought when she went still, perking up and fanning her jin out in a kind of satellite dish array, like she was listening.

What is it?

She only glanced at him, then back to the door. Something was wrong.

"What?" he repeated out loud, following her gaze to the door, too caught up in his thoughts to focus properly, until—

There.

He cocked his head, listening. There was definitely something there—the faintest muffled rhythm coming through the closed door. A drum beat, he realized, frowning in concentration. And an accompanying riff. A familiar one.

"Is that…" He turned to her, realizing as he did that there was almost no way she could know the answer to his next question. "Is that Spoon?"

"How… delightful," said the Gorgon named Sashia, her delicate fingers still hovering uncertainly over her omni controls.

She was considerably smaller than Iveera, and considerably less intimidating. And even after having studied only a sample size of one Gorgon, Jaeger was pretty sure she was just being polite.

It seemed a minor crime, given the layered nuance of pure musical gold currently pouring through the room in the form of Spoon's *Do I Have to*

Talk You Into It. But the Gorgon's musical appreciation was about the last thing on his mind as he glanced around to the swanky room's four wide entryways, wondering what the hell was taking his so-called ally so long.

"I am certain my Lord will be pleased with this gift," the Gorgon added slowly, delicately. "But may I, um…" She looked genuinely apologetic. "May I stop it now?"

No appreciation whatsoever.

Where the hell was that Troglodan?

"Just a sec," Jaeger said, taking a step closer to the Gorgon as he mentally shuffled through his options, feeling utterly ridiculous about this entire half-cocked ruse. "We're just getting to the good part, see? This right here" —He bobbed one finger in the air with the beat, silently praying the music would absorb her even as he saw on her face that it wouldn't—"this right here, that's the stuff."

And that right *there*, glimpsed right over her well-sculpted green shoulders, was Malfar's splotchy Troglodan face winking into sight, thank Christ and all his pals. For one relieved moment, Jaeger waited for the Troglodan to make his move, announcing the all-clear. Then he noticed the way Malfar was shaking his splotchy head, signing a rapid series of hand gestures toward the ceiling and the next room over.

Jaeger barely had time to process an inner *oh shit* before Malfar winked back out of sight.

"There are guests, Sashia," came a strange voice from behind them a moment later, jolting Jaeger into an involuntary jerk. He turned to the source of that oddly annunciated voice and almost jerked again at the thing he saw standing there.

"Yes, Zartan," Sashia said calmly to the thing that was vaguely resemblant of a fox, larger than a Saint Bernard, and entirely too intelligent in the eyes. "This is Lt Col John Jaeger, of the distant world, Terra. He has—"

"There are more guests, Sashia," the giant space fox interjected, its tone emphatic, the beginnings of a growl bubbling in its throat.

"No, Zartan. It's only—"

"Yes, Sashia," the creature insisted, sniffing at the air. "More guests. Can't-see guests."

Shit, was all Jaeger's racing mind could manage, as Sashia rounded on him with wary eyes, mental wheels clearly turning.

"Do I have to talk you into it?" crooned the speakers as he grabbed for her hand before he could think better of it, thinking maybe to distract with a soft touch and charming smile. Or maybe just to close the distance.

"Do we have to make sense of it?"

And close the distance he did. Smooth as butter. A regular Bond-freak-ing-James-Bond.

"They say I better seal you up in wax."

Right until the moment their skin touched, that was, and he *felt*—he didn't know how else to put it, but *felt*—her presence there, querying his intent, her jin gone suddenly rigid.

"So that you're never gonna bite me back."

Shit.

He lanced out with the short stun rod he'd slipped free with his other hand, distantly aware of the space fox Zartan baying wildly over the music, and watched with a kind of shocked horror as his polite Gorgon host flipped into a tight aerial, releasing his hand and dodging the stunner even as her jin caught onto his wrist and she landed, pivoting.

He was flying across the swanky living room before he knew it, clipping a luxurious red couch on the way. Flipping over to a hard landing on an equally posh rug. At least it was a *thick* rug, some part of his rattled brain pointed out, skull pounding to the rhythm of the music, right before he caught sight of the furious space fox charging in for the kill.

"Intruders, Sashia!" the thing howled, dipping up short on its forelegs and snarling at the stun rod Jaeger thrust out between them as he rolled over to hands and knees. "Interlopers!" It snapped its frighteningly powerful jaws and took a threatening step forward. "Fresh meat!"

"Heel, Fido," Jaeger growled, rocking up into a crouch and darting a sideways glance to where he half-expected to find the Gorgon bringing a nice marble statuette down on his head.

Breaking eye contact was a mistake.

The ferocious growl was all the warning he had. He triggered the stun rod and rolled to the side, thrusting the weapon blindly where he hoped it would catch Zartan's charge at the front shoulder. He caught a flicker of green motion—Saisha sailing in from above. Something hot and entirely too sharp clamped down on his left wrist.

His roll jerked to halt, searing fire radiating up his arm as Zartan's fangs crushed down on his wrist, yanking him up short. Jaeger rode the pain as best he could, trying to focus the burst of frantic adrenal energy on twisting the crackling tip of the stun rod to the side of the fox's head before the pain completely overwhelmed him. If he could just buy a moment...

But then Sashia landed on him, jostling him violently, and the pain roared into something blinding and unmanageable. He yelled wordlessly, trying to strike with his free hand to little effect.

Where were they?

Sashia caught him by the throat, plucked his stun rod free. Zartan clamped down harder, drawing a pained groan. The stun rod crackled to life, inches from his left eye. In the distant background, Spoon rocked on, unperturbed by any of it.

"Fine," Jaeger growled, resisting the urge to shout for help, silently praying for it instead. "Fine. If this is about the music…"

A pair of blessed mechanical coughs broke the unfinished statement. Jaeger groaned with a mix of relief and pain as stunner rounds tagged the rump of Zartan the murderous space fox from the two wide entryways where Elmo and Snuffy had just appeared. At the same time, a strong arm snaked around Saisha's midsection and hurled her off of Jaeger, down to the ground. The fire in Jaeger's forearm shifted qualities, intensifying in spots as Zartan drooped to the floor with a pitiful whimper of a growl, jaw loosening. Jaeger gave his own grunt at the sudden welling of blood and the cool kiss of air on his saliva-slicked forearm as he pulled it free.

"Fuck," he growled to himself, watching the blood come faster—too fast —and looking around for something to stop it.

"—and remain calm," the Troglodan was rumbling to Sashia, who he'd pinned neatly face down with a knee and one hand, his stun weapon pressed to the flat of her back where it was well out of reach of her lashing jin. "We have no desire to bring you harm." He looked up at Snuffy and Elmo. "You two, weapons ready. There are still two more—"

Two more *what*, exactly, Malfar didn't have a chance to finish before Snuffy disappeared with a strangled yelp, plucked around the corner by something that moved him like a rag doll. Elmo raised his weapon that way, then whipped around to the hallway behind him with a curse—just in time to take a devastating golden fist to the face. The big man hit the floor like a sack of bricks.

Jaeger scrambled to his feet, clutching the first lavish pillow his hands found tightly between his chest and his freely bleeding wrist. With his other hand, he scooped up his stun rod up from beside the struggling Gorgon— noting how dizzy he already felt—and rounded to go help his people.

"Wait," Malfar boomed. The Troglodan was glancing rapidly between the four gilded entryways, trying to track something over the driving beat of the music. Almost as a casual afterthought, he fired his stun weapon into Sashia's struggling form and stood to join Jaeger as the Gorgon went limp.

Something sped across the entryway to the right—a streak of gold at the edge of Jaeger's vision, gone by the time he turned. A sharp snap and clatter from the other direction sent him backing into Malfar's brick wall of a flank. He pictured Snuffy, broken. Pushed the thought down and rotated in tandem with Malfar, too busy trying to listen over the music to care that he was actually fighting back-to-back with a freaking Troglodan.

A gasp from behind whirled them both around to find a stunning platinum blond Atlantean woman staring down at Elmo's unconscious bulk, delicate hands clasped to her mouth in shock.

"Oh, uh, hello," she said, when her graze finally tracked up to Jaeger and Malfar. She gave them an uncertain smile and a polite little wave, like she'd simply walked in on a private but perfectly natural affair, then turned and bolted without another word.

Jaeger turned an incredulous look at Malfar. "Who the fuck was that?"

Malfar opened his mouth, then lurched down just in time to avoid the speeding obsidian statuette bound for his head. It crashed to a halt somewhere behind them as Jaeger caught sight of the one who'd thrown it—a golden god of a man, a juiced-up Eldari maybe, standing in the open entryway, buck-ass naked but for the oblong bronze shield strapped to one arm.

"What the piss," Jaeger muttered.

Then a wild bellow tore through the room behind them, and a second golden god came charging into the room, bound straight for them.

~

"THAT'S *DEFINITELY* SPOON," Nate said, propped up on his toes against the cell wall now as if it might somehow enhance his sense of hearing. "Who the hell's listening to Spoon out there?"

He shut his eyes, focusing in as best he could, and…

"Wait, is that—"

Lieutenant Colonel John Jaeger, confirmed Iveera, whose senses were clearly sharper than his. Her nostrils flared. *And the justicar too.*

What the hell are they doing here?

They aren't the only ones, Ex said.

"Someone is coming," Iveera said out loud, a second before Nate caught the faint sounds of someone tinkering with the access panel outside. Iveera's jin perked curiously as something plunked against the far door with a magnetic thud.

"Perhaps she forgot her key," she said quietly, almost to herself.

Then the door blew in with a low *whoomph* and crashed to the ground on a tide of smoke and debris. The energetic riff of Spoon's *Do I Have to Talk You Into It* poured in through the haze, along with the crashes and growls of what sounded like a genuine battle royale out in the main quarters. Through the smoke and the racket came Amelia Sundercaste, regarding the slain door with a curious frown as she strolled into the room.

"Hey Nate," she said, casual as could be. She turned from the door she'd just torched to look at their intact cell like she was eyeing up her next target. "Change of plans. We're getting you out of here."

"We?"

"Long story," she said, sliding a dark leather bag from her shoulder. "I'll fill you in on the ship."

"The…" Nate glanced at Iveera. "The ship?"

Something is wrong with her, Iveera sent.

Her pupils ARE unusually dilated, Ex added.

A wild bellow and a savage crash from the main quarters broke in before he could decide what to make of any of that.

"Asgardians," Amelia muttered, shaking her head disdainfully as she rummaged in her bag and withdrew something—a short pistol, he registered. Right as she leveled it straight at the cell.

He skipped aside with a surprised yelp as she started blasting, but his concern turned out to be preemptive. The sizzling orange projectiles, devastating as they looked, didn't fully puncture the outside cell wall. Just struck it in a string of shuddering smacks, each superheated shot embedding with a soft sizzle, a whiff of ozone… and the faintest beginnings of ghostly fault-line cracks, spider-webbing out from each point of impact.

Now's our chance, Nate thought to Iveera, not really sure what came next, but figuring the rest went without saying. Judging from the sounds outside, they didn't have long before Zedavian came swooping in to put an end to this. And if either of them could hope to crack open these fault lines with their bare hands, it probably wasn't him.

Iveera didn't move, though. Just stood there, arms crossed, jin flattened. *This is… not right, Nathaniel*, she sent. *I…* A shudder like he'd never seen ran through her. *I cannot defy the Order. We mustn't.*

He stared at her, wanting to be incredulous, yet painfully aware that he also had no plan here—no freaking clue what might actually happen if they stepped outside this cell, or how they were supposed to fix any of this if they were on the run. For a second, he stood frozen, wondering if maybe she wasn't right—about the Order, about their corruption, about all of it.

Then he thought of the Merlin and the Council that was apparently ready to write him off as a traitor. He thought of his friends waiting for him on Earth. Thought of his dream, and the uneasy sense of inevitability it'd left in his gut, whispering to him even now that he knew what had to be done––that he'd never again be able to trust that his home was safe.

He couldn't turn away from this. No matter what.

So he turned instead to do what Iveera wouldn't. Before he could take his first shot at the cell wall, though, Amelia stepped up close outside, murmuring quietly to herself as she withdrew a small brown brick-shaped device from her pack.

Looks like a thermal charge, Ex said, as she planted the thing to the cell wall.

He liked the sound of that about as much as he appreciated the highly uncertain look in Amelia's eyes.

"Take cover?" she suggested with a helpless little shrug.

Nate shuffled back a few steps before the pack ignited like a small white sun. He nearly fell backward in his hurry to distance himself, throwing his arms protectively over his eyes as his back smacked into the far wall. The light was blinding, the heat like a roaring bonfire from an inch away. Then something gave way, and painful heat became searing agony.

"Fuck!" he yelled as the miniature sun ran its course, and his vision began creeping in enough to show his blistered red forearms.

"My thoughts exactly," came Amelia's less-than-excited reply from somewhere ahead. He blinked the dying sunspots from his eyes, trying to focus. The charge had left a charred mess of the wall, tracing several of the hairline cracks black and maybe even deepening them, but the damn wall still held.

"I think I might've mixed up my explosives," Amelia said, frowning back at the first downed door.

Nate glanced at Iveera, who was still watching from her corner, seemingly unperturbed by the blistering burns across her exposed face and hands. "Just back up," he said to Amelia, scooping up a length of the dark shattered bench wood and stomping forward to do his damnedest.

Sturdy as his makeshift club felt in his hands, he was a little surprised when it shattered on the first impact, barely scratching the cell wall. He tossed it aside and squared off to put Ex's upgrades to the test.

The first kick was nothing to write home about. The second kick, jarring as it was, wasn't much better. The third kick, he was pretty sure, nearly broke his Ex-reinforced leg. But at least that one earned him a whisper of protest from the crystalline wall, the hairline fractures tracing out just a little wider.

Outside the cell, Amelia was rummaging in her bag again, like she'd just remembered something. Nate kicked again, in no hurry to find out what the Atlantean's next toy might do to them. Another kick, the fractures creeping wider, his leg half-numb with impact, knee positively throbbing.

You're doing great, Nathaniel, Ex said, too kindly.

Another kick.

You have no idea what you're doing. Iveera's voice this time, decidedly less kindly.

"A little help, then?" he growled in her general direction, kicking again, the wall holding firm despite its growing cracks, like some kind of indestructible impact glass. Iveera said nothing. He kicked again, and was rewarded with an odd pop and a frighteningly sharp pain in the knee.

I can fix that, Ex said. *Probably.*

Nate turned his glare on Iveera, who held his gaze evenly, waiting to see what he'd do. He wanted to plead with her. Wanted to beg. He switched legs instead, grunting with the pain, and prepared to kick again, noting with distant and morbid amusement the words drifting in from the main quarters.

"Do I have to talk you into it?"

Kick.

"Do I have to talk you into it?"

Kick.

"Well, here we go down a long dark road."

Ahead, Amelia was pulling something out of her bag.

"Been here m-many times before."

Nate raised his foot for another kick and faltered as Amelia raised the sinister gray capsule she'd produced for his inspection, eyeing it herself like she was weighing options that may or may not have included their imminent survival.

I do believe that's a miniaturized thermonuclear—

Ahead, Amelia went wide-eyed and scrambled desperately aside just as their cell's one remaining bench sped past Nate like a freaking freight train, too fast to follow. The cell wall exploded outward with a shattering crash of impact, plastering the wall and hallway beyond like a deadly flechette cannon.

"Lady's grace!" Amelia gasped from where she'd tumbled to the floor, clutching at her chest and gaping after the speeding debris storm that'd nearly taken her with it.

Iveera was already stalking through the wreckage, straight toward the Atlantean, copper armor unfolding from e-dim to encase her as she reached out one hand. The small gray doomsday device flew from Amelia's hand to Iveera's, then promptly disappeared into e-dim. Iveera stalked closer, reaching down for Amelia like she had half a mind to end the Atlantean right then and there.

"Iveera," Nate gasped, as the Gorgon snatched Amelia by the tunic. "What're you—"

He drew up short as Iveera yanked a petrified Amelia Sundercaste back to her feet and rounded on him with a fearsome glare, more openly furious than he'd ever seen. *If we fail to save the Merlin and somehow live to tell about it,* she sent, jin actually pulsing soft red, *we will almost certainly be slated for reclamation upon our return after this. Do you understand that?*

He wanted to argue. Didn't want to believe that Iveera Katanaga—a true, sanctioned Excalibur Knight—could really be swept under the rug so easily, even if Zedavian *would* no doubt delight in murdering Nate dead to reclaim Ex for a more deserving Initiate. He wanted to tell her that none of it mattered anyway because they weren't going to fail.

A crash and a strangled cry that sounded too much like Jaeger's yanked his attention to more immediate matters.

Iveera said nothing as he stepped out of the e-dim-dampened confines of the cell and immediately felt Ex's relief effort kicking into full gear, rushing aid to his knee and nourishment to his tired body, his armor folding onto him with barely a conscious thought, brimming with ready power.

First things first.

They needed to get the hell out of here.

Consciousness was little more than a disappointingly fleeting wisp at the edge of the endless darkness when a strong, sharp *something* came shaking the world. A voice, some part of Jaeger's tenuous awareness decided. A *familiar* voice, buzzing at the flickering edge of awareness. A jostling crash. Something tearing free from his throat. Something else rushing into it.

Air. Blessed fucking air. Too much of it.

Something crashed into the far wall as Jaeger coughed and sputtered his way back into the light, the room lilting drunkenly back into focus.

"What the hell?" came that familiar voice. Nate's voice. He was standing protectively over Jaeger, fully armored, staring at the crumpled heap of the big golden muscular chick he'd just pulled off of Jaeger and hurled across the room, buck-ass naked.

"Yeah, I got that part," he muttered with one of those trademark talking-to-himself gestures before he turned and hauled Jaeger bodily to his feet. "What the hell are you doing here?"

"Serving… Justice!" Malfar roared from his corner, right before he threw a savage shot into his own opponent's ribs, breaking their struggling dead-lock, and flipped the golden god of a man across the room to crash down on top of his naked counterpart.

Nate glanced from the Troglodan back to Jaeger with a clear *what the hell's HE doing here?*

"That… pretty much covers it," Jaeger admitted. "We came to get you out," he added, loosening his hold on Nate's disturbingly solid support, then grabbing back on as his spinning head pulled a surprise dip. "Obviously."

"Obviously," Nate agreed, bracing him by the shoulders.

On the floor, the two golden figures stirred, trying for their feet with a string of curses only to collapse back down in a fit of spasmodic jerks, each neatly tagged with a stun bolt to the forehead. Jaeger followed the trajectory and found Iveera had joined them, flanked by the same blonde chick who'd darted by earlier.

"Asgardians," said the Atlantean, wrinkling her perfect little nose at the golden gods in disgust.

Jaeger was still trying to push that one through his discombobulated brain when he realized that Elmo was no longer laying there where he'd been knocked cold. He turned, wobbling a little as he left Nate's support, then relaxed at the sight of Elmo shuffling into the room from the next entryway over, sporting a swollen eye and a severely disoriented Snuffy.

"Jesus Christ," Snuffy gasped, gaping around the wrecked room with wide eyes, finally settling on the space fox they'd stunned to the ground. "Is it just my imagination, or did that thing—"

"It talked," Jaeger confirmed, frowning as Nate took his left hand and sprayed something on the wrist he'd already lost too much blood from.

"Kitsune do not speak," Malfar said.

"Tell that to Zartan the Wonder Fox, here," Jaeger grumbled through the light burn, scowling down at his bitten wrist, then back to the culprit, noticing the thing's multiple furry tails for the first time. The Troglodan didn't seem to hear him, having instead locked stares with Iveera, something of obvious weight passing between them.

"So," Snuffy said, oblivious to anything but the two naked Asgardians in the corner for the moment. "Looks like Operation Eagle's Nest was a wild success, then?"

Jaeger was opening his mouth to put the kibosh on the chatter when Iveera and Malfar both turned smoothly and without warning to plunk another pair of stun rounds into Sashia, the Gorgon house attendant.

"Yeah," Jaeger said, looking down at the blinking red icon Sashia had triggered on her omni just before the bolts took her. "Yeah, I'd say we've graduated right up to Operation Get The Fuck Outta Here."

CHAPTER 20

LOCKDOWN

Nate pulled up to the corner beside Iveera, warily scanning the courtyard and pristine gardens where hundreds of nocturnal Forge denizens were scattered among the dancing fountain sculptures that reminded him vaguely of shape-shifting T-1000 terminators. Some shared food and drink near the open vendor stands, while others sat alone with their thoughts, adrift in clouds of exotic smoke and seas of holo stimulation. Odd tones sighed through the air from unseen speakers, melodious in a way, but also dissonant and erratic. Nate was idly wondering if it was meant to be music when someone ran straight into him from behind.

He bit down a startled curse and glanced back at their group, scanning the enhanced spectrum through his helmet display to count off all five of their shrouded tag-alongs, each of them half-blind to each other's cloaked movements, save for Amelia, who was fully blind and escorted by Elmo.

"Crap," came Snuffy's voice from the phantom outline that'd just walked into Nate and was now tapping at the side of its head as if to coerce his single tac lens to work its limited spectral magic better. "Sorry 'bout that. This is weird."

"You get Kalders yet?" asked Jaeger's voice from the next ghost over. Behind him, the much larger phantom of the Troglodan justicar shifted, seeming to check back the way they'd come.

"Working on it," Nate said, nervously following the Trog's gaze. The ambient sounds in his helmet quickly shifted, and Ex announced the channel was open. "Tessa?" Nate asked quietly, feeling the small extra touch of pressure that confirmed Ex had engaged his helmet's privacy seal.

"Mr. Arturi, as I live and breathe," came their pilot's vivacious tone. "I take it Operation Eagle's Nest wasn't a complete failure?"

"Well…" Nate considered. "We're alive."

"Hard to knock that."

"Yeah," Nate said slowly, as two Atlantean station guards marched into the courtyard ahead, heads on a swivel. "Might be more exciting once we make it through this next bit. Any chance I could interest you in a half-cocked escape plan this evening?"

"Oh my. We talking high speeds? Daring maneuvers?"

"The whole nine yards," Nate heard himself murmur, watching the two guards, telling himself they could've been looking for anything, or just stepping out for a routine patrol. But then four more Androtta glided into the courtyard and began fanning out behind them.

"Thought you'd never ask," came Tessa's voice, yanking him back to the task at hand.

"Yeah, well, I wouldn't get too excited before we make it to the hangar."

Tessa considered that. "I'm guessing our venerable Alliance hosts aren't going to be happy about all this?"

"That seems entirely possible."

She gave a soft huff of amusement. "I just can't *wait* to hear what you boys got up to over there." Her tone shifted a few degrees less playful. "Everyone's okay?"

"Yeah. Maybe a few concussions, but nothing we can't handle on the ship."

"Sounds like we're off to a tidy start."

"Still plenty of time for things to get messy."

"Eh, messy's fun too."

Something about the way she said it might've put a little heat in Nate's cheeks if he hadn't been so consumed with the sudden worry that they were making a colossal mistake here. On top of having already been a disappointment and garden variety pain in the ass for everyone involved, he was now endangering the future of all Earth-Alliance relations on what was, admittedly, a leap of faith.

But it was too late to turn back. They'd already assaulted Zedavian's aid and house guests. Christ, they'd stunned his freaking talking pet fox. There was no undoing that. The rest, he'd just have to worry about once they'd safely avoided landing back in alien prison together.

"Can you make sure everyone's ready to roll over there?" he asked Tessa. "Cammy too? Discreetly, if possible."

"I assumed that all went without saying, but… Ah."

Silence.

"Tess?"

More silence. "Well, this is awkward," she finally said. "Looks like we've got a call on the other line. Big strong Eldari chap, as far as Cammy can figure. No doubt wondering if we've heard from any fugitives tonight over here on the Knightship *Camelot.*"

"Shit. Be careful, Tess. He's…"

"I've got it," she said. "Hurry up and stay safe, Nate."

The comm line went dead, and Nate turned to Iveera's shrouded outline.

Zedavian's hailing the Camelot.

They will not deceive him, she replied, not seeming all that surprised.

Ahead in the courtyard, one of the Atlantean guards raised his hand, holo projector beaming to life, and Nate watched with a sinking feeling as a huge image of his face sprang into existence for all nearby onlookers to see, right next to a similarly billboard-sized wanted poster of Ser Iveera Katanaga. The Atlantean started shouting something to the crowd through a voice amplifier. Nate barely caught more than their names, unsettled as he was.

Time to run, then? he sent to Iveera, trying to keep the nerves out of his tone.

She was already starting forward, gesturing with a wave of her ghostly arm for them to fall in. *Time to run.*

ON PAPER, virtual invisibility should've been like cheat codes for slipping through the station unnoticed. In practice, though, it was much more of a "fucking charlie foxtrot," as Nate heard Jaeger mutter under his breath at one point, complete with far more slip-ups and accidental collisions than seemed statistically probable.

This is why you don't give shrouds to untrained operatives, Ex said in a tone that was half-amused, half-disgusted.

Nate kept his mouth shut, in no position to judge. Even with his superior enhanced-spectrum helmet display, his coordination was suffering. He couldn't imagine trying to juke through the crowd and around obstacles with nothing but one eye's worth of the faintest ghostly tac lens overlay of one's own shrouded limbs.

They hurried on as best they could, jogging through the courtyard like Iveera's invisible flock, whisking through maintenance tunnels. Out again, past a barracks of administrative-looking offices. Pausing as Snuffy bit it, vaulting a low divider. Then again, when Elmo did the same trying to skirt himself and Amelia around a crowd of drunk Hobdans.

Nate still wasn't sure what the hell Amelia *or* the justicar Malfar were doing there in the first place, outside of Amelia's hurried insistence that Calum Statecaste had sent her to "right the Council's wrongs" and the justicar's rumblings about seeing true justice done, whatever the hell that meant. There was no time to question any of it.

They hurried on past odd shops and through a tight pedestrian pass, Snuffy clipping a very confused and irritated-looking Troglodan along the way, Nate feeling a little too much like they were escaping the freaking Death Star. But at least the storm troopers couldn't see them, he reminded himself, as they emerged and followed Iveera behind yet another station security patrol. Maybe they'd be fine, as long as they didn't run into their golden-armored Vader, or… Christ, did Forge Station have tractor beams?

He didn't know. He filed it all away under Problems for Future Nate as they dodge-jogged through a crowded hub, toward the bass-thumping nighttime haze of the bazaar where they'd first come under Ooperian fire. The security patrols seemed to be growing in density. Maybe coincidentally. Maybe not.

He knew it'd probably take more than a few public security guards to stop them anyway, but that was about as comforting as "knowing" that this was really all just a huge misunderstanding that would *totally* be fine so long as they managed to slip the Forge, pop across the galaxy, and pry the Merlin back from the ungodly Black Knight before the Alliance and their mightily pissed First Knight could catch them.

Totally fine. Perfectly so.

Never mind that Zedavian and the Council didn't seem to *want* their Merlin back, or that Nate had no earthly clue what the wizard would even do about any of this giant charlie foxtrot of a situation if and when they found him.

So yeah. Perfectly fine. So fine that, for a second, Nate almost wanted to ask Iveera if maybe it wasn't too late for them to just turn around, slink back to their cell, and have a proper sit-down with Darth Zedavian. But the second passed, and Nate plunged into the bazaar crowd right behind the faint, rosy shimmer that was all his spectral HUD vision could detect of the Gorgon Knight, checking that the crew was in tow and nearly tripping over a trio of little demonic-ewok-looking creatures for the moment of distraction.

Not to complain my first day on the job, Nate thought toward Iveera as he caught up, *but does being a Knight normally feel this much like being a fugitive?*

If she had an answer, she kept it to herself. Nate glanced at a sputtering holo banner of their faces as they rushed past, turning his mind instead to what might be waiting for them in the hangar ahead. He didn't really see how it could be anything other than a small army. While there were no flashing alarms or blaring klaxons, their holo images had preceded them the whole way from the courtyard, leapfrogging ahead from one security node to the next like chain lighting, the faces of the SAS crew joining the bulletins somewhere along the way.

And it was no mystery where the crew of the *Camelot* would be headed.

Which was why Nate wasn't overly surprised when Tessa pinged back into his helmet, sounding less than excited. "We might be in a bit of a pickle here, Nate. Hangar control just—"

The channel hissed with static, then shut off completely. Ex grumbled something about jammers and rerouting to q-comms, but Nate was more focused on the wave of discontent rolling through the crowd like a game of pissed off telephone, several beings around them gesturing aggressively and smacking at their various omni devices.

"—onna let us go without a fight," Tessa's voice crackled back into his helmet.

"I kinda got that impression," Nate said, taking in the scene ahead. "Just a sec." They were nearly to their gate now, and he was peripherally aware of Carter falling in with them from somewhere in the churning crowd, bumping over to tell Jaeger something about how *he*—probably Zedavian— had slipped her shortly after leaving his quarters.

Nate was more concerned with the ring of at least a dozen gray and blue Forge Security uniforms waiting at their hangar gate, and the shimmering wall of hazy blue static that spanned the opening, buzzing across from two slender pylons behind the guards.

Disruptor field, Ex said. *They've anticipated our cloaking trick.*

Nate looked to Iveera, wondering what the play was—disrupt the disruptor, plow on through, or find another way around—but she was already melting into plain sight ahead, dropping her cloak and stalking toward the security line like the freaking goddess of war.

"Ah piss," he heard Jaeger mutter somewhere nearby.

"By the authority of the Order Excalibur," Iveera called at the guards, not slowing, "I order you to stand down and clear the way."

For a second, Nate thought the raw intensity of her command might actually do the trick. But after a comradely glance betwixt the two Troglodan guards on the line, the big bastards stepped forward to meet Iveera, refusing to back down—to a Gorgon, or a Knight, or just in general, Nate didn't know. Whatever their plan, though, they didn't make it farther than baring their ugly teeth before Iveera clamped an open hand to each of their oversized heads and dropped the pair of them like two heaping piles of butcher's scraps.

Nate couldn't tell if it was the work of concealed contact stun weapons or just some frightening feat of empath sorcery. More importantly, neither could the rest of the guards.

They all shuffled back a few startled steps, weapons held ready but not quite pointing at the Gorgon. *Come*, Iveera said quietly in Nate's mind. Then she strode forward, ignoring the guards completely, not slowing as she passed through the lightly crackling disruptor field.

Nate shook himself loose from his mental notes on How to Win Stand-offs and Scare the Shit Out of Everybody, glanced sideways at Jaeger, and moved to follow her. They dropped their cloaks at the same time, Jaeger beckoning the rest of the team to do the same and fall in. Nate didn't look back to see what the others thought of all this—just kept his eyes forward and his strained peripheral attention on the guards, trying to look Knightly and confident as he strode into their ranks.

The guards thought about trying to stop them. Nate could practically feel their quiet conflict building in the air. His eyes snapped to an Atlantean who'd started to shift his weapon, and to his surprise, the strong-jawed demigod of a man flinched back, dropping his gaze to the deck.

Nate marched on, insides straight up gelatin, and tickling with an odd trill as they passed through the disruptor field and into the hangars.

"Not exactly what I had in mind for an escape plan," Jaeger said quietly beside him, dark eyes tersely scanning the hangar crowd, checking their six, and finally settling dead ahead, where an entire goddamn battalion of Forge Security uniforms were waiting for them at the mouth of the *Camelot's* docking platform. Too many to quickly count, all stacked up behind a blaster cannon that was enormous enough to merit its own tripod. The Hobdan behind the trigger studs looked like he was dying to find out what the thing could do, and the Androtta who might've been in command beside him didn't particularly look like he intended to stop him.

On their flanks, more blue and gray uniforms were swarming out of the crowd, hedging them in as the rest of their party came through the pale blue disruptor field. Iveera marched on ahead, unperturbed, until she finally halted a few meters in front of the mounted cannon and its salivating Hobdan gunner, crossed her arms, and looked up at something above the gathered forces.

"Allow us to depart peacefully," she called, loud enough for the entire hangar bay to hear, "and no one need be harmed here. By the authority of the Order Excalibur, in the name of the Lady, we are on a time-sensitive mission, critical to the survival of the Alliance. Do you understand, lieutenant?"

The only thing any of them seemed to understand was that they had the biggest gun in the hangar bay.

"I understand only that the authority you seek to invoke has been temporarily suspended by the First Knight of your Order," the Androtta replied in its mechanical tone, violet-orange eye sparks unfaltering, business as usual. "Therefore, on behalf of the Joint Justice of the Galactic Alliance..."

Shield your people, came Iveera's voice as he spoke, *and get them aboard the Camelot.*

"... I hereby order you to lay down all armaments and—"

Iveera leapt skyward before Nate could ask how exactly the hell he was supposed to do either of those things, moving so fast that he only barely tracked the exotic staff weapon she called her *gaija* unfolding into her hands. Before he could blink, she'd broken the *gaija* into its constituent blades and was whirling around like an airborne dervish, one *gaija* blade rocketing out on a line of crackling blue energy like some kind of Jedi *kusarigama.* There was a sound not unlike a lightsaber hacking through a well-appointed battle droid, the Joint Justice League of Hangar Bay C-9 all staring up at Iveera for one slack-jawed instant. And then the entire damn docking platform fell out from under them.

Nate reached out a helpless hand, gaping at the glowing orange edge of superheated metal, and at the flailing, wide-eyed security army suddenly plunging to their doom. But Iveera was already plunging after them on gravitonic wings, lashing out with the same thin gray gravitonic whip she'd used on him at their first meeting. It sped after the falling platform faster than seemed physically possible, steel vertebrae segments lengthening from e-dim as it went, and snagged taut, jerking Iveera a few feet downward, like she'd just caught something incredibly heavy.

An army of vicious expletives and raw alien cries rang out below.

And they weren't the only ones.

If not for Iveera's warning, Nate might've been too stunned to react when their Forge Security flankers got over their own shock enough to level their weapons on him and the rest of the Eagle's Nest crew. Instead, he found himself lunging to the rear of the group, hands thrown out protectively, mind howling a desperate mantra of *shields, shields, shields!*

A wide swath of blue-green energy barrier hummed into existence just as the entire hangar bay opened fire, a hail of sizzling bolts splashing across his barrier like crackling lava. Blue for stun? He didn't know. In his mind's eye, he saw the smoking bodies of the Trogs he'd dropped with sizzling blue blaster bolts back in Atlantis.

"Bring the ship around!" he barked into his comms, not really sure who he was shouting to. The *Camelot*. Tessa. The Lady herself. *Someone* needed to get that boarding hatch closer to the molten edge of their missing hangar platform.

"Ship's mag-locked, kid!" Jaeger shouted somewhere behind him, Tessa's voice echoing much the same over the comms.

Perhaps we might try a useful order, Ex added, as if he actually thought it was a helpful suggestion amid the storm of blaster fire and guards pressing in, constricting, concentrating fire, seeking to rupture his barrier. Nate thrust his hands out harder, defiant, willing his raw panic into... Nothing. No Force push. No magical shock wave blast. Just a dozen blaster bolts per second, and—

"—thing to use as a bridge!" someone was shouting.

It happened so quickly Nate wasn't rightly sure it was even his doing. One second, he was whipping around, thinking desperate thoughts of Autobots and e-dim magic. The next, the *Camelot* was extending a plated metal walkway like Optimus Prime himself rolling out the red carpet.

"Let's go, people!" Jaeger cried, jabbing one hand toward the handy new boarding bridge and using the other to yank a slack-jawed Snuffy back to reality. "All aboard! Come on, Nate!"

Which sounded like a damn good plan, right up until Nate turned back to his barrier and took in the armada of guards who'd just decided to say *screw it* and charge.

Nate backpedaled, preparing to trade energy barriers for armored fists. The first two Androtta sprang forward, brandishing crackling batons. Nate cocked a fist, then drew up short as something slammed to deck beside him and disgorged a thrumming blast of gravitonic fury. Just like that, Iveera was at his side, and the rest of the guards were on their asses.

"Go," she said, in a tone that left no room for argument.

Nate turned and ran for the *Camelot's* thin bridge, sparing a dizzying glance below to where the severed docking platform had been deposited on the next level down, many of its disgruntled passengers dusting themselves off and collecting their scattered weapons. He faltered, thinking to turn back and cover Iveera's retreat, then flinched low as her smoldering gaija line flashed by overhead, searing through the mag lock arm on the *Camelot's* dorsal surface like a striking viper.

Back on the hangar deck, the cries and whines of discharging blasters redoubled, answered by another casually devastating grav pulse from Iveera's extended hand even as she lashed out with her gaija and severed the last mag lock arm. Nate watched with Looney-Tunes-esque surprise as the *Camelot* lurched free with a sharp crack, the bridge dropping out from beneath his feet as the ship settled onto its own gravitonics and his hand reflexively shot out and caught onto a hull-side handhold that may or may not have been there an instant earlier.

They were *free*, he realized in a rush.

I just hope the old man got the tractor beam out of commission, added Han Solo's voice in his head, shortly followed by a sharp bark of, "Get in here, kid!" from the open hatchway several meters aft, where Jaeger was waving furiously for Nate to get his shit together and start moving.

Which sounded like a singularly fantastic idea.

Nate shifted on his impromptu handhold, preparing to gun his thrusters even as he reached out to call for Iveera. He'd barely moved an inch when the weight of the entire world crushed in on him, like the air itself had suddenly frozen solid. He jerked to a halt against the invisible force, all but paralyzed, and realized the entire hangar had fallen still and silent—civilians gaping out from whatever cover they'd found while their disgruntled station security protectors quietly picked themselves up from the deck, all of them focused on one point just outside of Nate's view.

Oh, blackened hands, Ex muttered, adjusting the view on Nate's helmet display to show him the source of all the fuss.

Zedavian Kelkarin stood at the still-glowing edge of the severed docking platform, one hand casually draped in Nate's direction, attention fixed firmly on Iveera, who hovered before him, glowing gaija at the ready.

"Explain," was all he said.

Then invisible hands ripped Nate from the side of the *Camelot* and sent him hurtling across the yawning gap to slam down to his knees, right at the First Knight's feet.

CHAPTER 21
DESPERATE TIMES

"I gave you an order, Ser Knight," said Zedavian Kelkarin, in the dead silence of the hangar bay, towering over Nate with the deadly calm of a vengeful god.

From his lowly position on his knees, Nate turned to see Iveera hovering there, gaija held uncertainly at her side, and was quickly rewarded with another inexorable wave of force that smashed him face-down to the deck. Gravitonics? He couldn't even tell. It felt like freaking magic. Like he was being Force-smacked by Palpatine himself.

It is not magic, Nathaniel, Ex said. *He is every bit as mortal as you. Albeit several orders of magnitude stronger and more skilled with his Excalibur.*

Thank. You. For. That. Nate grounded out as he struggled to peel his megaton arms from the deck and get his hands under him. By some supreme force of will, he managed to start pushing himself up, at which point he saw that the First Knight had finally pried his gaze away from Iveera to watch Nate's struggles with something between disgust and amusement.

By Zedavian's will, then, Nate realized.

The bastard was toying with him.

"Look at yourselves," the Eldari Knight said, focusing his keen eyes back on Iveera. "Do you even realize what you're doing? How perniciously it spreads to your every thought and action?"

"Says… you," Nate grunted, fighting his way back to his knees. "The First Knight who sold his Merlin down the river."

He wasn't sure why he said it, what he was trying to prove—or even what Zedavian meant for certain. It just came out, ushering in a new silence. One that left him tensed, positive Zedavian would crush him back down for his insolence. His mind churned on with half-cocked escape plans even as his inner realist pointed out that there was no way in hell he was about to slip out from under the First Knight's thumb. He'd seen how fast Iveera could move, after all. There was no reason to believe Zedavian wouldn't be on par. Or faster.

"Is that what you think, Seven?" Zedavian finally asked, still watching Iveera. "That I am the traitor here?"

This time, Nate looked without looking, his display accommodating so that he could see Iveera without turning his head. She hovered there, unmoving, flattened jin tight and wrought with inner conflict.

Zedavian huffed in what might've been amusement, or maybe exasperation. "Very well, then. I *order* you to end this madness and release your armaments. In the name of the Lady, by all the power vested in me as First Knight and acting Merlin of this sacred Order, I *command* you to land here this instant and surrender."

Again, he watched her, waiting expectantly, as if there were simply no way she would—or even *could*—disobey. Waiting almost… eagerly. But Iveera made no move to land. Only shifted her gaija, ready to move, her inaction speaking the defiance her lips wouldn't. Nate tensed, waiting for the golden hammer to fall. Around the hangar bay, the assembled security forces did the same, shifting from wary sideways glances to more deliberate aims, ready to support the First Knight. But Zedavian didn't attack. Didn't even scowl, or curse, or do anything that Nate would've expected of a scorned commander.

He only began to smile, of all things—a slow, soft curl of the lips that bordered somewhere between amazed and deranged as it grew.

"I don't believe it," he murmured softly to himself.

"We are not slaves, Zedavian," Iveera said. "If you will not hear me, if you would truly demand I choose between the Order and my duty to the Lady, then I fear we have arrived at an irrevocable end."

Zedavian's smile only grew, building with amusement and something like wonder, building until his shoulders were positively shaking with it. Idly, Nate wondered if the Eldari was strong enough to put the gravitonic freeze on Iveera too.

I think we'd best prepare to move, regardless, Ex said, only deepening Nate's sinking feeling that the chuckling First Knight was indeed about to crack.

"Very good," Zedavian said, nodding slowly to himself, not seeming to notice as Nate tested his own gravitonic shackles. "I cannot allow you to leave, of course, but this has been most…"

He was still searching for the word when the first brilliant blue bolt lanced from the *Camelot*'s prow with a startlingly loud crack-hiss, nearly blinding as it washed over them, punching into Zedavian and…

And *nothing*, Nate saw, gasping for breath, insides still spasming with the electric fury of the passing shot as his brain caught up and realized the golden bastard had just caught the blast on one raised hand. He caught the three that followed, too. Palmed each furious bolt casually as fielding a string of softballs, then reached out with his other hand and plucked up the spectral phantom Nate hadn't even noticed the charging in on his flank.

There was a crackling sound and an acrid smell of burning, then Malfar the justicar sputtered into plain view, suspended a meter over the deck by Zedavian's unshaking hand and grunting with effort as he kicked fruitlessly at the First Knight's side. A thrumming rush and Iveera's grav whip caught Zedavian's ship-facing hand, cinching tight like a coiling serpent, catching him in an open cruciform.

Nate fought against Zedavian's invisible hold, readying his repulsors.

"Do it!" Malfar roared, and another brilliant blue bolt tore out of the *Camelot* and took Zedavian right in the chest. Nate gasped as the periphery of the blast washed over him, fighting against the spasms, entirely more focused on the loosening gravitonic resistance at his back. He thrust his repulsors out, blinking his fried eyes clear… and faltered at what he saw.

Zedavian was laughing—not stunned and staggering but full-on *laughing* at them—like he'd found himself under assault by nothing more than a squadron of snuggly puppies, Malfar's limp bulk still dangling effortlessly in his hand, out cold from the spillover of the last blast.

Nate gaped from the First Knight to his own charging repulsors, tasting the futility, electrified mind grasping for something—anything—that might throw Zedavian for a loop. And there it was, staring him right in the face from the corner of Half-Cocked and Crazy.

Nathaniel, I don't know how—

Just try, he growled, already lunging forward from his knees.

He wasn't sure exactly what he was expecting as he caught hold of Zedavian's golden ankle, pouring the entirety of his will into his wild half-plan. Black veins of corruption flowing from his gauntlets to Zedavian's pristine greaves, maybe. Jittery glitches running through their adjoined armor. Something. Anything. Anything to put the bastard off balance.

But nothing happened.

Nothing but the cold fall of dread over his heart as Zedavian looked down at him. Looked at him like he knew *exactly* what Nate had just tried to do and simply couldn't believe that anyone—even a stupid, lowly Terran—could be so foolish as to have actually tried it.

"You little shit," the First Knight finally murmured, his tone more astonished than anything else. Sensing what was about to happen, Nate threw his hands to the deck, shoving back. Too late.

Zedavian's kick was as casual as it was lightning fast—an understated flick of the foot that tagged him at the chest and turned the world into an instant blur. Bone-shaking impact and the coppery taste of blood were the next things that made any coherent sense in the chaos, shortly followed by the dizzy realization that he'd just struck the far side of the hangar bay hard enough to indent the bulkhead, and that it seemed a minor marvel his brain hadn't liquefied on impact.

You can thank our gravitonic "magic" for that, Ex said. *Now, were you planning to sit here all day, or would you like to help your friends?*

Nate tried to focus, his vision fighting him in odd dips and blurs as he took in the dizzying drop of open hangar space below, and the gold-and-copper whirlwind raging across it. Iveera and Zedavian moved in a blur of their own, too fast for human eyes to follow, trading blows with a storm of sound like a rapid-fire string of crashing cars. All of it oddly muffled, like they were moving so fast, they'd entered a world of their own.

Then there was an especially sharp crash, and Iveera smashed into the wall right next to him like a speeding bullet. *We should leave,* came her voice in his mind, entirely too calm and collected as she shook off the blow. *Quickly.*

No arguing with that, at least. Especially not as she wrenched free from her own deep indent and launched back across the bay at a waiting Zedavian with a commanding, *Get to your ship. Now.*

He pulled himself from his Nate-shaped nook in the wall, teetering between going directly after her or following the order. Then they met in another incomprehensible flurry of blows below and made his mind for him. He leapt for the *Camelot*, gunning his repulsors across the gaping drop of the hangar below, and landed roughly on the dorsal hull a few breathless seconds later. He spun, taking aim with his wrist blasters.

Get inside, Iveera hissed in his head, sounding properly strained now. *Use the Camelot.*

Nate glanced from his suddenly dainty-looking blasters to the ship, unable to argue her logic, unsure how quickest to get to the bridge. No sooner had he started looking for the nearest hatch, though, than he felt Cammy's frenetic intelligence there, querying his intent.

Let me in, he thought, not really sure what he was expecting—pretty sure in that moment, in fact, that he was as hopelessly useless now as he ever had been on Earth. But then the hull rippled at his feet, and he was simply sliding through, the *Camelot* absorbing him like a giant metallic phagocyte, interstitial paneling and hardware all smoothly parting to let him pass until Cammy spat him out on the other side.

He was nearly as surprised as Tessa looked when he smacked down to a heavy landing on the bridge deck, right behind her control station.

"Oh, hey," was all she managed.

Nate just rounded back in Iveera's rough direction, dimly aware of Jaeger barking orders from somewhere down the hallway, far more focused on feeding Cammy his next request. He felt the turrets reorienting. Felt it almost as if it were happening within him. Saw the feed in his helmet display, reticle forming on the clashing Knights outside.

"Uh, wait, are we sure we wanna—" Tessa started, but then Zedavian and Iveera broke apart from a storm of blows, and time slowed, beckoning Nate to take his shot while he had it.

Fire, he told Cammy. And fire she did.

Zedavian dodged the first bright emerald barrage so reflexively that he seemed genuinely surprised as he turned to track the damage it left slagged across the hangar behind him. Nate felt his own surprise blossoming, tinged with a cold horror at the realization of what he'd just done. Iveera was already speeding in to take advantage of Zedavian's lull, but he was ready, diverting her grabbing hands with what must've been a gravitonic parry.

Her diverted hands didn't go far, though, before they snapped back in place, as if caught in a magnetic eddy—gold and copper gauntlets locked mere centimeters apart, the air distorting oddly between them. Then Iveera lashed out with her grav whip, catching a nearby docking platform by a support strut and spinning through a complicated maneuver, Zedavian recoiling in surprise, and the warping force detonated between them with a low boom.

They both went flying, Zedavian cratering the hangar wall toward the bazaar, Iveera crashing port side into the *Camelot*, hard enough that Nate swore he felt it, almost like a punch to the side.

Go, he heard her groan, in his mind or via helmet comms, he couldn't tell. He was too busy nearly biting it as he turned to head for the hatch and found his feet half-immersed in the solid deck. He tripped his way clear, staggering into a sprint.

"Get ready to punch it outta here," he shouted over his shoulder at Tessa, no time to question what his ship was doing.

"Punch it out of where?!" she cried after him. "They're sealing down the—"

But he was already thundering out of earshot, past the ramp outside, bound for the main hatch, moving so fast he nearly plowed into Amelia and Snuffy as he rounded into the entryway. He felt a wave of relief as he caught sight of a battered Iveera hauling the unconscious Troglodan justicar in through the hatch. Then he took in the armada of Forge Security raising their weapons beyond, and the golden form launching out of the crumpled hangar wall, and the urgency clutched right back at his heart.

"Go," Iveera hissed, tossing the justicar to the deck. "Now."

"Let's move, people!" Nate cried—almost exactly as Jaeger barked the same words.

Jaeger shot him a startled *that's my line* look, followed by a terse, "Where the hell you'd come from?"

Then a hail of blaster bolts hammered into the *Camelot*, scorching the edge of the open hatchway, and they all took off for the bridge at a hard run.

"Punch it!" Nate cried as they thundered onto the bridge, the crew diving for their crash couches. "Get us the hell out of here!"

"Through what hole do you see us punching it?" Tessa snapped back, jabbing at a flashing red holo schematic that, amongst other things, included the words *hangar* and *lockdown*. Nate was considering the tight flight corridor and the distant hangar wall through the viewport ahead, numbly wondering what the harm was in one more act of war, when a rushing torrent of blue lanced out from the side of the ship, screaming down that long flight corridor, and punched a molten, *Camelot*-sized hole through the distant wall.

"I didn't do it!" Tessa cried, hands jerking into the air from her controls.

"Just go!" Nate and Jaeger both shouted.

Cammy was already punching it with a vigor that would've made Chewie proud. The *Camelot* roared with cosmic power, leaping forward—

only to lurch to an immediate, violent halt as something caught them in a King Kong sized death hug.

Zedavian, Nate realized, as Cammy conjured a port side holo window.

The First Knight hovered there, holding the roaring *Camelot* in place by the rigid end of the gravitonic lasso he'd just whipped around the ship's prow. He barely even looked strained. Looked, if anything, like he was only beginning to enjoy himself as he materialized a preposterously large blaster cannon from e-dim, plopped it to one shoulder, and casually took aim at the *Camelot*.

"That," Tessa muttered, "is one hell of a big gun."

"Shields," Nate heard himself hiss, echoing the thought more deliberately at Cammy along with a vague prayer to *punch it harder, Jesus, punch it* and get them the hell out of there. But even as he thought it, Zedavian's cannon began to glow—gold, some distant corner of his mind noted—and certainty struck in the rising whine and groan of the *Camelot*'s straining engines:

They were boned.

"Big gun, guys," Tessa was shouting. "*Big* gun!"

Her last words stretched oddly, time slowing as Nate turned from Zedavian's incandescent charging barrel, reaching for Ex's guidance, looking reflexively to Iveera… only to realize she wasn't there.

Shock and panic crested over Snuffy's shouting about how he wasn't ready to die in space, highlighting the collective death clench holding the entire bridge captive, drowning out Ex's streamlined something about *diverting power* and *destructive harmonics*. It occurred to Nate's screaming mind that he was the only one who hadn't had the good sense to strap into a crash couch.

Then a hissing blue *something* flashed by the holo window, and the Camelot sprang forward with a sharp cracking sound and a grateful roar of unfettered engines.

Nate had one last dilated moment to glimpse the unfathomable look on Zedavian's face. One last moment to feel that macabre certainty as steady golden hands tracked them with the raging supernova waiting to tear free from that barrel and consume them all.

Then they were rocketing out of sight down the flight corridor fast enough that even Cammy's sophisticated gravitonic inertial dampeners couldn't save Nate from staggering backward for balance. He caught himself on one knee just in time to register the shimmering emerald energy barrier that'd sprung to life ahead, across the gaping hole that someone—

Iveera, he suddenly realized—had blown through the hangar wall. Before he could utter so much as an *oh shit*, though, the *Camelot*'s prow tore through that emerald barrier like it was nothing, spitting them out into space like a ship-sized torpedo cutting into the black.

Straight into an ocean of Alliance fighters.

CHAPTER 22
RELAY RACE

The first scarlet lances of fighter fire splashed across the *Camelot's* energy shields, and the ship took a sharp dive under a massive external docking arm, buying them a moment's cover. They reemerged, screaming past sealed Forge Station hangar bays and a blur of cargo freighters and transports, all of them skittering for safety from the sudden violence.

"Eight drones in pursuit," Iveera announced from the nest of holo controls she'd spawned the instant she'd charged into the bridge, demanding full control of the ship. "More inbound."

Nausea roiled in Nate's stomach, watching the outside world of stars and Alliance superstructures spin and whip by in stark contrast to the steady pull of the artificial gravity at his feet and the more tenuous waves of Cammy's on-the-fly gravitonic inertial negation.

"Oh-shit-oh-shit-oh-shit," came a steady mantra from behind, seemingly in agreement with Nate's stomach.

"Shut it, Snuffy!" Tessa snapped.

"We just committed treason," came another incredulous voice. Amelia's. She was strapped down beside Elmo, looking like she'd just woken up and realized it hadn't all been a bad dream after all. "*I* just committed treason."

"Shut it, everyone!" Jaeger barked, before turning his Lt Col glare on Nate and Iveera from his crash couch. "You two have a plan to shake an entire goddamn fleet?"

"Calm yourself, John," was all Iveera said, her tone so perfectly flat and her every finger and jin so busy at work with the sea of holo controls floating around her that all anyone could do for a moment was stare, silently.

"Shots fired," Snuffy finally murmured back in his corner.

Then Iveera threw the *Camelot* into a hard barrel roll, gravitonics straining to keep up as she dipped them tight along the irregular underbelly of what looked to be the Capital Island's main cargo docks. The trailing fighter drones coughed a steady stream of crimson fire at their tail.

"ACTIVE CLOAKING ENGAGED," Cammy declared on Nate's helmet display and pretty much every other display on the bridge, right before Iveera yanked them into a violent switchback. They pulled clear from the Forge, angling around into open space, roughly bound for the main stream of traffic headed for one of the system's two gargantuan Beacon relay superstructures. Their pursuit raced right past, fanning out in a confused search pattern even as two more swarms of remote fighter drones swept in to join the hunt for the Knight ship that'd just dropped clean off their sensors.

"All right," Jaeger said. "Don't suppose that's gonna convince the fleet out there to just pretend like we *aren't* headed straight for the only two—"

"The fleet is scarcely our foremost concern," Iveera said, which seemed like a bold statement, as multiple sections of Nate's in-helmet display dialed in on the growing number of red blips on the viewport. Around the relay, several enormous Alliance warships were altering course to cut off all approach vectors from the station.

That seemed plenty damn concerning. At least until Cammy warbled another alert and keyed yet another holo window to show them Ser Golden Halo Kelkarin speeding after them from the Forge.

"Persistent bastard," Jaeger muttered, as another golden blip appeared on the holo, indicating that the First Knight's ship, the *Eldest Stone*, was also rapidly inbound from the other side of the Capital Island.

"Why am I getting déjà vu?" Tessa asked over the rest of the crew's uneasy murmurs.

Jaeger opened his mouth like he was about to tell them all to stow the chatter, then frowned instead, looking around the bridge. "Speaking of which, where the hell's the Troglodan?"

"If everyone could kindly shut their oral orifices," Iveera said over the sea of peaking mutters, "I am going to attempt to microjump us to safety."

"*Attempt?*" Nate heard Snuffy whisper over in the corner. He paid the mechanic no mind. He was too busy watching Zedavian rocket after them in the rearview, silently praying to the Lady.

Praying right up until the *Camelot*'s engines gave a sputtering rattle and died.

"Is this part of it?" Snuffy asked hopefully, even as the groan of dying electronics filled the bridge, some displays and lights flickering, most going out completely, casting them into sudden darkness.

ALERT, Cammy cried. *INTRUDER. INTRUUUU...*

Cammy's voice drained from Nate's mind as if she'd run out of batteries.

"What the—" Nate started, then abandoned the effort to instead clutch at thin air as the ship groaned again, and his feet left the deck. Weightless. Gravitonics dead.

"Blackened hands," Iveera hissed under her breath, whipping around like she'd just remembered something of vital importance. Her electric blue eyes cut through the panicked chatter of the crew and landed squarely on Amelia Sundercaste, who flinched under her stare, wide eyes darting back and forth between the viewport and Iveera like a frightened puppy who didn't understand what it'd done.

"Cammy?" Jaeger called up at the darkness like he didn't really expect it would answer. "You got a sitrep?"

"She's down, sir," Tessa said, confirming what Nate already felt as she futzed with the single display that was still flickering over her control consoles.

The intruder must have sabotaged Cammy's control nexus belowdecks, Ex said.

Nate's brain stutter-stepped down to the room of complicated conduits and whirring machinery that he'd only briefly had time to marvel at in his first full tour of the ship.

"Looks like we're on manual pilot for the moment," Tessa was saying, "but uh…"

"Without engines," Iveera finished for her, snapping back from her thoughts.

"Right," Tessa agreed. "That."

Iveera rounded on Nate with flinch-worthy intensity. "The justicar," she hissed. "He'll be in the nexus. Go now and stop him."

Nate, who'd mostly been floating like a baseless amoeba counting each precious second Zedavian was gaining on them, glanced from Amelia to Iveera to the rear of the ship, not following the logic one bit, but also pretty sure the *who* and *why* of the matter was absolutely unimportant at the moment.

He had to get down to the nexus.

"Go!" Iveera snapped, not looking away from her dizzying work. "You, Lieutenant Kalders," she added, flicking a few holo panes toward Tessa's consoles, which sputtered tentatively back to life. "Take the controls while I restore critical systems."

Tessa gave a *hey, why the hell not* shrug and took her fighter-jet-style control sticks with an, "Aye, aye, Ser Knight. But what about the engin—"

The words weren't even out of her mouth when Iveera finished working whatever holo magic she was working, and the *Camelot*'s engines roared back to life, throwing the ship forward and Nate backward with all the unforgiving force of true, undampened inertia. He hit the rear bulkhead like an armored sack of potatoes, vision going spotty as his heart struggled to keep up with the crushing acceleration.

You might want to brace yourself, Ex said, several seconds too late. *Might I recommend your personal gravitonics?*

Gravitonics, Nathaniel, Iveera added in his head scoldingly, before he could begin thanking Ex for his oh-so-helpful advice. *Get moving.*

Nate stowed his bickering and pried his head from the wall, trying to focus. Both took more effort than expected. Off to the left, Elmo had passed out in his crash couch. Snuffy didn't look far behind. Nate pushed them from his mind as best he could and focused on the thought of gravity's steady embrace, cocooning him from the ship's acceleration, holding him steady on the deck, business as usual.

It worked about as smoothly as expected, given how poorly he'd handled Ex's gravitonics in their rushed practice sessions, but there was at least a marginal wave of relief. More careful thought, and he managed to unpin himself from the wall and come to something like a controlled hover just above the deck. Iveera brought something else online, and the teetering balance became something workable.

"Go, kid!" Jaeger grunted, watching him out of the very corner of his eye from where the crash couch had immobilized his head against the crushing acceleration. The backseat Knighting might've been more annoying if Jaeger hadn't looked a few shades shy of passing out himself, but a deep groan from the belly of the ship reminded Nate just how much none of that mattered right then.

Golden Knight behind, saboteur below, and an entire Alliance fleet ahead.

Nate thrust himself out of the bridge and lurched off down the corridor like a drunken ghost on gravitonic wings, racing to go handle the one problem he could.

Be vigilant, came Iveera's voice in his head as he went. *I suspect the justicar and the Atlantean have both been manipulated by hostile minds. An Ooperian glamour, most likely.*

Ooperian—Nate lost control, bounced off the ceiling, clipped a wall, and skidded to a halt at the top of the ramp to the lower decks. *Glamoured, like... Like, fucking* vampire *glamoured? And you're just now—*

Just keep your eyes open and get your ship online, she snapped, attention clearly strained. *Broad-spectrum optics,* she added, just in case he'd forgotten the Ooperians' other tricks.

"Well fuck," Nate muttered as she withdrew from their contact, eyeing the dark descent belowdecks with a visceral chill. "Down the creepy hatch, then, I guess."

Preferably before the inevitable heat death of the universe, Ex added pointedly.

As if to punctuate the point, the *Camelot* lurched into a hard maneuver, lifting him a meter off the deck before he caught up with his shaky gravitonics. He shook the jitters off and launched down the rampway, trying to keep up as Tessa threw the ship into a roll, and the walls tilted dizzily around him. He skipped off the deck, caught onto the bulkhead at the "bottom" of the ramp, and levered himself around into the next corridor like swinging on a branch.

"Sure, come right on aboard, Mr. Malfar, sir," he muttered to himself, fighting down motion sickness as he glided down a narrow, wobbly systems corridor. "No, don't mind Nate. Not like it's his ship or anything. And oh, what's that? You've been mind-controlled by killer space vampires? That's okay. I'm sure that—Shit!"

The *Camelot* shuddered with what felt like a series of direct hits on the unshielded hull, and Nate missed the handhold he'd been reaching for. He over-corrected with the gravitonics and spent a jerky few meters making like a pinball until finally thudding to a landing on the wall just outside the sealed door his dizzy brain identified as the ship's nexus room.

You mind? he asked Ex.

There was a moment's unresponsive silence, then: *No such luck. Your turn.*

More blasts rattled the *Camelot,* demanding action.

Nate drove an armored boot into the door and was immediately rewarded with a hard lesson in both Newtonian mechanics and gravitonic directionality. The corridor spun, smacking the back of his head with the floor before he pancaked into the opposite wall with a bone-shaking thud—all to Ex's tangible amusement, even in the midst of their *sinking ship* desperation.

"Quickly, Nathaniel," came Iveera's voice, over the comms this time.

If only there were some way to cut through troublesome doors, Ex said, *or to stabilize yourself properly.*

Nate gritted his teeth, righted himself in front of the door with gravitonics, and leveled one armored hand, channeling all of his frustration into laser-tight, plasma cutting thoughts. He let rip. A blinding beam of white-hot fury tore from the aperture on his palm, dimming his HUD and splashing him with an unexpectedly sudden blast of heat. He moved quickly, tracing the outline of the door, too rattled by everything happening outside to really tell if he'd cut fully through or not. It hardly mattered, he decided, killing the beam and fixing back on his gravitonic control.

If Iveera could catch an entire goddamn docking platform and a few dozen guards in midair, he could sure as hell take on one obstinate little door.

So he lowered his shoulder and gunned the gravitonics, harder than he'd ever done. Harder than might've been strictly necessary, it seemed, as the corridor blurred, and the door gave way like a piece of cheap plastic. He smashed into the opposite wall, severed door pinned before him like a big shield, and blinked his way through a cloud of chirping tweety birds.

Across the nexus, Malfar didn't even look up from where he was strapped to the ship's innards by a few hastily-tied crash restraints, hard at work with an unidentified blunt object and a violently single-minded focus. Several mechanical manipulator arms were poised around him, frozen in place from the walls and ceiling, like Cammy had been reaching to stop the Troglodan just before he'd knocked her offline.

"Hey!" Nate shouted.

The Troglodan didn't seem to hear him—no more than he seemed to notice his thick legs and torso smacking against Cammy's frozen manipulator arms with each bludgeoning swing of his instrument, or the droplets of blood peeling from his battered fingers and trailing off to the rear bulkhead opposite their acceleration like some macabre jet steam.

There was definitely something wrong with Malfar.

"Bastards," the Troglodan slurred in a drunken growl, raising his bloodied weapon for another swing.

Nate launched across the nexus, caught him by his thick wrists, and yanked them both away from the *Camelot*'s vital innards with a firm gravitonic thrust. They yanked to a halt on Malfar's restraints, the Troglodan immediately wriggling to break free from Nate's grip. But only half-heartedly. With the strength of his Excalibur armor on hand, Nate knew he could out-muscle a Troglodan if push came to shove, but the way Malfar moved, it was almost as if the justicar were already at war with himself.

"Bastards…" he groaned, jerking erratically. "Jumped mmm… Sleep."

Nate severed the restraints with a careful pulse from his handy plasma cutters and hauled the Troglodan across the room, pinning him to the wall, taking stock of Malfar's beady, unfocused eyes, his alien face eerily vacant even as his mouth worked nonsensically and his body continued its half-hearted struggles.

He could've been sleepwalking. Or a Trog zombie.

At least until he bucked against Nate's restraining hands with a savage roar in a moment of frightening clarity. "Stun me!" he boomed, gripping the back of Nate's head with one huge hand.

Nate didn't argue. Just tagged Malfar with two darts from the nifty little wrist launcher Ex helped him conjure up with his finest sleepy thoughts.

"Not… leave… here," Malfar groaned, the sedative taking effect surprisingly quickly. Then he collapsed against Nate, well over two-hundred kilos of solid Troglodan.

"Well, that was weird," Nate grunted, sliding Malfar's weight safely down to the deck and wondering what kind of restraints he might conjure from their e-dim stores.

There's something else, Ex said.

What kind of something?

Biosynthetic explosives, unless my readings are scrambled.

He froze. *What, like…* He stared down at the slack pile of Troglodan bulk in his hands. *Like,* inside *him?*

Precisely.

Nate staggered back, raising his hands in reflexive defense. *What the hell do I do?! Is he about to—*

Detonate? A very brief eternity passed. *Oh, he definitely could. But not spontaneously. There will be a—*

"What's the holdup, kid?" Jaeger's voice cut in through the comms, startling Nate halfway across the room.

There will be a signal, Ex finished calmly. *Electromagnetic. The source would need to be rather close. On a pursuing ship, assuming the culprits are not suicidal. Or perhaps—*

"Are we down one saboteur or not?" Jaeger continued.

A pair of deep coughs rocked the deck from somewhere aft, like something had just thunked into the ship's hull, or...

Or perhaps aboard a departing escape pod, Ex concluded, with a grim tone of certainty.

"Oh shit," Nate whispered, chest tightening as the words sank in.

"Oh shit? Kid, I'm gonna need—"

Nate didn't exactly *mean* to mute Jaeger, but his subconscious must've thought about it hard enough, somewhere beneath the sudden screaming need to defuse—

—*shield*—

—the ticking—

—*electromagnetically triggered*—

—time bomb—

—*not a time bomb*—

—before—

Are you even paying attention, Nathaniel?

Nate was opening his mouth to snap back when the thought finally landed. A Faraday cage. They needed a Faraday cage, right this second.

As I was saying.

"Just help me!" Nate cried, thrusting his open hands toward Malfar, trying to convince himself that if Iveera and Zedavian could summon sophisticated e-dim cells from thin air, he should at least be able to manage a couple restraints and a simple wire mesh. He focused on the mental image of a strong sheet of chicken wire wrapping the Troglodan down to the deck —wonderful, electromagnetic-field-killing loops of wire, encasing the justicar, shutting him off from the nefarious signals of the outside world, and...

And there you have it, Ex said as the enclosure finished unfurling from e-dim, leaving Malfar strapped to the deck beneath a fine mesh weave. *Nothing to fuss over. You get so moody when you're tense, Nathaniel.*

Nate huffed an incredulous laugh, half-giddy relief at the close call, some small part of him still expecting Malfar might just spontaneously explode anyway. Finally, he took a proper breath, shoulders relaxing. They tensed right back up as the *Camelot* shuddered and groaned under a barrage of incoming fire.

When it wasn't one thing...

"Nate?!" Tessa's voice crackled in on comms, more strained than he was accustomed to. "We're gonna need—Just—Ah Christ, just see for yourself."

Ah, Ex said, apparently getting an early preview as he patched Tessa's feed to Nate's in-helmet display. *A full Knightship meld. A rare sight to behold.*

For a moment, he wasn't sure what he was beholding at all through the myriad flashes of blaster fire and searing tracer rounds raging back and forth between the *Camelot* and the swarms of angry fighter drones needling at her from all sides. Then he saw it in the not-so-distant space behind a pair of exploding drones—the golden streak of the *Eldest Stone* hurtling after them, strangely distorted, as if…

"What the shit?" Nate whispered, watching in disbelief as the thing that was supposed to be a ship finished its shapeshifting transformer act in the proud flying form of an honest-to-Christ, King-Midas-edition Gundam mech. Then it reached out for the *Camelot* with one enormous golden hand, closing fast.

CHAPTER 23

MELDED

"I've got it under control, people," Tessa was crying as Nate hoofed it onto the bridge, control stick in hand and a look of deadly, unshakable focus firmly ensconced in her eyes. "Just lie back and think of England. And Snuffy, for the love of Christ, will you stop giving me that look?"

What look? Snuffy's wide-eyed brow-speak beseeched the rest of the crew from his crash couch in the corner. *And how did she even know?*

"You know what look!" Tessa called before he could so much as open his mouth. "I can feel your little Snuffies ducking for cover from here." She yanked at the control stick, hurtling them through a dip and weave that would've left bits of Nate scattered on both walls *and* the deck if he hadn't been too gravitonically clenched to budge. "It's making me wanna move to Canada, man," she added, frowning at the hail of red blaster bolts zipping by the starboard side on the immersive holo panorama she'd managed to conjure around her consoles in lieu of Cammy's bridge-wide displays. "Honestly."

Nate was opening his mouth to give an update or request one—he wasn't even sure which—when he realized that Iveera was missing. And that Zedavian's giant *Eldest Stone* mech was closing in the rearview display. Too damn close, he decided, as a pair of fighter drones cut through the space between the *Camelot* and the *Eldest Stone*'s extended hand and simply imploded, crushed by whatever invisible forces seemed to be tugging at the *Camelot*'s tail, warping the space between them.

Nate sucked in a helpless breath as a nimbus of golden energy pulsed along the *Eldest Stone*'s outstretched arm and lanced forth, streaking straight for them. He heard Tessa's own surprised gasp, felt the Camelot responding, too late. Then a flash of copper streaked across the rearview display of the outer hull, and Iveera was there, hands thrown wide, siphoning a city's worth of raw golden energy straight into what was either e-dim space or a genuine micro-singularity, drinking it in until her armor radiated with it, and Nate was sure she'd collapse or explode under the weight. Instead, she pointed her gaija at the *Stone* and let loose with a tsunami of repurposed emerald destruction. The enormous mech rolled with impressive agility, dodging the worst of the blast and scattering the remainder off its shields in a crackling flare of golden-green brilliance.

Nate gaped from the display back toward the relay ring, where the blockade of Alliance frigates and cruisers was rapidly thickening, the two massive dreadnought capital ships spewing forth waves of fighters and a few targeting lances of emerald plasma that seemed nearly as large as the *Camelot*. He looked back to the bridge and noticed that Amelia's crash couch had been sealed off in its own little opaque cell. Back to Iveera, clamped to the dorsal hull of the *Camelot* via her grav whip now, firing one blinding azure blast after another back at their pursuit like a one-woman blaster turret.

"You call this *under control?*" Nate finally managed, pulling himself over to Tessa's side.

She spared a precious second to shoot him a sky-high eyebrow. "I'm sorry, M'lord, did *you* want to fly this here rudderless bucket of bolts through the alien apocalypse?"

"What happened to 'the finest piece of spaceship ass you'd ever dreamed to—'"

"Your Trog pal trashed every control system *and* its distant cousin down there, for starters."

"*My* Trog pal?" Nate was halfway into jabbing an accusing finger at Jaeger before he remembered himself and tried to shift to helpful thoughts. "Never mind. What do you need me to—"

"Just shut up!" she snapped, throwing the ship into a turn that squeezed a choir of strained groans from the crowd and left Nate clinging on for dear life. "That's kinda creepy, by the way," she added, shooting him a sideways glance as they leveled out. "Don't suppose you could get out there and give us a nice push with those fancy little gravity jets? Stabilizer controls are shot to shit, and main engines are flirting with the dodos."

He looked down at her, trying to decide whether she was joking about the *get out and push* bit, then remembered with an upward glance that Iveera was literally surfing the *Camelot*, smiting torpedoes and ship-sized blaster bolts into the void for them.

Maybe he freaking *should* get out and push.

—*FERENCE!* blurted a mechanical voice before he could.

"Cammy?" Nate half-cried, jerking around in shock before registering the voice had been in his head.

NA...TH-TH-THANIEL?

Lights and displays flickered on across the bridge, then sputtered back out.

"You there, C?" Tessa asked, not looking away from her flying.

CON... FUSED, the disembodied voice uttered. Nate leaned over and saw the word echoed on Tessa's main console display. *NOT... WHOLE.*

"She's still trying to regenerate," Nate reasoned out loud, thinking of the mess of cracked casings and frayed nexus connectors below—a mess Ex had assured him was "not as bad as it looked"—and trying to sound like he actually knew what the hell he was talking about.

Self-regeneration should begin shortly, Ex had said. *Provided we do not explode in the next five minutes.*

They still had a couple of minutes to find out.

NEED... Cammy burbled, voice undulating shakily. *NEED...*

She requires our strength, Nathaniel, Ex said.

Nate glanced up at Iveera's dorsal outpost, not following. *What, you want me to get out and push, too?*

That, or step into the command ring like a real Knight, and let her tap our power directly.

Nate eyed the subtle lip of the two-meter wide circle overlaid on the deck behind Tessa's and Jaeger's de facto command station. The ring, Iveera had explained, was meant to be analogous to a captain's chair for a Knight—once they were sufficiently acclimated with their ship and Excalibur to facilitate a proper merging.

No time like the present, he supposed.

"Help your ship, Nathaniel," Iveera's voice crackled in his helmet comms. "The coordinates are laid. She merely needs—"

A roar of static and a string of groaning impacts raked across the bridge, bringing Iveera up short as she danced across the Camelot, conducting a flashing symphony of blaster fire in and out. Nate hurried to the center of the command circle, anchoring himself firmly to the deck with gravitonics and reaching out to Cammy with open, inviting thoughts, searching anxiously for… something. Anything. Nothing.

Nothing at all.

"—ideas, kid?" Jaeger's voice broke into his third-rate sanctum sanctorum of rushed tranquility, rousing him enough that he almost missed it— the faint brush of Cammy's eclectic presence, like a frightened child reaching for a stranger's hand in the dark.

It was as touching as it was unexpected. Not that he blamed her for being rattled. He wasn't even sure which of them, if either, was the adult in this scenario. He just settled back into that open state as best he could and reached for her hand.

"—HELL'S HE DOING?" The voice was distant, oddly muffled like he was hearing it through several feet of water. "—the hell *is* that thing?"

Close by (or maybe from a hundred meters away), someone growled an incoherent curse.

Focus.

He tried. On some level, Nate was pretty sure he was still gravitonically anchored to the command ring on the *Camelot*'s bridge, where a multitude of spindly-armed *somethings* had grown from the deck and twined into his armor, cradling him like a secondary exoskeleton. But that experience was distant. Disembodied. No particular concern of his at the moment. Not compared to the thrill and accumulating stress of overworked, unregulated thrusters, and the entire humming spectra of electromagnetic and particle radiations showering his hull in a never-ending song of light and lost warmth.

His hull?

Don't freak out.

Ex's voice. And the *Camelot*…

Somewhere far away, a heart was thundering.

You're freaking out.

He *was* the Camelot?

*Well, I wouldn't put it quite—*Ex started.

"Why are we slowing?" someone growled through the murky depths, that thundering heart rocking closer on a confusing swirl of—

Bah, close enough, Ex amended quickly. *You ARE the Camelot. Now take a deep breath and stop clenching before you get us all killed.*

"—don't know!" someone else was snapping. "She's fighting me, sir!"

Tessa.

The thought jarred him back toward the bridge, where his eyes were prying themselves open, searching for something, anything, to orient his mind in the chaos. For one brief moment, he was besieged by an impossible juxtaposition of thrust forces and velocities, flashing mechanical stress alerts, and a million other incomprehensible datums, all soaked through with the raw sensory input of his own body. His mind threatened to tear in two with the dissonance. Then his eyes snapped shut reflexively, his body falling away to that distant place, and the rest rushed in to fill the void.

It was like drinking from a fire hose. Like trying to read that damned green-letter Matrix scrawl. Hundreds, thousands, of moving bodies dancing around them in the never-ending star song of the vast nebula they fled, each with a thousand metrics and factoids—size-weight-speed-crew-name-class-threat-arms-distance-intercept-and—

Focus, Nathaniel.

Ex's voice, tugging him toward the surface. Toward the place where twin dreadnoughts were cruising in to cut off their relay approach, dozens of Hellion fighters and Archon-class frigates leading the charge. Toward the place where they were trapped between a full-scale Alliance war fleet and a vengeful First Knight.

And Cammy wasn't fighting Tessa. *He* was.

"Sir, I think he's…" Tessa was saying somewhere in the distance, beneath the nauseous data swirl raging through his brain so fast he thought he tasted charred gray matter.

Oops.

In the visual feed of the bridge interior, Tessa was glancing from her consoles back toward Meat Suit Nate. "I think he's—Ah shit!"

Nate felt Cammy's proximity sensors flaring like an unnaturally sharp tickle in the tail bone, crying out in alarm as the *Eldest Stone* put on one last burst of speed and caught them by the stern with a violent crash and a horrible wrenching groan of sputtering shields and deforming metal.

It hurt.

It hurt as badly as if the *Stone*'s mighty grip were crushing down on the bony crests of Nate's own hips. He felt the *Camelot* bleeding velocity like a harpooned whale, suddenly dragging a thousand tons of the universe's most flashy golden emergency brakes. And the sharks were circling.

The jump, Nathaniel. Iveera's voice this time, cutting through the crushing pain as she danced across their back, soaking up the brunt of the intensifying fire. *Now. Right now.*

Which sounded damn good to him, given how the entire damn ship was flashing bow-to-stern with hull breaches, shield integrity alerts, and a hundred other alerts he couldn't comprehend. It just didn't fix the tiny little fact that he had no idea how to get the finicky wisp that was Cammy's rebooting presence to step into the light and do it.

Less fussing, more jumping, little hobbit.

Nate blew out a harsh breath, trying to sink beneath the pain, focusing on Cammy.

You have no idea what havoc you have wrought here, you fool, came another voice, somewhere toward the painful surface. Zedavian's voice, some part of him registered. He did his best to ignore it, sinking deeper to the heart of his ship's construct, until he could feel her there on some extrasensory level. She was shaking. Quivering like a frightened animal, confused and fragmented, and almost certainly in no shape to be pulling some sophisticated micro q-jump.

She wasn't ready.

Somewhere on the periphery, he noted the heart of the Alliance forces racing closer, the dreadnoughts' twin gunmetal prows coming alive with a rising emerald glow entirely too reminiscent of a pair of charging Death Stars. He resisted the urge to try to boost their forward shields, reaching instead to offer his hand to Cammy in the internal darkness of their shared nowhere.

It's okay, he thought softly, not really sure what it was he meant by that, only that it felt right in that dark place, with a world of danger screaming in all around them. *It's gonna be okay, Cammy. I'm not going anywhere.*

Nor am I, old friend, Ex added, stirring in the darkness beside them. *Not this time.*

It occurred to Nate that it was the first time he'd ever actually heard Ex speak to anyone that wasn't him. For a moment, it only reminded him just how much he still didn't know about his fated companions, and everything they'd been through before he stumbled along. But that didn't matter right then. No more than the crushing weight of Zedavian's grip on their hull mattered, grinding them to a halt as the dreadnoughts fired.

They watched it all happening from the darkness. Together. Time moving slowly in that place. Emerald columns of destruction creeping toward them through the black, belayed on a deep, foggy certainty that, together, they could fix this—this, and so much more. Together, they were safer. Stronger.

Together, they could be unstoppable.

TR-TR-TR- TRUST?

Trust, he agreed, surprised by the sense of unhurried calm that settled through him with the thought.

Trust, Ex echoed.

In the darkness, they felt Cammy's power stirring, rearranging itself to accommodate for her damaged Nexus, leaning on Ex here, Nate there, to fill in the gaps. Leaning until they hummed in triumvirate unison.

Outside, the front shields rippled with heat distortions on the leading edge of the plasma columns, bowing in as the lances struck and splashed out in slow motion, building to the inevitable collapse.

Time stopped. Space thinned. Or maybe thickened. For one eternity of an instant, Nate wasn't sure which. Wasn't sure, on some level, whether they even really still existed. All he knew was that Cammy took his hand more strongly in the darkness, and that reality flickered—morphed into something incomprehensible.

Then they snapped back into existence halfway across the Forge system with a roar of firing engines and mourning groan of warped metal, spewing a trail of debris where they'd torn free from the *Eldest Stone*'s death grip.

They were bound straight for the system's secondary relay super-structure.

Nate nearly cried out in relief. Then the rest of the Alliance fleet caught up from their moment of disoriented shock, and relief gave way to urgency. They felt the targeting lasers coalescing on the Camelot's hull and sensed the sudden flare of acceleration from the capital ships on the distant side of the Forge. The closest of their pursuers—the contingent squadron that'd been racing over from the secondary ring—wheeled around and began opening fire without hesitation.

Nate felt more than heard Iveera's explicit demand to get them to the ring, just as he felt her tight-beam message to the Beacon relay itself, demanding Knightship-level passage to the Tarkaminen system, Alliance orders be damned. Whoever's authority the relays answered to—that of the Merlin or the Lady herself—the superstructure obeyed, keying them in with an approach vector to where the manipulator arms were reaching for them with the blessed azure shimmer of a spawning gateway.

Not that the dreadnought and the two battlecruisers that barred their way seemed to give a damn. They just belched a sea of fighters and opened up with everything they had.

Distantly, they felt Tessa at the controls, preparing to go evasive.

Trust us, Nate thought—or maybe said, back on the bridge.

Then together, he, Cammy, and Ex lowered their figurative head and charged, accelerating with a wrenching groan and a few sharp snapping pains from the rear of the ship, he and Ex bolstering the forward shields with their own strength even as Iveera alighted on the prow, ready to lend her own support.

Fighter squadrons parted neatly ahead, sweeping wide to simultaneously open the line of fire for the larger ships and angle around for a run at the *Camelot*'s flanks. With the way fully clear, the dreadnought unleashed pure hell.

They pressed on, taking what punishment slipped through Iveera's e-dim sorcery on their shields without complaint, focused firmly on their waiting gateway. Distantly, Nate couldn't help but wonder how they'd fare on the other side. He could practically smell the Tarkaminen sister fleet waiting there thousands of light-years away, ready to hit them with torpedoes or tractor beams or Lady knew what else the moment they emerged.

They'd have to jump to crusher space or q-drive the moment they were through. He felt the same thought from Iveera—wondered briefly if it was even safe for her to take a relay jump strapped to the hull. He pushed those thoughts aside. She knew what she was doing.

All he cared about at that moment was clearing that ring.

They roared past the three capital ships, skirting the enormous underbelly of the dreadnought, and pressed on through the torrential 4th of July plasma show, rocketing toward the fully telescoped relay aperture in a blaze of smoking hull and whining engines. Almost there. Space unfolding through that heavenly target. A grainy haze of different stars waiting on the other side. Escape. Almost there. Lady's Light swirling in the depths. Almost—

Something is wrong, came Iveera's voice in his head, the moment before they tore through the portal. Nate tensed at her tone, gasping as the Light enveloped them, rushing over and through him like an icy river on a cloudy day. There was something wrong with this Light. Something unnaturally—

WARNING, Cammy cried through the explosion of tingling blue electrifying Nate's every cubic inch. He felt her pulling away. Felt their cohesion wavering.

LOCATION... There was a series of sharp starts and stops, like Cammy was attempting to say something she wasn't equipped to say. *LOCATION UNKNOWN.*

She was confused, Nate reasoned, as he tried to focus on their faltering meld through the rush of searing input, searching urgently for the telltale ocean of threat blips no doubt screaming in to catch them at the mouth of the Tarkaminen relay. Then he took in their surroundings and understood. It wasn't a glitch of her rebooting systems.

It was just hard to check the star charts when there were no stars. Nothing but radiant swirls of brilliant azure as far as the *Camelot's* indelible optics could see in any direction, in fact. Lady's Light. An entire sea of it. Untarnished, aside from—

Brace yourselves! Iveera snapped in his mind, just as Ex growled a sharp curse and his own breath caught in his chest at the sight his startled brain was still struggling to register.

There, awash in the endless ocean of nebulous blue, a pitch dark ship waited for them like a dread fortress on the eerie horizon. The *Avalon Eternal,* pinged a soft factoid from the *Camelot's* diligent sensors. The Black Knight's ship, Nate's numb brain translated with a sudden terrible certainty. He felt it in his bones.

And the blackened thing was headed straight for them.

CHAPTER 24

IN SHINING ARMOR

I t happened faster than Nate could react. No warning. No mystical time dilation to save the day. The *Avalon Eternal* merely gushed forth a terrible column of hyper violet energy, and the *Camelot* screamed its first dying scream.

Nate screamed with it, recoiling from the staggering pain, gaping in horror as his senses prodded at the damage and felt the several layers of ruined hull and decks the blast had just slagged straight through. Their shields were ruptured, weakly stirring to reassemble. Nate tried to bring his and Ex's strength to bear, mind racing with the power of that single blast, and what the hell they were supposed to do before the *Avalon Eternal* fired another.

My ship! Iveera's voice snapped him to order. *Release the Kalnythian W—*

The second blast caught her full-on, rending a deep gash across the *Camelot*'s dorsal hull, consuming the Gorgon completely in the ultraviolet inferno.

"—us the hell out of here!" someone was barking, somewhere too far away.

It was all happening too fast. Nate's entire world focused on the epicenter of that blinding blast, gritting through the pain, waiting for the storm to sweep by and reveal their mighty Gorgon Knight standing unharmed, defenses intact.

"Now, dammit!"

"Engines are full blast, sir. We're not—This place isn't…"

"—bout crusher drives?"

"—can't even—"

The second blast ended, the truncated edge of the column flying by like a train in the night, violet on blue, ad infinitum. Nate stared at the charred aftermath, uncomprehending.

Iveera floated there like limp, scorched bait, dangling from the *Camelot* by her gravitonic tether. Alive or dead, he couldn't tell. Couldn't feel her there at all, only the dark fortress of the *Avalon Eternal*, gliding closer, jet black prow coming alive with the glow of a third charging blast.

All that trouble. All the shattered alliances and sputtering fires they'd left behind in their daring gambit to fetch another shot at the Black Knight, and here the blackened bastard was, about to end them before they could so much as—

"Nate!"

Jaeger's voice snapped him back to the bridge, too close and urgent. He blinked with his own eyes, taking in Jaeger's dire expression, dimly registering he'd lost his meld with Cammy. He glanced down at the cradling exoskeleton of her interface arms, then back to Jaeger, who was watching him with a kind of grimly spreading acceptance, praying that he might kindly pull a Knightly miracle from his ass, but not really expecting it, which was just as well.

Nate had nothing.

Nothing but the sudden sobering certainty that he'd stepped worlds out of his league—that he deserved the soft anger burning in Jaeger's eyes, and the hollow ache that joined it when Tessa turned to face him, devoid of all that bravado. For the first time, she looked like a twenty-five-year-old pilot who'd somehow stumbled into a gig she wasn't ready for, never *could* have been ready for.

Ahead, the third violet glow reached a nightmarish pitch at the prow of the *Avalon Eternal*, gleaming with the promise of their imminent destruction. Nate watched helplessly, the image of Gwen's tear-streaked face flitting unbidden to his mind's eye.

We're not dead yet, little hobbit.

The words echoed in Nate's mind, a stubborn little challenge in the darkening storm, daring him to remember what he'd come here for—daring him to stow the sniveling and *do* something. Anything. Fight until he couldn't. He saw Marty and Gwen drifting there in his mind's eye. Saw

Tessa and Jaeger watching him, tinged with the hellish light filling the bridge.

He flexed fear-stiffened muscles and lunged to port just as the dark destroyer fired, not really sure what he could do that Tessa's straining engines couldn't, but demanding the *Camelot* to obey all the same.

And obey it did, lurching like a boat on phantom waters, not *moving* so much as *undulating* through the Light, as if it was Nate and Nate was it, paddling gently along on the azure currents they'd somehow found themselves trapped within. Searing heat scorched along the starboard hull before Nate had time to wonder at the enigma. He clenched his teeth against the pain and fired back with every blaster, torpedo, and sharp edge his mind could find. He spared a stray thought to pull Iveera's dangling body back into the *Camelot*, dimly aware his body, back on the bridge, was shouting for the crew to fight back and hit the bastard with everything they had.

Distantly, he thought he heard their battle cries joining his own. He was pretty sure he felt their hands helping to man the weapons systems as he poured everything he had into the singular thought of shredding the *Avalon Eternal* clean open. In the space of two seconds, the eerie blue void between them became a screaming storm of magnesium-flare-bright torpedoes, white-hot magnetic accelerator slugs, and searing green plasma lances. Enough firepower to core an Alliance dreadnought clean through several times over, he was almost certain. Enough that he feared Ex had been over-confident in his promise that the Merlin would survive to be excavated—if he was even aboard the enemy ship at all.

The *Avalon Eternal* consumed the entire damned firestorm like so much flak.

Through a murky fog, Nate was aware of his spent body hitting the deck in the shocked silence of the bridge. Then the dread ship let loose with another blast, and there was nothing but the pain. It spilled through his mind like fuming kerosene and sparked to life, flash-frying his entire world to a scream of raw agony. His guts, their lower decks, were on fire. Critical systems, losing power. Drowning in their own brilliant lifeblood. Drowning.

Yield, Terran, rumbled a dark voice, from somewhere in the depths of his nightmares. There might've been more, but he was too faded to make it out. Someone was shaking him and growling his name through the darkness.

On your feet, lad, whispered a hauntingly familiar voice, so thin he wasn't sure he'd really heard it at all.

Seconds passed. Scant seconds. Or maybe hours.

"—on, kid!" the voice growled.

He felt like he'd died and woken up.

Rough hands were yanking him up, shaking him. He tried to move, but acrid smoke choked his lungs with the stench of burning electronics, the coppery taste of blood thick in his mouth.

"Nate?" Another shake. He was on his back. "Hey, come on, Nate?"

Eyes open. Snuffy.

Snuffy *and* Jaeger.

He was on the deck, staring up at them through the smoke and winking red lights of a bridge in full meltdown.

"Something's happening," Tessa snapped from her control rig.

All things considered, it almost seemed like a laughable statement. At least until Nate's brain caught up and lurched him upright with alarm, startling a tense Snuffy and earning himself a violent wave of nausea.

Outside, the ocean of Light was rippling, agitated by some building storm, warping everything but the space around the *Avalon Eternal*, which sat there calmly, waiting, seemingly unconcerned with the smoking husk of the *Camelot*—waiting for what?

"The Merlin," Nate croaked, clawing his way to his feet, not arguing when Jaeger stepped in to steady him. "We have to—"

They both staggered as the perturbations intensified outside, bending the Light and seemingly everything in it. Judging by the groans across the bridge, they weren't the only ones who felt the inexorable wave of whatever it was. He didn't know what. Only that this place, whatever it was, felt like it was on the verge of collapsing.

Do you hear that? Ex asked.

Then a window of their endless blue infinity cracked open like a cosmic Coke can, offering an infinitesimal glimpse of dark space and stars before it belched forth a torrential flood of roaring golden energy. The beam tore past the *Camelot* and punched straight into the bow of the *Avalon* with a dazzling crackle of crimson energy shields.

And there, charging through that strange tear in the wake of the blast, was the magnificent golden mech form of Zedavian Kelkarin's *Eldest Stone*, cutting through the endless blue like he'd sailed these strange oceans a thousand times before, sweeping in for the kill.

The First Knight didn't give his prey a moment to calibrate from the surprise attack. The Black Knight didn't need it.

In the blink of an eye, both ships unleashed such unchecked hell on one another that Nate's head thrummed with the intensity of the exchange. And not just his head. His entire body. All of space itself, it seemed, as the two titans turned the azure ocean to flames, Zedavian charging headlong, the Black Knight standing his ground, neither attempting anything so coy as evasive maneuvers. The Light warped and hummed around them like a plucked string with each destructive wave, pulsing with ominous veins of black and purple, threatening to dissipate completely.

"Guys?" Snuffy asked, looking around with wide eyes. "Is anyone else feeling that?"

"Strap back in," Jaeger growled. "Now." He grabbed Nate and turned for his own crash couch like he fully intended to drag him there and go Dutch on the life-saving restraints. Nate stumbled along, trying to point out that he, unlike Jaeger, had his own personal gravitonics to fall back on. But it was too late.

The ocean of Light undulated on the back of a particularly spectacular explosion, warping Nate's head, the space between their three ships rippling like a desert mirage as the *Eldest Stone* sped to terminal impact with the *Avalon Eternal*.

"Brace yourself," Nate growled, shoving Jaeger down into the crash couch, unsure what the hell was about to happen, only that it wasn't going to be pretty.

No sooner had Jaeger's restraints latched on than the air—or maybe existence itself—shook with the unmistakable violence of impact outside. Nate whirled for the viewport, reaching for his gravitonics to brace himself against the inevitable turbulence.

He faltered at what he saw—the *Eldest Stone* plowing into the *Avalon Eternal* in an explosion of enormous sparks and sputtering shields, taking it in a full on tackle even as the *Avalon* shifted, folding, and springing jet black manipulator arms––making as if to match Zedavian's transformer act. And beyond that…

Nate squinted, the Light between them so warped now that it was hard to make sense of anything but the building thrum of power. There were shapes there—hundreds of them. Thousands of dark, splotchy phantoms ghosting toward them, ethereal in the Light, but unmistakably *there*.

Nate focused on one, dialing the optics in.

Then the clashing Knightships detonated with an all-consuming blast of rushing light, and with little more than a decisive rattle and a round of dropped jaws, the ocean of swirling blue simply winked from existence. Suddenly, they were staring through the display-dead viewport at nothing but the star-spangled blackness of normal space.

The *Eldest Stone* and *Avalon Eternal* were nowhere in sight.

For a long moment, no one spoke, the entire crew still tensed like they expected the two clashing Knightships might spill out into space beside them at any moment. Nate wasn't sure they wouldn't—almost didn't care if they did, as bone-dead tired as he suddenly felt, his insides shaky and feeling a little too much like they'd just been through the microwave.

"Where are we, Kalders?" Jaeger finally asked.

That was a damned good question, Nate realized, as he checked their few working displays and realized that they *didn't* have an angry Tarkaminen relay sentry fleet bearing down on them. There was no relay superstructure at all. Nothing but—

Tessa's gasp was the only warning before something smacked into the Camelot. Something big, by the sound of it. It screeched across the hull like a banshee family reunion, finally wrenching clear to drift past the viewport, a jagged dark mass, spinning lazily.

An asteroid?

Thousands of them, Nate realized, looking closer at Tessa's displays.

I believe we have experienced a slight detour, Ex said, as the rest of the bridge came alive with chatter. *But according to the star charts...*

"Report, Kalders," Jaeger said. "Where the hell are we?"

"I don't know, sir!" Tessa snapped. "Nav systems are down, and I—I..." She gestured helplessly at her sputtering displays.

Ah, Ex said, sounding unusually reserved about whatever he'd just finished digging up.

What is it? Nate asked, not sure he really wanted to know.

It... seems we have arrived at the Atlantean's missing Demeter colony.

Nate caught himself on the back of Tessa's flight chair, another shaky wave passing over him as he tried to process what Ex was telling him, and what it meant.

"What is it?" Jaeger asked, apparently noticing his sudden pallor.

He told them and watched the understanding dawn in each of their eyes.

"But then..." Tessa pried her eyes from him to the asteroid field, then back again. "This is...?"

"The Atlantean's dark colony," Nate confirmed.

The place was a graveyard.

CHAPTER 25
RUBBLE

"I still don't understand how we ended up here, of all places," Tessa said, not for the first time, as she finished limping the beaten *Camelot* more or less clear of the closest impending asteroid strikes, which was hardly to say clear from *all* of them. The debris field seemed to stretch on indefinitely, a steady shower of smaller particles peppering the hull wherever they went.

Was this really the graveyard of an entire *planet*?

"I still don't understand if it's okay to *breathe* again," Snuffy murmured quietly in the corner, staring into empty space with a permanently shell-shocked expression.

Nate knew what he meant more than he cared to admit. It was hard to process just how much shit had hit the fans in the short time since he'd been sitting in Zedavian's "brig" like a good little prisoner, arguing with…

His breath caught, the reminder of Iveera sweeping him like a landslide.

He turned for the exit without a word, only distantly aware of Jaeger's voice behind him, feet carrying him first quickly, then frantically off the bridge, senses questing out for guidance in the soft red emergency lighting.

How had he forgotten, even for a moment?

His ship was dark to his mind. Just plain dark all around outside the spill of the bridge's emergency lighting, but his helmet sensors picked up the slack quickly enough. He didn't have far to look.

Iveera's burnt husk was laid out in the middle of the main corridor, face down where she must've dropped after he'd bade the *Camelot* to drag her back in. She wasn't moving. Once-copper armor charred all to black. Motionless jin hanging limply around her head.

Nate dropped to his knees beside her, too sickened to breathe. He reached out a helpless hand, needing to check, needing to help, but unable to even touch her for the fear that she would merely crumble to dry ash.

"Ex," he whispered, practically a prayer.

Her Excalibur yet works to mend her wounds.

Does that mean she's...?

Even in his own head, the word dug in its heels, refusing to come forward.

An Excalibur Knight is not so easily slain, Ex admonished.

Nate let out a low breath and took in another, wanting to be relieved but not quite able to unhear the creeping uncertainty in his companion's voice.

An Excalibur Knight seemed to be a *lot* of things he hadn't been expecting when he'd first stepped onto the *Camelot* back on Earth. Fugitives, for instance. Fugitives who'd somehow bounced from bad dreams straight into the apparent remains of a dead planet, it seemed, with little to no idea what the hell they'd been thinking.

He looked down at Iveera's charred helmet, wondering if he shouldn't call for help, certain on some level that her Excalibur was already doing more than any of them could. He pictured the Gorgon's face wrapped in peaceful slumber rather than the more likely sight that awaited beneath the surface.

Why hadn't she stopped him?

What had changed her mind back in that cell? Even after Amelia had informed them of Zedavian's apparent decision to throw the Merlin under the bus for the Council, she'd stuck to her guns, insisting on loyalty to the all-important Order. And then, just like that...

He sighed, not sure what to think. She was six-hundred years old, for Christ's sake. Who knew what went on in her head, or in Zedavian's, or any of them? He didn't know the Alliance like they did. Hadn't understood what kind of shit show they'd been flying into, fleeing Forge Station like that.

Maybe she hadn't stopped him, he thought, staring at that blackened helmet, because she'd simply wanted to teach him a lesson about jumping the gun and trusting his gut in a world he didn't yet understand. Maybe all the collateral damage was a worthy cost in her mind.

Or maybe it was all his own damned fault, and he was just deflecting.

A shot at the Black Knight squandered. Zedavian missing. An angry

Alliance fleet, no doubt preparing to hunt them out to the edges of the galaxy. Or to wherever the hell they'd arrived. He still didn't know what to make of the drifting ruins outside. He only knew that they were too far from home and that they'd just gone farther.

The thought of home was a hollow ache in his chest, ripe with taunting images of Gwen and Copernicus cuddled up with him on the couch, Kyle and Marty playing games and ribbing them: *oh, to be young and in love.*

He waited for the inevitable pang of longing to follow, with all the same squirrely bargaining chips that'd played through his mind a thousand times since they'd left Earth. The vanilla college boredom he'd never again take for granted if only he could make it home. The childish dreams of mystical powers and fantastical space adventures he'd never again indulge.

The thoughts didn't come. Not as anything more than idle background chatter, at least. Instead, he just felt tired, content for the moment to merely hold on to the image of his friends and the less-than-concrete belief that he'd find his way back when this was all over.

Absorbed as he was, he didn't notice Jaeger coming until the sweeping flashlight beam danced over Iveera's body, and a curt whisper of, "Shit," broke the silence. The Lt Col knelt calmly down across from Nate and leaned in to inspect the Gorgon. The two fingers he started extending toward her throat went back to his side as he realized she was still fully encased in charred armor. He glanced back toward the bridge, probably thinking about calling for Carter, then thought better of it.

"Whadya got, kid?" he asked quietly.

Nate stared at him, brain crunching to catch up from its own reveries. Jaeger held his gaze, expression unreadable, then finally tilted his head toward their charred Gorgon in a silent gesture to focus up.

"She'll live," Nate heard himself say. "I think."

He didn't mean to say the last words. They just snuck out.

Jaeger nodded slowly, like he was filing that one away under *impossible things to remember moving forward.*

"We need to take stock," he finally said. "Figure out how we landed here. Figure out what's next. Should probably get her to a bed, at least," he added, glancing down at Iveera's unmoving body before looking back to Nate. "What happened to the Troglodan?"

"Locked him in the nexus," Nate said, still pulling his head on straight, still focused on Iveera.

"You left the saboteur locked with the ship's vital innards," Jaeger said, like he was testing to make sure he'd heard that right.

Nate pried his eyes from Iveera up to the Lt Col, releasing his helmet back to e-dim so that Jaeger could see his face in the jagged spillover of the flashlight beam and the flickering start-and-stop sputters of the corridor emergency lights. "I left him bound and electromagnetically shielded so I could hurry up and save our asses. Did you know you invited a walking bomb onto our ship?"

Jaeger held his gaze, not backing down, calmly tracing his words through. "Don't suppose that has something to do with why Ivy here wrapped Blondie up there in her magical Knight cocoon before she went out for her spacewalk?"

"Probably." Nate glanced toward the bridge, wondering if and how he should go about safely freeing the Atlantean from her cage. "She thought the Ooperians might've gotten to them. Brainwashed them, sort of."

"What?" Jaeger tensed, looking around like he half-expected to find one of the clammy bastards standing right there.

"It's called—"

"Fucking vampire glamour?"

Apparently, Nate didn't adequately hide his surprise that Jaeger would be familiar with the term.

"Yeah, I know how to read," Jaeger supplied. "Go figure. You have any idea where they…" He trailed off as something else occurred to him. "The escape pods."

Nate nodded. "I think they dosed Malfar and bailed. Should be safe from any detonation signals now that we're through the relay," he added, relaying Ex's comments in real-time, "but we still probably wanna get them, uh, disarmed before the biosynthetic explosives go into unstable decay or whatever. According to Ex," he concluded, in response to his companion's grumbling about second fiddles and the true brains of the operation.

There, Nate thought, as he moved to stand from Iveera's side. *Happy?*

Never, Ex shot back, though he sounded at least marginally pleased.

Jaeger, on the other hand, looked like he had something on his mind as he reached out and caught Nate by the arm, keeping him there. "About Mr. Ex," he started, before rethinking the unfortunate moniker with a dismissive head shake. "Whatever. About your Excalibur. You wanna explain why we had to find out from Malfar the freaking Trog justicar that you two caught a bit of the Knight plague from our dark friend back in Atlantis?"

Nate looked down at Jaeger's domineering hand, idly considering how easily he could've hurled the man across the room, and just how humongous the Lt Col's oh-so-casual stones must be.

"We didn't know."

"Yeah, well, that doesn't change the fact that this corruption stuff was enough to give His Golden Holiness the murder wood for all of us back there. Who's to say it wasn't how this Black Knight asshole knew exactly where to find us, too?"

That stopped Nate cold in his tracks.

"I... I don't think he was after us."

Of all the messy pieces refusing to make sense in his mind, he wasn't quite sure why *those* were the first words that chose to slip out of his mouth. Something about the look Zedavian had given him when he'd made the half-cocked mistake to try to infect the First Knight. The fact that they'd escaped the hangar and made it to the relay at all, only to be ruthlessly dismantled by the Black Knight and set aside like children in time out. Like they'd merely stumbled onto a stage set for another.

Had Zedavian *let* them escape?

Had he somehow known what they were flying into?

Yield, Terran, the dark titan's voice echoed in his mind, right there on the cusp of the words that'd followed, slippery as the details of some half-remembered dream.

"That's not an answer," Jaeger's voice broke into his thoughts. The Lt Col released his arm, stood from Iveera's side, and crossed his arms authoritatively, waiting for Nate's response.

Nate looked down at the charred Gorgon, wishing to the Lady and anyone else that she'd stir and tell them what to do next. Because Jaeger was right, it *wasn't* an answer. He didn't *have* answers—just more questions than he knew what to do with.

"I can't tell you why," he said quietly, not looking up, "but I think there's something more going on here. Something between Zedavian and the Black Knight. I feel it in my gut."

Jaeger looked none too impressed. "Funny, Malfar said the same thing. But here's the thing, kid. Unless that gut of yours can tell us how to fix this mess and keep my people clear of another blind-flying shit show like we just..." He trailed off, and they both turned to find Snuffy waiting there on the periphery of their conversation, head bowed apologetically.

"We've got a checklist from Cammy, boss," the mechanic said, looking tentatively between Jaeger and Nate. "You want me to get started on what repairs I can, or...?" He glanced awkwardly between them again, like he was wondering whether he shouldn't offer them the chance to finish having it out first.

Nate was already occupied reaching out for Cammy's presence, feeling too much like a parent who'd forgotten their kid in the car in all the excitement. And there she was—weak and only vaguely responsive to his probing thoughts, but slowly resurfacing from the beaten they'd taken together.

"Grab Elmo and get on it," Jaeger was saying, not bothering to ask Nate's opinion. "Pierce, too. Tell Carter we got a patient for her back here, and tell Kalders—"

Thump.

They all turned at the muffled sound, tracing it to the dark ramp belowdecks.

Thump, thump, THUMP, it went, more pronounced with each strike. Then an equally muffled roar, just barely recognizable as a single word.

"TERRAN!"

"Sounds like you did a real bang-up job securing the big angry Trog down there, kid," Jaeger said, shooting him a sideways glance.

"Yeah, well"—Nate splayed his hands, not sure how that even remotely compared to how generally boned their situation was out here—"maybe next time I'll just take my sweet time getting back to the bridge."

"Where are you going?"

Nate paused at the top of the ramp. "To disarm the walking Troglodan bomb, I guess. Then, I dunno. Maybe try to figure out how the hell we ended up..." He thought about the lifeless debris field that may or may not have recently been a populated Atlantean outpost. "... wherever we are."

Jaeger held him on the end of a clear *this isn't over* stare. Behind him, Snuffy shifted uncomfortably, looking like he'd give just about anything to have a wrench in hand and a discrete problem to solve.

"Let's get Cammy back on her feet," Jaeger finally said, shooing Snuffy back toward the bridge. "Then, we'll talk."

CHAPTER 26

WHO GOES THERE

In the short time it took to reach the narrow nexus maintenance corridor, Nate managed to conjure up exactly one disgruntled Excalibur and zero miraculous plans for dealing with their walking bio-bomb—or bombs, plural, Amelia pending.

Dearest apologies if the speed of my genius is not on par with your expectations, Ex said. *If you require a more immediate solution, might I point out that spacing both of them would be the easiest option.*

The thought alone was enough to draw Nate up short, hands curling into indignant fists.

Kidding, kidding! Ex insisted. *Hypothetically. Take a joke, Nathaniel. Though, really, while we are on the subject—*

We're not spacing them, Nate thought, so decisively that he was a little shocked to remember that it was a *Troglodan* they were talking about, here.

A Troglodan AND a rather Gwen-shaped Atlantean, Ex pointed out.

"Yeah," Nate muttered, telling himself that was the full extent of it. "Right."

But the rest of the thought wouldn't shake free as he set off, eyeing the door at the bend in the corridor. A full planetary invasion—eighty-thousand-plus humans killed and a not-so-harmless attempt to bring down the *Camelot* and his crew. And here he was, jerking away from the thought of spacing Malfar the Troglodan justicar.

Here he was, flinching away from the thought of *murder*.

Because that's what it would be, wasn't it? There was no denying it, not after everything he'd seen on the Forge. Somehow, the word hadn't even entered his lexicon when he'd been taking a shot at the attacking Ooperians, or back on Earth gunning down the big dumb brutes who talked in low grunts and growls. But now...

Now, he told himself, pushing the thought firmly aside, they had far more important things to worry about than the morality of self-defense. He drew up to the door he'd quickly melted back into place to keep Malfar contained, flushing a little as Jaeger's point about his rushed logic came dancing back to the surface.

Whatever. It had worked.

He raised a hand, preparing to slice his shoddy welding work back open, and faltered as the soft whine he hadn't noticed suddenly died on the other side of the door, and he caught a pungent whiff of scorched metal and carbon.

The door burst outward with a sharp crack, sailing at him like a spring-loaded booby-trap in some eccentric millionaire's trick mansion. He caught it by reflex and shifted it aside just in time to see Malfar the Troglodan justicar leveling a blaster and some kind of laser-cutting multi-tool at his un-helmeted face.

"What is your purpose here, Knight?"

Nate blinked dumbly at the laser cutter, trying to reconcile the tool's presence with the fact that he'd earlier found the Trog bloody at the fingers trying to bludgeon the nexus to pieces. "Feel like I might ask you the same thing. You get tired of your smashing brick or something?"

The Troglodan followed his gaze to the cutting tool with a dark scowl. "I was not myself," he said, tucking the device into his belt but keeping the blaster handy. "Now, where are those Ooperian scum?"

"What?"

"The Ooperians, Terran. Where have they gone?"

"They..." Nate frowned at the duraplate door in his hands and set it down against the wall, reminding himself what he'd come here for. "They bailed by escape pod back at the Forge. I shielded you"—he pointed at the heaped Faraday cage the Trog had somehow shredded his way out of—"before they could detonate whatever they injected you with. And now, if you don't mind, we need to get that shit out of your system before you blow my damn ship sky high."

The justicar stared at him, flatly.

"Space high. Whatever."

Malfar glanced warily down the corridor, one large hand drifting to his torso like he'd at least understood that bit. "Where are we? What has happened?"

"Still kinda trying to figure that bit out, but—"

"Bah." Malfar shoved past him with a grunted curse, muttering something about amateurs.

I think I like him, Ex declared, snapping Nate back from his impotent staring.

"Hey!" He splayed his hands at the retreating Trog's back. "Where do you think you're going?"

Malfar just kept marching on like he hadn't heard a thing.

Freaking Troglodans.

Nate was halfway into summoning up another round of sleepy darts to see about disarming the justicar, sans pesky consciousness, when Malfar halted and turned back as if something had occurred to him. Nate watched uncertainly as the blight-marked Trog fiddled with his wrist-mounted omnitool, then stomped back down the corridor, holding the device out for Nate's inspection.

The short runic scrawl danced before his eyes as the justicar drew closer, morphing through Ex's translation into four simple words: "Did you see them?"

It took him a few confused moments to realize Malfar was referring to the Ooperians. "No," he said, brow furrowing. "They escaped in the pods, like I said."

The Troglodan gave the neckless equivalent of a sharp headshake, shoulders and torso pivoting back and forth with gusto, then jabbed a thick finger to the side of his head and thrust the omni right in Nate's face with four emphatic pumps, as if annunciating each word.

Did. You. See. Them?

Nate opened his mouth, bristling with an irritated retort… and closed it again, insides icing over as he realized what the justicar was actually asking. Malfar, seeing that his point was sinking in, took a moment to key something else on the omni then turned the display back to Nate.

"Full-spectrum optics," it read. "Follow me."

"But…" Nate murmured, mind racing first with flashes of the pods breaking free back in Forge System, then with thoughts of the crew currently spreading out through the *Camelot*'s dead, darkened decks, going about their repair duties, perfectly unsuspecting. And out there, among them…

No. It didn't make any sense.

Malfar was being paranoid. That was all.

I can scarcely detect our own crew with the current state of the Camelot's internal systems, Ex said, before Nate could even coherently form the question. *But the Troglodan's logic is plausible.*

Plausible and *paranoid*, Nate told himself, but he called his helmet back from e-dim all the same. Full-spectrum optics. Malfar was already stalking off down the corridor like he didn't really care whether Nate fell in line or not. The Troglodan had some stones. Nate had to give him that much. Especially considering that the big bastard was still primed to explode at a light sneeze of radiation.

On the bright side, I believe I may have found a rudimentary fix for that particular quandary.

You believe? Nate demanded, wondering just how rudimentary they were talking as he set off after Malfar at a brisk shuffle.

You're right, Nathaniel. My sub-percent margin of error is unacceptable. Why don't we go ahead and employ YOUR designer serum to block off those highly-tamper-proof photo-detonators instead? I'll sit back and enjoy the show.

Just tell me what to do, Nate mentally grumbled, slipping quietly closer to the Troglodan, who was beginning to show the first signs of real caution as he approached the wide intersection hub at the base of the ramp.

Mayhaps you could conjure one of those nice little dart devices for us, Ex said, in the kind of tone usually reserved for speaking to children. *You know, the small pointy ones.*

"Gladly," Nate muttered under his breath, bringing his will to bear on the task.

Maybe it was petty, but he didn't bother trying to warn Malfar. He just stepped forward, taking aim with his materializing wrist launcher, and gave the Trog his rudimentary medicine, right in the back of his thick non-neck.

Bio-bomb defuser, Nate thought, carefully willing the words to take form on a small holo pane over his open palm as the growling Troglodan whirled on him for an explanation. *You're welcome.*

"Destroyer take you and your brood, Knight," the Troglodan muttered, swatting irritatedly at the injection site.

I'd rather that than you blow up my ship, Nate sent to the holo for the Trog to see. *Now, you wanna tell me where you're going?*

The justicar considered the holo, still clearly miffed, then turned and stomped off, ignoring Nate so completely he couldn't help but wonder if the message text had translated properly.

Sure, blame the Excalibur. I believe he simply doesn't like you.

What the hell did I do? Nate wondered, watching as the Trog paused to take his bearings at the base of the deck ramp ahead.

You mean aside from administering multiple unsolicited pharmaceutical agents, locking him in a small room, and most likely ending his career, to boot?

What, NOW you decide to develop a sense of empathy? Ahead, Malfar set off sternward, probably bound to investigate the escape pods.

And what do you mean, I ended his career? Nate wondered, starting after the Trog. *How is any of this...* He paused at the base of the ramp, assessment of faults taking a backseat, caught between the need to go check the pods with Malfar, and to first pop up to the bridge to check on the others.

They were fine up there, he told himself. All of them, fine. Aside from being derelict outlaws on the edge of a mysteriously missing planet, he couldn't help but remember, as the pitter-patter crackle-and-scrape of a passing debris cloud gave way to the *Camelot*'s faltering shields and hull. And aside from Amelia, who was still trapped in a cage up there, for Christ's sake.

He shook his head and turned sternward, reaching to open a channel to Tessa. A quick check-in on the way to the pods. Then he'd get Amelia out, disarm any lingering explosives, get his bearings on what the hell had happened back there in the Light, and—

"Nate? What's up?"

"Tess?" Nate said, double-checking with Ex that they were soundproofed inside his helmet. "Um, I just..." Suddenly, the truth sounded even more paranoid with another person on the line. "Is everything okay up there? Everyone's good?"

"Uh, yeah?" He could practically hear her brow furrowing. He stalked on down the corridor as she quickly rattled off the crew's whereabouts. Carter monitoring Iveera. The rest back in the engine room. Just her and Blondie up at the helm, though Blondie was still a little tied up, and what was all this about anyway, and...

"Nate?"

Nate surfaced from the tunnel vision he hadn't even noticed closing in from the soft red shadows.

"What's going on? You're acting weird."

"No, I'm just..." He scanned those ominous shadows, gaze flicking to the justicar shuffling into the grav lift ahead, idly wondering what the Trog planned to do if he actually ran into an invisible assassin.

Quickly as he could, he told Tessa about Malfar's suspicions.

"Well," she said, when he'd finished and was pulling himself up the rungs of the unpowered grav lift well, "creepy as that all sounds, I think the justicar's blowing his stack over ghosts. Cammy read lifeforms in both of those pods when they launched. So, unless a third suicide bomber decided to stay behind and for some reason *not* blow us all to hell the moment the justicar slipped his EM containment, I think our biggest concern right now is getting back online before we get pulverized by one of the big ones out there."

"Yeah, you're probably right," Nate said, clambering onto the upper deck as Malfar disappeared into the crew quarters ahead. But then why did he suddenly feel even more uneasy about all of this?

Probably because she's lying, Ex said, *in case that wasn't blatantly obvious.*

What?

"See you in a minute, then?" Tessa asked.

"Uh, yeah," Nate forced himself to say.

Cammy's nexus was thoroughly dismantled when those pods launched. I was unable to ascertain anything about the state of those pods. She's lying.

"Yeah, we'll just… I'll be up there in a minute. Just, uh…"

"Eyes open for ghosts?" she asked, an audible grin in her tone.

Words, Nathaniel, Ex prompted, as Nate dumbly stared into space.

"I'll be here," she promised, killing the connection.

With her gone, the halls of the *Camelot* suddenly felt silent as a mausoleum, every dark corner and soft red patch unnaturally still. Haunted. Nate turned his stare to the crew quarters where the escape pods had fired from, dimly aware of the sweat beading on his forehead, heart thundering in his ears.

Get me a line to Jaeger, he thought, starting forward. *To anyone. Just…* He trailed off as he stepped into the crew quarters and took in Ramirez lying peacefully in his softly-glowing medpod in the corner. So peacefully that, for a moment, Nate feared the worse. But the airman was alive. Doing well, even, judging from a cursory glance at the capsule's many readouts. Nate turned his attention to the far corner, where Malfar was sweeping the closed escape pod hatchways with a wide violet beam from his omnitool.

Not to alarm you, Ex said, *but—*

"Kid?"

Nate rounded at the unexpected sound of Jaeger's voice in the doorway.

And froze.

Malfar growled something. Nate couldn't have said what. He was too focused on Jaeger, and on the pistol pressed to his underjaw, grasped tightly in the Lt Col's own two hands.

There's something behind him.

Nate gaped, recycled air kissing at his perspiring brow, helmet display grasping to isolate the pale, slender outline that ghosted forward with long, sinewy steps, cloaked signatures all but invisible against the luminous red emergency lighting.

"Carefully, child," the Ooperian whispered, winking into terrible sight as Jaeger shuffled into the room, followed next by Snuffy, Elmo, Carter, and Pierce—all of them with weapons pressed to their own heads, all of them perfectly expressionless. "One false step and your entire crew dies."

CHAPTER 27
FROZEN

To Malfar's credit, the big Troglodan had his weapon drawn and trained on the Ooperian's pale forehead before Nate had even finished sucking in a surprised breath.

"Thaaat," hissed the nightmarish apparition, drawing the word out as it pointed a slender finger toward Malfar's weapon, "would be a falssse step, justicar."

The creature snapped its fingers, and Nate's stomach fell as Jaeger and the others obediently cocked their weapons, their faces still expressionless, seemingly unaware they were a light twitch away from painting the ceiling with their own brains.

"If I die, they pull the triggers," the Ooperian explained, perfectly matter-of-fact. "If I command it, they pull the triggers. If *you* do not cooperate…" It continued, fixing Nate with a level stare and leaving the obvious unsaid.

"What do you want?" Nate asked.

There are at least two more, Ex said, a red nav point appearing on Nate's HUD and quickly bifurcating, then *trifurcating.*

"Youuu will releassse your armor and surrender," the visible Ooperian whispered, as two lanky phantoms slid into the room behind it, splitting at the door and spreading out as their respective nav points did the same. "You will relllinquish your Excalibur to usss."

Make that four, Ex added, another point appearing in the distance, toward the bridge. *Tight-beam electromagnetics. Comms, most likely. Detonator handshake protocols as well.*

"It… doesn't work like that," Nate said slowly, trying to pretend as if he hadn't noticed their extra company, and hoping to all the gods above and below that their bio-bomb blocker had actually worked on Malfar. "The Excalibur doesn't just—"

The Ooperian breathed an airy sigh, and Jaeger jerked his pistol into a one-handed grip and jammed it roughly into his own temple, his face a sickening juxtaposition of helpless rage in the eyes and slack obedience everywhere else.

"I can't just take the Excalibur off, okay?" Nate cried, raising his hands in surrender.

"Weee are aware," whispered the pale outline in the shadows to the left, apparently not interested in trying to maintain its cover there.

"Weee offer a choice," added its counterpart from over by Ramirez's medpod.

Ex did something to attenuate Nate's helmet vision in the saturated red emergency lighting, and the specters took on a slightly more solid texture in his display, stalking the opposite sides of the room like wolves waiting for their pack leader's call.

"Ssspare your crew," hissed Lefty.

"Or do not," added Righty.

"Either way…"

"You die," finished their uncloaked pack leader, watching Nate with a crossed hand-on-wrist posture that felt absurdly courteous and profes-sional on such a garish creature, like it—*he?*—was a perfect gentleman at heart, and what they were discussing here was nothing more personal than a run-of-the-mill business deal.

"Why are you doing this?" Nate asked, before he could stop himself.

They didn't dignify the question with a response, or even a disdainful round of smirks.

"Relinquishhh your armor now, Terran," was all the pack leader said.

"And we will make it quuuick," added Lefty.

For a painfully long moment, Nate stared, head dancing with flashes of quick-fire attacks that might somehow drop all three vamps at once and gravitonic miracles whereby he might simply yank all the guns away from his glamoured crew. He'd seen Zedavian wield his gravitonics almost like telekinesis. But he could barely even control his own flight. It occurred to him that Malfar might at least drop the visible pack leader, moving Nate down to two targets, two wrist cannons. For a moment, it seemed possible.

Then the pack leader snapped his fingers, and Jaeger jammed his pistol down to his right thigh, weakly groaning his slack-jawed resistance.

"No!" Nate cried.

Jaeger pulled the trigger.

Inside Nate's helmet, the sound was far from deafening, the muzzle flash perfectly reasonable through Ex's combat filters. It was the look on Jaeger's face that hit him like a gut punch. The pained surprise as the man's leg collapsed out from under him, like somewhere deep down he'd still been sure he had the reins up until that moment. Instead, he hit the deck and crumpled forward, prostrated out like a faithful servant at the altar.

The Ooperian snapped its fingers again, and Snuffy snapped his pistol up to his temple in a macabre salute.

"Okay," Nate gasped, dropping desperately to his knees, hands up. "Okay, I'm doing it."

And true to his word, not knowing what the hell else to do in that moment, he ignored Ex's protests and made to release his armor back to e-dim.

"Terran," Malfar rumbled.

Nathaniel, Ex warned.

"Stand down," he snapped at the Troglodan.

We wait, he added to Ex.

Wait for *what* exactly, he didn't know. The Ooperians didn't seem the types to make mistakes and let their guards down. Ex was bristling—probably to say something to a similar effect, or to point out that these were four measly humans they were weighing against the fate of an Excalibur. Then his companion went unexpectedly still, perked at the edge of Nate's mind like a hunter catching a scent.

There's something else coming.

Much as Nate doubted that was good news, it almost didn't seem to matter as his helmet finished peeling back, and his chest armor began to follow, leaving him open and exposed to the waiting claws, disruptor rounds, and gods knew what else of his Ooperian assassins. He saw them there still, Ex feeding the data directly to his lens interface in lieu of the helmet display. Two cloaked Ooperian outlines, stalking closer, one fingering the wicked dagger he'd produced from somewhere like he simply couldn't wait to see what sounds a stuck Knight might make.

"Mooove, and they die," hissed the pack leader, without a single perceptible trace of smug victory. Such a goddamn professional.

Nate tensed as the leading specter moved within striking distance, body screaming at him to act, to fight. Mind paralyzed with the weight of those ready trigger fingers and the four lives hanging on his head.

Just wait. Just wait.

Wait for what? He didn't know. Couldn't say.

The specter raised its long arm, dagger ready to plunge straight into the back of Nate's neck, severing the spinal cord. Quuuick and easssy.

Not like this, Nathaniel, Ex said quietly. *Do something, damn you.*

Not yet.

Not—

Thunk.

Something smacked into the *Camelot*'s hull hard enough to rock the deck beneath their feet. An asteroid, Nate thought automatically, even as some glint of intuition told him that this was something different—that the mysterious *something* out there hadn't bounced off the ship like an inanimate object, but rather latched on.

"Wait," he gasped, watching the Ooperians' murderous reactions spill across the room. "I didn't—That's not—"

But it was already too late.

The pack leader winked under the cover of his shroud at the same instant the Ooperian beside Nate plunged his dagger down.

Nate jerked away, too late. A hard punch of impact rocked his shoulder, exploding into a sharp flood of pain. He screamed, twisting to grab his attacker's cold, spindly arm before his brain even finished registering that he had a hand's length of dagger blade buried in his trapezius.

"Toxins," hissed a voice, somewhere on the edge of that red roar of pain.

"Kill them all," growled another.

Nate lashed out at his closest attacker more with sheer blind fury than with any actual plan, shoulder screaming bloody murder as he sprang up from the deck. Somehow, he struck true. The Ooperian smacked into the far wall just as Snuffy toppled to the deck.

Nate whirled, the deck lurching strangely beneath him, and watched with a muddled mix of confusion and relief as Pierce, Carter, and Jaeger all thudded down on either side of the mechanic, all seemingly unconscious. No *gunshots*, Nate's swimming brain registered, even as Elmo teetered like a cut tree, pistol wavering beneath his bearded jaw.

Nate lunged for the big man. Watched helplessly as the weapon discharged, and Elmo jerked and crumpled like dead weight. He heard himself crying out and was surprised to find he'd fallen back to the deck, head positively spinning.

—r helmet, little hobbit! Ex's voice splashed through his mind, expanding and contracting like the ripples of a wave in slow motion. *—oxic gas.*

That was important, for some reason he couldn't quite grasp as Ex's voice warbled on. He shook his head, trying to latch back onto…

His helmet! The thought struck at the same time Ex bellowed the word, too loud to be ignored. Nate reached for his defenses on a sudden, powerful surge of adrenaline, his helmet unfurling from e-dim to embrace his head with a gush of cool, luxuriously clean air. He hadn't even noticed the way his eyes and lungs were burning—only noticed then how one of the ghostly shrouded Ooperians was staggering to its knees, tugging on its own mask.

The other one was rushing straight for him.

Nate raised a hand, calling his repulsors from e-dim. Something dark and pointy exploded from the back of his hand just before the armor enclosed his flesh. Another dagger blade, some incredulous corner of his mind noted, as his palm woke with a wave of pain that somehow barely seemed important in the wake of everything else.

He grabbed the Ooperian by the wrist with his free, fully-armored hand, vision waning with the pain and the effort, and squeezed for all he was worth. Bones cracked, the Ooperian hissed like a wild animal, and a pistol appeared in its other hand, barrel-first in Nate's face. For a precious instant, Nate could only gape, gripped by a flash of déjà vu, yet oddly devoid of the terror he'd have expected in such a moment. Then the Ooperian jerked backward, spewing a mist of dark ichor from its suddenly sputtering shroud. Then a second one. Then a third.

The creature hit the deck, it's face a ghoulish scene of gaping nightmare mouth and dimming amber eyes beneath the streaming ichor.

"The door, Terran!" boomed a muffled Troglodan voice. Malfar's voice, he registered, muffled by some kind of breather mask.

Nate lurched drunkenly to his feet, hand and shoulder screaming, mind burning rubber to catch up with what was happening. The sounds of struggle behind and the sight of the now-masked pack leader darting for the door ahead snuffed the rest out. He raised his good wrist and fired twice at the fleeing pack leader, but the creature was already cutting left, vanishing down the corridor as the blasts punched into the wall.

"Go!" Malfar boomed.

Nate took a reflexive step toward the door, then faltered as he registered that the Troglodan was caught in a wrestling match with the first Ooperian who'd stabbed him. He turned, eyes tracing unseeingly over Elmo's body. Darting back for a second look at the dark, angry-looking gash that ran the side of his rugged face in the hellish red light. A graze wound? He was—

Alive, Ex confirmed. *They all are.*

A roar of pain yanked his attention back to where the Ooperian's dagger had just found its way into Malfar's side. Before Nate could take so much as an unhelpful step, though, the Troglodan bellowed a war cry, smashed the Ooperian to the wall, and flipped the long-limbed creature to the deck in something like a hip throw.

"Go!" the justicar grunted breathlessly, yanking the Ooperian's arm behind its back hard enough to draw a wet pop and a yowl of pain. "The bridge," he added, reaching for something in his gear vest.

Nate gaped. *The bridge.*

Ahead, Malfar drew a stunner, gave the struggling Ooperian an unceremonious pulse dead center in the back of the head, and dug back in his gear vest for some restraint cuffs. Nate's thoughts were racing to the fourth Ooperian, and to the unaccounted for nav pin up front with Amelia the potential bio-bomb, and the fleeing pack leader, and—

Tessa.

"Go!"

Nate ran, head spinning. He clipped the door on the way out and kept running, bouncing down the corridor like a poorly thrown bowling ball on the rails. His head was getting worse. Everything was—shoulder and hand throbbing with every step. Vision thinning and blurring erratically. Deck unsteady beneath his feet.

Yes, yes, came Ex's voice, sounding more muffled and distant than it should've. —*'m—orking on it—tle hobbit. I'm working on—*

Something caught his foot. Flat goddamn deck, he mutely realized, as the floor rushed up to meet him. He caught himself on hands and knees, sliding a meter on armored momentum, then gasped a sharp breath as another flood of bright adrenaline seared through his veins.

—*asty stuff, really*, Ex said, coming back into focus. *Doesn't help that those daggers were laced with Death's Kiss, either. Twice the toxins and half the blood clearly does not a spunky Nathaniel make. Now, you'd best make good use of this pick-me-up. I'm not sure this squishy meat suit you call a body will hold up much longer before you require proper work.*

Nate pushed up from the deck and kept moving, too worried and nauseous to question or complain. He hurried past the main entry hatch and took the last stretch to the bridge at a slightly more cautious clip, painfully aware of how quickly Ex's magic combat boost already seemed to be fading. Over the dizzy rush of blood in his ears, he thought he might've heard voices somewhere belowdecks, but it was only as he crept past the ramp and got his first glimpse into the bridge that it really hit him. Hit him just like the *something* that'd hit the *Camelot* a minute ago, right before the mysterious nerve gas had come pumping.

Someone had docked with them.

And judging from the scene ahead, that *someone* hadn't come for a tea party.

Pirates usually don't, Ex agreed, *as I've been trying to tell you.*

Nate's eyes tracked to Tessa's limp body, alive by Ex's readings but far from safe as she dangled from her Ooperian captor's arm, a literal human shield held against the dark figure standing before them.

Their dark intruder was humanoid. No, *human*, he was pretty sure. Female. An Atlantean woman, then, dressed to the gills in dashing dark leather and well-worn plate armor, face hidden behind a jet black helmet. He took in the vibrant crimson scarf tying her whole debonair space pirate getup together and felt a very unknightly urge to giggle. His head was spinning again. And she was looking at him, onyx faceplate trained on him like she wasn't even remotely surprised to see him.

"Any survivors back there?" she asked, her modulated voice casual, like she'd been expecting him all along. Like he was merely reporting for duty.

Nate wavered on unsteady legs, unsure how to answer, completely clueless as to what the hell was going on. She just gave a casual nod, like he'd given her whatever she needed.

"Good," she said.

Then she drew her blaster and shot the Ooperian behind her before he could blink. A single blur of the motion, and a sizzling blue bolt caught the creature square in the forehead, just like that. She hadn't even turned to look, Nate's foggy brain pointed out. Which explained the murky anger that flared through his confused thoughts as Tessa's unconscious weight thudded to the deck with the Ooperian.

She'd nearly shot Tessa. Hadn't even looked.

Jesus, his head was spinning.

Well, perhaps if you would stop bleeding so bloody much, Ex growled on the murky edge of his awareness, his voice riding those strange waves once again, fading in and out in time with the pulsing red blurs rocking the world.

Two toxins. Half the blood.

He raised his wrist blaster and nearly fell over. "Who the hell are you?"

The woman only spread her hands in peace, onyx helmet cocked just so, and calmly holstered her pistol. "You must be the new Pendragon," she said. "Thought you'd be taller."

She might've said something more. He wasn't sure. The darkness chose that moment to rear up, and the next he knew, he was blinking across the cold bridge deck at Tessa's sleeping face, with no memory of having fallen.

"—t's our cue," came a faraway voice, pulsating in a dizzying wave over Ex's barely audible muttering. "Take him to the ship, Godfried," that voice said, through the rising darkness. "Then fetch the others."

CHAPTER 28

SHOW AND TELL

He woke with a start, waking from nothing, remembering nothing. Soft light flickering. Aches, and fiery pains, and the sickly, feverish itch of healing flesh. A bed. Not his bed. And at the foot of that bed…

"He's up," said the dauntingly tall Svendarian watching Nate with large, unerring golden-brown eyes, burly brown arms crossed across his dark jerkin above the topmost pair of his seven strong legs, which were folded to match down at the "waist," almost like a second set of arms.

Nate blinked around from the cushy white silken blankets and pillows, blearily taking in ornate chests, richly stained wardrobes, and an entire wall of neatly mounted artillery.

"You want we should show him who's boss, Boss?" squawked another voice at the foot of the bed. A squat orange Hobdan, Nate saw, eyes darting back to the vaguely equine Svendarian, then down. The little goblin was so dwarfed by his companion that Nate hadn't noticed him there at first.

"That won't be necessary, Belfric," came a woman's voice from the other side of the room. Nate glanced away from the little goblin's knuckle-cracking show long enough to follow the voice and was unsurprised, as the pieces began limping back to him, to see the Atlantean woman from the bridge sitting there, scribbling at something on the table in front of her.

As I suspected, Ex growled, stirring from whatever miraculous healing ministrations he was busy with. *The resemblance is uncanny.*

What resemblance? Nate wondered foggily, glancing quickly to his own body to confirm that he was indeed still safely encased in his Excalibur armor—no chains, no restraints of any kind, and decidedly not dead—then back to the debonair space pirate. There was no question the raven-haired woman was the same ruthless quick-draw shooter who'd been behind that onyx faceplate. Something about the calm, fearless composure on her brow and the precise movements of her ceaseless writing hand. Scratching away, he registered, on a leather-bound page of yellowed parchment via pen and honest-to-Christ candlelight, sitting there at a bench and table that both looked to be made of genuine old hand-carved wood.

This one's resemblance to the legendary Pirate Blackthorne, Ex said, drawing Nate's attention back from scanning the surprisingly spacious room, with its thick rugs, and rich furniture, and firelight dancing from wall-mounted braziers in bizarre juxtaposition to the star-filled holo viewport on the wall.

Blackthorne? Nate wondered, eyeing the two crossed-arms aliens at the foot of the bed. He vaguely recalled seeing that name somewhere among the throngs of the Forge bazaar, but he couldn't process what some old Atlantean pirate story had to do with any of this when said pirate must've been—

Dead for well over a thousand years, yes. But on her cultists rave, pillaging in the name of the Undying Blackthorne, abducting defenseless travelers, and—

"My crew," Nate grunted, moving to sit up as Ex's words registered, and the rest came rushing back. The two lackeys at the foot of his bed shifted like they might try to stop him. Behind them, their fearless leader's pen nib scratched calmly on, as if she hadn't heard Nate speak at all.

"Hey," he growled, voice stronger this time, shoulder and hand pains significant but manageable as he came to an upright position. He still had his armor. He could fight if need be. "Hey, I'm talking to—"

Her sigh was so monumental that it cut him short.

"Oh, don't stop now," she said, waving her pen in an exasperated conductor's flourish as she closed her leather-bound volume with a dramatic frown, her voice slipping into an overly masculine charade of Nate's. "Who are you, and what have you done with my people?" She flicked her pen idly across the table, not seeming to notice when it perfectly stuck the landing into its decorative holder in a highly improbable shot. She was too busy waving her hands dramatically, pressing on: "Why did you save my Terran-fried bacon back there? How did you even *find* my bacon?! What do you want with my bacon, you devious pirate witch? Answer, scurrilous wench! I am a Knight of the Sacred Order Excalibur, and you and your crew are no match for me!"

She broke her impromptu character, shooting him a conspiratorial sideways glance. "How am I doing here?"

Nate was trying to wrangle his thoroughly confused tongue around to tell her that she'd be doing just fine if she'd go ahead and spit out those answers right this instant, thank you very much. But something in her eyes drew him up short as she turned to meet his gaze in full.

Bottomless. That was the first word that came to mind as her eyes locked onto his, so dark they were nearly black. So bottomless and piercing that he completely forgot his face was even hidden behind the cover of his faceplate. She didn't seem to notice either, watching him without a single trace of her mocking charade act, watching him in a way that almost reminded him of Iveera, albeit indescribably more human. More open. Not threatening or taunting. Not even friendly or especially curious. Just holding him there, simply *seeing* him, until he had to look away for some irrational fear that she might actually absorb some part of his soul, straight through the faceplate.

Who the hell was this woman?

Lady's Grace. Spare me your superstitions and gather your wits. She is naught but a simple Atlantean.

"Your crew is safe and well," their raven-haired host said quietly, almost gently. "Or will be soon. My people are tending to them aboard the *Camelot*, as your companion can no doubt confirm."

She appears to be speaking the truth about the crew, Ex said. *But the Clanless One is in restraints and clearly none too pleased about it, and there are too many loose brigands poking around for my liking. I do not trust this, Nathaniel. I recommend you take control of the situation.*

That sounded like a plan, Nate decided, glancing back at those disconcerting eyes with a faint sense of… he didn't know what. Before he could so much as cross his arms and demand their surrender, though, another wave of animated spunk passed through their mysterious pirate host, and she plunked a hand to the table and hopped up from her bench, almost like another person was taking over.

"As for who I am and how I found that sizzling bacon of yours in your moment of dire need—stellar work on meriting yourself a round of genuine Ooperian assassins, by the way. They don't come out of the shadows for just anyone anymore. But, as I was saying… Ah."

Her eyes tracked back and forth like she was searching an invisible page for the place she'd just lost.

"You was saying who you are, Boss," offered the squat Hobdan Nate had nearly forgotten was standing there at the foot of the bed.

The shift was palpable. A sudden dark storm cloud hanging over the room, crackling in the pirate leader's eyes and thoroughly wilting her two lackeys as she turned to regard them.

"Leave us," she said.

The Hobdan tensed, breaking from his diminutive flinch to glance at Nate. "But Boss, he's still—"

The Hobdan fell silent as his partner reached down with a burly arm and placed a hand on his round shoulder. The Svendarian favored Nate with one last grave expression that seemed best interpreted as a frown, then dipped a deep bow to his raven-haired commander, and turned to leave, five of seven strong legs scuttling beneath him with effortless coordination and surprisingly little sound. After a few seconds, the Hobdan gave Nate a disapproving grunt and followed his partner out, the doors closing behind them with a low wooden thud.

Nate looked back to their fearless leader, thoroughly unsure what to expect next.

"So what?" he asked, testing his injuries as he slid to the foot of the bed. Far from painless, but he could move, and the lightheadedness was fading. "Is this the part where you tell me you're the Undying Blackthorne, reincarnate, and that you'll release my crew just as soon as I hand over the Excalibur?"

He pushed to his feet and turned to square off with her only to find her vacant, like she hadn't even heard him, too distracted with some distant thought or memory. It occurred to him she was the least flawless Atlantean he'd seen. Not unattractive by any means, but just more human than any of her kin from the Forge. Less plastic.

"You were out longer than I expected for one of your kind," she finally said, returning from her thoughts with an idle glance out to the stars. "Suppose that figures," she said, beginning to undo the fastenings of her dark overcoat. "How long are you bonded? Can't have been more than a Terran month now, sowaiy?"

He frowned at the unknown word.

Pirate gibberish, Ex provided. *Linguistic anarchy.*

Nate was watching the pirate's fingers work at the overcoat fastenings, more concerned with what to make of the rest of her question, and with the fact that he needed to establish control and get back to his crew—check on Iveera and figure out what the hell had happened back at the relay, what came next. And this strange woman was doing nothing but slowing him down.

"What do you want with me?" he asked, stepping closer, reminding himself that he was bigger and stronger, and that she was just a lone Atlantean. "Why did you—"

"Help you?" she asked, quirking one dark eyebrow at him, seemingly unconcerned by his proximity.

"Gas my ship with poison," he countered.

She let out a heavy sigh, finishing with the fastenings on her coat and moving to the clasp seal at the thick gear belt she wore over it all. "We have a saying aboard this ship," she said, releasing the clasp and beginning to slip her armored coat open. "Soway, sowaiy."

"Okay, well, I don't know what the hell that means, but what I do know is that you're gonna get your people off my—"

"Soway, sowaiy," she pushed forward, sliding out of her debonair pirate overcoat with not a care in the world, trading armor plating and her holstered pistols for nothing but a plain gray roughspun tunic beneath. Perfectly vulnerable. "Mayhaps we should've made it sowayto, sowaiyto," she added, holding her coat up to frowningly inspect something. "Rhymes with tomato tomahto." She fixed her attention back on Nate. "That's what they say back on that sweet old mother rock of ours, isn't it? Tomato, tomahto? Would've been catchier, I suppose."

"What the hell are you talking about?"

I believe she is inferring—

I know what she's inferring, Nate snapped back. Gas the ship or rescue the ship. Tomato tomahto. Same difference. Except it wasn't. Not one freaking bit. And he was getting tired of this game.

A knowing smile quirked her lips like she could see his frustration blooming. "Soway, sowaiy," she said with a soft shrug, and tossed her heavy coat aside. She didn't seem to notice when it came to a perfect landing on a hangar hook several meters across the room. "Unless you're going to tell me you had those Ooperians right where you wanted them back there?"

"I had it under control."

She studied him for a moment longer, then shook her head, looking slyly amused as her fingers drifted to the crimson scarf at her throat. "No. No, I don't think you did. You haven't had much of anything under control since you escaped Kelkarin's little Forge mausoleum, have you? Since Golnak, even. Or hells, since that crotchety old Merlin first found you back on Terra, if we're really being honest."

Nate stared in silence, wondering how the hell she knew any of this.

She's working you, Ex said. *Pirate parlor tricks. Nothing more.*

"When it comes down to it," she continued, stepping closer, slowly beginning to unwrap her scarf. "I suppose you've never *really* been in control in your life, have you? A leaf on the wind. That's you, right?" She smiled at the imagery. "A leaf on the wild winds, just hoping to all the gods above and below that the Gorgon knows what she's doing, at least enough to see you safely through all this madness and back to your banal Terran life, yes? Back to that sweet little blonde girl you dream of when—"

He'd covered the space between them before he knew it, Ex barking through the roaring storm of his mind to calm himself, that this was all part of her game. All he saw was Gwen's face. All he knew was the sudden icy terror in his chest that she wasn't safe, that somehow this woman knew too many things—impossible things—about his life.

"Tell me now," he hissed, fists trembling, one jagged breath away from grabbing her by two handfuls of roughspun and shaking the answers out. "Who the hell are you, and how did you find us?"

With maddening calmness, she finished unwrapping her scarf and peeled it free. "I didn't."

The fact that he managed merely to cross his arms in lieu of the wild outburst that fought to claw free from his chest at that moment made him wonder if Ex hadn't just slipped him a helping of the Excalibur-powered benzos.

"We've been here for days," she continued. "Since just after, well…" She looked distractedly out to the debris field, brow creasing, then back to Nate. "At any rate, you nearly crashed into us when you came spilling out of the Light. Neat trick, by the way, skipping the Tarkaminen relay by two lightyears." Something changed in her eyes. "I would dearly love to hear how you pulled that one off."

For a second, some part of him figured this would all go faster and less infuriatingly if he just spilled it all out for her and had done with it. Then his better senses caught up with the firm but polite question of what the hell he was thinking.

If I didn't know better, Ex said, doing something to adjust their faceplate filters. *I'd say this Atlantean just attempted to glamour you.*

But how could—

I don't know.

And that pretty much did it.

This time, Ex didn't protest as Nate took their little debonair pirate mentalist by the tunic and hauled her off the deck. He didn't care how many pirates there were out there.

Roughly three-hundred, by my approximations.

Or how exactly they were going to get back to the *Camelot*.

Drawing up escape routes, Ex chirped, beginning to sound pleased with this new direction.

Nate absorbed the information clinically, thinking of what Iveera would do.

"I'm only going to ask you this one last time," he said slowly, drawing her closer, letting her feel how easily he could heft her around. "Who are you, and what are you doing here? Tell me now, or I'll drag you back to the *Camelot* and lock you up until you're ready to talk."

"Well," she said, dark eyes darting toward the door, "fun as that sounds, I think—"

"Don't. We both know your pets out there won't stop me. Just talk."

To his infinite irritation, that fearlessly amused expression slipped right back across her face as she raised her crimson scarf up to eye level and let it daintily slide from her fingertips down to the deck. "Have it your way, then, Leaf."

And with that, she reached down past his hand and started tugging her roughspun tunic off from the waist up.

"What are you—" Nate stammered, catching her by the wrist, setting her down without really meaning too. She rammed a shoulder into his chest, bucking his grip. Startled as he was by the sheer unexpectedness of it all, his hands let go of their own accord.

"You want to know who I am?" she hissed, twisting free, grabbing at the hem of her tunic again. He backed away, raising his defensively, of all things, as she yanked the roughspun top up over her head, dark hair cascading freely back down.

"If this is, like, an Atlantean coupling thing," he said, averting his gaze to the deck, "you need to stop and—"

Her balled up tunic hit him in the face, sprawling across his arms as he reached to reflexively catch it, eyes shooting up, then away, then back again as he registered she wasn't naked at all, but rather stripped down to the form-fitting layer of navy blue thermal skin she'd been wearing beneath it all.

She quirked a dark eyebrow, clearly amused by his reaction. "Don't get ahead of yourself, darling," she said, hiking the hem of the thermal skin up to rest just below her breasts. "I'm not certain you'd *survive* a coupling with me, judging by that reaction. I merely need to show you something."

Nate was too distracted staring to be properly affronted. Staring at the shimmering fabric that wrapped her abdomen, like someone had taken a great swath of starry twilight sky, condensed it down, and made it into a silky bandage wrap, lightly swirling with the faintest azure trace of...

Impossible.

"Ah." She smiled, satisfied, as the realization hit him. "There it is. Now..." Slowly, she began to unwrap that shimmering fabric. "I wonder..."

Nate watched, mesmerized. Gently, delicately, she finished unwrapping and pulled the entire shimmering wrap away. His breath caught.

Beneath the fit figure, her abdomen was carved with a network of sickly dark veins of... he didn't know what. But even as he watched, they flickered with soft waves of azure, almost pulse-like. To look at it with no other input, he might've assumed she was terminally ill, or infected with some bioluminescent parasite. But he felt the trill in the air, as soft and subtle as it was unmistakable.

Beacon song.

And it was coming from her. Straight from the angry-looking dark spot right beside her navel, where something was embedded, burrowed in like...

"No way," he murmured.

Like a little black thorn.

"Does your companion still think I'm a clone?" she asked, with a coy smile.

This is... unexpected.

She's got a freaking Beacon shard in her abs, Ex.

As I said.

"I'll take that for a 'no,'" she said, beginning to wrap her dark little secret back beneath the shimmering fabric, the Beacon song waning as she did. "Good. Well then. On with the show, as they say."

She pulled her thermal skin back down and spread her hands, looking positively pleased as punch, like this was just the loveliest of picnics they were having.

"My name is Anastasiya Blackthorne. And I've been waiting for *you*, Ser Knight, for quite some time now."

CHAPTER 29

DARK TIDINGS

It was the kind of thing that had always been deemed impossible.

Instantaneous translocation, absent the target precision and massive dimensional stabilization proffered by one of the Merlin's Beacon-powered relay superstructures. Galactic teleportation, in other words. Deemed *impossible*, perhaps, largely by merit of the fact that no one of sufficient power and sheer, unshakable will had ever been mad enough to actually attempt such a feat.

And yet, as Zedavian Kelkarin gained his bearings amid the full-body storm of the *Eldest Stone*'s protestant alarms, there was no arguing with what his ship's extensive sensor arrays were telling him.

They'd jumped.

In he'd gone at the secondary C-Sec relay, and out he'd come in the middle of absolutely nowhere. Alone. No *Camelot*. No *Avalon Eternal*. At least four or five light-years out from the T-Sec relay, according to the *Stone*'s preliminary charting calculations.

Impossible, in short. And that was to say nothing of their joint, unnaturally prolonged journey through the Light, and the brief clash he'd shared with the *Avalon Eternal* therein. He'd never seen anything like that.

But neither of those soft impossibilities was even half as disturbing as what he'd seen in those final moments, colliding into the Black Knight's dread ship: a Synth protoswarm, closing in around them. Ethereal, as if it'd been caught on the edge between the Light and realspace. Only a few potential explanations for that. Most of them supremely troubling.

Once upon a time, he might've spent the effort of questioning his own senses, or praying that it had all been a mere hallucination. But he knew what he'd seen. Knew it as surely as his intuition now sung to him of how it was they'd blinked across the galaxy without the full aid of the Merlin's wizardly devices, and of what must've befallen the Tarkaminen relay for him to have seen what he had so unmistakably seen.

He patched into the C-Sec Net via q-node, unsurprised to see the exponentially accelerating flood of emergency alerts there, clogging the general feeds. Dispassionately, he eyed the incoming storm of personal messages from more chancellors and brazen senators than he cared to count, all of them demanding answers with varying degrees of grace and diffidence.

Zedavian looked at it all, feeling nothing, knowing at his core that not a single mortal soul in all of their mighty Alliance was prepared for the answers they sought.

It had begun.

For all he knew, it had already ended, too, right with the opening salvo—even if it'd still be several valiant centuries of bloody struggle before their children's children's children began to realize it.

He made another broad-range sweep of the sensors through the ship meld, half-expecting to find another protoswarm (or worse) closing in on the *Eldest Stone*. Almost welcoming the thought—a chance to flex his true power for the first time in longer than seemed worth recall. But there was nothing.

Come, said that infinite dark nothing, in a voice that tickled ancient memories. *Let us finish this once and for all, old friend.*

He considered the voice, considered the words, quietly contemplating.

"What have you done?" he heard his own lips mutter quite some time later, amid the decaying orbit of troubled thoughts of Beacons, and Black Knights, and faulty data logs. Stealthed q-nodes and corrupted Excaliburs. Corrupted politicians. And the Merlin. The blessed, cursed, thrice-damned wizard who'd been off at his drink and Lady only knew what else as the rising Darkness conspired at the unknown shadows of galaxy's edge.

"What have you done?" he murmured again.

He couldn't say for whom the words were meant. For that blackened abomination at the helm of the *Avalon Eternal*, perhaps. Or for the Merlin, or the Lady. Perhaps he merely asked the question of himself. The intention of the words hardly merited conscious thought, for Zedavian was infinitely more captivated with the infinitesimal stirring they seemed to awaken deep in his chest, beneath the millennia of accumulated apathy.

He regarded that stirring only indirectly at first, like a wild animal that might well bolt at the first sign of unexpected attention. But there it remained, as he reached out and experimentally stroked its tensed hackles. Quietly tremulous. Strengthening as the unmistakable call of Beacon song alighted at the edge of his mind from the darkness, clear and focused. Unnaturally so.

The thought of the raw power and mental control such a feat would've required…

It mattered not. For there was the call, crooning through the darkness like a cosmic welcome mat rolled out to his waiting boots. And here was the tremulous stirring at his very core. Alive, by all the gods above and below. Alive and… almost giddy. Some waking part of himself whose shape he scarcely recognized, whose name he couldn't quite recall.

It had begun. Faster and far more abruptly than before. So abruptly that he couldn't help but wonder if it had ever truly abated even as much as their infinitely pessimistic Merlin had declared all those many, many years ago.

It had begun again.

And perhaps, he thought, reaching out to align the *Stone*'s drives with that quivering line of Beacon song… Perhaps this time, there'd be a proper end.

CHAPTER 30

BLACKTHORNE

"Y̲ou're Anastasiya Blackthorne," Nate echoed quietly. "*The* Anastasiya Blackthorne?"

The raven-haired pirate gave the slightest of bows and made a little fanfare pirouette with one hand.

"But how…" Nate trailed off, not even sure where to start. Dead for well over a thousand years, Ex had said.

More like 1,500, Ex corrected. *She came to infamy back in Arthur Pendragon's time.*

"I doubt I need to tell a Knight how myth and legend tend to take a life of their own throughout the centuries," she said, clearly reading his confusion. "Or how even the wildest of them most often spawn from a kernel of truth." She smirked down at her abdomen. "Or a thorn of it, as it were."

I suppose it's possible that shard has managed to keep her alive all this time.

"But how did she… Where did you… How *old* are you?"

She made a soft tut-tut. "Never ask a lady, Nathaniel. Suffice it to say, I've been waiting for *you* for quite some time."

"Me?" Nate asked dumbly. He closed his gaping mouth, taking a moment to try to remake sense of their entire damned interaction through this new lens. He looked to the illustrious wooden doors, thinking of the pirates beyond, then back to Blackthorne, still entire lightyears behind. Not even behind. Just plain lost.

She placed a hand to her chest, softly pouting. "I must say, I'm a touch hurt you don't recognize me, darling. We *have* been sleeping together. Or didn't you notice?"

"What are you…"

Talking about, he didn't finish, as she stepped closer and gently, almost delicately took her roughspun tunic back from his hands, leaning in close and going up on tip-toe as if to share a secret with his helmeted ear.

"The choice is yours," she whispered.

The words rocked him back on his heels. The same words that'd tumbled from his dreams and spent an afternoon burning circles in his brain back at Zedavian's.

"You… saw my dream?"

"*Our* dream, thank you very much."

Nate searched her face for some sign of trickery. *Ex?* She looked so genuine. *Pirate parlor tricks? What's the deal?*

Ah…

What do you mean, 'ah'?

In front of them, Blackthorne furrowed her brow, mirroring Nate's scrutinizing expression even though he was pretty positive she couldn't actually see through his faceplate.

I'm going to be honest, Nathaniel. I think this one might be above my pay grade.

What does that even mean?

"There there, brave Knight," Blackthorne said, patting him jovially on the helmet and backing away to pull her roughspun back on. "You're here now, and we can sort out the rest just as soon as…" She trailed off, brow furrowed again as her eyes tracked back and forth with that same lost-on-the-page look she'd had earlier. "Scrumdugga."

"What?" Nate asked. But she was already turning away, shaking her head and stomping over to her candlelit table with a heavy sigh.

What are these words? Nate wondered as she plopped down to the bench with another sigh and pulled open her leather-bound journal. *Scrumdugga? Why aren't you translating?*

Because I am not fluent in pirate jibber-jabber. These words are not words, as far as the records of the civilized galaxy are concerned. If you want my professional opinion, that was an expletive.

Charming.

"Listen," he said, following her over to the table, "whatever's going on here, I need to see my crew and—"

She held up a crisp hand for silence, so intently focused on her reading that Nate drew up short. He frowned, watching her eyes hungrily scan the pages, irritation flickering up again. Quickly as it occurred to him that he didn't need her help to check on his ship, though, Ex stepped in and conjured in-helmet feeds from the *Camelot*, which indeed appeared to be safely docked in tow with Blackthorne's ship, whose ID tags appeared as a shredded scramble of nonsense. Nate watched as Ex manipulated the feeds, showing Jaeger and the others neatly arranged on their bunks in the quarters, an attentive Gorgon checking over their vitals, a surly-looking Malfar watching them from the corner where he sat between two armed Svendarians, his thick wrists bound in cuffs.

"You wanna tell me why your people chained up our justicar?" he asked, focusing back to Blackthorne's candlelit bedroom. It felt like a lie, calling Malfar *theirs* as if the Troglodan was anything but a justice-crazed tag-along whose presence Nate was still a little unclear about. But she didn't need to know that. Or to *hear* it either, it seemed, as she calmly finished the page she was reading and closed the journal, making no sign she'd registered his question.

"Hmm," she said quietly. "Ooperians, sowaiy?" Her voice sounded different. Weary. When she looked up at Nate, he saw it in her eyes, too. She almost looked like a different person. "Of course," she said, giving herself a tired nod, eyeing him up and down.

Nate frowned from her to the journal, unable to ignore the sudden feeling that she'd just forgotten their entire conversation and played catch-up with her notes.

"What, the Troglodan?" she asked, mistaking the source of his frown. "Admittedly, your colleague was less than cooperative with our, shall we say, *unsolicited invitation* to surrender his weapons and join us here aboard the *'Thorn*. Unsurprising, given his chosen vocation. But we made do. I trust you see that he and the rest of your people are unharmed. So, to business then?"

Maybe not mistaking, he realized. Maybe just changing the topic.

"Which business would that be?" Nate asked slowly.

"Hunting that blackened bastard down, of course," she said, swiping a fist through the air like they were old comrades. "Right?"

Nate just blinked at her, feeling the ground shifting yet again beneath his feet. Could she really mean…?

"Ah," she said, gauging his reaction. "We didn't get that far yet, did we?"

What was it with this woman?

I begin to suspect she's not entirely stable.

You think? Nate sat down on the corner of the bed, feeling as weary and impatient with this conversation as he was suddenly certain that this was far more than just some random pirate encounter. "Look, I'm getting whiplash, here. Can you just start from the beginning?"

Blackthorne looked at her journal, over to a flight-secured bookcase that held several dozen identical volumes, and back to him like she wasn't quite certain he was following. "That would be a very long story."

"Right. Yeah, well, maybe just the key notes, then. Like what you know about the Black Knight, and why I should trust a single damn thing you're telling me right—What's so funny?"

She shook her head, fighting to snuff out the last bubbling remnants of the chuckle that'd started to escape. "Apologies. It's nothing. I was just thinking how many times I've had this very conversation. Oh, the lips and timbre change, to be sure," she added, as if in response to some unspoken argument he hadn't made. "But the inane little sentiments—the who are you, what do you want, why should I trust you?—those remain the same, with shocking clarity. Hmm." She cocked her head at some thought. "The inane remain the same. Catchy."

"You're… kind of a confusing lady, you know that?"

She smiled and didn't argue.

Nate wasn't quite sure what it was that convinced him in that moment to release the protection of his helmet and faceplate back to e-dim. He knew only that he needed her to focus on the matter at hand. And focus she did, looking up to meet his eyes as soon as the faceplate folded out of sight.

There was power in her eyes. He was even more certain of it now, holding her unfiltered gaze. For a second, he thought that he'd made a mistake, dropping any part of his defenses, and that she might try more mind tricks. But the seconds passed, and by some deep-seated intuition he couldn't even begin to unwind, he found his certainty growing. This woman was not his enemy.

"You cannot trust me to do anything but that which is within my nature to do," she said, "just as I cannot trust you, Nathaniel Arturi. But as for the answer you truly seek, well, there is really only one thing you need to know."

"What's that?"

"The one you call the Black Knight. He was there the day my planet died all those many years ago. For that alone, I have sworn all my long life to find him. I don't particularly care whom he serves, or what conflict you have with him. I will not let him go for what he's done. And by our Lady's twisted Grace, I believe you and I are meant to help one another find him."

She watched him attempt to process that. He didn't have much to go by, what with his severe lack of galactic history knowledge.

Some legend has it that the Pirate Blackthorne rose as a spector from the arcane ruins of the Old Avalon colony. The very same Avalon after which the Black Knight's Avalon Eternal is ostensibly named.

More straws for the grasping.

"And you believe this because of the dreams? *Our* dreams?"

Blackthorne shrugged. He still wasn't convinced she wasn't somehow playing him on that bit, but he also had no idea how she would've gleaned such details.

"I suspect it's all connected," she said. "It usually is."

"What is?"

"Oh, you know." She waved a dismissive hand. "The Lady. The Knights. The Synth. A galaxy at war. All that shisaru. The endless dance." She frowned at the omni unit on the table in front of her, then over to the chamber doors. "Speaking of which…"

He followed her frown to the ornate double doors, catching the faintest buzz of muffled voices on the other side. Blackthorne sighed the moment before the doors were hauled forcefully open. Nate just gaped at the tall, charred figure standing there in the doorway.

"Iveera," he gushed, nearly as surprised to see the Gorgon standing there as he was by the flood of relief that washed over him at the sight. He hadn't realized just how worried he'd been until he found himself halfway to his feet, like some part of him had half a mind to go and hug her. The ridiculousness of that thought sobered him up as much as the gratuitous burns still scorched across her face.

"And so the mighty Huntress rises again to stalk her immortal prey," Blackthorne said softly, almost to herself. "It's okay, boys," she added to her tense Hobdan and Svendarian lackeys who lingered uncertainly in the doorway as Iveera stalked into the room.

The Svendarian closed the doors with a troubled frown. Iveera drew straight up to Blackthorne's table, not quite limping but unmistakably moving slower than usual.

"Knight," Blackthorne said.

"Pirate," Iveera replied, eyeing her warily

"You two…" Nate started, glancing confusedly between them. Know each other. Obviously. But… "Are you okay, Iveer—"

Her name died in his throat at the look the Gorgon shot him.

"What are you doing here?" she asked, deadly intense. Nate was fumbling for the words to explain when Iveera turned back to Blackthorne, having apparently been addressing the pirate. "You shouldn't be here. You've been warned before."

To her credit—or maybe to her madness—Blackthorne didn't look any more intimidated by Iveera's threatening presence than she had been by Nate's. She just shrugged. "Blame it on your Lady if you must, Knight. It's hardly my fault she's seen fit to fill my dreams with this one's visions."

She tilted her head at Nate, indicating to which *this one* she was referring. Iveera's phosphorescent eyes flicked to follow, studying Nate for a moment, absorbing the claim without question, like it was entirely within the realm of possibilities. That might've answered that if not much else. Nate was half-sure she was about to tell Blackthorne to piss off anyway.

"Very well," she said instead, focusing back on the pirate. "Let us hear what you have come to say. But be quick, pirate."

"She's looking for the Black Knight too," Nate said when Blackthorne didn't answer. Partly to be helpful, and partly to break their lengthening staring contest. At first, he didn't seem to have accomplished either. But then something passed between them, and the tension shifted.

"You're certain he was here?" Iveera asked.

"Reasonably," Blackthorne replied.

The Gorgon crossed her arms. "What is he to you?"

Nate got the impression Iveera would've rather asked the more basic question they were both still wondering: what *is* he? Period. But that would've been showing their hand, letting Blackthorne know just how clueless they still were.

Not that the pirate seemed to need much help arriving at that conclusion. "I'm sure you have your theories," was all she said.

Iveera considered her for a long moment, then turned disinterestedly for the door. "Come, Nathaniel. We cannot trust this one, and we have no time to tarry. We must search the wreckage and—"

"Wait."

Nate was surprised to hear himself speak up. Even more surprised to see Iveera pause, jin twitching, and look back for the explanation he hadn't yet found.

"I'm just saying, if we can all set aside the disagreements for a second... I think we need her."

"So sweet of you to say, darling," Blackthorne said, touching a hand to her chest and shooting him an affectionate smile.

"Why?" Iveera asked, ignoring the pirate completely.

Nate opened his mouth, intending to explain—over Ex's muttered comments about *superstition,* *feminine wiles,* and *pathological suckerhood*—what Blackthorne had already told him about her home planet and the Black Knight. He closed it again, realizing he wasn't sure any of it was actually true. Truth be told, he wasn't really sure why he felt they should give her a chance at all.

Someone clearly wasn't listening to my expert diagnosis, Ex grouched.

"For what it's worth," Blackthorne said, inspecting her nails with a disinterest to match Iveera's, "I *have* already spent some time searching the wreckage. I can tell you what happened here."

"You can?" Nate asked, feeling mildly betrayed that she hadn't thought to lead with that.

"I already know what happened here, pirate," Iveera said.

Nate turned to the Gorgon, feeling more incompetent by the second. "You do?"

"Then you'll also know it's going to be damn near impossible to find what you're looking for without an eye witness, sowaiy?" Blackthorne fired back, both of them eyeing one another like a pair of mighty jungle cats, neither making any sign they'd heard Nate at all.

"I suppose you just so happen to have one aboard," Iveera said.

Blackthorne smiled, spreading her hands like a circus conductor preparing to reveal the next act. "I *just so happen* to have one aboard!" Her smile turned a few shades more glib. "Not to mention a pair of Ooperians with whom I imagine you both might have a great interest in speaking."

Iveera stared the pirate down, jin lightly swirling, clearly not delighted. Blackthorne didn't flinch.

"Not to interrupt," Nate said, hooking a thumb toward the planet-sized debris field in the holo viewport, "but can someone please tell me what I missed here? What *did* this? Was this… Was it the Black Knight, or not?"

The two traded one last standoffish look, then seemed to come to some unspoken agreement.

"He *was* here," Blackthorne said, turning to face the debris field, all lingering traces of coy amusement bleeding a cold death on her face.

"But he did not do this alone," Iveera finished.

"But then"—Nate glanced between them, sensing the gravity—"who else…"

But he already knew, he realized, as he searched Iveera's eyes.

"You would have already felt it, had you been paying attention," Iveera said, quietly reprimanding, as she came to face the viewport beside them. "This is the work of the Synth. It's already begun."

He swallowed and dropped his gaze to the deck, knowing on some abstract level that he should be terrified by those words. Instead, he just found himself eyeing his own lack of experience yet again. He didn't *know* enough to be properly terrified. All he felt was a twinge of hot-cheeked embarrassment, capped over with a nice, vague layer of existential doom.

"Who would've guessed the Second Age of the Great War would kick off with naught but the senseless slaughter of a harmless mining colony?" Blackthorne asked quietly. She looked at them in a way that made it evident she wasn't looking for an answer—wasn't looking for anything so much as an end to all of this. "Now, would you like to meet our lone survivor, or not?"

CHAPTER 31

SUNDERED

Their lone eyewitness survivor, it turned out, was a trembling Atlantean girl named Lena, who couldn't have been much older than eighteen, to look at her. Nate listened in mute horror as she described her chance encounter crashing her dune skimmer straight into the Black Knight only to come to a few hours later, with a smoking village on the horizon, and an indescribable cloud of death descending from the sky.

Nate found himself glancing to Iveera at each bizarre detail, attempting to gauge the reality of what he was hearing. A planet. An entire damned planet, ripped open by an endless, shapeless swarm of rock and accumulated space debris. A swarm that only seemed to grow as the destruction spread, like it wasn't a discrete attack force so much as a self-replenishing virus, tainting all it touched, turning the very bedrock of the planet against itself.

It all sounded impossible. Iveera's face was an ivy green mask, giving nothing away, her jin making only the slowest of thoughtful swirls, as if in deference to the tragedy.

"I... I just watched it all," the girl, Lena, whispered, eyes painfully empty, quiet tears streaming down her cheeks. "I wanted to help. Tried to go back, but... but they just... The homestead was gone. Just gone. Just like that. And before I knew it, I was running the other way, and crawling into my pod, and"—she sucked in a wet, shuddering breath, holding back a sob—"and I just watched. And now they're all dead, and I'm just... I'm here."

She said the last part like she wasn't really certain it was true—which was understandable enough, given what little Blackthorne had told them of how they'd pulled the girl out of a drifting, atmos-depleted pod, oxygen-starved and more than half frozen to death. A Terran wouldn't have survived what she'd been through. Nate felt the soft weight of tears pressing at his eyes as he watched the girl, wishing there was something he could do to alleviate her pain.

"Did you observe any change before the swarm departed?" Iveera asked, in her version of a gentle tone.

"There was..." Lena sniffed and wiped her face, mastering herself admirably. "There was something on the rad sensors, I think. I mean, they were going wild the whole time, but... Well, at first, I figured they were all just malfunctioning, or... I mean, the entire magnetosphere was... I don't know. But right before they broke away, my entire panel spiked, like... I don't know." For the first time since they'd entered, she found it in herself to look up and meet Iveera's eyes. "I don't know what does that."

"You have shown great bravery in telling us your story, Lena Miner-caste," Iveera said, kneeling before the girl in something like a bow and reaching one hand for her light brown cheek.

Blackthorne stepped in and caught the Gorgon's hand before she could touch Lena, shaking her head. "Not like that," she whispered.

To Nate's surprise, Iveera didn't argue. Only showed Lena something like a gentle smile, then stood and turned for the med bay door, gesturing for Nate to join her. He considered Lena, wanting to give her something—anything. He fell in behind Iveera, feeling heavy. Behind them, Blackthorne gave the girl a touch on the shoulder, murmuring soft words, then moved to follow them.

"Ooperians next?" she asked, as she stepped into the corridor, Lena's door hissing shut behind her. "Or have I already made the team?"

Iveera waited until a pair of Blackthorne's approaching dark-garbed Atlantean crew finished giving her and Nate the distrustful stare-down and passed by.

"There's something else," the Gorgon said quietly. "We'll discuss it on the *Camelot*. In private. The Ooperians can wait."

"So I *have* made the team, then," Blackthorne said, drumming at an elbow with one crossed hand and somehow managing to sound both glib and bored at the same time.

"I'd simply rather keep you in my sight, pirate, if you insist on interfering with our business."

"What's going on?" Nate asked, trying to bring them back on track.

Iveera considered him, looking unusually hesitant as she crossed her arms to match Blackthorne. "We have a few problems."

Nate briefly considered the grand total of all the shitstorms currently raging around them. "That kinda feels like an understatement."

"And yet, it gets worse."

"What's worse than this?"

"I admit you've teased my curiosity as well," Blackthorne said, straightening from her wall lean and looking a touch more serious. "What do we have? Juicy new lead? News from the Capital?"

Iveera searched the pirate's face, earning herself a finely arched eyebrow. She seemed to confirm something. "You *haven't* heard then. The Tarkaminen Beacon is gone. The relay is dead."

Blackthorne stiffened. "How?"

"Not here," Iveera said, looking up and down the corridor.

Some dumb part of Nate's was still reflecting that it was the first time he'd seen the pirate look so openly surprised by something when Iveera's original words finally caught up with his rudimentary understanding of interstellar travel like Diet Coke to Mentos.

No Beacon, no working relay. No working relay…

"Come," Iveera said, starting down the corridor. "We have much to discuss."

No working relay…

"Fuck," he gasped.

A thousand meters away, down the oddly dilating corridor that thrummed with every pulse of his racing heart, Iveera marched on, expecting them to follow.

"Relay dead," Blackthorne murmured beside him, so close he nearly jumped. "You know, I really don't get to say this often, but I did *not* see that coming."

He looked at her dumbly, searching her dark eyes for some saving grace, some lifeline to counter the terrible conclusion his short-circuiting brain cells were feebly sputtering toward.

"Come now," she said, clapping him encouragingly on the shoulder as she set off after Iveera. "It's only the end of life as we know it."

Nate watched her go, head buzzing, feeling very small and alone, and horribly aware of the fact that he was but a tiny speck drifting on the wrong side of an indescribably vast galaxy.

No working relay, no trip home.

They were trapped here.

They were all trapped.

~

BY THE TIME they'd reached the *Camelot*'s bridge, and Blackthorne had dismissed the two pirates she'd left to safeguard their docked trajectory, Nate was still watching the outside world move by in a blur, hopelessly stuck on the words splashing across his brain again, and again.

The Beacon is gone. The relay is dead.

The Beacon is gone. The relay is dead.

Over, and over, and over again, building to the crescendoing tune of Oh Shit in F Major.

You're overreacting, Nathaniel, Ex said. *Worst case scenario, it takes us a few years to return to civilization via staggered q-drive and crusher jumps. From there, it's still a quick jump back to Golnak. Well, provided the Forge relays are still there by that point. And, of course, that the Synth haven't already...*

Nate stood there mutely, waiting for his companion to finish the chain of thought.

You know what? Let's focus on the here and now. 'Live in the moment.' That's what you squishy meat bags always say, right?

"How did this happen?" Nate croaked, turning to Iveera as the heavy bridge door slid shut behind Blackthorne's people. Dimly, he noted that Amelia's crash couch cell was no longer there in the empty corner and that he should probably go check on the crew and bring Jaeger into this conversation. But Iveera was playing this one cautious, and he needed answers now. "Was this the Black Knight?"

"Most likely," Iveera said. "Quite possibly with the aid of the same protoswarm that consumed the Demeter colony."

"Might explain why they left mid-assimilation," Blackthorne said, earning herself a distrustful look from Iveera. She shrugged. "I'm no expert, and it has been a *very* long while, but as far as I recall, protoswarms don't tend to leave scraps behind without good reason."

The words were of little comfort to Iveera.

"Don't give me that look, Knight," Blackthorne said, crossing her arms, "As I told the Terran, I don't particularly care who is working for whom here. My only aim is finding the Black Knight. We have unfinished business, he and I."

A testy silence settled between them. Nate was still trying to wrap his head around how this had happened.

"What about the fleet?" he asked. "The relays are all guarded, right? You're telling me this… And all the other traffic…" His head spun, thinking about thousands of civilians they'd seen queued up for the relay back at Golnak. "You're telling me this swarm wiped them all out?"

The tension between Iveera and Blackthorne eased a touch as they traded a look.

"Yes," Iveera finally said. "Most likely."

"At least a few thousand souls lost on Demeter-12," Blackthorne said quietly. "The colony was only beginning to establish itself. At the relay, we're talking about at least another twenty-thousand casualties in the patrol fleet alone. Perhaps only a quarter that many more in passing civilian traffic, Lady willing. The Tarkaminen relay is… er, *was* the least trafficked by far in Alliance space. Mostly large ore freighters and the like. Lower than average crew densities."

She looked like she might keep talking—like maybe if she didn't stop, the actual horrors of the numbers wouldn't quite set in. Nate wasn't sure if the kindness was intended for her or for him. He was just gaping numbly ahead, plenty horrified all the same when something struck him out of the blue.

"I saw them."

They both looked at him.

"Back in the Light, I mean, when Zedavian was attacking the Black Knight, and the place was collapsing around us. I think I saw this swarm out there, just before we spilled out. I thought they were ships or something, but…"

Iveera watched to see if he'd say more, jin bobbing a slow affirmative. "You weren't the only one who saw them," she finally said, coming to some decision and waving her holos open. She flicked a frozen, half-sized hologram of Zedavian Kelkarin onto the deck between them, then fixed them both with a grave look. "Observe."

With a jab of her jin, Iveera triggered the recording.

"Seven," Zedavian's hologram said, coming to life before them. He looked for a second like he couldn't quite decide whether to be cavalier or flatly sober about it. "Iveera," he said, settling for the latter.

Nate had never seen the ancient Eldari hesitate before.

"I have a line on your Black Knight," the recording said. "You may too, by the time you're hearing this." He hesitated again. Seemed to come to some decision. "You were right about his wielding of the Terran Beacon. Which, if you haven't already realized, means he might well be beyond any of our powers to stop. Do with that as you will. I'd order you to stay away—*am* ordering you to do just that, in fact—but I think we both know we've already crossed that threshold. You are bound by his corruption, whether you can see it or not. You can no longer trust your judgment in this matter any more than I can trust you at my back."

A humorless smile pulled at his lips.

"Perhaps you'll even believe what I'm telling you. But, if not, do rest assured that I will take great delight in personally rendering all punishment befitting your insubordination if and when we should see each other again, Ser Knight."

The smile faded, his golden face turning thoughtful.

"In the interim, there are a few things you should know. You've probably already noticed the Tarkaminen relay is down. What you might not realize is that it was attacked by a protoswarm. Mid-class and recently gorged, I'd guess, by the brief look I had before the relay collapsed." He huffed. "Not that that will mean much to anyone alive. Well, no one but our dear old wizard, of course. And Silas, wherever the hell he's gone."

Again, a moment of hesitation.

"And perhaps this Black Knight, too, if I make my guess correctly. And if I do…"

His golden eyes went distant.

"His name was Mordred, once upon a time. Mordred LeFaye. Don't bother with Alliance records. You won't find him there. He was one of us. I know the wizard already told you as much. What he didn't tell you was that our dear Ninth Knight turned on us not so very long after the Great War. Not hard to understand why we wouldn't want that in our esteemed histories. A lot of people died. We were six Knights back then, not counting him. Mordred LeFaye slew four of our Order, the Terran's predecessor included, before Silas and I brought him down. He was… unnaturally gifted. Even for one of us. Unnaturally angry, too. But trust me when I say I cannot conceive of how any living being, mortal or otherwise, could've survived what we wrought on him at the end."

A moment of silence before Zedavian's hologram returned from some memory.

"Perhaps he didn't. Perhaps the wizard was right, and this foe is nothing but a dark shell, risen on the power of the Synth and bound in his image. But I do not believe that. I…"

Zedavian's golden brow creased ever-so-slightly, like he'd only just realized he was still talking.

"Lady's Grace be with you, Iveera," he said. "Stay away if you can."

The message abruptly ended, Zedavian's likeness winking out of sight.

They all stood there in silence. It was only then that Nate noticed Iveera was watching Blackthorne like a hawk, almost like she was waiting for some reaction or explanation.

"That's the most I've heard him say in a thousand years," Blackthorne finally said. Nate glanced at her, still too wrapped up in Zedavian's words to be overly shocked by the statement. A thousand years? Sure, why not?

"He expects to die," Iveera said.

"I think you're right," Blackthorne agreed, trading a meaningful look with Nate, "in a manner of speaking, at least."

Nate's mind drifted to the last moments of his dream. The crossed blades. Zedavian bowed at the Black Knight's feet; swords crossed over a crackling portal as the Merlin hung impaled on a great dark thorn. The weight of his sword in hand.

The choice is yours.

But *what* choice?

He looked at Blackthorne, wondering for the thousandth time at what he'd seen—what *she'd* apparently seen, too. She watched him right back.

A dream. It'd been a disturbingly *real* dream, granted, and one he'd somehow shared with another person from tens of thousands of light-years away. But still a dream, nonetheless. And now…

Now that he knew about Blackthorne's connection to his so-called vision, he didn't know what to trust. It all felt tarnished, somehow. Less pure. And as for Zedavian, well, he *had* saved their lives back in the Light, hadn't he?

Sure, some paranoid corner of his mind pointed out, *leaving us safely in Ooperian hands for the* second *time counting.*

Still, the Zedavian who'd sent them that message hadn't *sounded* like an evil mastermind going to turncoat and join forces with his secret dark ally. He'd sounded like a man, or an Eldari, preparing to go face an unwinnable fight in the line of duty.

Lady's Grace, Ex murmured, *at this rate, he might actually die of old age before you make up your mind.*

Nate narrowed his eyes at nothing in particular, focusing back on Iveera and Blackthorne, who were both occupied on their own thought. "I think we should try to find Zedavian," he said. "Whatever else is happening, he did save our lives back there."

"Sounds more to me like he saw a foe and attacked," Blackthorne said. "You'd be wise to refrain from imagining you understand anything of his motives based on that single outcome."

To Nate's surprise, Iveera didn't argue.

"At any rate," Blackthorne continued, "I gather finding Zedavian and finding our Black Knight might shortly become one and the same, so count me in, or whatever you'd like to call it."

"We have limited options," Iveera said, jin flicking softly back and forth. "The First Knight remotely disassembled the q-node he used to get this message to the *Camelot*."

Nate frowned. "What node?"

Iveera pointed to the console Jaeger had been using, near Tessa's larger command station. The paneling had been ripped off from the side, internal cabling and circuitry all spilling out with a hastily picked-over look. "For future reference," she said, "you should tell your Lt Col to think twice before accepting devices from strangers, and twice again before interfacing them with this ship." She frowned at the open console. "Not that he would've been able to spot anything amiss. It was quite the clever microassembly Zedavian's data key left behind. I nearly missed it myself."

Nate stared at the console, digesting this new piece of information.

Friends didn't install tracking nodes in friends ships, did they?

Not unless they were worried said friend might lose their mind and go rampaging across the galaxy, he supposed.

"So what do we do, then?" he asked.

"We need more information," Iveera said. "Without knowing precisely what we are looking for, it seems our best option is either to follow the trail of the missing Beacons or to pray our Lady sees fit to bless you with further insight."

"Needle in the haystack," Blackthorne muttered, glancing at Nate. "That's the saying, sowaiy?"

Thinking of how long it'd taken Iveera to dowse the Beacon's location on Earth, Nate kind of saw her point when one considered even his laughably inadequate understanding of just how damned *big* space was.

"And since only one of those options appears to be within our control," Iveera continued, ignoring their reservations, "I intend to begin preparations. The *Kalnythian Wilds* should be nearly ready to come out of e-dim for final repairs. We'll be able to triangulate more quickly if we part ways and make a systematic sweep of the sector."

Nate tensed inwardly at the thought of splitting up now, here on the trail of some planet-eating swarm and the dude who'd apparently killed at least four Knights *before* he'd had a Beacon or two on hand. He couldn't bring himself to ask how long she expected such a sweep might take. He was pretty sure he didn't want to know.

"Perhaps the two of us should take a nice nap and pray for the best, in the meantime," Blackthorne said.

Iveera regarded them both with a flat look, then turned and stalked off, waving the bridge door open and disappearing without a word.

She may be an ally, for now, came her voice in his mind a second later, *but do not make the mistake of trusting the pirate.*

Duly noted, he thought back. He still wasn't entirely sure where Iveera's stalwart disdain for Blackethorne stemmed from, but then again, he'd probably missed a few centuries of interpersonal history. Who knew with any of these people?

"So what do you say, partner?" Blackethorne asked beside him, wiggling her raven-dark eyebrows in a gesture entirely too frisky for a thousand-year-old lady. "Care to join me in the bedroom?"

He looked after the spot where Iveera had disappeared, too drained to even blush at the comment as he once might've. He wasn't sure he should have a *say* at all, lost as he felt in all of this. He was kind of surprised— maybe even a shade irritated—that Iveera hadn't simply taken control and told him what to do.

Yes, how dare she trust you might be capable of thinking for yourself? Ex muttered. *Honestly. The outrage.*

Nate frowned. *Not sure now's really the time to be pulling off the training wheels.*

Well, perhaps she isn't quite so in control as you'd like to believe. Either way, I don't see any reason you can't at least try to be useful.

His frown deepened right along with the sinking feeling in his gut. He didn't argue. Blackthorne was still watching him expectantly, but also with the patient air of someone who unmistakably had the time. It occurred to him that she was the oldest of them all. At least several centuries older than Iveera, as far as he'd gathered. Maybe that counted for something where wise plans were concerned. Maybe not.

If he *could* get back to the dream… well, he wasn't sure what he might find.

It wasn't much of a plan. Not at all. But then again, neither was blindly feeling around the galaxy for the effervescent flicker of Beacon song he could vaguely feel even now—as faint as it was hopelessly directionless—if he closed his eyes and really focused. He looked back to Blackthorne, weighing piss poor options, getting nowhere fast.

"I think I need to talk to my crew."

CHAPTER 32

FINDER'S FEE

"So let me get this straight," Jaeger said, groaning a little as he hefted himself shakily to his feet from the edge of his bunk. "In addition to somehow dropping out of hyperspace on the remains of the Atlanteans' missing colony, which was coincidentally eaten by a friggin' fleet of rocks, we're now friends with the lady—

"Pirate," growled Malfar from the corner.

"—With the *pirate*," Jaeger amended, "who just gassed us all and—"

"And saved you all the trouble of a round of self-inflicted gunshots to your pretty heads," Blackthorne interjected from where she was standing against the wall with crossed arms, her smile delightfully saccharine. "Except you, of course, darling," she added toward Elmo, whose square face sported a thin adhesive wound strip where his near-miss bullet had grazed from the jaw right up past the eye socket. "But I think you're positively dashing."

Elmo's burgeoning frown quickly shifted to a pained scowl as his wound informed him that facial movements were unwise. Jaeger just fixed Nate with a firm look of *who is this lady, and why aren't we venting her right now?*

Nate looked around the crew quarters and saw a similar question echoed in most of the SAS team's eyes. The displeasure ran at least triply high in Malfar's case, but the Trog had kept it quiet. He seemed acutely aware of what was happening here, maybe because he hadn't been born in Alliance space yesterday like the rest of them, or maybe just because he'd been conscious throughout the attack thanks to the handy breather mask in his gear vest. The more Nate observed of the Trog, though, the more he saw a sharp, astute mind turning behind those beady eyes. Sharper than his own, he was starting to think.

He'd just finished recounting Lena's disturbing tale of the attack on Demeter-12. Having been only tenuously conscious when he and Blackthorne had walked into the room, the crew had listened without much interruption, save for the introductory round of *who are you and what are you doing here* as they'd roused to the sight of Svendarian guards and a strange Gorgon medic—not to mention the odd little blinking medical apparatuses fixed to each of their chests like mini versions of Ramirez's medpod.

Most of them were sitting up now, in various states of bleary-eyed suspicion and discombobulation. Pierce and Tessa both looked and sounded like they'd had a rough night on the town. Snuffy seemed to be wondering if this entire situation might just magically go away if only he laid down for a quick nap. Only Carter looked particularly lucid beneath her dark, ashen frown.

Amelia, on the other hand, looked no less worse for wear. After her initial skepticism, the Atlantean had even seemed a touch riveted with the presence of their legendary pirate guest. At least until they'd gotten to the news of Demeter-12. She'd barely moved or spoken since then, sitting in the corner like a powered down android, posture immaculate but for the faintest droop in her shoulders and head. Eyes distant and expression vacant. Nate wished he could do something for her. Wished he had anything but a long list of more bad news.

"That pretty much sums it up," he admitted to Jaeger's expectant look, hesitant to push on with the rest of it before they'd all had a chance to at least try to process the scale of the destructive forces they were up against here.

"Well," Pierce finally broke the silence. "'Least we didn't get caught by our Alliance friends straight outta the gate, right? That's something."

"This doesn't really feel like a silver lining kind of situation," Snuffy said quietly, eyes on the floor.

"Oh fuck off," Pierce shot back, waving a vague hand toward the endless space outside. "Any other day, you'd all be riding my ass for being Ms. Debbie Fucking Downer. This is what we came for, right? Find the wizard? Stop the Black Knight from raising the ancient evil and sacking the goddamn village? All this… shit? I mean, Christ." He came to his feet with an unsteady lurch, hands spread wide as he looked around at the crew. "Are you guys even hearing this bullshit? Evil asteroid swarms? The fucking *Merlin*?"

"Lieutenant," Jaeger said, in a voice even made Nate pucker a little bit. "That's enough."

Pierce rounded on his superior, clearly more than a little tempted to give the good Lt Col another steaming piece of his mind. Amelia spoke quietly from the corner before he could.

"Turns out, you're a little too late for the village, Terran."

Pierce whirled on his new target, anger spiking then evaporating as he took in her empty expression. For a second, he looked like he'd apologize, but then he got stuck on the words and sank back to his bunk instead, burying his face in his hands with a steady muttered stream of, "Christ, Christ, Christ."

Jaeger gave the room a moment to breathe before turning back to Nate.

"First things first. Where are the Ooperians?"

"Safely aboard my ship," Blackthorne said, "ready for interrogation."

"But we have bigger problems," Nate said.

"Bigger than the alien vampires who almost just killed us all?" Pierce asked, looking up from his cupped hands long enough to show what he thought of that.

"Dude," Tessa said, hooking a thumb at the holo pane that was currently displaying Demeter-12's drifting remains.

Jaeger silenced the chatter with a raised hand, then fixed Nate with a serious look. "Floor's yours, kid. But if you're gonna tell us what's happening here, you're gonna tell us the whole damn thing, you copy? Starting with why His Golden Holiness was so keen to throw you and Iveera in the clink in the first place."

In his silent corner, Malfar stirred for the first time. Nate eyed the rest of the crew, wondering how much they'd heard, how much Malfar had even figured out.

"No," Jaeger said, shaking his head. "No more calculating. No more thinking you can lie to protect us. We're done flying blind, kid. This here's the reckoning. You want us on board watching your back, you're gonna tell us what the hell it is we're standing in. Zedavian and the corruption, the swarm, our magical relay jump right to ground zero. All of it. The whole Shitstorm Special."

Nate didn't need to glance around the room to sense that the crew felt the same way. The air was thick with it, Carter and Elmo with their somber stares, Pierce with his accusatory scowl. Malfar and Amelia watched with something more like professional curiosity, and while Tessa and Snuffy at least looked amicably supportive about the whole thing, they clearly wanted answers too.

Jaeger wasn't backing down anyway.

Nate glanced at Blackthorne and caught her watching him with a curious expression. It evaporated the moment he looked at her, and she gestured to the others, cordially inviting him to go ahead and spill his guts and make it pretty.

And if the immortal old lady said so…

"Fine," he said, turning back to the crew. "One Shitstorm Special, coming right up."

BY THE TIME Nate shambled out of the crew quarters an hour or so later, his throat was uncomfortably dry, his spirits low, and his readiness to witness any more stoic heartbreak from the crew about on par with his desire to blast his own foot off.

It is for the best, I think, Ex said. *You did well in there.*

He didn't even sound sarcastic about it, which might've sounded the warning bells had Nate not already been too busy feeling like the Anti-Santa Claus—Ms. Debbie Fucking Downer, to borrow Pierce's phrase.

He wasn't really sure what he'd been hoping for, laying it all out for them—the whole Shitstorm Special, as it were. A miracle, he supposed, looking back now. He'd been hoping for a miracle. A brilliant stroke of inspiration. Or at least some fresh perspective, or a slight loosening of the cold-packed dread in his gut. What relief he'd found confiding in the others, though, had quickly been replaced by the guilt that'd sunk deeper with each falling face, each downward glance.

To their credit, they'd listened to most of it with minimal interruption. Zedavian Kelkarin's theories about this so-called corruption, the Synth protoswarm, and the identity of the Black Knight Mordred LeFaye. The name still felt odd on Nate's tongue. Easier to imagine a faceless agent, a dark protrusion of this unknowable Synth's will beneath that black helmet. He still wasn't sure that wasn't the case. But the bad news had been far from complete.

On the matter of which punch to save for last, he'd been a bit torn. That the Tarkaminen relay was dead along with the thirty-some thousand souls and an entire colony settlement was plenty devastating. That the path home was closed for business, though, with a Black Knight and a planet-eating army of darkness standing between them and their only hope of fixing it, was decidedly more personal. That their best intel for *finding* said Knight boiled down to a rather cataclysmic dream—not to mention the fact that one of the most powerful beings in the galaxy was unconvinced even *he* could face a Beacon-powered Black Knight if they did… well, that was just plain old terrifying.

In the end, there'd been no stroke of inspiration, only heavy words leaving his mouth, and the progressively heavier weight of somber realization settling through the room, one downward glance at a time. There'd been a lot of silence, a lot of brave faces. It was the first time Nate had seen through them all—even Jaeger's and Carter's.

But they were professionals. They'd kept it together and turned to discussing plans and options once they'd gotten the initial shock and pithy comments out of the way. Nate, thoroughly talked out and circling the brim of his own despair, had only half-listened to most of it. Jaeger's talk of finding reinforcements among whatever Alliance forces must still be scattered throughout the sector on their side of the busted relay at least caught his full attention, but he also couldn't bring himself to argue as Pierce questioned whether conventional reinforcements would even matter against the magic swarm that had apparently ripped apart an entire relay patrol fleet.

The fact that he found himself agreeing with Ms. Debbie Fucking Downer himself, Nate figured, probably meant it was time to take a break.

"Well, he needs to go have his fairy dream sleep, right?" Pierce had practically cried out, as Nate's quiet move for the door was met by a hail of questions. "How else are we supposed to know how to stop the devil and his army of darkness?"

Whatever else could be said about the man, he didn't play favorites. His nay-saying was absolute, without boundaries. It was freaking transcendent.

"I'll settle for finding them first," Nate had said carefully, gauging the rest of the room. They'd all looked as tired as he felt. As hungry for a proper plan, too. At a tired murmur from Cammy's slowly rebooting systems, he saw that Iveera had pulled the *Kalnythian Wilds* out of e-dim.

"If it comes down to it," he'd said, "maybe we can take the Black Knight by surprise in Iveera's ship while the *Camelot* runs interference."

"Interference against the heart of fucking darkness," Pierce muttered.

"You watch the hands," Nate said, turning for the door. "We'll hit the heart. That's the best I have for now. I'm gonna go see if the Lady can do us one better."

They didn't stop him, but he didn't make it far himself before remembering he might need Blackthorne. Luckily—or not—she was already standing right there at his elbow when he turned, watching him like *what's the holdup, here?*

Add *silent ninja* to the list of her odd skills.

"Your plan is quite shit, you know," she said, with a friendly grin. "No offense, of course."

"No, of course," he echoed, frowning as he searched her face. "So, should we go test this dream theory," he started slowly, getting the distinct impression she had something to tell him, "or is there something you wanted to…?"

"Ah. Yes. Well, you see, I haven't been completely honest with you, sowaiy?"

Nate glanced down the corridor toward the crew quarters, less than thrilled at the thought of more secrets after the past hour. "I feel like I shouldn't be surprised."

"Oh, darling," she said, placing a hand to her chest and affecting a hurt expression.

He sighed. "What is it?"

"Well, the thing is—and, mind you, this isn't me saying 'no' to your sleepover—it's just that…" She ran her fingers through the air as if searching for the proper words. "I already know where the Black Knight is going."

"What? How?"

"Oh, how does anyone know anything, really?" she said, waving a dismissive hand. "If you *must* know," she added, when Nate didn't waver, "I recognized the ruined city in our dream from the start. On top of that, it *is* written along the prow of his ship, so really…" She waved her hand along like the rest should've gone without saying.

Nate was still frowning, trying to follow. "Wait, Avalon? Avalon's… a real place?"

"Was a real place," she corrected, "a very long time ago. I don't suppose you happen to remember that home planet I mentioned?"

Nate felt his eyebrows trying to touch. "But if it was destroyed…"

"It wasn't. Not completely, at least. Catastrophically demolished, yes, and utterly devoid of life. But part of the planet survived its jump."

"It's jump?"

"Long story. Listen, darling, the important part is that I have a reasonably reliable idea where to find what's left, and I'm astronomically certain that that is exactly where we want to be."

"Well, is it reasonably reliable or astronomically certain?"

Her grin went lopsided. "Sowayto sowaiyto, darling."

Nate gritted his teeth. "Why the hell are you just telling me this now?"

She pursed her lips thoughtfully. "Perhaps I was… stirred by your admirable display of honesty back there. Call me inspired."

Nate held her on a hard stare, not really expecting to rattle her, but also determined to get a real answer.

She finally shrugged, like *have it your way*. "If you hadn't noticed, the Gorgon doesn't find me exactly trustworthy."

"Again, can't imagine why."

"You're so sweet," she said, cupping his cheek and smiling like she simply refused to believe he'd meant it sarcastically.

"If you already knew all this," he said, pointedly removing her hand from his cheek and glancing worriedly down the corridor again, "if you already had what you needed, why even involve us in the first place?"

She gave him one of those odd looks of hers. "Well, I'm not about to bloody cross swords with that blackened bastard, am I? I might have a long life and a few tricks up my sleeve, darling, but this fight is above my pay grade, sowaiy?"

"So you figured you'd just tag along and watch us do the heavy lifting in the name of your—Your vengeance, or whatever?"

"Consider it something of a finder's fee," she said, smiling warmly as she reached up to brush his cheek again with the back of her hand.

"Charming," he said, taking her hand and pushing it back down to her side with *stay put* force. "Just…"

She pitched her brows expectantly, hovering ever-so-slightly on tip toes and affecting the most innocent little puppy dog eyes he'd ever seen. It was kind of unsettling, how this woman could just shift from the thousand-plus-year-old-lady-with-all-seeing-eyes vibe to the cutesy thirty-year-old-girl-next-door act at the drop of a hat.

Ex cleared his throat. Loudly. Which seemed kind of impressive for someone who didn't really *have* a throat.

"Just give me some time to think about this," he finished, stepping pointedly back from the pirate.

"Of course, darling," she said, glancing past his shoulder to where Amelia was emerging from the crew quarters. "I'm sure I can find some way to keep myself busy for an hour or two," she added, lips curling in a predatory grin.

"Just remember," she said, coming back to Nate and placing a gentle hand on his shoulder, "one wrong move, and we're all dead and gone for eternity."

"Right. Yeah, that's…"

But she was already patting his shoulder and moving on, bound for Amelia, who leaned against the corridor wall and watched her approach, exhibiting the kind of timid apprehension one might expect from someone who was about to meet their favorite celebrity.

"… Real helpful," Nate finished to no one in particular, watching with quiet fascination as the pirate strolled right up to Amelia and shamelessly twirled a lock of the Atlantean's platinum hair on one deft finger, speaking soft words he couldn't make out. "Lecherous old… goat."

Atlanteans, Ex grumbled.

Are they about to…

Before he'd finished the thought, Snuffy poked out of the crew quarters, scanned both ways, and did a double-take of the unfolding Atlantean situation, seeming to wonder the same thing. At a raised eyebrow from Blackthorne, he stiffened, remembering himself, and hurried down the corridor toward Nate.

"Hey," he said, drawing up somewhat breathlessly. "I just, uh…" He glanced back for the brief triple-take. "Do they, like, know each other from somewhere, or…? Nate?"

"Hmm?" Nate's mind had been drifting in everything Blackthorne had just told him. "Oh. I think that's more of an Atlantean thing, actually." He focused back on Snuffy. "What's up? Did you need something?"

"Oh, uh…" With a force of will, Snuffy drew his attention firmly back to Nate. "No. No, actually, I just thought you might wanna know Ramirez seems to be waking up if you wanna come."

"That's…"

Great news, said his brain, even as his tongue caught on the words, held fast on a confusing wave of more relief and sudden guilt than he knew what to do with.

"You seemed like you needed a bit of good news," Snuffy said, tilting his head toward the crew quarters in invitation.

Nate fell dumbly in step with the mechanic. "I'm just glad he's… Thank you, Snuffy."

He kind of felt bad, defaulting to the beloved-yet-degrading nickname the crew had branded him with, but the cheerful mechanic didn't seem to mind, chatting on about how it was a good omen that things were really looking up.

"You'll see," he said. "We'll find this Mordred dude, snatch the goods right out from under him, and—Huh?"

They both drew up short, trading a round of uneasy looks with the two Atlanteans down the corridor as a medium-range proximity alarm chimed through the *Camelot*.

"Ah, piss," Snuffy muttered as Nate waved open a holo for all of them to see. "Not again. Please, not again."

The sight that greeted them on the holo was not an encouraging one. More ships than Nate could quickly count. Troglodan maybe, Nate guessed, based on the craggy dragon's head shapes and his relative lack of other options. Seventeen ships in total, according to the figures that appeared in the corner, with three enormous capital ships at the heart of the formation.

They didn't look like they'd come for a tea party.

Nate traded one terse look with Snuffy then hurried into the crew quarters to find most of the team gathered near Ramirez's medpod, most of them looking to the holo display that was still fixed on the Demeter-12 debris, Cammy's recuperating systems apparently being too distracted to manage such minor details.

"I miss anything, Boss?" came the dry rasp of Ramirez's voice from within the huddle, just before a second alarm bleated through the room.

At a look from Jaeger, Nate flicked the feed from his personal holo over to the wall display, and the tight silence of the room gave way to a round of soft curses as the fleet appeared there, fanning into wider formation and dumping several fine-specked clouds of smaller fighters into space. The most massive of the capital ships, the *Blood Moon*, pushed decisively ahead, leading the charge.

"Few things, Ramirez," Jaeger said, straightening from the airman's side as the first flashing red *targeting scans detected* warning blinked across the display. "Just a few."

CHAPTER 33
NEGOTIATIONS

For a long second, Nate could practically feel the whole room silently hoping that maybe—just maybe—if they were all still and silent enough, this whole damn mess might somehow just blow right by. Then the holo display gave a disappointed chirp, and the *targeting scans detected* text toggled to a big red *target lock* warning.

"Don't suppose that's our backup?" Ramirez asked weakly from his open medpod.

Someone—Tessa, maybe—gave a kind of delirious giggle, then the room exploded with every held-in comment at once.

"What did *we* do?" Snuffy whispered beside Nate, like he was still kind of afraid the ships might hear him from two-hundred-thousand kilometers away.

"More like what did *they* do," Pierce said, having somehow heard the mechanic. He turned his accusatory stare on Nate. "Those ships look Troglodan to me. Dollars to fucking donuts they're looking for Arturi and the Gorgon who killed their big bad Knight, right?"

The last bit, he turned to Malfar, and as one, the entire room swiveled to follow his attention.

Malfar regarded them in grim silence from his corner. "The Terran is correct," he finally said, rising from his couch like he expected he'd just had his last good sit-down for a long while. "I suppose now may be the time to mention that a sizable Troglodan war party was granted diplomatic travel access to Tarkaminen from Golnak roughly two standard days ago."

"Sounds like two days ago might've been the time to mention that," Pierce said.

"I was preoccupied having my life's work suspended over the pursuit of those involved in the Terran incursion," Malfar said calmly, holding Pierce's gaze until the pilot sat himself down. Malfar looked to Jaeger and Nate. "They arrived at the Golnak relay shortly after Ser Kelkarin escorted you to Forge Station."

"Any idea what they want?" Jaeger asked.

Almost as if in reply, the main holo display chirped with an incoming hail from the largest of the three approaching capital ships, the *GTA Blood Moon*.

"I am not privy to that information," Malfar said, following their stares to the winking alert, "but my most workable hypothesis is that they have indeed come to visit vengeance on Ser Groshna's killers. That is the personal flagship of Groshna's primary next-of-brood sire leading the fleet."

"Like, Groshna's son?" Snuffy asked.

"Groshna has hundreds of sons," Malfar said, crossing his arms. "Varga is merely the top of the brood. He is not a particularly reasonable bull."

Jaeger looked at the display, processing that. "Well, shit."

Nate couldn't argue with the sentiment. Especially not as the comms pinged again, and the intercept timer continued ticking down. He tensed at yet another incoming ping on his own holo, then saw the name, accepted the connection, and watched with relief as Iveera's hologram sprang to life in the center of the room. She didn't appear all that worried either. But then again, it was Iveera.

"We could use them," she said, without preamble.

"Unlikely they are looking to be used, Knight," Malfar said, stepping forward to address her holo directly. "Least of all by you."

"By another then, perhaps," Iveera said, holding the Troglodan's gaze.

Malfar's nostril slits flared with a harsh snort. "Have you seen my hide, Gorgon? They would sooner copulate with a herd of harfarners than speak with me."

"Shall I do the talking, then?"

Nate was surprised to hear Iveera ask such a question of anyone. Even more surprised at the begrudging spark of amusement that flickered between them. Judging by the sideways look Jaeger shot him, Nate wasn't the only one who was a tad taken aback.

"We should contact the Council," came Amelia's voice from the doorway, where she was watching on with a look of professional apprehension. "This is all… highly unsanctioned. Ser Katanaga, your ship has q-comm links with the Forge, yes? If I could access your connection—"

"I think not."

"But if I could merely speak with Calum and Chancellor Adamus, I'm certain that an appropriate armistice could be reached."

"Any chance it'll be reached in less than two minutes?" Jaeger asked, with a pointed glance at the closing fleet on the holo.

"It matters not. A fleet of this size couldn't have arrived here to begin with without a Council conspirator. Quite possibly the very same conspirator who engineered the murder of a Kalnythian Elder and multiple assassination attempts against us. There's no reason to expect Council aid, nor to expect this fleet to hold itself accountable to Alliance law or even to their own Troglodan Emperor now that they're here."

Amelia looked like she wanted to argue that that level of corruption and shady dealing simply couldn't be, but then she followed Iveera's gaze to Malfar, who gave a grim nod like Iveera had nailed the same conclusions he'd arrived at on every front. Amelia's brow steepled Malfar just touched his spotted cheek with a thick finger in response to Iveera's questioning gaze.

"Very well," Iveera said, as if that answered that. She glanced briefly at the rest of them. "Best you all stay quiet and allow me to handle this."

A few jin swipes later, the holo display on the wall expanded, bifurcating to spawn a second window to the left of the fleet display. Iveera's hologram turned to face it alongside them as the two-dimensional feed populated with the gloomy interior of the *Blood Moon*'s bridge, where dozens of Troglodans were busy at work in bulbous clusters of consoles and holo displays. Several more were posted up along the large room's interior, armed and armored, most of them staring curiously at the feed that must've just appeared at the helm of their bridge, and at the mighty Troglodan who stood proudly in front of it.

The size, Nate was starting to get used to, even if the one Nate took to be this Varga was notably thicker and bulkier than most Trogs. It was more the sophisticated crimson armor that Nate's attention drifted to, battered and battle-dented, but still quite obviously superior to that of all the armed Trog soldiers behind him. His hide, too, was a shade of bronze-copper like Nate hadn't seen on other Trogs. He looked rather regal, in a bloodthirsty warmongering kind of way.

"Knights." He growled the word like a curse, beady eyes shifting back and forth to take in each of their feeds. "Which one of you has my Excalibur?"

Nate traded a sideways glance with Jaeger. He'd expected more captain talk. Formal threats and demands for surrender. Not a blatant show of hand, right off the bat.

"Admiral Varga, Clansire Groshna," Iveera said, perfectly calm. "If you refer to the Excalibur previously wielded by Ser Groshna—"

"Let us not bandy words, Katanaga. You know damned well what we're here for. My sire was unrightfully slain, and we have come to collect what is ours."

"Ser Groshna led an illegal incursion—"

"Incursion?" Varga boomed like the word was utterly foreign. "On that backwater piss pot?"

"Terra is protected by Alliance charter, as I'm sure you're aware."

"Lies and shit, Gorgon. Your Order is bound by no such petty law."

Down the line, Malfar stirred like he had more than a few things to say about that, but he held his tongue as Iveera replied.

"You wish not to bandy words? Very well. Ser Groshna acted in error, even by the most extreme interpretation of my Order's capacities, and neither you nor your Empire has any rightful claim to a fallen Knight's Excalibur. No more than will the people of Kalyria have claim to mine when I should perish. The dominion of Excaliburs is that of the Lady, and the Lady alone."

"You speak many words, Gorgon, but I—"

"I am not finished, Admiral. If you wish to express your personal enmity with me, then that is your prerogative, for it was by my hand and my sworn duty that Ser Groshna came to his end. But if you wish to align your blame with the one who orchestrated the event, then you and your Empire should know that Ser Groshna was manipulated to his actions by another. An unknown interloper, armored all in black and wielding uncanny power. It is this individual whom we currently hunt, and it is in the name of Groshna that I invite you to combine your strength with ours and see this Black Knight brought to justice. After that, I will, of course, submit to the ruling of Alliance Law and that of my own Order on the matter of what punishment is owed for my actions on Terra and since. What say you, Admiral Varga?"

For an uncomfortably long time, Admiral Varga said nothing, right along with everyone else. Behind him, the Troglodans of the *Blood Moon* were still and silently confident, like they knew all too well what came next. On the *Camelot*, there were only tense sideways glances, and Malfar was unusually agitated, eyes shifting from Iveera to Varga, to Nate, and back again like he was turning over a particularly unfavorable idea in his head.

"My Empire," Varga finally said, wringing the words with violent loathing, "would sooner cast itself to the fiery pits than align itself with the self-proclaimed murderer of Ser Groshna. So allow me to rephrase, Gorgon: I am going to—"

"Be a shame if they chased us headlong into a real fight, wouldn't it?" someone murmured in Nate's ear, so close enough that he lost track of Varga's tirade completely, and nearly jumped out of his skin to boot. Blackthorne. He hadn't noticed her ghosting up behind him. She held him on the end of one pointedly arched eyebrow, her words echoing through his mind another two rounds before her meaning struck like a proton torpedo straight to the thermal exhaust port.

"I care not for your dust-ridden accords, Gorgon!" Varga was roaring, in response to something Iveera had just said. "I would sooner copulate with a herd of lame harfarners than relinquish command of this fleet to a snake-headed—"

Nate tuned back out, pretty sure he saw where this was headed, trying instead to focus on his bond with Iveera. If he could just get word to her, let her know what Blackthorne had told him… Maybe *between a rock and a hard place* wasn't the worst place to be stuck when they had the faster ships and were in desperate need of a nice angry rock to fling at that hard place anyway.

He was only beginning to wrestle with the burgeoning moral questions behind the half-formed plan—not to mention the haphazard logistics of arranging such a thing—when Malfar cut them all short.

"—ry it from our dead fingers, Gorgon wench," Varga was roaring.

"Then let us fight for it," Malfar said, stepping front and center.

"Who the—" Varga growled, expression dancing from confusion and annoyance at being interrupted to pure, disgusted scorn as his beady eyes found the blight-marked speaker. "You *dare* speak to me, runt?"

For some reason, Malfar only gave an amused grunt at the wave of shock and outrage his apparent audacity had sent reeling through the *Blood Moon*'s bridge. "I dare challenge you, sire. By the Old Ways."

Iveera's hologram shot Malfar a rapid sideways glance like she was wondering what the hell he was playing at. Varga just bellowed an ugly spew of laughter, looking around his bridge to take in the increasingly incredulous reactions of his crew. "What claim have you to the Old Ways, Clanless One?"

"None by letter of law," Malfar admitted. "But seeing as it seems we're not overly fond of that construct at present, and as the claim would be mine by birthright anyway, were it not for the spots on my hide, I challenge you all the same."

A dangerous silence stretched, the first notes of uncertainty spreading among the *Blood Moon*'s crew. What did he mean, by birthright?

"Who are you?" Varga asked.

"Do you not recognize me?" Malfar replied. "You saw me often enough, peering on from the outside."

"I tire of this game, runt. Speak plainly."

"Sire," Malfar said, snapping a smart fist salute to his wide chest. "My name is Malfar, Clanless One, justicar of the Galactic Alliance and first descendant of Groshna, Clansire Groshna. Born by Tarmina, Clanmatron Groshna in the brood of the 5,022nd year of our Great Empire's reckoning."

The effect on the *Blood Moon*'s bridge was instantaneous—a veritable explosion of snarling faces and curse-heavy accusations that was only barely contained by the domineering fist Varga snapped high for silence. More than a few beady-eyed stares fixed on their fearless leader's back, waiting to see what he'd do as the commotion died.

On the *Camelot*, the looks were more of the confused *did I hear that right* variety. For possibly the first time ever, Iveera and Blackthorne looked more surprised than the rest of them, like only they fully understood what manner of bomb had just been dropped. Nate, for his part, was only beginning to register the nature of that bomb himself when Malfar took another step forward, his expression positively predatory.

"Do you not remember me, brother?" he asked, quiet and confident. "Do you not remember the young spotted runt who'd watch from the southern crags on those rare hot fielding days when they let us see the sun? I know you saw me. I remember how you pointed. Remember how dear Mother bade you to ignore the dirty little runt and go back to thrashing the rest of your brothers, how your sire would be so very proud of y—"

"Silence," Varga hissed.

Malfar considered him for a moment, then pressed on, unconcerned. "I bet you still wonder sometimes why she never allowed you to call the guards on that dirty little runt. I know I do."

In the background, several of Varga's Trogs were giving their mighty leader sideways looks now, like they were starting to wonder if this blighted runt was actually speaking the truth. At a look from Varga, though, the entire bridge of the *Blood Moon* snapped to smart attention, deadly silent as he turned back to the screen with a kind of practiced apathy.

"You are clanless, runt. Unfit to hold my station. You have no right to challenge me."

"And yet I do, brother," Malfar interjected before the next words could leave Varga's mouth. "But not for your station. In the name of the Destroyer, I challenge you only on the condition that, should I win, your war party will first seek justice on the true culprit behind Ser Groshna's death, the Black Knight Mordred LeFaye, before pursuing any action against Ser Iveera Katanaga and her allies here aboard the *Camelot*. After that, I care not."

Nate couldn't tell if Malfar meant the last bit, or if he was merely selling the act, but the Troglodan wasn't done.

"I'd swear it on our fallen sire's honor," he continued, with something like grim amusement, "but then, I've also seen what you do to those who make the mistake of trusting you to be a creature of honor and dignity."

Varga bristled, raising a hand like he was about to either command his crew to open fire or to reach through the holo display and take Malfar by the throat.

"I kept watching through the years, you see," Malfar pushed on, determined to maintain his momentum. "Through all the deaths. Through more accidents than seemed believable. I was careful, mind you. Especially after the day I witnessed you tampering with brave brother Fargin's rattler just before your tragic race down Death's H—"

"Enough."

Nate was surprised to register it was Iveera's voice, not Varga's, that cut Malfar's accusations short. The surprise only deepened when he took in the sideways glance Malfar shot the Gorgon—not a look of indignant irritation, as Nate would've guessed, but rather one of flat acknowledgment. And despite having only vaguely grasped at what Malfar had been driving for, Nate felt it then, too: a dangerous swelling of Varga's pride and impugned honor, cracking tight as a lion tamer's whip.

"You have the location of this Mordred LeFaye?" Varga asked, deadly quiet, looking pointedly to Iveera as if Malfar were already dead and gone.

Iveera held the admiral's murderous gaze, jin swirling calmly, thoughtfully. Thinking what, Nate didn't know. But he found himself stepping forward, all the same, Blackthorne's words echoing through his head. Iveera's eyes flicked to him, seeming to understand. She didn't argue.

"We do," he said, hoping to all nine of their mythic hells that Malfar knew what he was doing.

The words drew looks of quiet surprise from the crew around him, but Varga only had eyes for Iveera, and if she was surprised by Nate's news, she hid it like a cold-blooded pro. The admiral nodded once, like that was that.

"Then you will share this information with me once I have cured your ship of this deranged blight spot, and we will have words concerning what is owed the Troglodan Empire." Finally, he turned his beady eyes back to Malfar, and there was no mistaking the hatred there. "I will end your suffering by the Old Ways an hour hence, runt. Destroyer take your tarnished soul."

With that, the connection cut to black, and the display quickly rearranged itself back to the single large feed of the approaching fleet.

"What just happened?" Snuffy asked the silent room.

"Justice," Malfar said, not sounding particularly pleased about it. "At long last."

CHAPTER 34
TO THE DEATH

"You're… sure about this?" asked the Terran Knight for what felt like the thousandth time, craning to peek out of the top slit of the shoddy, makeshift gladiator's cage before glancing back to Malfar. "We can find another way."

He was a kind soul, Malfar decided. Too kind for what his sacred Order Excalibur and the unnatural centuries would do to him, provided the boy actually survived that long. Given their present circumstances, it all looked rather less than certain.

"There is no other way," Malfar said, flexing his fingers, fixating on the feeling of the drying war paint cracking at each knuckle. Truth be told, he wasn't at all sure that Varga's war party wouldn't immediately take up arms against them in the unlikely event that he actually managed to bring his behemoth of a bastard brother down. If there was any single truly binding covenant among Troglodans, it was in the glory of battle and in the honor of the Old Ways. But he was a spotted runt, as evidenced by the war paint running up from knuckle to shoulder, and streaked across his bare chest—jet black for his blighted soul, whereas Varga and any other true-blooded Troglodan would be wearing white. It was why his sneering kin had funneled him into this ramshackle holding pen of cargo crates and other gear when the *Blood Moon*, like most any large Troglodan ships, already had two perfectly serviceable gladiator pens ready and waiting. He just wasn't fit for them.

"I watched an entire occupation force surrender to Iveera," the Terran said, clearly still stuck on the idea of getting out of this thing some other way. He was eyeing the deck now, apologetic to his last. Perhaps the boy wasn't quite so naive as Malfar had originally thought.

"I'm not exactly chopped liver, either," the Terran added. "And we've got Anastasiya here. And the faster ships. I'm just saying we've got options."

"Justice demands this," Malfar said, though, in truth, he wasn't even sure about that anymore. Here he was, after all, a fugitive from Alliance law, challenging his own blood in a desperate attempt to gain leverage and resources for a fight whose stakes were well beyond his comprehension.

Demeter-12. The Black Knight. The Synth.

Zedavian Fucking Kelkarin, and the second coming of the Great War.

Malfar was undoubtedly in light-years above his pay grade now. Whether the legendary Huntress Iveera Katanaga *could* or *couldn't* dismantle an entire war party with the help of her fledgling Terran Knight and the rest of their friends hardly seemed to matter anymore, though. They needed allies here, not another fight. He'd smelled as much back on the *Camelot*, watching the Terrans' insides shrivel as they struggled to wrap their heads around what they'd gotten into. They needed hope.

Besides, if anyone deserved to feel the wrath of Justice, it was Varga. That much, he was certain of. And while he hadn't allowed himself to dwell on it over the decades, Malfar had always quietly hoped he'd one day be the one to deliver it. Perhaps he'd even *believed*, in some twisted, self-important way, that it was his destiny to do so. Varga was, after all, more or less the reason he'd eventually become a justicar.

His dip into the investigatory arts may have begun with tracking down his own lineage, but it was Varga's murderously competitive streak that had pushed Malfar to truly begin honing his skills of deductive reasoning. While most of his casework would've been thoroughly inadmissible in the Alliance courts, there was little arguing with what his so-called brood brother had done over the years. Poor Fargin and his fatal rattler crash had been only the first in a long line of accidental tragedies.

Prodigious fratricide was hardly unheard of among the Troglodan people, of course. Next-of-brood competition was fierce, and even among the lower clans, sirehood came with many pleasures to ease its concurrent pains. For the most part, such power struggles were met with a blind eye and a stoic *such is life* mentality, so long as the victors took care to at least marginally cover their tracks.

But Varga had enjoyed what he'd done—had in fact prided himself on his work. Which had always struck Malfar as especially repugnant, seeing as the vicious brute really hadn't been clever at all. The more Malfar had learned how to look, the more he'd begun to see the same essential fingerprint on each messy accident throughout the years, the fine details changing while the guiding hand remained quite obviously the same to the discerning eye.

There'd been a time when Malfar had spent the nights dreaming, weaving plans of how he'd contact his aging birth mother Tarmina, or even Ser Groshna himself, and expose Varga. Show them what their prized heir truly was. Make them see. Sometimes, he'd even allowed himself to imagine that, on that day, they'd realize he wasn't such a worthless runt after all and welcome him back into the brood. It had been quite the fantasy. Then the days had come when he'd anonymously shared his findings, and Groshna had publicly appointed Varga as his junior next-of-brood sire not long after. The line of tragedies had continued to grow around him. Such appointments were hardly ironclad, after all.

Malfar had scraped together what savings he had, bartered passage to the Forge, and left it all behind him as best he could. But there was a part of him that'd never let go. A part that still raged at the injustice of it all. A part that still felt pity for those foolish brutes who'd clamored to unseat Varga, blind to what manner of beast they provoked. A part that even now wondered what their bloated Emperor Harsgard would think of it all, were he ever to hear the full extent of the new Clansire Groshna's transgressions.

It was from decades and worlds away that Malfar came back to the growing din of the *Blood Moon*'s cargo bay and looked up to find the Terran Knight and his compatriot, Lt Col Jaeger, both watching him. Both entirely more concerned for his imminent well-being than any of his own kind had ever been, save for maybe Heilga. Dimly, he wished he could've heard her brood song one last time. The thought brought the beginnings of a grin to his mouth, thinking of how chest-pounding soldiers out there in the cargo hold would taunt and cajole to see a grown Troglodan sitting here with his Terran pals, wishing for brood song. It would've been like a Hobdan or a Sven asking for the teet one last time at the ripe age of fifty.

But he didn't care anymore.

Outside, the ceremonial drums sounded, summoning forth the two mismatched combatants. As per the customs, Malfar had yet to witness Varga with his own eyes since coming aboard, but it wasn't hard to remember the frightening presence of that devastatingly powerful build. Not after watching Varga thrashing his brothers around the yard. He still remembered the way his heart had practically stopped, those first few times he'd watched from afar as Varga pushed a beating too far, teetering on the brink of smashing in the head of a yielding opponent here, or prolonging a stranglehold on an already limp calfling there—each time only barely restraining himself in the end.

Then he'd grown up and stopped playing around. So too had Malfar. In a way, it was almost as if he'd been training all his life for this moment. It was with that thought that, for the first time he could remember, Malfar stood without a trace of shame for who and what he was.

"In the name of Justice," he said, to no one in particular. Then, remembering his Terran company, he added to them, "I will do my part."

After one last worrisome glance outside, the Terran Knight drew himself upright, facing Malfar with a forced air of confidence. "We'll be right behind you."

"Hooah," the Lt Col said more comfortably, giving Malfar a grim nod, like he knew exactly what came next. "Give him hell, Spot."

HAD SOMEONE TOLD NATE, as he'd stood in the ashes back at State College or at New York, that he'd one day soon find himself fearing for the life and well-being of *any* Troglodan, he almost certainly would've pointed them straight to the jarring eighty-thousand-plus casualties the brutish bastards had just finished wreaking on his planet. Now though, there was no denying the trepidation he felt as he marched through the roaring crowd on Malfar's flank, headed for the clearing at the center of the *Blood Moon's* cargo bay.

The justicar was bare-hided from the waist up, and painted across the front and back with glyphs Ex had translated to roughly mean *truth* and *justice*. Blackthorne had done the honors when Malfar's so-called kinsmen had plopped the black paint—apparently an insult in itself—down outside the makeshift ready room and made it clear they wouldn't be touching his tainted flesh. For some reason, it hadn't seemed like her first time. All Nate could really focus on, though, was just how deeply these Troglodans seemed to hate Malfar for nothing more than the milky pink splotches dotted across his hide.

The level of rejection was staggering, and Nate felt real anger flickering in his chest as they approached the open center of the cargo bay through a solid corridor of Malfar's so-called kinsmen, who shook their fists and poured a steady stream of awful curses at the justicar. By the time they reached the opening at the center, Nate's jaws and fists were clenched tight against the very real urge to snap back at this howling mass of... *bigots*, he finally decided, surprised not so much by that realization as by the fact that, even after everything he'd seen on the Forge, he'd still somehow been clinging to the hope that such petty, vile beliefs simply wouldn't exist outside the bounds of humanity.

Judging by the curtailed jin twitches, Iveera wasn't a fan of the spectacle either, but she also didn't seem especially surprised by any of it. Which was probably sensible. They *had* come to essentially fight for temporary control of this entire fleet, after all, once all other issues of Troglodan culture were set aside here.

"Goddamn, I hope he knows what he's doing," Jaeger muttered softly beside Nate.

That made two of them, Nate decided as they split off from Malfar and took up a position at the inner edge of the crowd.

He'll be fine, Ex insisted. *He's a clever Troglodan.*

It sounded a little too much like wishful thinking for Nate's liking, but it was kind of hard to form coherent thoughts back at Ex with hundreds of packed-in Troglodans howling for spotted runt blood. Nate watched Malfar trod across the rust red deck plating, toward the yawning gap where one of the *Blood Moon*'s dorsal cargo hatches had been left open, sealed only with a shimmering green atmos containment field. It wouldn't stop a Trog from tumbling out into the cold vacuum of space, if either combatant managed to pitch the other through. But that was probably the entire point.

A shudder of unease rippled through Nate's insides at what was about to happen, coupled with unbidden memories of his first experience aboard a Trog cruiser, with Marty, Gwen, and a hundred other terrified Nittany Lions at his back, shackle chains a-jangling, a ruthless Gorgon killing machine tearing through the ship after them. He glanced sideways at Iveera, thinking of how he'd fought to escape her grav whip in a cargo bay much like this one.

How far they'd come.

"If this goes South..." Jaeger said quietly.

"Stay behind me," Nate finished.

"Gladly," Blackthorne said, before Jaeger could return anything but a nice, blistering sideways scowl.

A second sounding of the ancient war drum drew their attention across the Trog-encircled arena, to where the gates of Varga's considerably more ceremonial gladiator pen were pulling open with a rattle of chains and grating metal. An anticipatory hush fell across the crowd, which seemed a little odd to Nate, given that they ostensibly saw their commanding officer somewhat regularly. Then the rumbling laughter and raucous war cries sounded from the first side of the crowd to spot their emerging leader, and Nate understood.

On-screen, Varga, Clansire Groshna, had been a monstrous mountain of a Troglodan, thick and beefy in all the scary places. In-person, he was much the same, but there was another intangible quality about the behemoth—a kind of animosity that poured from his every powerful movement, filling the air with the promise of bloody brutality to come. But it was the glyphs painted across his body in bright white—Nate realized, as the laughs spread through the arena—that really seemed to steal the show.

Breed purity, the first one read, as Ex's translation took effect before Nate's eyes. The second one wavered an extra instant before Ex sighed and pared it down to: *'runt-fisting' would be the most literal translation, I believe.*

"Bloody Troglodans," Blackthorne muttered beside him, apparently having no trouble reading the glyphs herself.

Nate just watched as Varga stomped toward Malfar, wincing inwardly at the size discrepancy between the two Trogs. It wasn't quite a David vs. Goliath situation—Malfar was hardly scrawny for a so-called runt—but nor did it look anything like a fair fight. He tensed as Varga bore down on Malfar, wondering if this was it, if they'd simply rip straight into it. Then Varga stomped right on past his little bastard brother without so much as a beady-eyed glance, like he hadn't a thing in the world to fear in turning his back on this particular opponent.

"My noble bulls!" he cried, throwing his bulging arms wide. "Let us not delay the true justice."

If that was a deliberate jab at Malfar's own chosen glyphs, the justicar didn't take the bait as Varga pushed on.

"You have heard this filth speak naught but lies! The jealous lies of a soul too blighted to know it's place among our great people. May the Fathers forgive me for sullying the Old Ways with this farce." Finally, he looked at Malfar. "But such an insult cannot be left unanswered."

And with that, he charged—no fight bell, no anything. Just a half-ton of bellowing Troglodan rage, thudding across the rust-red deck for the defiant justicar.

Malfar was ready.

For one brief moment, they met in exactly the kind of colossal clash

Nate expected, Malfar catching Varga by the wrists, taking his momentum head-on as the two bellowed furious war cries into one another's faces, like they were introducing their inner demons to one another. Then Malfar cut back, pivoting clear of Varga's forward drive even as he yanked the Trog along by one wrist and leveraged a savage elbow blow at the side of his head.

Varga moved with a boxer's tight efficiency, not dodging the attack so much as allowing it to brush off at an ineffectual angle, keeping Malfar close at hand. Malfar, sensing the impending death grip or uppercut, forewent any obvious target and instead punched Varga directly in the biceps—or whatever bulging Trog arm muscle—as the admiral swung after him.

The justicar sprang clear, not exactly light on his feet, but fast enough to buy a moment's distance. His posture was ready, his eyes calculating, like he was documenting everything he'd just learned from their brief spat. Varga, on the other hand, just shook his arm loose, looking irritated, and moved in again.

What followed over the next few minutes was some unsettling combina-tion of terrifying and inanely underwhelming. Two hulking soldiers in their rights, slogging their way back and forth across the deck, their labored grunts echoing eerily through the unnaturally silent crowd. Varga attacked with a kind of terrible mechanical efficiency, while Malfar countered again and again with a pragmatic fluidity that'd probably come from years of handling stab-happy criminals in the streets.

Savage and relentless as Varga's blows were, though, Malfar always seemed to be one step ahead, expecting them, catching each strike with a clever twist or surprising reversal. At one point, Varga caught Malfar against one of the broad grav lift housing columns perilously close to the open cargo hatch, but Malfar broke free with a quick groin strike/straight knee kick combo that fanned the low-murmuring flames of the crowd and set the cargo bay roaring with cries of blighted cowardice.

Varga, battered but hardly defeated with his bloodied cheek and brow and his degrading body glyphs, ignored it all and kept after Malfar with a vengeance. As they fought on, Nate almost guiltily found his attention drifting to the riveted, blood-hungry crowd, watching with mouths agape, fists frozen in raised anticipation as the two tiring combatants grunted through yet another exchange.

Suddenly, he couldn't even begin to fathom what the hell they were all doing here, entertaining a goddamn cockfight when they were literally floating in the graveyard of a planet, with a *real* enemy out there, building his protoswarm for Lady only knew what. It was preposterous.

Someone had to stop this, he thought, glancing toward Iveera only to freeze as Jaeger tensed beside him, eyes whipping back to the fight. He didn't see whatever critical misstep must've preceded what was happening. Just the look in Malfar's eyes as he teetered past the point of recovery, and Varga's full-weight punch contacted with a wet smack that sent him staggering, eyes unfocused.

The next punch came quickly and without mercy, and it hit hard enough to lift Malfar from the deck before he came crashing back down with an ominous thud and a far more thunderous roar of approval from the crowd.

Just like that, the brutally long dance was done. Varga stomped on Malfar's chest once, twice, laughing as the justicar weakly tried to scramble away and the crowd began pelting him with bits of food and spare gear.

"Get up," Nate growled, fists clenched, pulse rising. "Get up." But Varga was already descending on his fallen foe with a kind of slow, confident finality that turned Nate's stomach more than any bloodthirsty roar ever could've.

Nathaniel, Ex warned, alerting him to the fact that he'd just taken a step forward, drawing hostile looks from every Trog in the vicinity.

Ahead, Malfar's head made a sickeningly wet crunch as Varga slammed it to the ground, bloodied hands groping weakly, then going slack as Varga slammed him down again. Nate looked to Iveera, heart thundering desperately. The look on her face drew him up short.

Shock. Sheer, open shock like he'd never seen on her face before. Like she'd just been stabbed in the back. A thud from ahead as Varga hauled Malfar's limp body from the ground and slammed him into the support column beside the open hatchway with a victorious roar, cocking one mighty fist back for the killing blow.

"Stop," Iveera hissed, practically gasped.

But Nate already lunging forward—utterly done with this pointless Bloodbath Honor Sport bullshit. He braced himself, ignoring Ex's halfhearted protests, gathering his strength to plow into the wave of Trogs bounding to head him off.

A pale red bolt of *something* ripped straight between them from Iveera's direction, sending them all jerking back a step. Nate watched with wide eyes as that bolt smashed straight into Malfar's chest, and the smaller Troglodan snapped to life with a roar to match Varga's.

He caught his brood brother's speeding fist in an open palm, bones cracking with a wet pop. Varga's bones, Nate registered numbly, as the huge admiral howled in pain, trying to jerk away. Malfar held tight to Varga's shattered hand, hauling back with the other fist.

The punch sent the behemoth sailing halfway across the arena. There was a collective gasp as Varga slammed to a messy rag-doll landing on the deck, then sudden and total silence as they took in the gory damage. Nate could only gape.

Varga was almost certainly dead. His head a bloody, caved-in mess. He looked more like he'd been brained by a full-power grav cannon blast than struck by a fist. And as Nate's stunned eyes tracked to Malfar, then to Iveera's shocked expression and back again, it dawned on him what'd just happened.

He turned his attention to the crowd, trying to watch every way at once, waiting for them to erupt into roars and cursing jeers—to yank their weapons free and start shooting, or to charge in and try to rip Malfar limb from limb. He prepared to spring in and try to stop them. Wondered if there was any way he *could* stop this many enraged Trogs. But there was only silence as Malfar rose from where he'd tumbled to his knees with the momentum of his own strike. He rose, shakily at first, then with proud shoulders and high head as he faced his gaping onlookers.

"By the Old Ways and all the honor of the Troglodan people, I bid you: see to the admiral's remains and then prepare this war party for departure. We must make haste. Until our terms are met and justice is delivered to the Black Knight Mordred LeFaye, you answer to Ser Iveera Katanaga."

And with that, he turned and set stiffly off, marching for the docking seal like he couldn't be bothered to wait for a response. After a stunned moment, Nate and the others gathered themselves and hurried after him amid a darkening sea of silent, murderous stares.

It was only when they caught up to Malfar that Nate noticed the odd grunts coming from him, and the way his gait seemed to be decaying with every few steps. Instinctively, he stepped closer and discreetly caught a bit of the bloody Troglodan's weight as Malfar weaved just a little too far sideways. The justicar caught his balance, murmuring nonsense, and pushed on ahead, beady eyes unfocused, blinking drunkenly.

Around them, a tight corridor of vengeful Troglodans stared on, trading glances amongst themselves here and there. There wasn't a single doubt: every Trog in that cargo bay was half a twitch away from taking a crack at finishing Varga's work, Trog honor be damned.

Nate was almost more surprised than he was relieved when they finally reached the docking seal, and the last two Trogs begrudgingly stepped aside to allow them passage. They all marched through without a word, barely even daring to breathe until the *Camelot*'s hatch sealed behind them.

Then Malfar took a single incredulous look at Nate and Iveera and collapsed where he stood.

CHAPTER 35

TOUCHED

"So, uh…" Snuffy said, pulling his eyes from where Carter and Elmo were hovering over the several hundred kilos of beaten Troglodan they'd just failed to catch and looking to the rest of the crew that'd just stumbled in from the *Blood Moon*'s cargo bay arena.

"What the fuck just happened?" Jaeger finished for him, turning to Nate and Iveera. "Was that what I think it was?"

Nate looked to Iveera, wondering the same thing, pretty sure he already knew the answer. That ghostly flash of crimson—crimson, just like their late Dread Knight Groshna's armor. That burst of freakish strength. He'd had something similar, back when he'd first been touched by Ex's power.

And then came the sniveling, Ex said, in a tone that suggested he was recalling the Dark Ages.

A series of muffled cracks perforated the silence from the sealed entry hatch, making them all tense. All of them but Blackthorne, at least, who was leaned in the corner with arms crossed, thoughtfully drumming her fingers on one elbow.

"Blood Moon successfully undocked," came Tessa's voice as a small holo window winked into existence on the entryway bulkhead. "Did we, uh—" Her gaze flicked downward, like she was taking in Malfar's appearance. "Is he okay? Did we win?"

"Come with me," Iveera said, presumably to Nate, turning on her heel like she didn't have time for any of this.

"Hey," Jaeger said, splaying his hands wide, "what about—"

"The Troglodan will heal on his own," Iveera said, pausing and glancing back at Malfar's lightly breathing form. Her jin were visibly agitated. *She* was visibly agitated. "He's well beyond our technological ability to help now."

"So that really was Groshna's…?" Jaeger trailed off, looking to Nate for some kind of confirmation.

Nate, unsure what to say—not even rightly sure what the hell had just happened, save for the one glaringly blatant detail—instead made a request to Cammy's tenuously rebooting systems. He watched with an empty feeling as a padded platform that was half-bed, half-crash-couch rose uncertainly from the deck, lofting Malfar's unconscious weight into its cushioned embrace.

"I think he'll be okay," he said to Jaeger, as Iveera took him by the arm and pulled him impatiently along the corridor.

"Great. Yeah," Jaeger called after them. "We'll just… We'll just be here then!" They'd already pulled out of sight when Nate heard the Lt Col mutter to himself, "Freaking Knights."

"Okay," Nate said, shaking his arm from Iveera's grasp. "Can we just pump the brakes a tad, and—"

"Not here."

"Well…"

Nate teetered for a moment on trying to explain how they'd *just* had a whole trust breakthrough on this ship, and that it had been a whole big thing, and that now really wasn't the time to be sneaking off to swap secrets. Then he remembered what Blackthorne had told him, and what he'd declared to Varga in front of everyone. Iveera was already floating off anyway, drifting up to the dorsal hatch in the alcove just aft of the bridge, helmet unfolding from e-dim like she was planning to go outside for a spacewalk.

"Freaking Knights," he muttered to himself, reaching for his gravitonics.

SPACE, it turned out, was unconscionably enormous.

That much had pretty much gone without saying each time he'd stared out of the *Camelot's* holoports. Tens of thousands of starlight pin-points in every direction, each home to Lady only knew how many planets and asteroid belts and funny little quarks of alien life. Multiply that all by ten million times to even begin to account for all the additional bits you couldn't see when you looked out those ports, and factor in the sheer amount of black *nothingness* between each and every one of those stars—not to mention the fact that this was all just for their single little galaxy—and you began to feel it in the tiny little flecks of space dust you called bones: an entire universe of empty nothingness, dotted ever so faintly with all the matter in existence.

It was wondrously overwhelming, seeing it without the protection of the *Camelot*'s hull securely around him. How he'd managed to avoid his first spacewalk this long since leaving Earth, Nate couldn't say. As soon as he popped his head and shoulders out from the second hatch of the airlock, though, it hardly mattered. For a long minute, all he could do was stare out into the black, clenching to the precious safety of the ship with his gravitonics—and with pretty much everything else he could clench, too.

It was only when he poked out far enough to see the heart of the exploded Demeter-12 debris field, framed against the long lines of Iveera's legs and battle-scarred armor, that the frightful wonder settled back down to something more grimly appropriate for the situation.

Something is foul with this place, Ex said.

Before Nate could even think to respond, Iveera stooped down, caught him by the wrist, and pulled. He felt his fingers slip the rungs and watched in a kind of slow-motion horror as the ship fell away beneath them, dark space engulfing them, stomach in free fall, heart suddenly *wump-wumping* like a freaking bass drum in the confines of his sealed helmet as they flew out, out...

Calm yourself, came her voice in his mind as they pulled to a halt some two hundred meters from the *Camelot*, and she released him. He swiped for her hand on a spike of agoraphobic panic, gripped beyond reason by the intensely proximate fear of flying off into the endless abyss, never to be seen again. The movement only sent him spinning ass over teakettle— Iveera, the Camelot, and the endless abyss all trading places at a dizzying rate in his field of view, breath quickening, chest tightening.

Nathaniel.

Iveera's voice hit him like an anchor, reminding him who—and what— he was. Or was supposed to be, at least. He blew out a hard breath, cheeks beginning to burn as he leaned gently onto his gravitonics and began to correct his spin relative to Iveera. A few moments later, he was drifting back to her side, racing heart slowing beat by beat.

Well done, little hobbit. You're getting better at this.

Nate was too busy gaping at the scene ahead of them to marvel at his companion's seemingly sincere compliment. Much like the endless expanse of space around them, the sight of the Clan Groshna war party was a vastly different experience in person than it had been on the viewports. He'd gathered well enough from inside that the *Blood Moon* and its capital brethren were significantly bigger than the Trog cruisers he'd seen on Earth, but seeing them dwarfing the *Camelot* and the *Kalnythian Wilds* by size multiples he couldn't even accurately guess at still drew him up short as he reached Iveera.

She didn't turn to him, occupied as she seemed to be with her own ruminations. He hovered there without complaint, ogling the breathtaking expanse of the cosmos and the fleet before them. It wasn't long, though, before the multi-headed hydra of apprehension began to reawaken in his chest, turning his thoughts to what had just happened to Malfar and the commander of this war party, and what was about to happen to them.

He looked at Iveera, wanting to ask. Even with her face hidden beneath her helmet and her jin drifting oddly in zero g, she still looked uncharacteristically unsettled.

How did it happen? he wondered at her. *I thought only the Lady and the Merlin could assign an Excalibur.*

Now that he thought about it, he wasn't really sure where that assumption had come from, especially since Iveera had made it perfectly clear there was no shortage of people who'd gladly try to eliminate a Knight in hopes of scoring themselves a nice superweapon. Iveera wasn't in any rush to give him an answer. She just hovered there, her head turned a few degrees his way, still seemingly lost in thought.

Zedavian was right, she finally said.

Nate quelled the urge to immediately ask *about what,* instead waiting for her to speak her mind.

I didn't give Calitha permission to release Samael back there. She looked at him, her faceplate going transparent as if she'd just remembered she was speaking to him and not herself, and that he didn't have a clue what she was talking about. *Groshna's Excalibur,* she explained, to Nate's dumb stare. *It... escaped.*

They have names? Nate wondered before he could stop himself, or even try to process what she meant by *escaped.*

Of course, we have names, Ex said. *That's hardly the point here.*

But why didn't you tell me?

Well, you didn't ask, did you? Besides, I don't recall my having to ASK for your name.

That's different. Wasn't it?

Is it? We are bound, are we not? Ex gave an amused huff. *FULLY bound, according to you.*

I speak carelessly, Iveera's voice cut in. She was watching his expression. He hadn't even noticed he'd subconsciously matched her transparent face-plate style. *An Excalibur's name is not a secret to be freely given, but such matters are hardly our most pressing concern at the moment.*

Told you so, Ex said.

The chief concern remains, Iveera continued, *I did not consciously intend to release Groshna's Excalibur from the considerable safeguards I had placed upon it, and yet it is now free within another host.*

Are you saying it's... what, thinking for itself? Or that your Excalibur let it go?

That is not... Something like a frown bent her green brow, and he got the impression that, much as she'd rode him for failing to mask his talks with Ex, she must be having a separate and rather involved conversation with her own companion beneath the surface. *The boundary between a Knight and their Excalibur is not so easily distinguished as the bond deepens,* she finally finished.

He thought about it. *Well, maybe this is a good thing. Maybe it was the Lady.*

It wasn't, Iveera said.

But Malfar might actually be able to help us bring down the Black Knight now, right?

Wielding the very same Excalibur that fought in his service not a fortnight past? No. Her jin sliced at cold space. *We cannot trust this. I'm...* Again, that look of internal conflict. *I'm no longer certain we can trust ourselves, Nathaniel.*

He considered that statement, trying to weigh it objectively, knowing even as he did that it was hopeless.

And what about Blackthorne? he asked instead. Because at the end of the day, whether Iveera was right or not, he wasn't really sure what else they could do but keep on with their mission.

Iveera's lips pulled tight like she was making one of those soft hissing sounds of hers, but it didn't come through their mental link or the vacuum of space. *I trust her still less. She may not be our enemy today, but I assure you, everything that woman does, she does by her own design and for her own reasons. The years have made her cunning.*

Somehow, he didn't find that especially difficult to believe. But that didn't really change the fact that he had naught but a few dream fragments, the word of a pirate, and a strong feeling that the Clan Groshna war party wasn't going to sit patiently by and stick to their word while they fretted over the details here.

What did she tell you, Nathaniel?

He held her piercing stare, hesitating only out of some fear that she wouldn't believe him—or maybe that she would.

Do you trust this dream of ours? he asked.

She studied him closely. *My trust lies with the Lady and our Merlin,* she finally said, hesitating only a moment before adding, *but also with you, Nathaniel. Your senses, and yours alone, can tell you whether what you see is a product of our Lady, or merely a clever manipulation. Attune your senses to the Light, and you will have your answer.* She looked out to the sprawling remains of Demeter-12. *Just as you will sense what happened here.*

He followed her gaze, thinking of what Ex had said about the place feeling foul and wondering if that explained why he felt so damn nauseous right now. Bad Synth mojo fouling up his humours, or what-the-hell-ever. It wasn't as if there weren't plenty of other explanations for his crawling insides. Once she'd said it, though, he couldn't quite un-notice the faintest little dissonance scratching at the back of his brain, like a few tiny voices in the already infinitesimally quiet choir of the Lady's all-pervasive Light had struck a flat note. Had that been there since they'd arrived?

Is this why you brought me out here?

That, she agreed, considering the looming Troglodan fleet, *and the small expectation that we might require rapid mobility should our tenuous allies decide to break their bond and open fire.*

Nate felt a slow smile creeping across his mouth. *Guess we really lucked out today then, huh?*

Clearly, she replied, and if he hadn't known any better, he might've thought her lips actually gave an amused twitch. After a thoughtful pause, she turned from the war party to look at him. *I also wished for a moment of solitude, if I'm to be honest with you. You might find this hard to believe, but I do have emotions of my own.*

Nate stared dumbly, trying to think of something to say. That *of course* he realized that she, as a living breathing sentient being, had emotions of her own. Except he'd barely thought of her that way through any of this, had he? Mostly, he'd just looked to her for instructions, expecting her to have the answers at every turn. Expecting her to be unbeatable. Infallible.

But maybe six-hundred-odd years of life and Knightly experience wasn't quite the panacea cheat code he'd wanted to believe it to be.

At any rate, her voice broke into his thoughts, *this destruction smells of the Synth, and you would be wise to commit it to memory before we go. There is much more I would've taught you before we faced such foes, but alas...*

He pulled his eyes back to her and found her watching him like she needed to be sure he understood her next words.

Our true enemy has joined the fight, Nathaniel. Whatever happens, moving forward, the only safe bet is that our odds are going to be worsening every step of the way. Even if we liberate the Merlin...

She left the rest unsaid but for a soft flick of her jin.

For vague words, they sure did cast a shadow over his heart. He swallowed, fighting down the sudden urge to tell her that he wasn't ready for this—that he *hadn't* been ready for any of it since the day the Merlin had yanked him into this mess, and that she *should have* taught him more, rather than hiding in her alcove and letting Jaeger and the others handle his so-called training the only way they knew how. But it wouldn't change anything.

He didn't need to hear Iveera's response—or anyone else's—to know that she'd done what she thought was best with what little time they'd had, and that probably *no one* was ever really ready for something like this. She'd done what she could. Some lessons just weren't so simple. Some lessons... what was it? Skirting around at the edge of his memories. Something he'd heard once, about learning and rebirth. Something that had sounded like extreme melodramatic hyperbole at the time.

He looked at the Gorgon, studying the tranquil drift of her jin in zero g and wondering just what kind of lessons had rendered her so thoroughly unshaken in the face of all the death and bodily injury she'd been through. Then he looked to his own hand, still throbbing in kind with the matching Ooperian stab wound in his shoulder as Ex put the finishing touches on mending the internal damage.

Fallible or not, Iveera wasn't really in the same boat as him here. Probably never had been. She had the training. The experience. The natural-born warrior's grit. She had a thousand things he didn't, probably more. But maybe he wasn't doing so bad, all things considered.

He looked to the *Camelot,* decision made, and was starting to reach for his gravitonics to return to the ship when he remembered that there was nothing holding him to Iveera but his own gravitonics. All he had to do was let go. And that's when it came to him—that fickle little tidbit at the edge of his mind.

To be reborn, you have to die first.

That was it.

I'll go get us a location, he told her.

Nate was still turning over Iveera's words as he thudded back to *Camelot*'s deck below and turned to go find Blackthorne.

It wasn't exactly the finest pep talk he'd ever heard. Especially since their odds already seemed plenty shot to shit. Even *with* the murderous Trog war party on their side against the planet-eating protoswarm and the Black Knight. The Black Knight, who'd taken them out twice like last week's garbage and now ostensibly had two Beacons at his command.

But it was those two little words that saved it for him. *Moving forward.* Because what the hell else were they supposed to do? Lay down and die? That was the only other option here, wasn't it?

That's the spirit, Ex said. *Piece of cake, as they say.*

So maybe the stakes had changed, Nate thought, angling down the ramp to the ship's lower level. Maybe the odds had shifted. A lot. But the plan hadn't changed. Find the Black Knight. Recover the Beacons. Save the Merlin. Nothing had changed. Not fundamentally. Nothing but the fact that they were decisively cut off from any other reinforcements, and probably even more hopelessly outnumbered and outgunned than they realized.

But moving forward, as you were saying...

Nothing but the cold realization that Earth was over fifty-thousand light-years away, and that, if they failed, he was never going to see his home or his friends again.

I think we may be regressing here.

Nothing but the terror of the thought that they might actually *succeed* in catching up to the Black Knight again. What would happen then?

We will be ready, or we will die. I see no point in sniveling about it, either way.

Despite everything, he actually huffed a chuckle at that.

At least we have—Nate started, then frowned as he realized he was drawing up to the door of his own quarters without a clue where he thought he'd been headed, or why his subconscious had apparently been under the impression Blackthorne would be in his quarters.

Because I just told you she was, Ex said, sounding a touch confused. *Pay attention, Nathaniel.*

Nate frowned, then pushed the oversight aside, chalking it up to overwhelm and fatigue. He was entirely more concerned with what the hell

Anastasiya Blackthorne was doing in his room anyway. He palmed the access panel—and froze solid at the frantic moaning and unmistakable wet schlicking sounds that spilled out into the corridor in prelude to the sight of a half-naked Amelia Sundercaste spread across his bed, back arched in ecstasy from whatever Blackthorne's fingers were doing to her.

Well, that answers that, at least, Ex said, sounding positively chipper, as the two Atlanteans turned at Nate's incoherent noise of surprise.

Amelia, for her part, gave him a warm smile and the kind of little wave one might expect passing a friendly co-worker in the hallway. Blackthorne just arched one raven dark eyebrow at him in question, deft fingers carrying on their business like discrete professionals that couldn't be bothered to stop for anything less than open war or a natural disaster. Unlike Amelia, she was still fully clothed, and she looked pleased as punch at whatever reaction was etched across his face. They both did.

"Can you just—" Nate started, caught in stutter step between looking or not looking, backing away or demanding to know what the hell they thought they were doing in his bed. "I came to—Jesus, can you just stop doing that for a second?!"

The sounds paused.

Amelia, whose head had been tilting back in pleasure, opened her eyes and perked up, joining Blackthorne in shooting Nate a quizzical look.

"People are, like, dying out there," Nate murmured, waving a hand in the vague direction of *out there* by way of weak explanation, his traitor cheeks burning hot despite his best efforts. "Or Varga is. Did. Look, we've got some serious shit going on out there, and—"

"Oh!" Amelia crooned, covering her mouth with what might've been amusement or fascination as she looked at Blackthorne and back to him, understanding dawning across her face. "Oh bless me, this is uncomfortable for you, isn't it? Unusual, I mean," she quickly corrected herself, raising her hands in a *no offense intended* kind of way. "Culturally shocking, that is. It's a —Oh, what was the word? A faux pas. That's it, right?"

A faux pas.

The words echoed through the empty shell of Nate's brain as he stared, and then un-stared, and then stared again at the pantless Atlantean and the devious pirate woman sharing his bed.

"Yeah," Nate said slowly. "Yeah, you… You nailed it. Faux pas." He forced his focus to Blackthorne, trying to make it clear he meant business. "I came to talk about the thing. Privately."

She tried on a thoughtful expression. "*The* thing, hmm? *That* one? Surely not the—"

"You know which thing, Anastasiya."

The name felt strange on his tongue, but his tone seemed to do the trick.

"Right then," she said, raising her hands in surrender. "That thing. Very well. Excuse me, darling." She patted Amelia right at the pale juncture between thigh and hip, pausing for a bit of a squeeze, then sighed and stood. "We have to talk about the thing, you understand. You stay right here, and we'll be back in just a moment."

"We won't," Nate said, stepping aside to let Blackthorne pass. "I mean, she won't. I mean, I won't either, but—Jesus, is this like, standard Atlantean protocol? You guys just lock eyes across the room and get coupling on whoever's bed happens to be nearby?"

"Pirate, darling," Blackthorne said, patting his chest as she padded past him. "Pirate."

Nate glanced down at his chest, registering which hand she'd just used, then almost guiltily back to Amelia.

"Most settled Atlantean worlds *are* well-populated with privacy pods, should the need arise away from more personal quarters," she said with a soft shrug. "To answer your question."

"Right. Good, I guess." He started to turn, reminding *himself* now that there was some serious shit going on out there, then paused. "This… this isn't gonna be in your assessment, is it?"

She just gave him an innocent smile and—maybe it was his imagination—spread her legs a few centimeters wider.

"Jesus," he muttered to himself, slipping back out the door—right into the line of Snuffy and Tessa, who by some stroke of awkward magic chose that moment to come strolling up the corridor from the aft engine rooms, talking over something on a shared tablet.

They both slowed, eyeing Nate and Blackthorne. More on sputtering reflex than anything, Nate slapped the access panel, closing the door, but not before they got a glimpse at the disheveled, rosy-cheeked Atlantean spread-eagled across his bed.

"That's not what it looks like," he blurted, even as Blackthorne asked if they'd care to join like it was the most normal question in the world.

Freaking Atlanteans.

"We've got… engine stuff?" Snuffy said, eyeing the door and then Blackthorne with an audible swallow.

"That's *right* we do, Mr. Snuffleupagus," Tessa said, curious eyes flicking from Blackthorne to Nate as she looped an arm over her mechanic's shoulder and turned him along his axis like a man-sized puppet. "Real, real big engine stuff to get all up in." She shot Nate a look. "Balls deep, you know?"

He opened his mouth to explain it to them, but they were already skirting away, Tessa nudging Snuffy along. "You crazy kids have fun," she called over her shoulder, with one last bemused glance between him and Blackthorne. "Let us know when we have a plan outside of 'hope that big fleet doesn't shoot us now,' yeah?"

Nate's jaw worked through half a dozen more failing attempts to explain before he finally gave up and nodded, but Tessa had already turned away. He heaved a heavy sigh, already blushing inwardly about what the crew would make of all this if and when Tessa and Snuffy told them, and turned back to Blackthorne.

"Thanks for that."

For a long second, she looked genuinely confused as to what the issue was. Then it hit in a long, "Ohhh." She shook her head, smiling softly. "Terrans. That's right." Her smile widened. "Bunch of perverts."

For a moment, his breath caught on a spike of irritation. Then it whooshed right out, and he was laughing in spite of himself. "What the hell were you doing in my bed?"

"Would you believe me if I said I thought I was extending a polite invitation?" she asked, chuckling with him now.

"Bullshit," he said, trying to rein himself in, reminding himself that she wasn't to be trusted. "That's not how you work. You were"—he waved a hand, searching for the right fit—"trying to throw me off balance, or get me to…"

He trailed off at her patient look, like she was waiting for him to put two and two together. Waiting for him to register that he wasn't in Kansas anymore, Toto.

"I thought you might be wanting a clear head and sweet dreams for the journey ahead," she said, with a shrug. "That one in there seemed quite well-suited for the task. Tell me, have you noticed how much she resembles your pretty friend back on—" She paused at the look on his face. "Ah. But of course, you have. Small world, no?"

"What do you know about that?" he asked, no longer smiling.

"Not a thing, save for that small worlds are rarely so very small at all when one finds themselves huffing one's ass across the surface under a hot sun."

"What the hell's that supposed to mean?"

"Call it naught but the ramblings of an old hag, if you will, but between the Ooperians, that sweet Sundercaste in there, and this entire pile of Council assessment scrumdugga she was so kind to tell me about, I'd say it seems you've caught the devoted interest of a very determined *someone* back Forge way, sowaiy?"

He studied her expression. "This from the outlaw who just so happened to be floating nearby at the exact moment we came under Ooperian attack, right?"

The comment lit a fire in her eyes like he'd never seen before, and when she spoke, her words were clipped and desolate, and utterly devoid of any of her usual quippiness.

"My sweet boy, you know not how my heart burns at the very allegation. I'll have you know that I, Anastasiya Blackthorne, am the prime reason their foul kind have dwindled thin as they have throughout the centuries. I am no friend to the Ooperians."

"I'm… sorry," Nate said, reeling at the terrible intensity in her eyes and the sudden storm cloud aura hanging over the corridor. At that moment, for the first time since they'd met, it was no stretch at all to imagine that this woman was ancient well beyond her appearance. Then she drew a chesty breath, relaxing her shoulders, and it was like the clouds had lifted.

"Well, you didn't know, did you, darling?" she said, waving it off like she *hadn't* just about gone Dark Side on his ass. "Now, I take it you want to talk about our missing planet?"

CHAPTER 36
SUPERMAN

For reasons he didn't particularly care to dissect, it wasn't the Synth, the Black Knight, or even Blackthorne and her laissez-faire attitude toward the sanctity of a man's bed that Nate was thinking about as he sat listening to the quiet hum of the *Camelot* cruising crusher space and bade Ex to reach out to the q-node on Terra. Instead, it was a scene from the movie adaptation of Stephen King's *The Green Mile* that was loitering in his thoughts, and the way he remembered watching it, thinking how profoundly, heart-wrenchingly fucked up it was: the entire concept and awkward ceremony of the last meal.

It was just occurring to him that he hadn't eaten in a while when Ex thankfully interrupted his reveries with a pointed clearing of his nonexistent throat. Nate brought himself back to his quiet bedroom corner and watched with more trepidation than he'd expected as the holo in front of him resolved into oily darkness, interwoven with the faint glow of what might've been a streetlight permeating window blinds, and the soft sounds of breathing.

Nighttime. Copernicus was sleeping. The realization made him feel a tad self-important. He hadn't even thought to check what time it was back in State College. Like some part of him had just expected his friends would all be sitting around at all hours, waiting to hear from him before he flew off into the next harrowing encounter. But this was fine.

On a hunch, he closed his eyes, inviting his senses more fully into the connection, and felt a sense of homey peace as he felt his State College bedroom taking shape around him—dark and quiet and perfectly ordinary, Copernicus' two front paws stretched out languidly in front of him from his q-node collar point of view. It brought a pang to his heart, thinking of the little corgi sleeping in Nate's bed all alone. Then there was a sleep snort, and the room spun dizzyingly on its axis as Copernicus rolled over to settle on his other side with a heavy doggo sigh. Rolled right over to face the bed's other occupant.

Fifty-some-thousand light-years away and Nate's heart still leapt at the sight of Gwen lying so close. Sleeping in *his* bed, he noted, with a preposterous little swelling of animal pride. In the dim light, he could just make out the pale ghost of her platinum hair and the fitful pinch of her sleeping brow. He opened his mouth, thinking to whisper soft midnight greetings, but seconds ticked by, then maybe minutes, and he still hadn't said a word. He just sat there, watching her troubled dreams pass. Watching her face settle back into perfect, beautiful peace. Wishing to Christ and all his pals he could reach out and touch her.

If things went poorly tomorrow…

If he couldn't get back to them…

A soft change in breathing pulled his darkening thoughts back to Terrra, where his Goodest Boy was beginning to stir like his sleeping mind was finally catching on to their nighttime visitor.

Nate had closed the connection before he even knew it.

He sat there in silence for a while afterward, wondering at his own action, then stood and turned to go check on what, he didn't know. The crew. The ship. Malfar. Anything that wasn't the quiet of his own room. It was an unusual thought for a lifelong introvert, but then again, he also hadn't had many occasions to contend with his own restless mind on the eve of battle.

If battle truly was what they were flying into.

If Blackthorne hadn't somehow duped them, for reasons of her own.

If this wasn't all some arcane trap, and the Black Knight wasn't waiting with his protoswarms and Beacon black magic to simply atomize them all the moment they dropped out of crusher space.

He definitely needed a distraction.

Momentarily, his lowly lizard brain drifted to Amelia and Blackthorne, and to the standing invitation they'd offered to join them in the guest quarters where he'd insisted they move after what the crew had immediately and uproariously taken to calling Operation Spread Eagle. Then he thought of

Gwen, feeling doubly guilty for having flaked out of the call, and moved for the door before his overactive brain (or Ex) could start in on the sticky question of *why* he'd done it.

"Sorry babe," he mumbled to himself in a poor imitation of Todd Mackleroy's voice. "You looked so pretty sleeping. Didn't wanna wake you before I up and died."

That wasn't it at all. Or not the whole of it, at any rate. But he didn't want to face the whole of it right then, no more than he wanted to wait around and see how long Ex's spell of oddly judgment-free silence would last. So, he jabbed the door panel and kept moving before the rest could catch up. Or tried to keep moving, at least.

Tessa was standing there when the door whooshed open, knuckles cocked like she'd been about to knock. Nate rocked up on his toes, catching the door frame to avoid running into her with the momentum of his escape velocity.

For a long second, neither of them spoke. He didn't miss the way her gaze darted past him, though, seemingly checking the vicinity for any gyrating Atlanteans. When her attention came back to him, it was with a soft smirk. Wordlessly, she proffered a bottle of something—whiskey, he thought at a glance—and cocked an eyebrow in question.

"One last hymn before battle?" she asked.

"Uh…" Nate glanced back into his quarters as if some part of him was expecting to find a reasonable answer lurking on the bed or among the flight-sealed shelves. When he met Tessa's eyes again, her smirk had definitely deepened a notch or two.

"Other plans?" she asked, glancing meaningfully down the corridor, probably not coincidentally in the direction of the guest cabins.

"No. I mean, not—That wasn't what it looked like earlier, for the record."

She chuckled. "I'm just yanking your Excalibur, Nate. Shit, end of the world, ancient forces of darkness, no one could blame you for wanting to wet your whistle one last time anyway."

"But that's not—"

"I know, I know," she said, waving down his indignant fluster. "None of my business anyway, dude." She caught herself on that last word, her lip twitching in amusement as she searched his reaction. "Captain. Ser Knight."

"Nate works fine."

"I sure hope so," she said, not missing a beat.

He wasn't positive how she meant it. Friendly banter. A casual reminder of how much was currently riding on him and his patchy dreams and broken sword. Or maybe it was more to do with the silence stretching between them, and that petulant little thrill tap-dancing its way across his heart as she didn't look away.

This wasn't okay.

"Welp," she said, stirring from the moment like she'd read as much on his face, "I'm gonna go hit up Sesame Street, then. We'll be upstairs if you wanna join us for a round."

"I'll, uh…" His cheeks were burning again. "I was just gonna check on Malfar. Maybe I'll join you guys in a minute."

He'd been planning on doing no such thing, but now that he'd said it, it didn't sound like the worst idea. Tessa just cocked the whiskey bottle to her brow in salute and sauntered off down the hallway, whistling a rather intricate rendition of Muse's "Knights of Cydonia."

He found himself smiling at her selection as she dipped into the grav lift. Martian Knights. Clever. And a great song, all around.

Lovely whistling voice too, Ex said. *Canoodler.*

Nate took a breath, thinking of the many colorful ways he might tell the voice in his head to shove it, then gave up with a sigh and went stomping down the corridor in search of less flummoxing distraction.

So what IS your name? Nate wondered idly at Ex, when he'd tired of staring silently at Malfar the justicar-Knight's unconscious bulk.

If you need to ask…

I can't handle the truth?

It is merely a name, Nathaniel. An arbitrary smacking of air on tongue and lips.

Nate made a noncommittal grunt of reply, too absorbed in everything else to bicker over this too. Malfar was, unsurprisingly, just fine. Or not fine at all, depending on how you wanted to look at it. Either way, the Troglodan didn't seem to have changed much since the last time Nate had poked up to see him. He was still unconscious, probably in some manner of Excalibur-induced "super sleep." Still neatly packaged in the ship's main entryway, where Iveera had conjured him a nice e-dim cell to keep him contained if and when he awoke, demanding answers—and, quite possibly, justice for Groshna, or subservience to the Black Knight, or Lady knew what else.

Nate wasn't sure what to expect from the justicar. More accurately, he wasn't sure what to expect from Samael the corrupted Excalibur, and neither was Iveera, regardless of what she might say. Personally, he still wasn't sold on the wisdom of keeping their potential ally imprisoned. Especially not when the only real strike against him was that his Excalibur was packing the same corruption they'd both already been touched by anyway. A corruption they still didn't understand the first thing about.

He wasn't sure what to think about any of it, really. But he also couldn't help wonder, staring at those transparent e-dim dampening panels, why it was that not a moment seemed to have passed since he'd entered this mess that at least one member of their sacred Order Excalibur hadn't been actively trying to trap or stop another.

It felt more than a little bit rich—and, coincidentally, more than a little reminiscent of good old Terra—flying out to save the world when they apparently couldn't even get their own house in order. And here he didn't even know his own Excalibur's name.

You'll know it when you hear it. Don't be dramatic.

Yeah, I'M being dramatic, Nate shot back, shaking his head. He looked idly down at his own hands, still thinking. It was an odd thing, knowing the strength those hands could summon while still feeling so completely clueless as to the true depth of the power they might hold, if only he could find the way to it. But that was the crux of it, wasn't it? Finding the way. Finding their way through the endless void of space to the one objective he'd been clinging to so tightly that he hadn't even stopped to consider that maybe they had that part wrong too. That maybe, the Black Knight *wanted* to be found. That maybe, even the mighty Iveera Katanaga wasn't ready for this. That maybe, people would get killed, either way.

Where was this feeling in the movies?

Where had his gritty hero's determination ran off to? It'd been there before. Now, though? He just felt lost—like a guy who'd just seen an entire planet destroyed and suddenly couldn't even bring himself to talk to his girlfriend. Couldn't bring himself to tell her or anyone else that he *wasn't* okay. That he was goddamn terrified, actually. That, in addition to his own life, he'd definitely just plopped the lives of Jaeger, Tessa, and the rest of the crew into the shifty hands of an infamous pirate. That he was leading them all even farther from home, and that he didn't have the faintest clue how he was going to get them all back.

Christ, maybe he *was* being dramatic. He found himself thinking, bargaining almost like a prayer: if only this all worked out. If only…

He'd never watch another superhero movie again, for starters. Never ogle another pair of spandexed demi gods super-slamming each other through concrete walls. Not without flinching at all the bone-shaking pain such highly-tuned eye candy would never truly convey. Because, how could they? More importantly, why *would* they, when it wasn't even part of the fantasy they were selling? Effortless power. That was the real dream. So much power and strength and damn-near invulnerability that a good hero just couldn't help but make it all look easy on the big screen. So much natural born heroism that even when the chips were down, and they were getting their face pounded in the final fight, you couldn't *really* believe that it hurt all that much. Not when it was them. And especially not when they emerged from the pounding with no more than a bloodied lip, or a frayed costume and a quippy one-liner.

That shit was fun to watch.

That shit made you feel invincible without the pesky investment of actually *trying*.

Getting your teeth kicked in by an unstoppable Black Knight, on the other hand…

Feeling your ribs snap as he slammed you straight through one of those damned concrete walls…

Nate huffed at himself in grim amusement, feeling a little sick as he stared at the aching pink flesh where the Ooperian dagger had pierced his hand, his mind's eye turning with the image of Iveera's charred remains after their relay scuffle.

"Fucking Superman," he muttered, to no one in particular.

"What do you got against the Man of Steel, kid?"

Nate looked up, startled to find Jaeger watching him from the corridor, arms crossed. He hadn't heard the Lt Col approaching, lost as he'd been in his own thoughts.

"Oh, just asking myself the age-old question," he replied, not really sure what else to say—only that he'd be damned if he was going to start complaining to his non-powered allies about how his inner nerd had been lied to all these years.

"WWSD?" Jaeger guessed. "What would Superman do?"

"Something like that."

Jaeger considered him for a few seconds, then broke into a tired smile. "Well, maybe you can ask him yourself, one of these days. Way things are going, I'm starting to feel like it's only a matter of time before we run into him out here, too."

Nate huffed a tired chuckle. "Guess we could probably use the backup."

Jaeger didn't argue as he settled down on the other end of Nate's bench. He pursed his lips marginally, looking like he had something to say. Maybe something more than the same tired *get-some-sleep-while-you-still-can*s he'd been dishing out to the crew like candies since they'd made the jump to crusher space. But the silence stretched on.

"So Spoon, huh?" Nate finally said, when it'd become borderline uncomfortable.

Jaeger considered him, slightly taken aback by the abrupt change of topic, then shrugged. "They're a national treasure."

"Can't argue with that. Surprisingly relevant anthem for a jailbreak, too." Nate shot him a sideways glance. "You ever listen to the Wombats, by any chance?"

Jaeger started to say something, then pursed his lips again and fixed Nate with a look that seemed to say *we're not here to talk about music, kid.*

It was Nate's turn to shrug.

"For what it's worth, I *am* sorry I let that Golden prick trick me into slipping a tracker aboard your ship," Jaeger said after a while, frowning a little like the words tasted wrong. "Granted, I only did it so we'd have a convincing cover to bust your asses out of his palace, so…"

"Hey, apology accepted," Nate said. "No harm and all that."

He said it more to rustle Jaeger's jimmies than anything else. But the Lt Col didn't bristle, or start in, as Nate half-expected he might, on the categorical breakdown of all the myriad ways Nate had put their lives at risk since then. Instead, Jaeger just turned his pensive frown on Malfar, clearly thinking about what came next. He'd been quietly thoughtful since their initial strategy session a couple hours ago. They all had.

"Carter and Cammy both seem to think he's already more or less healed in there," he finally said, dark eyes still on the justicar. "Still kinda freaky, even after everything we've watched you and Iveera slog through."

He pulled his gaze from Malfar, focusing his attention on Nate.

"Any idea whether we're gonna be looking at Groshna 2.0 when he wakes up?"

"Iveera said—"

"I know what Iveera said. I'm asking you."

Nate considered the blight-spotted Troglodan. Brutish as his outward appearance still was to Nate's uncultured eyes, Malfar looked rather peaceful in sleep. Even after watching him knock Varga's head in on an unexpected burst of Excalibur strength, it was hard to imagine the creature in front of them could ever be like Groshna. "I really don't know. He seemed like such a…"

"A good dude?" Jaeger offered.

Nate looked at Jaeger, slightly surprised to realize that *was* pretty much what he'd meant. A good dude. A devout servant of justice. Maybe even a decent person. He'd never expected to think of a Troglodan that way. Wasn't sure he really wanted to now. Especially not as Jaeger nodded to himself, watching Nate like he'd just confirmed something important, and resettled himself on the bench like they were about to have themselves a Talk, capital T.

"You ever hear the stories about how many soldiers went through World War II without ever actually firing their weapons?" he finally asked.

Nate searched the Lt Col's face, trying to extrapolate where this was headed, suddenly unable to think about much of anything aside from just how many Trogs he'd gunned down back in Atlantis. Before that, too, back on their prison ship. How many Troglodans had he killed? How many decent soldiers, just following orders? *Was* there even such a thing?

"What's your point? What are you asking?"

Jaeger shook his head as if to say he wasn't asking a thing. "You've done good, Nate. Getting us away from the Forge. Coming through in that scrape with the Ooperians. Even fighting the Trogs back on Earth. You've done real good."

"But?" Nate asked. There was definitely a *but* in the air.

"*But* willful violence doesn't come naturally to well-adjusted college kids, and you're still running around out here with a fully-loaded conscience, all the heavy artillery you can shake a stick at, no proper training, and no clear chain of command."

"Oh, is that all?"

Jaeger just watched him with that inscrutable commander's stare, inviting him to defend himself, or at least to flounder around trying. He wasn't in the mood.

"So what, you just wanted to come tap in for one last round of the hoo-rah bullshit before we hit the dirt? Now's not really a good time to—"

"Now's the only time, kid. You're about to go twelve rounds with the goddamn devil, and you've got a floppy sword. The only thing now's *not* the time for is sitting here pretending that you've got your shit sorted, and everything's just going to magically work out."

The words were so casually scathing that for a second, Nate could only stare, watching with a kind of morbid fascination as the cuts opened, showing their true depth. He felt like he'd been slapped. Felt quite suddenly like a snot-nosed child who'd just been unceremoniously reminded he'd actually been playing make-believe all along. Jaeger watched him, waiting to see if he'd fight back, but Nate had nothing to say. Nothing but a thoroughly pierced ego and a sudden desperate thirst for an answer to the fear that'd slowly been freezing over his insides with every passing light-year they drew closer to the Black Knight.

"It's not bullshit, Nate," Jaeger finally said. "The hooahs, the training, the chains of command you thumb your nose at. That shit all exists for a damn good reason."

"What, so you don't have to think about all the shit you've done?" he asked, hope deflating. This wasn't going to help. His wounded ego pushed on anyway. "So you can just call it duty, and offload it to the next guy up the line?"

"You're goddamn right," Jaeger said, leaning forward with a darkening intensity. "And you wanna know why that doesn't bother me?"

"Enlighten me."

"Because we're not goddamn holy knights, Nate. We're not built to do this alone. Shit goes wrong somewhere, people do bad things to one another, and there's no guiding light shining down to show us how to fix it —how to fight the monsters without becoming one of them. So you outsource it. You defer your conscience up to your superior. Follow orders. Trust they'll do the same. Trust that, somehow, together, maybe you'll all manage to do the right thing, the good thing. Because the moment you start thinking you've got it figured better than the rest of the world, that's the moment you might just start down your own path to darkness."

"I don't believe that," Nate said, though truthfully, he wasn't so sure.

"No shit. You probably believe the system's broken, probably think it's the top of the food chain that's the problem. The fat cats calling the shots with nothing to lose and everything to gain from pushing the next war into the pipeline, right? How am I doing?"

Nate shrugged. "I don't see the Atlanteans bombing each other over material rights out here."

Jaeger sighed and shook his head like he was missing the point completely.

"But that's not what I meant, anyway," Nate finished, deciding the feeling was mutual.

"Enlighten me," Jaeger said, echoing his own words back at him with a notable hint of derision.

Hell, maybe he deserved it, because the longer Nate searched for a starting point to the righteous counterargument he was so sure this conversation deserved, the more he floundered, thinking of all the injustices out there—back on Terra, and everywhere else. All the greedy assholes and all the costly power they abused. All the pointless conflict and even *more* pointless dick-measuring that seemed to rule the entire damn galaxy.

He raged at it all. Raged like a good little make-pretender. But when he finally opened his mouth, it was only four frightened words that fell out.

"What if I'm wrong?"

Jaeger watched him, waiting to see if he'd elaborate. "'Bout what?"

"About the dreams. The Merlin. About all of it. What if…" He shook his head, turning to Malfar's cell just for an excuse to escape Jaeger's vigilant stare. "What if I'm not the guy they need me to be?"

"Well then, congratu-fucking-lations, Mr. Knight. You just unlocked the key to the universe."

Nate looked at him, some combination of incredulous and plain pissed.

"You want me to tell you you're special, kid? That some mystical Lady's guiding your steps, and it's all gonna be okay?" He shook his head. "I can't do that. I don't know. But you know one thing I *am* pretty damn sure about?"

Nate splayed his hands, not really seeing how much worse this pep rally could get. "Enlighten me."

"These 'special' paragons you're building up in your head? The ones who get the distinct honor of knowing beyond a shadow of a doubt that their way is *the* way, and that their shit is going to come out squeaky clean no matter what? I'm pretty damn sure those people don't exist—back home or out here. I know Iveera's struggling. I see it, and I think you do too. And maybe your Merlin or that Golden Boy asshole have something different to say after however the hell long they've been around, but me? I'd put money on it not a day goes by even *they* don't question the things they've done, and prop that guilt right back up their Lady's divine skirts. Hell, maybe she's got questions too."

"That's… probably heresy or something."

Jaeger smiled. "Sure is a good thing no one's ever going to hear a fuckin' peep of any of this then, hooah?"

"Hooah," Nate murmured flatly, still chewing on what he'd said. Jaeger's sudden grip on his shoulder was as firm as it was unexpected.

"Hey, I'm trying to tell you we've got your back here, Nate. You get into the shit down on that planet, you just remember we're right there with you, and that no one lives without fear. Not even Mordred fucking LeFaye, you hear me?"

Nate looked from Jaeger's strong hand to his dark eyes, rattled by the man's sudden intensity. "I hear you."

Jaeger held him at stare point for another long moment, then nodded and dropped his hand, seemingly satisfied. "And if you *are* wrong someday, and you happen to be self-aware enough to actually see it, then hey"—he shrugged—"you clean your shit up, and you try again. You learn your lesson, take your licks, and get the hell back on your feet. And you trust that we'll be here when you can't do it alone." He gave Nate a meaningful look. "Just to answer your question."

Nate nodded slowly, real gratitude bubbling up as he processed Jaeger's words. "This coming from the guy who literally just said now's not the time to be counting on magical second chances," he pointed out anyway, unable to help himself.

"Kid," Jaeger chuckled, shaking his head, "you think too fucking much."

Hear, hear, Ex chimed in. *Though 'thinking' may be a generous word for it. Floundering, perhaps. Or—*

Sniveling? Nate wondered, surprised and oddly satisfied to find himself smiling.

Ahh, Ex sighed in a sound of pure relief. *And now I've truly nothing left to teach you, Nathaniel. The student has become the master. I couldn't be more proud.*

Nate just smiled wider and focused back on Jaeger, realizing he hadn't said anything. "Well, Tess said they were gonna have a round, if you wanna help me work on that thinking problem. 'One last hymn before battle,' she said, or something like that."

He gave Nate a curious look. "Did she." It seemed more like a thoughtful placeholder than an actual question. "Well"—he straightened his pant legs with his palms and stood—"I need to check in on Pierce and Elmo's Knight-ship orientation, make sure Iveera hasn't killed the both of 'em yet, and then I'm gonna get some damned rest. You should all do the same. We meet again at 0500."

"That's it?"

"What?" he asked, grinning a little. "You think I was gonna tell you my whole life's story, and how we're really not so different, you and I, and how you have to learn from my mistakes, so you don't repeat 'em?"

Nate shrugged. "I mean, when you put it that way..."

For a moment, Jaeger looked like he might say something, but then he pushed the thought away with a grimace. "Much as I'd love to share my cock-eyed leadership wisdom with you, kid, I think it suffices to say there's a damn good reason I ended up annexed to the alien squad well before our sad asses had any reason to believe there *were* aliens. The rest is a story for another time."

"After we survive the doomsday battle?"

It was Jaeger's turn to shrug. "Nothing else for it. We rest up, we rehash the plan until we're sick of it." He looked to Malfar's cage, a slight frown creasing his brow. "And then we pray to your sweet Lady his cousins or whatever don't try to stab us right in the ass before we get our shot at that swarm."

CHAPTER 37

WAKE UP CALL

They stood in a loose semi-circle: three Troglodan captains—two holograms and one solid—facing their present acting admiral across the holo banks. In front of them, a trio of ship schematics rotated in slow, tandem cycles: two sleek Knightships and a third custom job whose dark hull looked to have been built on an old heavy Atlantean freighter skeleton but had been so heavily modified that it now resembled something more like a small battle cruiser.

It was the *Blackthorne*, and it was the first ship to be waved aside as the first holo captain stepped forward to speak.

"We should open with anti-atomics the moment we arrive."

"No," said the second holo captain. "If we're going to do this, we should wait until we can safely hit them with the SID and be done with it for certain."

"Nonsense. Think of the waste. Have you no faith in our ability to cripple a few tiny ships?"

"Have you no respect for common sense? These are not some shiny pleasure yachts to be casually disabled."

"Have neither of you any respect left for the Old Ways?" asked the third captain, who'd listened to the exchange with visibly growing disgust. "You speak of respect and faith, yet neither of you seem to recall that a deal was struck. A deal that should be sacred by our Ways. What of our honor, brothers?"

"Honor?" The two holo captains traded a smugly amused look. "You speak of honor in bowing to a blight-stained runt? Listen to yourself, you old fool."

"And what of this Black Knight and his fleet?" asked the third captain, not shrinking under their disdain.

"Don't you mean his *swarm*?" countered the first captain. He spat on the deck—or spat on his own deck, at least, on the other side of the holo connection. "Fist the Knights and their ghost stories."

"You saw what happened to the Atlantean colony."

"Hardly beyond the scope of modern weaponry," said the second holo captain.

"Or the mystic powers of a Knight, if one were to simply believe all they hear," added the first. "Perhaps this Black Knight fellow cored the planet with an anti-atomic of his own."

"You both know the drift diagnostics disagree with—"

"Enough," said the only other Troglodan physically in the room, their acting admiral who, at a glance, did not command even a quarter of the respect Varga had from his three dragonhead captains. "You bicker like children."

They all three of them looked like they had thoughts about that. Funnily enough, their shared disdain might've been the only thing that unified them at the moment. They all waited more or less obediently, though, as their acting admiral drummed his fingers thoughtfully on the arm of his commander's chair, taking his sweet time coming to his decision.

"Much as I stir to think of turning the Knights' own weapons against them," he finally said. "I will not condone such mindless waste. Not before we've exhausted all other options."

The three captains traded a look.

"What would our admiral have us do?" asked the third.

"We will take them all before they know what's hit them. We will take back what is rightfully ours." He showed them an ugly grin, leaning forward in his commander's chair. "We will return to our people as heroes."

The room rippled with the last words, beginning to fade as the four Troglodans continued speaking. In its place, there was nothing but drifting darkness and the tenuous, baseline itch of a solitary presence suddenly threatening to disturb it.

Wake up, damn you.

Not solitary, then, that presence reflected of itself. Nor, apparently, awake. Which didn't—couldn't—seem to make sense from any angle.

Not until Malfar blinked his bleary eyes open.

Awareness flooded into the depths, fuzzy light and shapes greeting him, wrong for reasons he couldn't place, hands shooting out reflexively, defensively, as if expecting a blow from…

Varga.

The memories hit like a flood. He jerked upright, yanked immediately to a halt against full-body crash restraints, and thudded back to the cushions, pieces slamming together like lightning and thunder in his pounding head. The fight. Those last moments. That crimson bolt of…

"No," he groaned, head spinning.

Yes, replied a rusty metal voice, undeniably in his head. *Time enough for that later. Listen now.*

"Listen to…" He blinked again, hearing another voice, trying to get his bearings. He was strapped to some kind of crash cushion inside a transparent cell in the *Camelot's* entryway. One of the Terrans—the dark-skinned medic they called Carter—was watching him warily from the holo display she'd just been speaking into.

"You're safe and secure," she told him, speaking slowly and clearly, and only half-convincingly. "What I need you to do is take a breath and tell me how you're feeling. You've been out for a while."

Out how long, some part of him wanted to ask, before the thought brought him back to the dream that he'd just—

Not a dream. Brought your mind aboard Blood Moon.

Malfar clenched his teeth, wanting to roar at the voice, caught instead trying to parse its meaning. His mind. The *Blood Moon*. The low hum of crusher drives. How in nine hells could he have—

Varga belonged to Groshna. Groshna trusted no one. Kept surveillance on all threats. Wisely. Varga's bottom feeders planning to slag Knightships on arrival.

There was a sharpening then, almost like the mental equivalent of a clearing throat, and the voice added, in a decidedly more Troglodan tone, *I recommend you pull head from ass and do something about it, runt.*

Malfar looked back to Carter, mind racing, the reality of the situation uncomfortably ambiguous in his head. "How long until we arrive?" he asked, trying to sit up, nearly losing it and bucking like a wild bull when he came up against the restraints.

She gave him an assessing look. "You don't need to worry about that until—"

"HOW LONG?!"

The Terran didn't flinch at his tone so much as reset, reevaluate. She was a steady one. That was good, he thought, forcing himself to breathe, to calm down.

"The Gorgon," he said. "I must speak with the Gorgon. Now."

"Why?"

"Because I strongly believe we are in imminent danger of betrayal at the hands of my kin."

She studied him a moment longer, gauging his statement, then gave a curt nod and turned back to her holo display. "We're almost there," she said, tinkering with the display controls. "Crew's making final prep, and— Dammit." She waved the display away, scowling, and glanced toward the bridge.

"I'll be right back with the colonel. Just—"

For a moment, he thought she'd simply decided against telling her restrained patient to *stay put*, or whatever she'd been about to say. Then he noticed that her eyes were tracking something from the corridor behind him. Something he couldn't see. Her hand hovering closer to her holstered sidearm. Slowing.

"It's okay, darling," came a smooth, honey-sweet voice. Atlantean. Buzzing with an odd, barely perceptible energy that nevertheless strummed at something deep inside him.

Malfar watched with a sinking feeling as Anastasiya Blackthorne stepped into the edge of his view.

"There's nothing to fear," she said, sauntering toward Carter, who stood stiffly frozen in place like she'd been hit by some low-grade neural stunner, or—

Or *glamoured*, he realized, as Blackthorne spared a sideways glance his way, and he caught the unnatural golden-orange sheen glinting in her eyes, like the reflected light of a sunset that wasn't there.

"What the hell are you doing, pirate?" he growled, setting aside the impossibility of what he was seeing. "What do you want?"

He saw the corner of her mouth pull into a grin as she focused her full attention back on Carter. "Oh, galactic peace," she said, stepping closer to the Terran. "A decent hot bath." She reached out to stroke Carter's dark cheek, and for a moment, a fire sparked somewhere beneath the Terran's petrified expression. She actually tried to take a swing at the pirate, but her movement was like that of a drunk, limp-tentacled Kelgen under the influence of Blackthorne's enchantment. The pirate caught her advance easily, cupping her face almost tenderly and whispering soft words as Carter sank unsteadily to the bench beside them.

"Perhaps a few quality hours with this one," Blackthorne continued as if nothing had happened, hooking a thumb back at Carter as she turned to Malfar. "Lady knows I love me a good fighter. But if you'll do me the honor of not screaming for a moment, and forcing me to do something we might all regret…"

He felt her will boring into him as she held him on the end of that unnatural stare—tiny little fingers seeking purchase in the cracks of his mind, waiting until he reluctantly closed his mouth from the roar he'd been sure he was about to make for Lt Col Jaeger or anyone else.

"Well then," Blackthorne said, pressing up to the wall of his cell and looking, for all her many ancient years, like a satisfied, borderline giddy young woman. "Given recent developments, I thought we might forget about me and take a moment to discuss what *you* want, my honorable justicar friend."

CHAPTER 38

RAPID DEPLOYMENT

For all the times he'd hammered on Murphy's Law and espoused every conceivable variation of *no plan survives contact with the enemy* sentiment in the past twenty-four hours, Jaeger had to admit he'd left out the one glaring little detail for which he had yet to find any solution:

A dick punch—whether encountered out of the blue in the wild or meticulously planned for in advance—was still a goddamn dick punch.

And as he watched their plan fail to survive even the first instant out of crusher space, there was no denying it: it didn't feel good.

"I do *not* like that," Kalders said from her flight chair beside him, her main personal display showing a zoomed copy of the same story being told across the *Camelot*'s main bridge display.

The *Blackthorne* had just slipped their yoked crusher drive course, kept their drives engaged for an extra few seconds, and dropped back to real space on the dark side of the barren, rather small planetoid that was supposed to be the lost colony of Avalon. *Supposed to be* feeling like the operative phrase now more than ever, as Jaeger took in the spread of the Clan Groshna war party dropping to real space on the tactical display, in neat formation around the *Camelot* and the adjacent *Kalnythian Wilds*.

"Evasive actions, Kalders," he snapped, fumbling to open comms with Iveera. "Now."

He heard the others gasping and clenching up behind them. Saw Kalders swinging into action almost before the words were out of his mouth, no questions asked. Felt the *Camelot* groan and wobble, like they were already caught in the pull of their neighbors' gravitonics. On the tactical displays, the first alerts sounded, red blips pinging from the Trog's three Nova-class dragonheads to come racing toward the *Camelot* and the *Kalnythian Wilds*.

"Get us outta here, Cammy," Jaeger amended, taking in relative speeds, and the ominous "Anti-matter Weapons Detected" alert flashing across the displays, and remembering what Iveera had recommended for any such contingencies. "Microjump. Now. Anywhere within mission radius."

"Q-DRIVE PROTOCOL SPECIFIES—"

"Override!" Jaeger snapped, as the torpedo impact timer ticked danger-ously low. It was only as the *Camelot* whined with the building charge that his brain registered the remainder of Cammy's previous warning above her cheerful, "AFFIRMATIVE," and he remembered that Nate would be popping out onto the hull right about then, preparing to drop planetside with Iveera.

They winked across the system before Jaeger could blink, carried on a rushing pulse of sound and an intangible energy that left his head buzzing, heart palpitating in his ears and throat.

"Oh god," Nate's voice groaned from the consoles, right before a quar-ter-sized hologram of his likeness appeared, looking a little green at the gills. "That didn't feel right."

"Sooorry about that one, Mr. Knight," Kalders said, biting her lip as she checked the updating displays. The jump had landed them on the "bright" side of Avalon, where a kind of twilight haze lit the surface from the distant white star the computers projected the planetoid to be passing by at about a billion kilometers. "You still got all your bits and pieces out there?"

"All the ones I can see, anyway." Nate wrinkled his nose and mouth, like he was trying to get his ears to pop. "Might be tasting sounds, though. That doesn't seem right. Just trying to get a fix on—"

"Holy nuts!" Kalders barked, at the same time that Nate cried out with a decidedly more colorful exclamation.

Kalders was already whipping them around into a tight course change as Jaeger processed what he'd just seen on the displays: a loose pack of rock and ice, roughly the size of freaking Texas, abandoning its deadened drift to come darting directly at them. And darting *was* the right word, freakish as it seemed. The accumulated debris came alive like something organic—the reanimated appendage of some colossal galactic octopus, driven by Lady only knew what. Whatever it was, it sent half of the *Camelot*'s instruments haywire. Something in Cammy's systems adjusted the readings, calming the rough edges until they could see a kind of spectral blue *something* reaching through the writhing mass, guiding it straight toward them, scary fast.

Jaeger was opening his mouth to give the *open fire* order when a brilliant column of blue lanced by on their starboard. It punched into the leading edge of the surging swarm, holding it there on a tide of superheated matter that swelled with frightening speed, almost immediately threatening to spill over. Then the *Kalnythian Wilds* rushed by, disgorging a lone torpedo into the surging mass before arcing off, and for a few seconds, the *Camelot*'s displays simply bleached out at the ferocity of whatever hell had just been unleashed.

When the storm cleared, there was nothing but a dissipating scatter of pebbles and atomized space dust, blessedly devoid of whatever specter had convinced its previous constituents to defy all worldly physics.

"So that's, uh… That's a protoswarm, huh?" Kalders asked, finding her voice.

"That was not the swarm," came Iveera's voice over the bridge comms. "That was a stray tendril. *That* is the swarm."

A wide section of the main display shifted as she spoke, zooming to whatever fix she'd just shared.

"Holy nuts," Kalders repeated at a quiet murmur.

Jaeger couldn't really disagree with the sentiment.

To say it was more of the same might've technically been true on a surface level, but the sheer size of the thing defied comparison. Calling it an ocean would've almost certainly been underselling it. It looked a lot more like they'd just found all the missing bits of Demeter-12. And maybe they had, he realized, numbly. Right along with a few other planets' worth of mass fodder.

The swarm undulated and churned like a living thing, an entire ecosystem of thickening arms and infinitely diverging tendrils, drifting through the cosmos on the creeping storm system of that spectral blue energy. The energy itself was concentrated most densely at the heart of the swarm—and was also apparently invisible to the naked eye, Jaeger realized, with a few toggling flicks of his controls.

"So, uh…" Kalders said, slowly pulling her eyes away from the spectacle to turn to Jaeger. "Time to give 'em the ol' razzle dazzle then, boss?"

"If that's what we're calling a bait and switch these days," he said, noting the distance and spread of the Trog war party, and their incoming velocity relative to the closing swarm. They needed to move.

"You good to drop out there, kid?" he asked, turning his attention briefly planetside. A storm was gathering down there, in one discrete sector of the murky twilight. Almost like an invitation, he couldn't help but think.

"We have a fix on our target," Iveera answered instead, pinging planetside coordinates dead center of that ominous darkness.

"But the Trogs," Nate argued. "And—And fucking *that.*"

Even without his pointed swarm-ward jab, it wasn't hard to figure out which *that* he was referring to. But even so.

"Space battle's our problem, kid. Stick to the plan, hooah? The sooner you grab the wizard and the orb, the sooner we're outta here."

Nate looked less than convinced, but after a few moments of that distant, voices-in-the-head look he got sometimes, he came back with a sigh. "Fine. Be careful, guys. I…" He looked dangerously like he wanted to start with an *if we don't all make it…*

"Window's closing, kid," Jaeger said, sincerely meaning it as he eyed the ticking intercept counters. "Save it for afterward and get your ass moving."

"Not a scratch up here," Kalders chimed in. "Promise."

Nate hesitated another moment, then he nodded and jetted off after Iveera, two glinting specks bound for the planet below like a pair of speeding missiles, sans the drive trails.

"Kick his ass, Nate," Kalders said quietly to herself.

Jaeger allowed himself a second to silently echo the prayer, then he put his commander's face back on.

"Lieutenants Pierce and Kalders," he said, checking to make sure their comms were open with the *Kalnythian Wilds*, and the moody pilot Iveera had reluctantly left in charge of her beloved craft. "If you'd kindly bring us around, I believe we have two armies in desperate need of an introduction."

Quiet and almost peacefully surreal as the dark rush of their space dive was, Nate was actually flirting with forgetting to be afraid when the first bright flashes of battle lit the darkness over Avalon and brought his nerves crashing back down. He resisted the urge to cock his head around, relying instead on Ex to feed the visuals to his helmet display.

He didn't love what he saw—two Knightships weaving into a storm on incoming Troglodan fire, threading the gaps in the war party. Nate watched in sinking disbelief as the Trogs split their attention, fighters and a few smaller support ships still peppering at the *Camelot* and *Kalnythian Wilds* while their battlecruisers and three mighty dragonheads opened on the closing protoswarm with a blinding display of plasma fire.

Apparently, it was going to take more than an ancient, planet-eating evil to convince the Troglodans to set their grudges aside.

It was only when Ex killed the helmet feed, and Iveera sparked into a full-on Super Saiyan fireball ahead of him, that he realized he had more immediately pressing concerns. She plunged into the thin alien atmosphere, energy barriers crackling around her like a spearhead. Fast as he was moving, he didn't have more than a second to grit his teeth and do his best to follow suit.

To his surprise, whether it was thanks to Ex's help or his own deepening relationship with discomfort, neither the rushing heat nor the skull-rattling turbulence of atmospheric entry seemed all that bad.

Probably, he was just too busy worrying about his friends above, and the enemy below.

He'd caught sight of them as they'd fallen toward Avalon, remotely borrowing on the *Camelot*'s powerful optics to make them out from that distance. Through the gathering storm and erratic interference, it'd been hard to make out much more than a few glimpses of the gold and black figures. He was pretty sure he'd seen the wreck of the Black Knight's ship down there as well. Hopefully, that was a good sign. But as the thermal distortion of entry faded and the thin air began to clear, there was nothing but dread in his gut at the sight below.

Avalon was a tiny planet compared to Earth. Not that it felt especially small, plunging from kilometers above. Mostly, the twilight sprawl of ash and dust below just felt dead, and maybe a little bit haunted. But at least it was easy enough to see where they were headed.

He gunned the gravitonics a little harder, catching up to Iveera, and saw with a quick zoom of his helmet optics that his first glimpses above had been accurate enough. Zedavian Kelkarin stood facing the Black Knight beneath a gathering storm. The soil was scorched in areas around them and cratered and thoroughly upended in several more. The downed wreckage of the *Avalon Eternal*, gouged open along the port side, left little doubt that there'd been fighting. But there was none now, Nate couldn't help but notice, as he and Iveera shed their horizontal velocity and began to cautiously descend.

The two Knights only faced each other, both standing tall and confident. They looked to be talking. Warily, maybe. But talking all the same.

What is this? he wondered at Iveera.

Be ready, was all she sent back, but he was pretty sure he could feel her discomfort.

He kept his barriers raised, half-expecting the Black Knight might turn and blast them out of the sky. Briefly, he wondered if they shouldn't take their own shots from afar—if maybe that was exactly what Zedavian was waiting for. But Iveera continued her descent, and Nate followed, trusting she had her reasons.

Avalon was a dead planet—the soil almost perfectly flat to the horizon, save for the occasional soft swelling of a dune, and the ashy bones of the city village that had clearly once stood here but had since been mostly lost to time and erosion. Those bones looked even more broken and desolate than they had in his dreams. Beneath the frosty swirling of the unnatural storm clouds gathering above, the thin air felt utterly still. Enough so that the Black Knight's voice easily carried up to them as they descended the last length.

"The choice is yours," he said, in seeming conclusion to whatever they'd been discussing.

The words made Nate's skin crawl. The same words from his dream. Too casual. Too trusting and familiar, as the dark titan turned his back on Zedavian and stomped off for his downed ship, not even bothering to look as Nate and Iveera set down on the ashy dirt of Avalon.

Nate glanced at Iveera, waiting for her to take the lead, but she only stared at Zedavian, her gaija held loosely at her side, jin flattened in something that looked too much like defeat.

"What are you doing?" she finally asked, her voice quiet.

"Fighting," Zedavian said quietly, gaze fixed absentmindedly through the dusty soil. "Fighting and talking. Talking and fighting. It's all we ever seem to do, isn't it?" The silence stretched without an answer, and he finally stirred, focusing on Iveera with an almost desperate energy. "Isn't it, Iveera?"

Lady's Grace, came Iveera's voice in Nate's mind. *His Excalibur. He's been corrupted too.*

Somehow, Nate was pretty sure he'd already felt as much. Or maybe it was just that look in the Eldari's eyes.

"Zedavian," Iveera said aloud, her tone more quietly pleading than he'd ever imagined she was capable of sounding.

Above them, the clouds began to churn more thickly, cold currents twisting down to rustle the dead air.

"I told you to stay away," Zedavian said quietly, golden eyes distant again. Maybe even remorseful. Like he was about to do something he sincerely wished he didn't have to do.

Nate opened his mouth as the Eldari turned to them, thinking to reason with him—to point out that the two of them were still here, still on task, despite this mysterious corruption. That they could talk about this. Turn things around. That no one needed to get hurt.

But then the First Knight flash-stepped across the distance between them, and all hell broke loose.

CHAPTER 39
TITAN FALL

Words like *fast* and *strong* didn't begin to cover the capacities of Ser Zedavian Kelkarin.

Before he could so much as blink, Nate found himself laid out in the dirt with little notion of how he'd gotten there save for the screaming ache in his head and the fine spiderweb cracks across his face-plate. A string of sharp crashes off to the left announced the beginning of Iveera's own engagement with Zedavian. On some combination of scrambling hands and gravitonics, Nate lurched up to his feet and threw himself after the combined copper-golden blur of their clash, reaching for a weapon—any weapon—that might knock a Knight flat on his ass for a moment.

He felt the weight forming in his hand. Took aim on the golden half of their whirlwind blur as best he could. Swung as the gravitonics carried him over the last dozen meters at frightening speed. Then the copper half of the whirlwind rocketed away with a sound of impact like cracking thunder, and Nate yanked to a violent halt, caught in impossibly strong hands by the throat and wrist, impromptu stun club crackling uselessly in his hand.

Zedavian said nothing. Just threw him what felt like halfway across the planet at roughly the speed of light, fast enough that the Gs squeezed his vision to straight blackness. He crashed to the dirt—*through* the dirt—an instant later, as another pair of unyielding hands caught him and slammed him down. Still Zedavian, some part of Nate's ringing brain registered, having moved fast enough to catch him on the other end of his flight.

Rather than marvel at the feat, Nate thrust a palm up and let rip with a full power repulsor blast. The First Knight absorbed it with little but a shimmering ripple from an otherwise invisible energy barrier, then curled a golden finger, and gravitonic force flung Nate from the dirt straight into Zedavian's waiting hands.

"You don't... wanna do this," Nate groaned between pained breaths, struggling against his iron grip to no effect, the full extent of the last few blows only now catching up to his reeling body. He'd never felt so useless in his life.

Over Zedavian's shoulder, Nate glimpsed Iveera charging the Black Knight, flashing out of sight only to reappear an instant later with half a dozen identical doppelgängers, each moving with its own individual will—half of them for the Beacon and half for the Black Knight himself—so quickly and convincingly that Nate couldn't even make out which one was real. Not until the Black Knight raised the Beacon and released a thrumming pulse that swept the illusions away like so much sand in a gale force wind. The real Iveera hit the dirt thirty meters later, moving fast enough rip an explosive gouge across the planet's surface. Nate redoubled his efforts on Zedavian's grip, desperate to help—to do *something*. The First Knight turned back to him with a bored sigh, like he'd expected better from both of them.

"He's using you," Nate grunted through his exertions. "I've—I've seen it. You don't wanna do this."

Zedavian showed him a contemptuous smile, those golden eyes perfectly alien. "And what makes you think you could even begin to comprehend what I want, Terran?"

He didn't wait for an answer. A flick of the wrist, a bone-shaking impact, and Nate was embedded back in the dusty topsoil, gasping for air with a paralyzed diaphragm as Zedavian towered over him. Somewhere in the distance, he heard the sounds of Iveera clashing with the Black Knight.

"Perhaps you deserve to be forgiven," Zedavian said, crouching down over him. "You haven't been around long, after all."

Smash.

The casual ferocity of the punch left Nate sputtering, bloody drool dripping from his mouth as his senses struggled to reassemble the blurry colors and sounds into something coherent.

"Please," he groaned, raising a badly shaking hand. "Please d-don't."

"Oh, I'm not going to kill you, Eight."

Smash.

The world lost focus.

"You have no idea what you can endure."

Smash.

"Please." Consciousness hung by a bare thread, little but a soft roar of white noise and rushing blood. He felt like he was pinned beneath a waterfall, the blurry likeness of Zedavian's face coming in hectic starts and stops. "You're the… only one… can stop… stop him."

He wasn't sure the words were audible. Wasn't sure they made it out at all. There was nothing but the sick reeling in his gut and the buzzing vibrations in his splitting head.

Another sound pierced the buzz. A voice, he thought. The voice from his nightmares, vibrating from the air itself. He couldn't make out what it said. He only saw the blur of Zedavian glancing off at something, then turning back to him.

Nate flinched as Zedavian reached for him, expecting the worst, but the First Knight only stroked Nate's helmet with the back of his golden-armored fingers, almost tenderly. "It's nothing personal, Eight. Perhaps you'll understand one day."

"P-p-portal," Nate sputtered, blood bubbling in the back of his throat.

Zedavian faltered, already halfway to his feet. "What?"

Hope welled, faint and weak as his voice as he tried to explain.

"Kelkarin," called the Black Knight's voice, seemingly from all around them.

"Very well," Zedavian sighed, rising the rest of the way and turning to go join his dark ally casually as if he were being called to the dinner table. "Let us have done with it, then."

Nate caught him by one golden greave, desperate to be heard before it was too late. "—'s try'n open… p-portal."

Whether Zedavian heard or understood, Nate didn't know. All he knew at that moment was the bemused look in the First Knight's eyes high above, and the terror of the golden boot rising to stomp his face in.

There was an impact after that. He was pretty sure. That was the only reasonable explanation. But he couldn't seem to recall the moment itself as he lay there, not quite unconscious, but only by the slim technicality that some part of him seemed to be clinging to that singular thought. The world was certainly dark enough. His body oddly cut off. Unresponsive. For a horrible second, it occurred to him that—

You're not paralyzed.

Somewhere deep in his numb body, something gave a sickening pop, and a searing fire shot through him.

Not permanently, anyway. Though I would recommend you try to keep your head on straight for the next round.

Next round?

An incoherent grunt escaped him, fingers curling weakly in the dirt. Muffled voices and buzzing ahead. Incoherent thoughts.

With painstaking effort, he lifted his head. Something gave way, light and sound pouring in, streams of dirt showering down from his wrecked helmet. He stared dumbly at the head-sized hole he'd just excavated himself from, strength slowly ebbing back into his fingers right along with all the pain his battered body had been too shocked to feel.

"—ven't been completely honest with me," came Zedavian's voice ahead, less muffled now, albeit still not quite right past the ringing in his head. Squinting at the resolving blurs, Nate saw the Black Knight facing the First Knight near the base of his wrecked ship, holding a long, dark bundle under one arm: the *Merlin*, Nate realized with a jolt, thinking of the dream. The wizard was wrapped head to toe in some kind of charged film.

"What are you really looking for?" the First Knight asked.

"An end to it all," the Black Knight finally answered, his deep voice heavy, almost resigned.

"Oh, is that all?" Zedavian said. "Curious, you forgot to mention—"

"Do not pretend you do not wish for the same thing, Kelkarin," the Black Knight said, tossing the Merlin roughly to the ground. "I have seen your heart."

"My heart," Zedavian echoed, for some reason looking genuinely amused at that. "Well then, perhaps you might point the way, for I've seen neither hide nor hair of that fickle thing since you were last alive and well, LeFaye."

"You challenge my patience," the Black Knight said, and there was nothing haughty or indignant about the threat.

"I find that hard to believe for a man who spent 1,500 years staring at rocks," Zedavian said anyway, unimpressed by the warning. "I need only speak with the wizard one last time."

That was probably his cue, Nate decided, chiding himself for wasting precious seconds lying around in the dirt.

"No," the Black Knight replied flatly, as Nate looked carefully around, searching for Iveera, gathering his bearings from what he remembered of the dream. "We are too close now to let the wizard's foul tongue undo your resolve. Have faith, Kelkarin."

She wasn't lying where he expected. He didn't see her at all.

"Ah, now there's another fickle thing," Zedavian was saying. "Faith. Faith in the dark specter who says he's a man yet wields a Beacon and commands a protoswarm as effortlessly as any Archon. You *do* remember the Archons, don't you?"

"You know better than to believe the old man's lies. I told you, the swarms are not mine."

"And yet they do not come for us," Zedavian said, looking skyward, to the growing spectacle of the battle raging on above. "I wonder why that is."

Something passed between them when Zedavian returned his golden gaze to the Black Knight's jagged, inscrutable helm—a silent understanding that seemed to suggest the end of the discussion, even if Nate couldn't tell why. He didn't have time to ponder it anyway, as he spotted Iveera creeping out from behind the wreckage of the *Avalon Eternal*, more than a little battered but clearly planning to fight on. He eyed the Beacon in the Black Knight's hand. If they could just get that damn thing away from him, or free the Merlin…

"It's going to take more than three of you," the Black Knight said.

The quiet warning sent a shiver through Nate, hairs standing on end as he registered that the words were intended for him and Iveera, too, and that neither of them had gone unnoticed. Seeing no reason to keep pretending, he pushed himself to his feet and prepared to move.

"You really think I would've hobbled this pair if I needed them?" Zedavian asked, paying Nate and Iveera no mind.

"Three thousand years, and still, you do not understand." The winds were building now, kicking a light swirling of Avalon's ashes into the air.

"Still, you do not fathom how your precious Merlin has stacked the game against you," the Black Knight said, looking to each of them in turn. Iveera was stalking warily closer, eyeing the bundled Merlin near his feet. Zedavian began a leisurely circle around the dark titan, naturally dividing his attention between the two of them.

"Still, you cannot know how he has betrayed you," the Black Knight continued, wholly unconcerned.

Nate watched the Knights circling one another, unsure which way to go in the brewing storm, bloodied mouth and aching everything reminding him that he had no godly clue whose side the First Knight was even on here. He was just starting forward, deciding that the Merlin should be his first priority regardless, when the three Knights froze ahead, like the violence was about to explode.

Nate was the last to hear it coming. By the time he looked up, it was already too late.

The asteroid was at least twice the size of the *Camelot*. Probably larger. And it was rocketing straight for the Black Knight, driven both by gravity and the golden burn trails of what looked like several externally rigged thrusters. Nate didn't have time to ask questions. He just hunkered down, raising every shield he could think to raise, preparing to charge on the aftershock.

Then the Black Knight turned, raising his Beacon hand high, and Nate watched instead as untold thousands of tons of speeding rock and ore simply ceased to exist—disintegrated on a blinding white column of energy whose heat burned painfully hot, even at a distance and through several layers of armor and energy barriers. The Black Knight moved seamlessly back to the fight, blasting an incoming Iveera away from the Merlin, whirling to meet Zedavian's rush.

Only to jerk to a startled halt as the First Knight flashed into existence behind him and ran him through with his glowing blade. Before the Black Knight could gasp, the Eldari flash-stepped to his front and unceremoniously jammed a second slender blade through his armored navel at an upward angle. Nate watched in stunned silence as the Black Knight coughed and sputtered, reaching for Zedavian, twin bloody swords skewered through him like a lopsided X buried at his core.

"You think so little of me, Ser Knight," he gasped, voice wet with blood and thick with pain, searching hands finding Zedavian's chest, "as to try the same trick twice?"

Zedavian showed him a humorless smile, red hot tears of molten rock raining down around them in the stark silence with little zipping *whoosh* sounds as he reached almost gently for the Beacon in the Black Knight's hand. "You'd think I would've learned my lesson by now."

The Black Knight jerked his Beacon hand back as if preparing to fight the First Knight for it.

"Perhaps I have," Zedavian said softly.

Then the sky cracked overhead, and the speeding golden blur of the *Eldest Stone*'s mech form came crashing down on the two of them like a falling mountain. Nate pitched backward, sure that the speeding ship was about to crater them all, right up until it stopped, just *stopped*—Lady only knew how many thousands of tons of speeding metal wrenching to a perfect halt just shy of the Black Knight's raised hand without so much as a whisper of impact.

"Well, fuck," Zedavian muttered in the chilling silence, both hands clasped to the Beacon as it came to life in the Black Knight's palm, setting the winds howling, an azure inferno rushing down the Black Knight's arm, crackling through his armor, setting the dark eye slots of his helmet aglow beneath the jagged horns and blood-red plumage. Zedavian's golden helmet unfolded rapidly from e-dim, like he was tensing for the inevitable blow.

Then the Black Knight gave a terrible bellow, and the air detonated around him with a monumental shock wave that raced out in all directions. Nate had a glimpse of Zedavian's blades ripping free from the Black Knight's torso in twin gouts of azure radiance, then the rushing wave punched him off his feet like a roaring tsunami, and he was thudding across the dirt, Ex stabilizing his flight with their gravitonics before Nate could even think about.

The planet shook, a thick cloud of dust erupting into the air as the *Eldest Stone* toppled to the wayside from the Black Knight's Beacon-powered grip. Nate righted himself to the sounds of clashing armor and blades, Iveera and Zedavian already moving in on the Black Knight through the dusty miasma, attacking in tandem. Nate launched himself toward the dizzying flashes of copper, gold, and black, covering the ground quicker than expected, and was almost surprised to find himself ripping through the swirling dust storm to catch onto the Black Knight's sword hand from behind, opening him up to Iveera's incoming gaija thrust. Then there was a flash of azure and a blur of motion, and he hit the ground hard enough to leave him coughing for breath, half-buried in the dry Avalonian soil.

A few thundering impacts later, a brilliant flare of energy lit the darkening storm of the battlefield, and Nate's insides clenched at the comparatively soft sound of an armored body thudding to the ground nearby. He clawed his way from the ground in the raining dust, coming around on his knees.

Right into the makings of the scene from his dream, he realized with a sudden rush of cold horror.

Iveera's charred form sprawled limply in the dirt off to the left, right where she'd been. Stormy winds clearing the air of dust. He turned just in time to watch Zedavian yank to a halt mid-flash-step, caught in the Black Knight's gravitonic grip, golden arms and legs prying wider and wider open as if the dark titan intended to rip him limb from limb. Then Zedavian roared a battle cry of his own and let loose with a golden river of energy that poured straight from his chest, washing them both from sight with its brilliance.

When the blast finally faded, the Black Knight stood unharmed at the center of the storm, the molten ground glowing red hot and sputtering with flames beneath him. Then the Black Knight clenched his fist with an audible crack, and Zedavian Kelkarin screamed. The sound turned Nate's stomach. It was horrifying in a way he couldn't describe. The Eldari who hadn't flinched at the best Nate and Iveera could throw at him. The only one Nate had truly believed, deep down, might actually be able to stop this evil bastard.

And he was screaming. Screaming mindless pain, right up until the Black Knight jerked his hand down, and Zedavian followed, smacking down to the molten ground, grunting with pain and rage as the heat set his barriers crackling and smoking. He didn't cry out again. Merely strained against the Black Knight's control. But it was over. Nate saw it in the Eldari's weakening struggles. He watched, caught somewhere between disbelief and a dreadful sense of inevitability, as the First Knight was made to rise back to his feet—movements stiff and jerky, like a badly-controlled puppet—and hold out his gleaming sword just so, even as the Black Knight unsheathed the dark greatsword from his back and moved to match.

It was happening.

Two titans facing off in the windswept ruins of Avalon, swords drawn. Searing streaks of green and blue lancing through the stormy haze above. Blinding flashes of orange and white flooding the angry heavens as his friends fought for their lives.

Blackened hands, the Troglodans just unleashed a singularity bomb.

Nate didn't need to ask what that meant to know they were losing above. He felt it deep in his gut. Felt it in Ex's resignation as he tried and failed to reach the *Camelot* through the storm, and in the sickening déjà vu at the scene unfolding ahead. Iveera down. The Merlin's dark bundle stirring. In his mind's eye, Nate saw the wizard emerging just like in his dream. Robe tattered. Face hidden by a tangled mess of filthy gray hair. Then Zedavian's blade met the Black Knight's with a voluminous boom, and Nate knew it for certain, the howling winds all but screaming it in his ears.

It was happening, just as he'd seen it.

They were losing.

And he didn't have a single clue how to stop any of it.

CHAPTER 40

BLACK HOLE

"Get us out of here, Cammy!" Jaeger shouted over the blaring alarm and the laughably unnecessary "Gravitational Anomaly Detected" alert flashing across the main display.

It was kind of hard to miss, after all, staring down the angry black hole that was currently sucking them straight toward oblivion.

"What the piss was that?!" Snuffy cried, probably in reference to whatever the massive *Blood Moon* had just launched into the heart of the swarm to start the doomsday collapse. Jaeger was too busy snapping orders to Pierce over on the *Kalnythian Wilds* to even try to answer. The details hardly felt pertinent, anyway, as the *Camelot* whined around them with straining engines and building power.

He got a clipped "Copy that," from Pierce, and then a thrumming head rush later, they'd blinked across the system to a moment's peace in low orbit over Avalon. The bridge let out a collective breath, Jaeger wondering if it was time to try to get Nate—if the planetoid was even going to survive this unfolding weapon of mass destruction. Then Kalders yanked on the stick with a curse, and they were jetting off again, yet another huge tendril of rock and ice speeding after them as Snuffy and Ramirez opened up with multiple rear-facing turrets.

The fighting had gone from bad to worse almost as fast as Nate and Iveera had hit Avalon's wispy atmosphere, then straight to hell in a hand-basket shortly after that. To call it a shit show would've been too high of praise. The Trogs had split their focus like a pack of dogs trying to decide which car to chase, driving any hope of a united front clean out of the picture from the start. Whether it lacked the guiding intelligence or merely didn't care, the so-called Synth hadn't shown much interest in tactical decision-making either. The swarm had just come head-on, crushing itself against Troglodan fire until one rushing tendril broke through, and then another. Just like that, the fleet had begun to fall—breaking ranks and disappearing in bright plumes of fire as ruthless torrents of space debris tore them open like tin cans. And now…

Jaeger looked at the display as the distant *Blood Moon* and the rest of its few surviving allies pitched toward the gaping maw their doomsday device had spawned, battered along by the steady tide of protoswarm mass collapsing inward with them.

He'd expected destruction. But not like this.

A whole damned fleet, gone in minutes flat.

Later, he might actually feel bad for the Trogs. For now, he could only hope the battle was going better planetside. They'd lost contact with their two Knights thanks to whatever hellish storm was building down there.

"*Blackthorne*'s gone," Kalders said, her jaw tight as she juked another tendril, dipping low enough to rake the *Camelot*'s ventral hull against the outer reaches of Avalon's thin atmosphere. "Must've landed somewhere down there. Or got eaten."

Jaeger checked the displays, solidly impressed their maverick pilot was able to notice anything outside of her own wild flying. In the distance ahead, whatever was happening down on Avalon's surface pulsed brighter, odd arcs of azure energy flashing horizontally through the swirling clouds. The Camelot's optics couldn't pierce the shroud. On the tactical display, he saw the far reaches of the swarm diverging out, those bits that could still escape the pull of the growing singularity peeling off to branch around the far side of Avalon. Somehow, their ranks didn't seem to be thinning, despite the destruction. If anything, those reaching branches seemed to be thickening—more and more matter creeping in from god only knew where. All of it converging on Avalon.

The fight was lost up here.

"Time to go pick up the kids," he said, making the call. "Take us down, Kal—"

A distant roar echoed up from the innards of the ship, shortly followed by a muted crash and a quickly erected holo display from Cammy.

They all watched in a stupor as a burning crimson figure streaked away from the *Camelot*, bound straight for Avalon.

"Okay," Kalders said. "That sure looked like—"

The sound of thudding footsteps cut her off, turning them all to the rear of the bridge just in time to see Anastasiya Blackthorne come sliding through to a halt, red-faced and doubled over.

"Justicar… escaped," the pirate managed, between heaving breaths. "He's… lost his mind. Thinks he's… the Dread Knight."

Jaeger felt the crew trading looks, then turning his way.

"Where's Carter?" he asked. Or started too, at least, before a wrenching impact from the rear of the ship cut him off. Kalders threw them into a hard roll, sending Blackthorne smacking into the wall as the inertial dampeners struggled to compensate, but effectively shaking the rest of the incoming tendril that'd just scraped their portside flank. Jaeger skimmed the displays amid Cammy's chirping damage report, painfully aware of the crimson speck cutting into the atmosphere below in a glowing nimbus of entry friction, speeding toward their only hope of winning the day—whatever that even meant at this point.

"Get us down there," he told Kalders.

She didn't argue, just tossed them into a rapid descent as Jaeger relayed the same orders over to the *Kalnythian Wilds*.

He glanced back at a recovering Blackthorne, feeling the crew's collectively held breath as if it were his own, uncomfortably aware of the feeling they'd somehow winked away from one black hole only to fall straight into the inevitable gravity of another. The *Camelot* shuddered with the fury of their atmospheric entry. Jaeger focused his attention on the displays, trying to sift through the distortion to get a fix on their rogue Knight-justicar. They'd just broken through the worst of the turbulence when the comms hissed a burst of static, and Nate's voice crackled across the bridge, only barely audible through the distortion:

"Get as far away from this rock as you can," he said.

They all traded one last look, all sensing the finality in the kid's tone.

"Well, fuck that," Kalders said.

"Fuck that," Jaeger confirmed. "And while we're at it, prepare to open fire."

CHAPTER 41

DECONSTRUCTION

Somehow, even after all of the macabre waiting of the trip here and the explosive violence that had gripped them since the moment they'd arrived, it was only then, kneeling in the ashed ruins of Avalon, staring at the unharmed Black Knight and the failing space battle overhead that the realization truly settled over Nate's heart.

They were all going to die here.

There was no one coming. Iveera was down or dead, Nate didn't know which. Zedavian had just run the blackened bastard through with two blades and dropped the heavens on his head, and there the Black Knight still stood, tall and unfazed at the center of his swirling cocoon of power. The *Eldest Stone* and *Avalon Eternal* laid out behind them like great tired beasts waiting for their masters to conclude their business. It was happening, just as he'd dreamed it.

He had to do something.

That does seem highly advisable.

Nate planted a hand in the dirt, trying to force himself up from his knees, but it was like a lead blanket had fallen over him. His beaten body couldn't find the hope to listen. Not in the set of Zedavian's golden shoulders. Not in the half-focused eyes of the Merlin, as the wizard feebly pried his face free from the dark bundle, positively emaciated, just in time for the Black Knight to raise a hand and pull him closer, dragging him through the dirt on an invisible gravitonic leash. The wizard mumbled and sputtered all the way, trying to say something to the Knights, something that was impossible to make out over the howling winds.

A look passed between the two titans, unreadable behind their gold and black helms. Nate tried again to rise and realized it wasn't all in his head. Something resisted the movement, like the thrumming Beacon had rolled out a tremendously strong gravitonic rug beneath him, keeping him riveted in place. He couldn't even lift a hand.

"Nathaniel," whispered a familiar voice on the wind.

Nate jerked around, looking for the absent speaker as best he could under the increasing pressure, heart racing, beating faster as he turned back and found the Merlin looking straight at him with those faded eyes and the exact same expression Nate hadn't been able to fathom from his dream.

"—*will* open it, wizard," the Black Knight's voice boomed over the howling winds, which only redoubled their buffeting fury at whatever the Merlin replied. The air between the Knights began to crackle with an eerie blue energy, that awful black monolith erupting from the ground between the Black Knight and the Merlin, beckoning with its razor-sharp protrusion as it rose from the crust.

Nate gathered his strength and *pushed*, getting one leg up, the other knee still planted, his head spinning with strange whispers on the wind.

"OPEN IT!" roared the Black Knight ahead, splitting the sky with the ferocity of his bellow. Then he thrust a black hand toward the Merlin, and Nate watched in helpless horror for a second time as the wizard sprang into the air, weightless as a feather, and thunked wetly onto the slender obsidian spike, unceremoniously impaled.

The crackling line of Black Knight's would-be portal pulsed brighter, as if the wizard's lifeblood excited it. Zedavian fell to his knees, drawn by the same crushing force holding Nate down, maybe. His golden hand, though, remained locked to the hilt of his sword, which was, in turn, locked to the Black Knight's blade by whatever arcane process was underway, holding firm until Zedavian was practically dangling by the weapon.

Nate gulped in a labored breath past the crushing weight, looking for direction, looking for Iveera, but she was still down—a broken copper figure strewn in the ash. He was reaching for her mind anyway, thinking to jolt her back to it, when the air smacked him with a deafening upswing of power, casting her copper armor brilliant azure. Casting over everything.

The rest came in a confused blur. The commanding boom of the Black Knight's voice, demanding the Merlin's subservience. The pop-and-crackle white noise of the *Camelot*'s comms trying to break through the maelstrom.

The terse tone of Ex, telling him that they had about two minutes before the Trogs' growing singularity started having Avalon for a snack.

In the moment, though, all Nate really registered was the firm weight materializing in his tired hand and the cool, clear voice that whispered to his ears from the air itself, as foreign and wild as it was hauntingly familiar.

"The choice is yours."

At that moment, he no longer wondered where the Lady was in all of this—why she'd led him here with nothing more than a nebulous wisp of a dream. He felt her there, vibrating through the air all around in, easing the gravitonic force from his bones. And at that moment, watching the Black Knight towering over the Merlin and his First Knight, glowing Beacon raised high, Nate understood.

He gripped the lead weight of his sword, far heavier than it should've been in the gravitonic field. But whole, he knew without looking. Whole because it *had* to be whole. Because it no longer mattered that he didn't know how to stop this. Because even Ser Zedavian Kelkarin didn't know. Because the Black Knight was unstoppable, and they were all about to die anyway.

There was only one thing left to do.

Nathaniel, you cannot—WE cannot...

Doesn't mean we can't try, he mustered, grunting with the effort of rising against the gravitonics. *You got a better plan?*

"OPEN IT, WIZARD!"

Ahead, the color was bleeding from the air, darkness accumulating like a fog through the crackling lightning of the Knights' crossed blades. The Merlin's hands spread wide like some arcane crucifix, coming alive with a power of their own.

It didn't matter anymore.

"Get as far away from this rock as you can," he broadcast on the comms, willing the *Camelot* to hear him by whatever means necessary, Gwen's face swimming in his mind's eye, right alongside Marty and Copernicus. Kyle. His parents. All of their faces dancing before him in the screaming winds, lit by the hellish glow of the one thing that could've gotten him back through the Tarkaminen relay. The one thing that could still take him home.

It didn't matter anymore.

No more rules. No more waiting for someone else to do the job. We're ending it. Right now.

Keep this up, Ex said, with a resigned air, *and you might just make me proud to be your Excalibur.*

A precious huff of air escaped his struggling lungs, a grim smile tugging at his lips. *Wouldn't dream of it, buddy.*

Then he pushed up from the ashes of Avalon and gunned his gravitonics into the maelstrom with everything he had.

Time slowed, then actually stutter-stepped like a skipping record; gravitonics, Lady's Light, and raw adrenaline all crashing into a roaring stream of sound and disjointed, hyper-focused details. The crackling energy lengthening down to the ground between Zedavian and the Black Knight, like a doorway preparing to open wide. The flash and roar of ships descending on them at speed, fleeing the singularity or coming to attack, Nate didn't know which. He caught one unexpected glimpse of the *Camelot* barreling down toward them. One of the crimson figure blazing the way ahead of it—Malfar, he realized with a jolt, jetting down in full Samael armor, howling like the winds and all the hells above and below.

Then the blazing blue sparks of the Black Knight's eyes snapped straight toward Nate, Beacon arm raising, and Nate's entire world condensed to the horrible realization that he was about to be disintegrated before he could do a thing.

A barrage of sizzling blue blaster fire punched into the Black Knight's back from the incoming *Camelot*, staggering him just enough that he didn't see Zedavian coming. The Eldari lunged forward, still tethered to his bound blade, but plenty long-limbed enough to catch their foe with a devastating kick to the knee.

The Black Knight spun with a curse and savagely smashed the Beacon into Zedavian's temple, sending the First Knight sailing, both of their blades still hanging in perfect alignment over the burgeoning portal. Nate sped on as the dark titan cut the sky with a wild blast that scorched the *Camelot* and clipped the bellowing justicar, sending both tumbling out of control. Sped on as the Black Knight whirled back to him, Beacon raised—the source of all his godly power, held out without fear, for not even the mighty Zedavian Kelkarin could pry it from his hands.

And there, at the end of the steady arm that no longer felt like his own, Nate saw the glowing tip of his own sword racing forward in the Beacon's glow. Saw the terrible Black Knight himself flinch as he realized what was happening, what Nate was doing. Then Nate felt the bizarrely silky *thunk* as his blade slid home, piercing the one target no true Knight would've ever attacked. Smooth as butter, some stupefied part of him noted. As if the Lady herself had reached down and opened the way.

Time seemed to have stopped—the entire world bizarrely silent, frozen storm and all, like a crowd that'd hushed itself to have a better look at the unfolding spectacle. Nothing but a soft gasp from the Black Knight. One that sounded impossibly of fear.

Nate looked down in the rushing silence, aware of the growing pressure in his chest, and was dumbly shocked to see that the Black Knight's greatsword was no longer hanging over the frozen portal but rather buried straight through his sternum, right up to the wicked cross guard, and that his own blade had continued on through the Beacon far enough to pierce through the Black Knight's shoulder on the other side, practically skewering them together.

"What have you done?" the dark titan whispered, holding Nate in something perversely akin to an embrace.

Nate tried to say something, and choked on blood instead, dimly aware that the Beacon's burbling whine seemed to be slowing, decaying. It sputtered and died completely, and for a short eternity, time truly did stand still, but for the slow, deep creep of the singular thought that this was the end and the silent, immovable companionship of Ex waiting there to face it beside him. Then whine of the Beacon returned with a trillion-fold vengeance, pure radiance blasting out of the artifact and up through his sword arm, tearing through his body, consuming him from the inside.

He tried to scream. Tried to do anything. He could only watch in a petrified stupor as the world began to bleach to white, reality disintegrating around them. Evaporating completely from the outside in. From some deep corner of his awareness, he had the vaguest abstraction of the Merlin gasping to life on his disintegrating obsidian shrine and then suddenly diverging, multiplying until he seemed to be everywhere at once—gathering Iveera and the others to them in the glaring white void, manipulating some dark machinery as it grew from the shrine. The wizard was there, prying Nate from Mordred's blade, touching a hand to the Black Knight's helm, almost as if in apology.

Then the Beacon detonated, and reality collapsed entirely.

CHAPTER 42
COCKED-UP

When Nate came to, it was like being reborn on a nimbus of pure white light. There was no murky rise from the darkness. Just the first delicious breath of air, tinged with an almost divine quality, like he hadn't been "out" so much as merely held in the arms of the Lady herself for an indeterminate time. He sat up, mind pleasantly still, refreshed. Then he began to register the familiar carbon-paneled walls of his *Camelot* quarters, and the memories came trickling back in, right along with the realization that he wasn't alone.

He felt a wash of relief at the sight of Iveera seated on the opposite wall, decidedly not dead, idly watching him through the fog of her own thoughts. And beside her…

"Welcome back, lad," the Merlin said, staring at him from the corner chair and absentmindedly stroking his beard.

"You look… better," were the first words that found their way out of Nate's mouth. In his defense, the wizard looked like a new man. Face fuller, wild gray mane straight and flowing. Tattered robes replaced by pristine ones of deep, intricately silvered blue. He looked like the latest winner on Extreme Wizard Makeovers. He looked almost regal.

"Ah, yes," the Merlin said, following Nate's gaze down to his vastly enhanced appearance. "Well, 'dress for success,' as they say on our favorite third rock from the Sol. If the time has truly come to retire from exile and wrestle control of this unfortunate situation from those Capital pissants—and indeed it seems it has—well…"

He gestured to the illustrious robes as if they spoke for themselves.

Nate nodded dumbly at the Merlin's words, only fractionally registering. He was still playing catchup, trying to process what was going on.

We're back in C-Sec, Ex provided. *Almost to the Forge. It's only been a few hours.*

A few hours? A few hours since…

With a start, Nate clamped a hand to his sternum, remembering the last sight he'd had of the Black Knight's greatsword rammed clean through his chest. But there was nothing there. No gaping hole or bloody bandages. Just tender flesh and an oddly deep itch. Nate gaped back at the Merlin, who seemed content enough to let him find his own way back to words.

"The Beacon?" Nate asked.

"Kaput. Gone. Dust in the wind, as it were."

Iveera stirred from her reveries long enough to fix Nate with a thoroughly disapproving, possibly accusatory stare, her jin tight and agitated.

"Which is to say," the Merlin pressed on, "that I struggle to find the language to accurately express just how thoroughly you've stuck your foot in it this time." He cocked his head as if weighing his options. "It mightn't even be an exaggeration to say you've gone and doomed the Alliance from the outset of this war. And with a single thrust of the sword, no less. Not a lie among it, lad, the nihilist in me rather wants to be impressed with your work."

Nate dropped the wizard's gaze, cheeks burning, too mortified to even try to point out that he hadn't seen any other way, that he'd only been trying to do the right thing. He just stared at his hands, feeling indescribably childish to be blushing at all, given the scope and gravity of this situation, and even more so for the selfishness of the question he couldn't help but ask.

"Does this mean I failed? Are you gonna take Ex away from me?"

"Failed?" The Merlin traded an unreadable look with Iveera. Nate's stomach sank. Then the wizard gave an amused huff. "I don't believe a day goes by that we don't each of us fail one way or another. But reclamation? I don't think so, lad. Not yet."

It was like someone had let the air back into the room.

"Besides," the Merlin continued, "I reckon 'twas a bit of a devil's dilemma you faced back there, seeing as we might well've lost the whole damned caboodle today if you hadn't done what you did."

"What I did?" Nate echoed dumbly, too relieved in the moment to make much sense of anything else.

The Merlin gave a sharp bark of laughter at that. "Were you not paying bloody attention, lad?"

"I just meant, the Black Knight. Mordred. What was he trying to make you open? What did we stop back there?"

"The end of all things, I expect."

Nate chewed on that, wondering how literally the wizard meant that, and why it was that he would *expect* rather than *know*.

"I saw it in my dreams," Nate said quietly, before he realized the Merlin almost certainly would've heard it from Iveera by now anyway.

But the Merlin was shaking his head like Nate had it all wrong. "It wasn't a dream. Not exactly. I saw it too, albeit from a few layers under. As did Mordred, I expect. And that squirrelly little Blackthorne."

"I don't understand."

That seemed to amuse him. "No one under*stands*, lad. We under*crawl*, at best. And vaguely, at that. Beacons are mysterious things. The death of one is not a casual affair. The natural order of things breaks down. Things like time and space can get a bit wobbly. Those present at the time of collapse— and conscious," he added, with a glance at Iveera, "might even catch a fleeting glimpse of what's to come, provided they're adequately attuned to such phenomena."

Nate frowned, trying to follow. "You're saying I saw those visions *because* the Beacon collapsed?"

The Merlin just waggled his bushy eyebrows mysteriously and pushed on. "Of course, premonitions are merely one mildly interesting side effect of the main event. We've neither the numbers nor the cognitive capacity to shake a stick at how much power that Beacon released back into the galaxy. We don't *want* to shake a stick at how much of it was gobbled up by the Synth."

He paused, eyeing Nate and allowing that thought to sink in.

"Mordred and Anastasiya might well have suspected the root cause of our visions, of course," he continued. "They were there, after all, at the original fall of Avalon, when the ninth Beacon was destroyed. My fault, I'm afraid. Shoddy engineering from the start, my hopeful little worldship."

"Avalon," Iveera explained, at Nate's openly confused look. "It's how the Merlin got us home."

Nate felt Ex hovering at the edge of his mind with the tentative offer of some visual explanation. He accepted it, slightly confused why his companion was suddenly bothering to ask permission, then forgot about the behavior completely as the otherworldly image laid itself across his visual field.

Outside the *Camelot*, he could just make out the distant flurry of activity around Forge Station, framed against its breathtaking backdrop of stellar superclusters. Much closer, though, drifted what looked like the ruins of Avalon, cracked asunder by whatever had happened. It was plainly crumbling into pieces, though several of the larger chunks were slow to drift apart. Nate noticed several thick veins of what looked like the same obsidian material the Merlin had been impaled upon here and there among the exposed sections of crust, like some great scaffold networked throughout the planetoid.

"An ancient dream of mine," the Merlin said, like he knew what Nate was seeing in his private ocular feeds. "The galaxy's first true wandering planet. A beacon of peace and hope, 'twas to be, powered by a Beacon of our own beloved Lady. A new way to travel the cosmos. A better way." He let out a great sigh, looking very tired. "Alas, Old Avalon has seen its last days."

Nate stared at the drifting spectacle, struggling to comprehend how so much matter could've conceivably jumped halfway across the galaxy—and on only a portion of what the collapsing Beacon had had to offer if the Merlin's comments were any indication. But here they were, home against all odds. Or close enough to the relays that would take them there, at least.

"What about the others?" Nate asked, forcing his building relief to wait its turn. "My crew?"

"Present and accounted for, I believe," the Merlin said, looking to Iveera to take over, like he'd already spoken more than enough for his liking.

Nate listened with a kind of mentally fried numbness as Iveera broke down the details of what she'd gathered of those final moments in speaking with the crew and the Merlin. What little remained of the Clan Groshna war party had either been lost to the swarm or consumed by their own last-ditch singularity weapon. The *Camelot* and Malfar, as Nate vaguely recalled, had escaped the same weapon and touched down to Avalon just in time to come along for the Merlin's ride. Reports from C-Sec scanners seemed to suggest the *Blackthorne* had done the same on the planetoid's dark side, only to hightail it outsystem moments after Avalon's miraculous jump back to the Forge. And as for the dastardly captain herself…

"Blackened pirate stole my ship," Iveera said.

"What?" Nate sat up straighter. "But how—Pierce and Elmo?"

"Glamored happily onto Avalon's before she fled the system with her new prize," Iveera said, in a tone that suggested that better men wouldn't have fallen for such simple tricks.

"What a pirate she's become," the Merlin said, seemingly to himself. He almost sounded proud. "But not to worry, my dear Huntress," he added, to Iveera's stiff-jinned glare. "The *Kalnythian Wilds* will be recovered in good time."

He said it like he'd already seen it happen. Or maybe just like someone who'd lived so long as to feel confident that, given a sufficiently long window, any such declarative statement would eventually prove itself true. Iveera hardly looked convinced, but the Merlin didn't seem to notice.

"And there you have it, lad," the wizard said, spreading his hands like *ta-da*, and moving to stand like that was that.

"But wait, what about Malfar and Zedavian? I mean, what's gonna happen to them? And the corruption. And Mordred, is he...?"

"Gone for good this time, I should hope. Along with his blackened corruption."

"I still don't understand what the corruption even was."

"A tricky little beast is what it was, lad. A conniving collaboration between Mordred and his Synth masters, lest I miss my guess. Delimiting a Knight's control over their Excalibur. Slowly driving that Excalibur's processes rampant." He shook his head. "It might've felt like progress at first. Difficult abilities suddenly coming like second nature, and so forth. But eventually... Well, you saw the way the justicar made his entry at the end there, fully armored and in control on his first day. That wasn't a Knight flying his Excalibur, lad. Other way around."

The thought sent a little chill through Nate, turning his attention inward to the weight of Ex's presence lingering there at the edges, listening to all of this.

I assure you, the Merlin has rectified my imbalances.

Ex didn't sound particularly excited about it, and Nate suddenly wasn't sure whether he should be grateful or not for said rectification, but that was probably to be expected on both accounts.

We'll figure it out, buddy, he told Ex, meaning it.

"In the end," the Merlin said, stroking his beard thoughtfully, "Mordred's crowning achievement was likely also his downfall. A properly functioning Excalibur never would've been capable of so casually destroying a Beacon, you see. But so it goes. If you wish to understand this galaxy well enough to serve it meaningfully, Nathaniel, you could do worse than to begin by noting how frightfully often our greatest ambitions prove to be the stepping stones to our own self-destruction."

The wizard settled back in his chair once again, lost in thought, like he'd forgotten he was about to leave. Nate watched him for a stretch, thinking about what he'd said, thinking about the nature of Mordred LeFaye's ambitions, hesitant to speak the question on his mind.

"If he really knew what those visions were," he finally said instead, "why go through with it at all? Why risk losing his Beacon?"

"Were you not just listening about the blinding nature of ambition, lad? None of us saw how it was going to end. He walked into that fight because he wasn't prepared to live in a world where he didn't win." The wizard scrunched his brow thoughtfully. "Well, that, and becasue I might've played a wee bit of head games with him, lettin' him think he'd finally tricked me after all these years. In the end, he still didn't understand what he was truly looking for. If he had…"

Nate waited, but the wizard didn't finish the thought.

"All those things he said about you…"

The Merlin stirred. "That I'm a traitor, et cetera?"

Nate nodded. Iveera stared him down with a thoroughly reproachful look, like even he should know better than to ask such insolent questions, but the wizard didn't particularly seem to mind.

"Well, I am, aren't I?" he asked. "I had the man killed, lad. Or thought I had, at least, all those years ago."

"But why?"

"Because it had to be done. Because even back then, he would've brought the entire galaxy down with him, if he'd had his way. Because I failed him if I'm to be honest with you, and that failure meant choosing between betraying his trust and betraying the galaxy. I've lived with that choice ever since, just as I've lived with all the others. But it's over now. Leastways everywhere but here," he added, tapping at his own temple.

Nate was quiet for some time trying to digest that. Neither Iveera nor the Merlin seemed to mind, lost as they were in their own thoughts.

"Still," the Merlin finally said, sometime later, "plenty left to fear in the present, I think. An entire quadrant of the Alliance, good as dead in the opening salvo. Two Beacons lost to the swarms in as many days. All told, I do believe that makes this one of the finest cock-ups in galactic history." He popped to his feet with an unexpected vigor and looked down at Nate. "Try not to do it again, eh lad?"

CHAPTER 43

ALL HELLS

The following days passed in something of a blur.

To say the Council was pleased by the Merlin's triumphant return would've been a bold-faced lie. It probably didn't help that very few of the sitting chancellors had ever actually met the wizard, given that he'd apparently been living in his self-imposed exile for the better part of five-hundred years. But then again, Nate wasn't entirely sure it hurt things, either. For the most part, the rulers of the mighty Alliance—along with a surprisingly large majority of Forge Station—seemed hellbent on pretending that the wizard simply didn't exist, and that he never had.

Nate might've had more trouble believing the cold reception if they hadn't been so equally hellbent on extending the denial out to the plainly demonstrable facts that it had indeed been the Synth—not pirates, not terrorists, not solar flares—that had destroyed the Tarkaminen relay, Demeter-12, and very nearly all the assembled ships and crew who'd returned upon the very real, very observable hunk of Beacon-powered worldship that'd popped into C-Sec. But Avalon drifted on by, crumbling in glorious slow motion on its long fall into the gravity wells of their neighboring superclusters, and still, the heels dug in. Then the day came when the Merlin hauled Zedavian Kelkarin out of his golden palace to, in turn, haul the Small Council in for a very private, very mysterious meeting, and things changed.

Nate could only guess what might've actually happened in there.

Conjurer's tricks or a whole line of good, old-fashioned spankings. It was anyone's guess. All he knew for sure was that Supreme Chancellor Priatus and his eight core chancellors—including Adamus—eventually emerged looking rather frazzled, and that a sharp change of tune spread through the Capital like wildfire after that day. It would've been patently false to say that change was one of support for the Merlin and his Knights. Mostly, Nate noticed it as a sudden and prolific rise in the number of dagger-sharp glares that followed them everywhere they went, scolding hottest toward the mysterious wizard who'd returned after half a millennium to drop the ax on the longest, most prosperous run of peace the Alliance had ever known. But at least the Council was listening, beginning to accept what'd happened out there, and what was coming for them next.

The fact that Zedavian had played a part in bringing about the changing tides—not to mention the fact that he was roaming free at all—still left Nate unsettled. He and Iveera both asked the Merlin on more than one occasion how he could possibly still trust Zedavian, much less allow him to continue as First Knight after everything he'd done. The golden bastard had practically staged a coup, after all. He'd stood by, perfectly willing, maybe even eager, to let the Merlin die. If nothing else, the fact that Iveera was actually willing to side with Nate and question her precious Merlin about this particular call among all others should've been evidence enough that the whole damned thing was unconscionable.

"His actions were not his own," was all the Merlin said to their concerns. "None of yours were. And while I do not for a moment delude myself into believing there remains any shred of love or fondness for me within our First Knight's tired heart, I can promise you both this much: Zedavian Kelkarin is not our enemy. You've nothing to fear from him any longer. You're going to have to trust me on this."

The words were hardly reassuring—were, in fact, only additionally troubling, the more Nate analyzed them. He watched the Eldari from afar the few times Zedavian appeared from his golden palace, wondering what the Merlin wasn't telling them, wondering why Zedavian hadn't spoken a word to either of them since their return. No apologies. No explanations. Nothing. That golden face was nothing but a flat, empty wall. No relief. No joy or anger. He just looked tired. Resigned. And something else, Nate thought, the one time he witnessed the Eldari watching the Merlin across the brimming Council amphitheater when he thought no one was looking.

Nate was almost positive that there was some deeper, more complicated history there that the Merlin wasn't telling them about. There had to be, after more than three thousand years of shared trials and tribulations. But the Merlin puttered on, unconcerned, and Nate and Iveera had their own problems to deal with.

In the first days, there were more meetings and debriefings than Nate could count. At times, he couldn't even remember who he was talking to, or why. He just stuck to the script as best he could, hoping it would be enough, at times worrying it might, in fact, prove to be too much. Even to a complete outsider, it was obvious that Forge Station—and possibly the entire Alliance—was just a few more unpleasant surprises away from shredding into total chaos, and maybe even civil war.

The one thing the Council and pretty much everyone else seemed to be able to agree on, though, was that they categorically disapproved of just about every action Nate and Iveera had taken since the incursion of Terra had begun. In a weird way, amidst the rest of the chaos, their unified outrage at him and Iveera almost made Nate feel useful. More than ever, the people of Trogarra longed for Iveera's head on a pike, and now Nate's name was on their tongues as well. It didn't matter that Groshna's Excalibur had allegedly ended up back in the hands of a Troglodan. No one particularly seemed to care that their Golden Boy Zedavian had by all accounts become equally complicit in the whole mess by the end. Indeed, even when it came to the issue of the destroyed Beacon, the most cacophonous avenues of complaint had little to do with the Merlin's fears of what the development might mean for the rate of Synth expansion, and everything to do with the fact that Nate had effectively destroyed one of the eight most economically valuable objects in the galaxy.

For the most part, it just seemed everyone wanted a few easy targets at which to aim their considerable fear-born anger as the uncomfortable turbulence of change swept over their dominion.

Politicians, Ex grumbled, time and time again. Nate had to admit, even after a few days, he was starting to understand why the Merlin had gone into hiding for a few hundred years.

When the Merlin finally decreed an end to the still hopeful talks of assessment and reclamation, and the time came for the official Knighting of Ser Nathaniel Arturi, Eighth Knight of the Order Excalibur, the whole thing felt more like a funeral or a strong-armed corporate acquisition at gunpoint than an actual ceremony. Nate retreated from the assembly as soon he could, accepted the beautiful bottles of Atlantean wine Calum Statecaste offered him along with one of a scant few congratulations, and returned to the *Camelot*, where he shared the wine with the crew and refused to call it a celebration.

More than a few times, he and Jaeger tried to see about visiting Malfar, but the Merlin wouldn't even tell them where the Troglodan was being held —or treated, or whatever the hell was going on.

"Please," Nate told the Merlin, on one of the increasingly rare moments he could find in private with the wizard. "Just tell me, are you planning on… reclamation?"

The word tasted bitter on his tongue.

"If I'm to be honest, I don't rightly know yet," the wizard admitted. "In his corrupted state, I fear Samael did quite a number on the man's head. I'm still seeing what I can do for him."

How long? Nate wanted to ask. *And what can I do to help?*

"He's a good Troglodan," he said instead, still not really one-hundred percent sure what he even meant by that, but sure that he did mean it all the same. "If I deserved a chance, I'm pretty sure he does too."

"Rest easy, lad," the Merlin said, hands raised in peace. "I'm of the mind that enough blood's already been spilled over this mess. If the Troglodan can be helped, that's one less vacant role I've to worry about filling for what comes next."

Nate couldn't help but think it sounded like a rather laissez-faire way to think about appointing one of the eight most powerful walking weapons in the Alliance, but he sure as hell wasn't about to complain.

Mostly, he just stuck to the *Camelot* as often as he was allowed, fretting about what *did* come next, and puzzling over what had come before. Black-thorne's betrayal continued to eat at him, not so much because he was ashamed at having been wrong about her but because of the lingering hope that this was all still some big misunderstanding—that they just didn't yet know the punchline to the joke the pirate was telling. He was being naive, he knew. Probably because some part of him had actually been starting to like the pirate, in spite of his and Iveera's better judgment.

Still, he couldn't help but be a little impressed as the crew recounted the escape pod acrobatics the pirate had apparently employed to hop over and board the *Kalnythian Wilds* in those last moments. From the sound of it, Nate had Jaeger to thank for the fact that it hadn't been the *Camelot* the pirate had made off with. He'd been the one to head her off during the descent, after she'd cracked Malfar out of his cell and come to make her move. Carter wasn't fond of the story, and Nate had a feeling Malfar wouldn't be either, when he finally had a chance to hear it in his right mind.

Iveera, for her part, quietly took back to her makeshift quarters in her isolated nook of the *Camelot*'s greenery and pointedly refused to accept Nate's ham-fisted apologies for the loss of what must've been the closest thing she'd had to a true home for the past six-hundred years.

It wasn't a great feeling. Nor was the weight of the rest of the unresolved questions circling in his mind about the Synth, the Beacons, and Mordred LeFaye. What the man had truly been looking for, and why. Why Zedavian and Groshna had gone Dark Side on his corruption juice when Nate and Iveera had still been willing to oppose the Black Knight, albeit with a few apparent kinks in their operating systems.

With each passing day, he grew more hesitant to ask the Merlin about any of it. Like the further they left it all behind, the more dangerous it became to disturb it. He doubted he'd get more than cryptic answers from the wizard anyway. Why, indeed. Lady only knows. No need to fret over it, lad.

If only it were that easy to stop.

On the many occasions he was forced to leave the secure comfort of the *Camelot* for the chaos of Forge Station, Amelia and Calum Statecaste became quick best friends in his efforts to navigate the churning maelstrom of Forge activity and Alliance politics. They stuck by his side as often as they could, though Calum was often absorbed off into meetings of his own. Divergent social ticks and constant promiscuous coupling offers aside, he truly began to enjoy their company.

One day, over a peculiar lunch of spicy roots and a slimy yet delicious aquatic delicacy, it was floated that Nate should perhaps consider taking Amelia on board the *Camelot* as an adjunct crewman and a working liaison between Nate, the Atlantean Empire, and the people of Terra. It was on that same day, at that same lunch, that it suddenly struck Nate that an entire week had passed by in the blink of an eye. He was immersed in a whole new world. Immersed to the gills. Yet somehow it hadn't felt remotely as real out there chasing the Black Knight as it did now, sitting there amid a bustling civilization that wasn't his own, to the sobering realization that it'd been days since he'd last thought of the one he'd left behind.

He needed to call his friends back home. He'd left it for too long. Left it out of guilt, he supposed, though he still couldn't quite put his finger on what exactly it was he felt guilty about. Wasn't the entire point of being out here to protect them, after all? To protect Terra and all the other worlds that would be in danger if the Synth weren't burned back down into oblivion?

For some reason, that logic felt about as noble and sound as the grand posturing he'd watched bouncing back and forth between the Council's evolving war strategy sessions like an endless volley of tennis.

"Have you ever seen it like this?" Nate asked Iveera quietly, on one of the rare occasions that they were both in attendance but not in the heated spotlight of one such assembly.

She thought about it for a time, watching from their high amphitheater module as so-called civilized chancellors and senators spewed baseless threats and infantile insults back and forth. "The chaos, yes. The fear, no. This is… different."

"Kinda feels like the end of the world."

"Then your instincts serve you well, for it almost certainly is the end of more worlds and more innocent lives than either of us will ever be able to comprehend.You must never forget that."

He flinched under the weight of her words, but he held her gaze, knowing she was right. "Thank you, Iveera. For not giving up on me."

She considered him for a silent stretch, looking like she was still warring on some level with the part of herself that would've liked nothing more than to remain furious with him for his every bumbling misstep from the very beginning. Finally, though, she nodded and touched him lightly on the shoulder.

"Welcome to the Order Excalibur, Ser Arturi."

WHEN HE FINALLY SAT DOWN FOR the long overdue call, recounting his adventure to Gwen, Marty, and Kyle proved to be an odd experience.

It wasn't that the story was too outlandish, or that there was any part of it they didn't believe. It was more the nagging feeling throughout that they were listening to him the same way they might've listened to some kind of audio dramatization—a serious adventure, to be sure. But still one they were experiencing from the comfort of their State College couch. No amount of his own self-reported terror could quite snuff out the soft gleam of amazement and envy that shone in their eyes at the highs and the lows.

Because they didn't understand. They just couldn't.

He felt like a self-important prick for thinking it at all. It wasn't like he was some grizzled veteran himself, to be judging his soft-bellied friends who so clearly just didn't "get it." Yet the more he talked, the more that nagging certainty was there, inching its way slowly between them, blunting their every reaction and supportive comment in his mind.

"So, what happens next?" Kyle asked at the end, almost like he was waiting for the auto-play timer to start the next episode. "How long will it take the Synth to reach Alliance space with the Tarkaminen relay gone?"

"No one seems to have a clear answer on that," Nate admitted.

"Sounds like we should be more worried about how quickly they'll start assimilating all the settled worlds that are cut off out there," Marty said.

"And the unsettled ones too," Nate agreed. "The Merlin's saying we need to kick the entire Alliance into full wartime economy and start sending fleets in graduated waves by crusher drive to head them off in stages before they can reach critical mass."

"That sort of sounds like…"

"Like he's planning one hell of a long war of attrition," Nate finished for him. "Of course, if *someone* hadn't destroyed the Terran Beacon, a Knight-ship could've reached the Tarkaminen relay a hell of a lot faster and tried to reestablish military transport to the sector, but yeah."

"Dude, I think you need to give yourself a break," Marty said.

"Definitely that," Gwen agreed, scratching a happily panting Copernicus behind the ears.

"You did save the wizard *and* prevent the rise of the Dark Lord Sauron, right?" Kyle added. "That's like—" He burped. "Like not insignificant," he finished, guiltily setting his beer aside.

Nate had caught them on a Friday night.

"Sounds like a pretty critical mission success to me," Marty said.

"Yeah," Nate said, unconvinced. "Well, half the Alliance is still crying that the Synth aren't even real and that was all some elaborate terrorist attack anyway, so I guess first things first."

A silence stretched, less comfortable than it should've been.

"So," Gwen started, looking uncharacteristically hesitant.

"Does this mean you'll be coming home soon?" Marty finished for her. "I mean, they're not, like, trying to deploy you straight back into battle, right? Not until there's a real plan?"

"I'm not really sure," Nate said slowly, both because he really wasn't, and also because he didn't know how else to answer. "Calum said his people will be sending envoys to help the Ter—to help you guys start ramping up your defenses and spacefaring capacities as quickly as humanly possible, so…"

So what? So he'd talk to the Merlin? Find out how soon he could slip out of here for a casual social jaunt?

"We'll be ready," Marty said, saving him the need to finish the thought.

Or so he thought, at least, before Gwen sat forward, and Kyle and Marty seemed to divine that she wanted a moment alone with him.

"Good job out there, dude," Kyle said.

"We're really proud of you, Nate," Marty added, taking Copernicus from Gwen's lap as she stood and gathered up the q-node.

"I've been sleeping here, you know," Gwen said, once they were back in the privacy of his bedroom—or maybe it was *her* bedroom, now. He kind of liked that thought.

"I'm sure they've been glad to have you around," Nate said, forgoing the lame rent jokes, not to mention the little tidbit that he'd already kind of gathered as much when he'd called in and opted not to wake her the other night.

"Nate," she said quietly.

"Gwen," he whispered back, his chest tightening unexpectedly. "You need to know, when I was out there, when I decided to do it… All I could think was that I was stabbing my only chance of getting back to you right in the heart."

"You had to do it, though."

He shook his head, surprised to find tears welling, surprised to hear the words pouring out of his mouth. "You don't understand. It's not that. It's not that I stabbed that chance in the heart anyway. It's the fact that you were all I could think about in that moment. It's the fact that I was about to destroy one of the most important artifacts in the galaxy, and I couldn't bring myself to think about anything but my own petty shit."

"Oh," Gwen said quietly, and the look on her face told him that she understood the ugly heart of what he was telling her, even if the specifics were too alien to grasp. "Oh. Well, that's…"

He saw the pain blossoming up from down deep, coloring her eyes and pinching her brow. It hurt his heart, how far apart they were in that moment.

"I don't know," he said.

"If you're coming back?" she finished.

Maybe she understood it all, better than he thought.

"I'll be back," he said. "Someday. Maybe soon. I just don't know. It's out of control over here right now. The things that are coming for us, Gwen, they're…"

He shook his head, lost for any words that could possibly explain it.

"We should've gotten on that ship with you," she said quietly.

"What?"

"We've been talking, Marty and I. Pretty much every day. There's…" She bit her lip, searching for the words. "It's different here, Nate. I mean, the world's trying to get back on its feet, you know? People are talking about resuming classes, and the economy, and all that menial shit, but—But none of it really sounds important anymore, you know? Like, I'm gonna just go back to basic muscular dystrophy science when they have things out there that might treat every single form, just like that?"

"That's not necessarily—"

"I know, I know," she said, running an anxious hand through her hair. "But you understand what I'm saying."

He nodded somberly. "I understand what you're saying."

She looked at him, and for a second, it was almost as if he really were back there, and all the rest of it had just been a strange dream.

"I love you, Nate. I wish I'd said it sooner. I wish I'd gotten on that damned ship. But I love you, and I miss you, and I just need you to hear it."

"I love you too," he said quietly, meaning it. Meaning it more than he'd expected to at that moment, but unable to ignore the rest of it anymore. "Gwen, that's why I can't—"

"Don't," she whispered, shaking her head and blinking back tears. "You don't have to do that. Just…" She bit her lip, composing herself. "Just know that we're here for you, always, and that Marty and I are ready. I mean it, Nate," she added at whatever she saw in his face, her voice coming alive with a fire he'd rarely heard from her. "We're ready. We're scared, and we're light on the training, but we're ready for anything you need. Just…" Some of the fire bled from her eyes. "Just think about it."

"I will," he said. "I promise."

His fingers lingered over the holo long after he'd ended the call, feeling leaden, too heavy. He stared at the textured wall paneling until he couldn't stand to stare any longer, and then he left his quarters in a haze, not really sure where he was going. Not really willing to think enough to figure it out. He let his feet wander until the buzz of a nearby voice and the tap-tap of a firm finger on the shoulder brought him to a mechanical halt.

When he turned, Jaeger was squinting at him like he was observing a specimen under the microscope.

"Earth stuff?" he finally asked.

Nate opened his mouth, closed it. Nodded dumbly.

"Hmm," Jaeger grunted sagely. They hadn't really addressed the question of if and when the SAS crew would be trying to return to Terra. Not head-on, at least. There was a lot they hadn't discussed in the past days, as much as they'd chatted about this and that.

Jaeger seemed to be thinking along similar lines.

"You did good out there, kid," he said after a length of silence. "Don't think I ever actually told you that."

Nate blinked at the Lt Col, only half-processing his words. "I did the exact opposite of what you told me to do. Head down, trust the system and all that?" He huffed a humorless laugh. "I went and stabbed the system—"

"Right in the dick," Jaeger agreed, with a rebellious, lopsided grin. "And you did good."

"Huh," was all Nate could think to say to that. Then, thinking of that talk they'd had: "You know, I never did get that whole cock-eyed leadership spiel you promised."

Jaeger cocked a dark eyebrow. "Promised? 'Story for another time,' I'm pretty sure the deal was."

"*Now's* another time," Nate pointed out, looking up and down the empty corridor. "You saying you don't wanna tell me how I can learn from your mistakes? We're not so different, you and I?" he added, when Jaeger didn't take the bait. "Hooah?"

Jaeger watched him flounder with an amicable frown, then shook his head. "Story for another time, smartass. I think it's safe to say you're already getting acclimated with the moral of the story anyway."

"What's the moral of the story?"

"War is fucked, kid. War is fucked, and sometimes—most of the time—there's nothing but living on with your decisions once it's done." He held up three fingers, like he was about to expand on the thought by counting something off, but then he shook his head, thinking better of it.

"C'mon," he said, thumping Nate on the shoulder and pulling him toward the crew quarters. "Plenty of time to brood yourself to death later. Ramirez found some kind of Hobdan rum he says would put hair on a… well, I actually don't remember what he said, but you look like you could use a drink, regardless."

"You *do* remember you guys are supposed to—"

"We checked, we checked," Jaeger said, hands raised in mock surrender. "Safe for Terran consumption."

"Glad the recovery's going so smoothly," Nate muttered, but he couldn't deny that the tension in his chest began to loosen as he heard the sounds of laughter from the quarters ahead, punctuated by the sputtering of an indignant Snuffy trying to defend himself.

He felt a smile stretching his lips as they reached the doorway and Elmo and Ramirez held up twin bottles of some dark liquor with a pair of questioning looks. Nate thought unbidden of that chilly autumn night not so very long ago, when he'd stormed out of the Iota Nu Nu house with a drowned phone and ordered himself a whiskey at Zeno's, trying to escape the pathetic confines of his own personality. The same night he'd first met the Merlin.

How far we've come, little hobbit.

It was the first time Ex had called him that in a while.

"New round, new round," Pierce was saying, gathering up the deck of cards that were strewn across the table between them in the aftermath of whatever game they'd been playing. "Someone get the boss a cup," he added, as Jaeger strode in and pulled up a chair.

"What about you, Mr. Knight?" Tessa called from the head of the table, handing Jaeger an empty cup and brandishing another his way with a mischievous grin. "You in?"

For a long moment, he held her gaze, meaning to answer, but caught up in something that felt, for the life of him, oddly like the peace of coming home. For a moment, he allowed himself to simply enjoy it. Then Nate blew out a shaky laugh and went to join his crew.

EPILOGUE - TO THE VICTOR

"Any way you like, Senator," she gasped, hips thrusting up in perfect time, pulling him closer to the edge despite his resigned boredom. "Use me any way you like."

Calum Statecaste's hands trembled, burning to take her by the throat, to feel her pulse throbbing beneath his fingers. She was offering, after all. Any way he liked. But he couldn't. Not here. Not with her. He clenched tighter to the bed linens instead, imagining the feel of her throat, picturing with each thrust the soft indent of his hands crushing down, crushing down, until he ejaculated into her with a throaty grunt and collapsed. For a moment, there was something akin to relief as he lay limply on her lithe body, panting. Then she twirled a finger through his hair, and that was that.

"Thank you," he said, pulling himself out of her with a light shudder and padding across the room to the open shower unit.

She was still watching him from the bed when he turned around in the cascading rain. Idly, he wondered if she felt as dissatisfied as he did deep down. Probably not, if the three shaking orgasms had been any indication. Each one genuine, he'd noted, in the rosy blushing of her breasts, and in the transiently elevated heart rate and abdominal wall contractions. Calum always checked, more out of mechanical curiosity than any real feeling of obligation to satisfy.

Then again, the glistening trail of his own sterile ejaculate oozing down her leg as she stood to come join him was proof enough that a simple orgasm wasn't always the epitome of satisfaction.

He actually missed Amelia Sundercaste, he realized.

Missed the things she let him do to her, at least.

"I have a good deal of work to see to," he said, as she stalked closer, delicate and sweet as could be. Thoroughly uninteresting. "I've enjoyed this coupling with you."

She could decide for herself which one of those statements was the lie.

"And I with you, Senator," she said in the traditional response, reaching for his flaccid sex with a rather untraditional smirk. One that very nearly caught his interest, right up until her hand entered the shower stream, and she jerked back with a surprised breath.

"It's ice-cold," she said, as if maybe he wasn't aware.

"Have a pleasant evening, Aradnia."

When she'd gone, he quickly toweled himself dry and pulled on a fresh tunic and trousers. It was going to be a long night of calls with the Triton builders, figuring out what they were going to be needing for the shipyards —and, more importantly, how to procure it at a reasonable enough rate to keep pace with the Merlin's insane requests for warships.

He finished dressing and let out a controlled breath, taking stock. He might miss Amelia at the moment, but it did nothing to dim his pleasure at having successfully maneuvered her into an adjunct crew position aboard the *Camelot*, pending Ser Arturi's official authorization. The Terran wouldn't say no, of course. Who *would* say no to such a delectable creature? Especially when she so resembled the one he'd left behind on Terra.

Calum smiled, still appreciating just how perfectly the stars had aligned on that one. (Not that it hadn't been without a small bit of nudging.)

On one level, it almost felt as if everything was finally starting to fall into place.

On another, though—the one steeped in cold, hard reality—he had to admit that it only happened to feel that way because the entire plan had been a spectacular failure thus far.

His hands clenched to fists again, just thinking about it. He glanced at the door, idly wondering if maybe he'd been too careful, if maybe he shouldn't have simply taken the sweet Statecaste girl as she'd asked. Taken her properly. Soothed his ragged nerves.

Someday, perhaps.

Someday when he no longer had to fear the razor's edge balance of reputation and power.

Someday when he had the means to better his failing empire without having to worry about wagging lips and what those above him might think of his proclivities.

Across the room, his omni buzzed on his desk. He padded over, beckoning for the holo display, feeling the faintest thrill of surprise (chased quickly by a hefty dose of irritation) as he took in the caller's identity.

It wasn't as if his agents could've made any relevant progress ever since he'd lost what little track he'd had of them in their mad, sloppy rush from the Forge. He knew for a fact they hadn't finished the damn job. He'd stared the proof in the face, not three days earlier. Which was beyond unacceptable, given how much trouble he'd gone through to procure them in the first place.

One did not shell out the credits to hire Ooperians unless they bloody well meant to see their target ended for good. Even the Svartalfs he'd hired to silence Elder Teedath of Kalyria at Ser Groshna's request, following the Golnak incident, couldn't compare. Or shouldn't have, at least.

The plan was too far gone now for any of it to matter.

"You'd better have a good reason for calling," he said, as the connection established through the myriad of proxy nodes, and his vocal scrambler pinged active.

"I have been informed to tell you that the associates in question failed to make the remainder of their appointed check-ins," came the monotonous voice on the other side of the line, unmistakably that of an Androtta. Not a surprising choice, given the nature of this particular subsidiary's most common services.

Calum was opening his mouth to give the quartz-bot a very organic *no shit* when the Androtta continued.

"There was, however, an untraceable contact with an unknown entity on the final occasion. Likely a female Atlantean, sir, though vocal analyzers were unable to reliably ascertain any coherent data beyond that."

"What do you mean, coherent? Was she employing a scrambler?"

"More likely a vocal emulation suite, sir."

"And you arrived at that conclusion *because*?"

"Because vocal recognition matched the recorded signature with a very commonly emulated voice, sir."

"*Whose* voice?" Calum all but growled, uniformly cursing the Androtta people and their undying mechanical literalness in all things. "What did she say?"

"The voice matched that of the deceased pirate, Anastasiya Blackthorne, sir. I'm transferring the recording now."

Calum killed the connection as soon as the data packet arrived, engaging his Net scrubber routines and running the mental circuits, confirming it for himself multiple times before he allowed himself to react at all. He was safe. He'd properly managed and scrambled each point of contact. Even if she'd pried the check-in protocol out of the assassins, the Ooperians themselves had no idea who'd hired them. Everything went through multiple layers of obfuscation. Everything.

He was safe.

He keyed the scrubbed data packet.

"You'll pay," said a dangerously calm female voice. Not an emulation suite, he knew. Not after what Nate Arturi had told him of their adventures in the deep. The Pirate fucking Blackthorne, threatening his life.

"You'll pay," she echoed, the recording looping itself, her voice a thing of predatory beauty. "You'll pay."

He felt himself growing hard.

"You'll pay."

The plan had most certainly gone to hell.

"You'll pay."

But Calum was nothing if not adaptable.

～

Deep in the dark reaches of the unbroken void that spanned the cosmos beyond the small but booming oasis of Forge Station, Anastasiya Blackthorne draped herself back against her chair and cupped her head in exasperation.

"I want it ready as soon as he is, Godfried. Sowaiy? Can you tell me what's so bloody damned hard to understand about that?"

In the disheveled clutter of her chambers aboard the *Blackethorne*, Godfried shifted nervously on five of his seven legs and glanced at the squat Hobdan beside him.

"Don't look at him," she snapped, slamming her pen down to the parchment. "Me, Sven cur! Look at me!"

"Yes," Godfried said, head bowed, back legs still shifting. "Yes, my lady. It will be done, of course."

Blackthorne stared the two of them down. "Belfric?"

"Yeah, boss? M'lady, that is," he amended, little Hobdan face scrunching in upon itself like it was trying to hide.

"How goes it with the Gorgon's Knightship, Belfric?"

The Hobdan's face contorted a little further, emitting an uncertain sound, not unlike a deflating air sac.

"Then would you tell me, Belfric, why the two of you are still standing here when you have your orders?"

The Hobdan tensed like a wild thing just realizing it'd been caught in a snare, glancing at Godfried, both of them trading one of those damned *walking on eggshell* looks of theirs.

"Go!" she cried at them, springing forward from her chair and waving her arms like the bloody madwoman they thought her to be at that moment. "Go! Go! GO!"

The door thudded shut behind them, and Blackthorne collapsed back against her high-backed wooden chair with an explosive sigh, staring with unseeing eyes at the mess of her chambers. Smelling her own unwashed stink.

How long had it been since she'd slept?

Weeks now, probably, if one were to rule out the occasional restorative trance—as one very might well should in any sleep deprivation case ranging into the territory of *weeks now, probably.*

She looked down at her notebook and sighed again at the sight of the dark glob of ink oozing across the page from the pen she hadn't noticed cracking on impact. Her last words were lost to it, but she didn't have to look far to imagine what they might've been about.

It would do no good, she reflected, taking any of this out on her beloved little Belfric and her strapping Godfried. But they simply didn't understand, she told herself, reaching for a cloth to begin wiping up the mess. How could they understand, those poor, dear mortals?

Wrong, is what it was. So much wrong. Lifetimes of wrong, rendered in blind faith to the force that'd been supposed to guide her. Supposed to bring them back together, after all these years.

"Supposed to," she muttered, pausing with the bloody ink mess of her notebook. "Supposed to."

She sighed and threw the cloth down with another sigh. It was pointless. All of it. The Knights. The Beacons. The bloody Synth, and those infinitely damned Ooperians.

"Why do I bother?" she asked, rising stiffly from her chair, knees popping from the prolonged disuse. She stretched her arms high, eliciting a chain of similar pops throughout her body, then turned for the humming grav slab that rested beside her bed—doubtlessly the prime source of her beloved crew's suspicions that she'd truly gone and lost it properly this time. Far more concerning than any tantrum she might throw. But what was she to do?

So much wrong.

Lifetimes of it.

And all of it for this body of ash and dust, held in place by little more than a humming containment field.

Alive? Not by any conventional meaning of the word. But he had been a Knight, once upon a time. Just as the Lady had once been kind.

Blackthorne didn't know what else to do. She only half-noticed the flickering buzz as she reached her fingers carefully through the containment field, occupied entirely by the frail black form she reached for. She shuddered as her fingers delicately traced the ashy edge of a bracer. Choked on a quiet sob as her fingers hovered over the charred remains of that black helmet, blood red plumage burned to dust, face sunken and obliterated in the few horrible slices she glimpsed through the cracks.

So much wrong.

"I'm sorry, my love," she whispered, tears forming in her eyes as she bent her head down, leaning in until the containment field crackled against her wetting face with an electromagnetic tingle. "I'm so sorry."

END BOOK TWO

Author's Note
(June 21st, 2020)

Dear Reader,

Much as I originally imagined I'd want to cap this story off with a charming little love letter to you, the awesome person who just came along for this ride, I have to admit: upon finishing this adventure, I'm a tired little Pen Monkey.

Suffice it to say, this book was a beast to write—an entirely new challenge for me on several levels. (I say this fondly, and in the best possible meaning of the word "challenge.")

The Excalibur Knights universe is drastically more expansive than anything I've ever written before. (And holy wow if it doesn't just keep expanding with a life of its own the more I write!)

If you've made it this far, I can only hope you've enjoyed the adventure as much as I have, and I can't wait to share what comes next!

That said, if you're ready for more, I have two recommendations (*plus some free Excalibur Knights extras you can read today!*):

1. You can hop on over to *lukermitchell.com/books* to grab Book Three (*Spoils of War*) and keep the adventure rolling!
2. You can ALSO go to *lukermitchell.com/black-knight-signup* join my mailing list and get immediate access to two exclusive Excalibur Knights special features, *Flight of the Huntress* and *The Last Good Boy*.

The former throws you into the weathered copper boots of Iveera Katanaga for the opening shots of the Terran Incursion. And the latter... well, you'll see.

Sign up at the above link to grab them both today, and enjoy! (As a welcome gift, you'll *also* get the lowdown on all of my other published works and receive free books from each series. But more on that once you're in.)

Whichever way you go, I hope you find plenty to enjoy there. Me? I'll keep teasing this expanding universe out, one page at a time. I can't wait to share Nate's next adventure with you!

Cheers,
Luke Mitchell

ACKNOWLEDGMENTS

As always, I'd be remiss if I didn't start by thanking my ever-loving wife, Marina, for all of the wonderful things, big and small.

Thanks go as well to my obscenely supportive mom, to my family and friends, and to my steadfast publishing team, without any of whom I'd undoubtedly be lost at sea. (Except not sea, because I definitely wouldn't have left the house in this particular hypothetical. "Lost in chair," let's call it.)

Special thanks go to Rob Shores for stepping into the copy-editor's booth with gusto in the middle of what was undoubtedly the most hectic production process of any book I've written to date.

Penultimately, my uproarious love and gratitude to the following Patrons, who directly support my work, rain or shine:

Mildred Ann Mitchell — James Mallison — Linda Lestha
Mark Frink — John Munson — Bartholomew Bacak
Bob Laughner — Simon Danner — Joan M. Combes
Janet Ober — Robert Stuart — Grant Wilson
Letcher Ross — Eldridge Newlin —Sharon Kenneson
Mary-Anne Mitchell — Andrea Johnson — Tony Tieuli
Toni Mcconnell — Steven Mathis — Howard Wolfgang
John Barnes — Lisa Hoffman — Ron Williams
Yaakov Bright — Aj Jain-Perkins — Debra Franklin
James M Blaine — Nicholas Ruppert — Daniel McNeese
Andrew Staples — Karl Hakimian — Faith Hakimian
Gordon Keller — Dan Andrews — Adam McIntosh
Sam Higby — Robert Poet — Dagmar Preusker

You gentlebeings are the blessed wind to my authorship's funny little sails. Love and peace to each and every one of you.

(Side Note: If you loved this book and would like to support more like it, hop on over to patreon.com/lukermitchell to learn more about the perks of becoming a Patron!)

Finally, my deepest thanks to you, Dear Reader, for coming along for the ride. I sure do enjoy you spending this time with my work. Thank you. And here's to many more stories to come!

Sincerely,
Luke Mitchell

ABOUT THE AUTHOR

Not a llama. Mostly human.

Luke is a storyteller whose dreams include learning the ways of the Force, becoming a sentient robot, and maybe even one day growing up. Also, lots of zombies… Don't ask.

Oh, and that "growing up" bit? That was a lie.

After studying engineering science at Penn State and neuroengineering at Drexel, Luke finally decided to throw in the towel on building a working Iron Man suit and opted instead to simply make things up and write them down. Boy, is he having more fun now.

When he's not holed up in his writing cave trying to string words together, he can often be found powerlifting, video-gaming, reading, and/or drinking the darkest, most roasty beers he can get his mitts on. Sometimes all at once.

But you know what? That's enough about Luke. He's really not that interesting. Still, if you'd like to say hi to him for whatever reason, he'd probably be glad to hear from you!

Go to **lukermitchell.com/black-knight-signup** to join up for fun emails, free books, and lots of other great deals and exclusive content you won't find anywhere else. (Content like the Excalibur Knights specials, *Flight of the Huntress* and *The Last Good Boy*, which you can read today by joining the list!)

~

Additionally (as you wish)…

Follow me on BookBub for new release alerts
bookbub.com/authors/luke-r-mitchell

Browse the rest of my published titles
lukermitchell.com/books

Join the Patreon team for digital copies of ALL of my work (past, present, and future) — and much more!
patreon.com/lukermitchell

Thank you for reading!